Maneater

THOMAS EMSON

Proudly Published by Snowbooks in 2008

Reprinted 2009

Snowbooks Ltd.
120 Pentonville Road
London
N1 9JN
Tel: 0207 837 6482
Fax: 0207 837 6348
email: info@snowbooks.com
www.snowbooks.com

British Library Cataloguing in Publication Data
A catalogue record for this book is available from the British Library.

ISBN 13 978-1-905005-84-0

Printed and bound in Great Britain

Maneater

THOMAS EMSON

PART ONE.

PREDATORS.

CHAPTER 1.
EASY MEAT.

CANAL ST, MANCHESTER — JUNE 7, 1999

"SHE'LL eat you alive."

"She's only human," said Matt, gaze fixed on the girl.

"She's out of your league."

"I'm up for promotion."

Dan laughed, then said, "She'll chew you up and spit you out."

"No way. Look at her. She's easy meat."

He considered the girl for a moment. Then, swigging his Budweiser, he thought, *Yeah, I'm right: she is easy meat.*

The music throbbed up into Matt's chest. The lights flash-gunned as bodies jerked on the dance floor below. He leaned over to Dan, whose eyes roved the club in search of other prey. "I'm making my move," he said, his stare never leaving the girl at the bar.

He swaggered towards her. She crossed her legs, and Matt's gaze drifted to the darkness beneath her silver dress. The glimpse stirred something in his balls. He groaned in appreciation, heat shuttling through him. The girl sipped from the straw sticking out of the watermelon Bacardi Breezer. She swept a hand through her pitch-black hair.

He said, "I'll get you another one of those."

She snared him in her gaze. Her autumn-coloured eyes fixed on him, and a shiver creeped down his back. Matt flashed the smile, all teeth and dimples.

"Would you like one?" he said.

She said nothing. Her nostrils flared as if she was sniffing him. Her eyes were locked on Matt, and he felt the confidence drain out of him. *Look away, babe,* he thought, *like you're not interested because you really are. Smile. Frown. Shake your head. Do something.*

Matt leaned forward. Her perfume saturated his nostrils. "What's your name?" he said, hoping the noise would hide the trembling in his voice.

"Laura Greenacre."

"Matt Grundy." He offered a hand. She didn't take it. "There's no need to be like that."

"Like what?"

"Rude."

"I'm not interested. That's all."

"But we've only just met."

"Well, nice to meet you. Bye."

Shit, he thought, *lesbian.*

Dan and Matt guessed the gay club would be brimming with straight girls. Straight girls liked gay men, didn't they? Felt safe in their company. No complications. So for straight guys like them, the odds of pulling were high. Or should have been. Just his luck the hottest babe on the block was a butch. They never considered that a gay nightspot would pull in the lesbian crowd. Didn't they have their own clubs?

"Hey, I'm sorry." Matt held up his hands up in surrender. "No hard feelings. You're just the most gorgeous girl here. I didn't know you were...you know...I'm sorry. Can I buy you a drink anyw–"

"Didn't know I was what?"

"You know, that you like...girls."

She laughed and shook her head. Her long, dark hair swished over her bare shoulders. Then she said, "I don't. I mean, I'm not like that. I'm just not interested in you." She laughed again.

It was like a punch in the guts.

"Okay." He could feel his face flush. "Don't take the piss."

"I'm not taking the piss." Her laugh drifted away into the babel of music and voices. "It's just you thought I was lesbian because I didn't fancy you. How sad's that?"

He didn't know where the rage came from, but it came, and it was blinding. He flipped the beer bottle towards her, spilling it across her breasts. She sprang to her feet and stared down at her Budweiser-soaked dress.

The fury left Matt's head like it came: in a spark. He gawped at the girl, a coldness sweeping over him.

He tried to say *sorry* but no words came out, only a bumbling sound. He shook his head like a man rejecting an impossible vision. He didn't see her arm lash out, but he felt the nails dig through his shirt and into his chest. A flash of agony surged into his brain. He dropped the beer bottle, and it shattered. He grabbed the girl's arm, squeezing. It was so slender he thought it would snap in his fists.

It didn't.

It raised him off his feet.

Clubbers turned to ogle as the girl forced him upwards, the pain in his chest searing as her nails dug into his skin.

Matt looked down at her. She looked up at him. Her eyes were yellow. Animal eyes. The pupils were black slits. Matt's scream pierced the cacophony.

He felt his neck jerk as the girl tossed him away. The air rushed out of him. As he spiraled, clutching at nothingness, he glimpsed the whirlpool of faces watching him fall.

Their shrieks rattled his eardrums as he soared over the balcony and plunged into a lake of dancers. The dancers parted, and the floor hurtled towards him. The audience gasped as he crash-landed. As unconsciousness swept over Matt, he saw those yellow animal eyes: the eyes of the girl Dan warned would eat him alive.

★ ★ ★

Elena McIntyre saw the girl push her way through the crowd.

Ice water rushed through Elena's veins.

It can't be, she thought.

It's impossible.

Light drowned the club. The music died. Shouts and screams criss-crossed. Revellers babbled and thronged to the balcony to see where the man had smashed into the floor. Clubbers shoved past Elena as they dashed to secure the best spot.

It can't be her, Elena told herself, staring at the girl who was using her arms to hack a path through the forest of bodies.

It *is* her.

The girl had her back to Elena. They were ten feet apart. But Elena could see it on the younger woman's shoulder, nestling below the scapula.

It's you.

For Elena, the recognition was like being switched on. She started pushing through the crowd. Black shirted bouncers did the same. They were headed for the girl.

"Run!" The racket swallowed her shout. But the girl heard, and she turned to face the warning. She bolted, forging a path through the bodies. A have-a-go headcase lunged at the fleeing girl. She swatted him away as if he were an insect.

Elena followed her as the bouncers shoved through the crowd. She watched the girl bound the stairs three at a time.

The girl crashed through a door marked BOYS. Three boys spilled out, tripping over each other.

Elena reached the door. She heard glass shatter from the inside. She rushed into the toilet. Cool air brushed her cheeks. She went to the window and leaned out, careful not to wound herself on the jagged edges of glass spouting from the frame.

"I know who you are," she said as the girl got to her feet three floors below. No street lights illuminated the alley, but the younger woman was held by the moon's glare. She gazed upwards to the voice.

Elena shouted again. "I know who you are. I know *what* you are."

The toilet door crashed open and Elena turned. Three bouncers stumbled into the toilet. Elena leaned out of the window to shout an alert. The warning locked in her throat. The girl was gone.

CHAPTER 2.
KILLER.

THE blow shattered the rottweiler's ribcage.

The dog was in mid-flight, pouncing on its prey, when the monster burst from the thicket. The crack of bone snapped at the night.

The rottweiler yelped as the impact hurled it off course. The animal crashed into undergrowth.

The dog squealed and struggled and shat as teeth and claws ripped through its fur and flesh, tearing it to shreds.

The other two dogs stood statue still. They were no longer interested in chasing the prowler who had activated the alarm, which got them freed from their cage. The dogs' hesitation gave the intruder time to escape the grounds by scaling the ten-foot perimeter wall.

But something else lurked in dark, tangled undergrowth. Something huge and terrifying and lethal.

The rottweilers locked eyes with the gloom that had swallowed their pack leader. They sniffed. The scent was fat with blood and danger.

One dog whimpered. It barked a warning, stepped forward. Then it faltered.

It stepped back.

It turned and bolted, and its companion followed.

Ears back, tails between their legs, the dogs fled.

And something pursued them, bearing down on its prey.

* * *

The alarm wailed. John Thorn raced from the house. He yanked the Browning automatic from its holster.

Security lights flooded the front lawn. Thorn hurtled through the glowing pool created by the light, his heart punching at his chest.

Lucky he switched the alarm system back on after the fool who was supposed to be responsible forgot. Thorn pledged to report the guy to the security firm.

He headed for the woods at the far end of the lawn.

His grip on the gun tightened.

Thorn stopped at the edge of the lake of light and crouched. His breathing was steady, drawing the August air into his lungs. He squinted, forcing his eyes to grow accustomed to the dark. It seemed thicker, darker in the trees.

He shouted into the dark. "Armed police. If you've got a weapon, put it on the ground and step out with your hands above your head. Now."

Silence and darkness.

Voices babbled from the house two hundred yards behind him. Thorn glanced over his shoulder and clenched his teeth. A cluster of guests had gathered at the front entrance.

Get them inside, he thought.

Tuxedoed security men tried to herd the flock back into the mansion, but Sir Adam Templeton's guests scented action. They wanted to see what tripped the alarms and the security lights, what had made the dogs bark and howl.

The guests were business leaders, politicians, family, and friends of Sir Adam, formerly a Northern Ireland minister during the Thatcher regime. They were launching a venture that promised to create hundreds of jobs. Thorn had no idea what kind of jobs, or if they'd ever materialise. He didn't let that worry him. The police sergeant was focused on his job: protecting Sir Adam.

He stared into the knot of beeches and oaks. A shiver seeped through him.

Seconded to the ex-MP eighteen months earlier, Thorn had two months left before returning to duties with the Northumbria force at their HQ in Ponteland. He craved it. Wished he could fold the calendar and make those eight weeks disappear. Accompanying the insular and sullen Sir Adam to functions and meetings had been tedious; ensuring the former minister's arrogant son, Michael, kept out of trouble had been wearisome.

This latter function was secondary and unofficial, but Thorn felt it part of his responsibilities to protect the whole clan. With a host of Templetons at that evening's do, Thorn felt his duties had multiplied. The burden was a heavy one.

He whistled, hoping the dogs would react. Nothing moved in the trees. His palms were sweaty on the Browning. The gun had been unholstered only once before, but never fired in action.

Right, in you go, Johnny-boy.

He glanced over his shoulder again. The guests were being penned into Templeton Hall's Georgian structure. Two security guards hired for the night jogged down the lawn towards Thorn. With back up on the way, relief brushed away some of Thorn's tension.

He stared back into the woods.

Dark and still and silent.

He straightened and moved forward.

His feet crunched on the gravel path that circled the house and lawn. Crossing into the blackness of the trees, he felt the atmosphere tighten. The pleasing temperatures that August nights brought with them turned clammy. The beeches lurched above him. Leaves rustled and twigs cracked beneath his feet as he treaded deeper into the maw.

Swallowed by darkness, Thorn gazed upwards. Summer made the trees thick and he could only glimpse a hint of sky, a sliver of moonshine above him.

"Shit."

Thorn's legs felt like hundredweights. His bladder became heavy. His eyes watered as they fought to penetrate the blackness.

He spun round as the ground shook, twigs cracking, heavy shoes crunching through the undergrowth.

"You couldn't make any *more* noise, could you?"

The two security men who followed him from the house halted. They glanced at each other like schoolboys caught smoking.

"Found anything?" said Finch, built like an oak tree with a bushy goatee.

"Found anything? I can't *see* anything." Thorn wished them away, but he felt safer with some muscle.

The skinhead named Norton, who played rugby for the Newcastle Falcons' second eleven, drifted off to the left.

"Stay close," said Thorn. "It...whatever...they might still be out here."

Finch said, "'It'? What do you mean 'it'?"

"The dogs are dead, Finch."

"I thought you hadn't found anything."

"That's why I think they're dead."

"You called them?"

Thorn nodded, wanting to end the conversation and delve deeper into the trees. "And I heard them make a right fucking racket," he said. "Something was killing them."

Finch seemed to tense. His gaze flitted from side to side. "You think we should get some more men? Some guns?"

Thorn waved his Browning. "I've got a gun."

"Jesus Christ. Thorn. Come look at this."

It was Norton. Panic pinched his voice into a higher pitch.

Thorn's heart lunged at his ribcage. "Where are you, Norton?" He hurried through the darkness, Finch at his heels, the security man's breathing as heavy as his footfalls. "Keep talking. We can't see you."

"Here. Over here. Christ. Hurry. It must still be out here."

Thorn could hear the panic in Norton's voice.

It must still be out here.

Thorn could see the skinhead standing like a mourner at a grave. The sergeant kicked on through the undergrowth. A stench struck at his nose: a coppery smell, heavy and warm.

"There's fucking blood everywhere, man." Norton's voice was a whine.

Thorn wanted to puke. His throat locked, dry like sandpaper. Behind him, Finch coughed and spluttered and swore at the sight.

"What the fuck did that?" said Norton, as if hoping someone would make sense of the carnage.

Thorn's stare fixed on the two heads. Torn away from the bodies, the black fur on both was matted in blood. The eyes were white and empty, and the mouths gaping. The pink tongues lolled like giant slugs over the jaws.

The animals' remains were scattered about the undergrowth: a paw, a flank, a leg, bones, guts, blood.

Steam rose from the meat. Thorn felt it cling to his skin, creep up his nostrils. The hairs on his nape stiffened, and he shivered.

It must still be out here.

"Get back to the house. Call the police," said Thorn.

"Should we tell Sir Adam?" said Norton as he turned his back on the carnage. Finch had already skulked into the darkness.

"No. Don't say anything."

Finch and Norton threaded their way out of the woods. Thorn listened until their footsteps faded. He gazed at the rottweilers' remains. He still had to find the other dog. Thorn knew it would be in a similar state of dismemberment.

But whatever killed it, and these two...

His grip on the Browning tightened. Sweat leaked from his armpits. A chill leached through his bones. His eyes roved the darkness.

...could still be in here.

He stalked backwards, watching the blackness about him as best he could. If an animal (what kind of *animal* could do this?) lay in wait in the murk, it could see him. It had an advantage. A voice in Thorn's head urged him to run. But his nerves held firm against the flight instinct. A dash would only trigger an attack. He'd probably get one shot off before being downed.

Thorn kept moving. The only sounds were his breathing and the crunching of twigs as he stepped away from the bloody scene. His eyes searched for danger signs. The lights of Templeton Hall shimmered through the bulk of the beeches. It would be good to get inside; sink a brandy to temper his shakes. It would be good to –

It crashed from the thicket to his left.

He spun to face it, eyes half-closed to take the blow, gun hand ready to fire.

But it was too close.

He thrust up an arm to protect his face. The figure smacked into him. He heard a crack, and his elbow jolted. He staggered away, swiping at the darkness. Thorn gasped, ready for the attack.

It never came.

He leaned against the trunk of a tree, the bark rough against his skull. His stomach muscles knotted, and his belly lurched.

The girl lay on the ground. She was naked. Her dark hair fanned around her head and shoulders. She wiped what looked liked blood from her mouth and chin. Her cheeks were streaked pink. A bruise cupped her left eye.

CHAPTER 3.
TERRITORIAL.

"IS that your blood, pet?" asked PC Susan Pendle, struggling to twist her bulky frame in the passenger seat of the police car. "How did you hurt yourself?"

The girl said nothing.

"How's she doing?" asked Sergeant Ken Travis. He glanced in the rear view mirror at the suspect. He winced at her swollen eye. That's where John Thorn's elbow cracked her, he thought.

Seated in the back, she was wrapped in a blanket.

Pendle turned to face the front and shook her head. "She looks in shock to me, Sarge."

"We'll get her looked at. Get those arms patched up. Dogs gave her a good going over."

"And something returned the favour. What do you think did that? Butchered the poor animals."

Travis shook his head. "Let's look after this young lassie before we do anything else."

The five-mile drive from Templeton Hall took them through open country. Up ahead, Travis saw the Abbey dominate the dark blue skyline. Everything felt better when that building came into view. The Abbey was founded in 674AD, and loomed high in the town of Hexham. Seeing it made Travis feel he was home. Born and raised here, he was proud to serve as a sergeant in the local police station. The joy that filled him on his wedding day, and on the birth of his two sons, also filled Travis whenever he saw the Abbey. He loved the embrace of a homecoming. Even the stress of having this feral stranger in the back seat was tempered when the monument came into view.

The girl had been found naked and caked in blood at Templeton Hall. Was it her blood, as Pendle inquired, or blood from Sir Adam's mutilated guard dogs?

"What were you doing on Templeton land, pet?" said the policewoman, huffing again as she turned to face the prisoner.

Travis heard a guttural noise.

He said, "What did she say?"

Pendle faced front once more. Travis glanced across at her. The policewoman's face was pale.

"Nowt, Sarge. She growled."

"Better leave her be for now."

But Pendle persisted. She spoke into the rear view mirror this time. "You've got to tell us your name, you know. Sir Adam may want to prosecute you for trespassing. Do you understand what I'm saying, pet?"

"Do you speak English? Can you understand?" said Travis, guiding the patrol car into the town. He'd be glad to get this girl out of range. He couldn't see how such a frail little thing could have killed the Templeton dogs. But she was found in the vicinity, and that made her a suspect. Travis watched the RSPCA guys scrape up what was left of the rottweilers. He didn't like the idea of being near anyone linked to such violence. The smell of the dogs' remains had been stomach churning, and its trace remained with the girl in the back, an invisible passenger. He wanted to get home to Joanna, to a beer, and the Thai curry she'd promised him that afternoon as he left for his shift.

Travis steered the car into Hexham General Hospital's car park on Corbridge Road.

Then the girl spoke. "What are we doing here?"

Travis jammed the breaks and the safety belt bit into his chest. Pendle gasped. They twisted in their seats to face the girl.

"You *do* understand," said Pendle, glowering at the younger woman.

The girl said, "Why are we at the hospital?"

But she didn't wait for an answer. She grabbed the door handle and rattled it, whining at its refusal to budge.

"Calm down," said Travis as Pendle reached over and held the girl by the shoulders.

The girl snapped back into her seat and scowled at the officers. Strands of raven-black hair threaded over her face. Her eyes were autumn leaf crescents, deep and dark. Travis could sink into those eyes...

He sensed his flushing cheeks and coughed, turning away from the girl. "We're...we're going to have your arms looked at. Get you checked out. Then we're going to have to have a chat down at the station."

"I could kill you both, you know," said the girl, her voice calm.

But it shook Travis.

Pendle jabbed a finger at the girl. "Are you threatening us, young lady? I'm warning you—"

The girl said nothing. She stared defiantly at Pendle, then hitched her feet on to the seat and squatted there.

"Oh, my God," said Pendle.

"What is she doing?" said Travis, gawping into the rear view mirror.

"Oh, my God," said Pendle again, hand covering her mouth.

Travis heard the hiss as liquid struck the carpet, and a sour stench filled the car.

CHAPTER 4.
THE TEMPLETONS.

GUNFIRE barked and zombies groaned as Michael Templeton destroyed the undead.

This was Michael's domain. Locked in the games room, he could drown out the dullness of life at the Hall. The centrepiece of the oak-panelled room was the full-size billiard table. Skirting the walls were arcade-type games. He was playing The House Of The Dead on one of the machines. In one corner a 61-inch TV boasted a DreamCast logo, the console itself perched on a beanbag where the player would lounge. A rack of shelves on one wall brimmed with games, arranged alphabetically by Michael. A considerable stereo system was stacked at the front wall next to the door.

John Thorn sat on a stool at the bar that was set into the back wall.

Like a landlord, Sir Adam Templeton stood behind the bar, a brandy glass in his hand. The room reeked of polish and tobacco, the nicotine a clue to last night's party. Thorn guessed that Michael and the Templeton clan's young turks spent the evening in the games room, scheming and drinking and snorting.

Sir Adam's grey eyes stared into the tumbler as if he were reading the booze like a fortuneteller reads tealeaves. He said, "How old would you say she was, John?"

"Difficult to tell. She was a mess. But I'd say early to mid-twenties."

Michael was killing zombies. He grunted as another green-skinned monster exploded under a rain of bullets.

Thorn glanced at the young man and clenched his teeth. *Stop your fucking playing you little git,* he thought.

Michael's black ponytail bobbed as he squeezed the console's trigger.

"Did you get a good look at her tits?" The younger Templeton spoke into the screen as another of the walking dead was sent to video game hell.

"What?"

"Come on, John." Michael spun to face his father and the sergeant. Behind him a zombie filled the screen. The screen turned red. "She was naked. Out cold. You must've had a look."

"Enough, Michael." Sir Adam's eyes were still fixed on the brandy.

"Dad's a bit worried, you see, sergeant. He thinks the past's come back to haunt—"

"Enough, Michael." Face turning red, the older man stabbed a look at his son.

Thorn wondered what Michael meant. But he left it. He didn't like to get involved in their father-son arguments. There were too many to recall, and they all concluded with Michael storming out of the house in a blaze of threats.

Michael leaned against the arcade machine and folded his arms. His face muscles danced in anger as he clenched his mouth shut, holding back the battery of abuse he wanted to fire at his father.

"I don't want her charged," said Sir Adam. He gulped at the brandy.

Michael stepped forward. "You've got to." He crossed to the bar and slammed his hands flat on the counter. He glared at Thorn. "Father," he said, eyes still locked on the sergeant. "Father, we should discuss this. Alone."

Thorn didn't budge. He held Michael's gaze.

"Alone," said Michael more forcefully.

Thorn looked away. His gaze dropped to a copy of The Journal, the local morning newspaper, which lay on the bar. He scanned the front page. The splash told of the bid by Sir Adam and his partners to bring hundreds of jobs into the area. Next to it, a picture of Alan Shearer celebrating a hat-trick in Newcastle United's 3-0 win over Everton. "Full story: Back Page," offered the caption. A single column story to the right of the picture was headlined: "Masked rapist's third victim." He turned the paper over and read the first few paragraphs of the

Newcastle United story.

Sir Adam poured himself another brandy. He asked Thorn, "Can you let your colleagues know I've no intention of taking action against her?"

The officer nodded. "If that's what you want."

Michael huffed, and pushed himself away from the bar. "This is madness. She...she killed the dogs."

"She was about five-foot-four, weighed not much more than eight-and-a-half stone, and carried no weapons." Thorn directed his words to Sir Adam. "There's no way—"

"What the fuck do you know?"

Thorn glared at Michael.

The younger man's cheeks reddened, and his brow furrowed. He was so like his father: the wide-set eyes, the Roman nose, thin lips, sharp chin. You're daddy's boy, all right, thought Thorn, quelling the urge to smack Michael in the face, but you'll never be your father's son.

"Do not use foul language in my house," said Sir Adam.

"Then tell this beat cop to mind his own business." Michael jabbed a finger in Thorn's direction. "Tell him he doesn't know what he's talking about. Or just *tell* him."

Silence fell on the room.

Thorn had to speak to the girl. Sir Adam and Michael appeared to know her, and why she'd been there. Did she know the Templetons? Sir Adam wasn't willing to tell. Thorn didn't want Michael to tell. The younger Templeton's voice grated. It made Thorn think violent thoughts.

"Could you leave us, John?" said Sir Adam. "Thank you for tonight."

Thorn headed for his room, pacing through a corridor lined with portraits of long-dead Templetons. Voices blared behind him. The words were muffled, but father and son spat vitriol, he was sure of that.

Thorn paused at his door and glanced at the portrait staring down at him. The Templeton features were vivid, framed by snow-white hair and thick sideburns. The brass plate on the frame read: Sir Richard Templeton, MP: 1835-1902.

Slipping into his room, Thorn thought about the past and if it could come back to haunt.

CHAPTER 5.
BLOOD MATTERS.

"JUST a little prick."

The woman's head snapped round. She glared at Dr Lawrence Procter as he leaned forward. He saw her eyes shift to the needle approaching her bicep. Procter smiled and dropped his gaze to the injection.

She lashed out.

Her hand was a claw on his face. The thumb and little finger pressed into his cheeks. Her index and second finger forced their nails into the spongy temples. The long middle finger drilled into his forehead.

The doctor yelled. He dropped the syringe and grabbed the woman's wrist with both hands, trying to pull the claw from his face.

She sprang off the examination table and pushed Procter backwards. He was much taller than her, so her arm stretched out at a 45-degree angle to make sure her grip on his face was maintained.

His skin at the pressure points was turning red. Procter smacked her arm, once, twice, three times. But his struggle to dislodge her vice-grip from his face proved hopeless. She smacked his head back into the wall, cracking the back of his skull against plaster. The doctor screamed. Nausea swept through him, and he fought to hold back the vomit spewing up his throat.

The door crashed open. PC Pendle, a nurse, and two porters rushed in. Procter's attacker turned to look. The quartet froze when they saw what was happening.

Procter shouted, "Get the bitch off me."

Pendle and the others lunged forward. The young woman picked Procter up by his face, and hurled him across the room. He crashed into Pendle, bowling the PC to the floor.

The two well-built porters grabbed the patient by the arms. She kicked out, missing her targets.

"Jesus Christ, man, she's strong," said one of the porters, an immense black man the doctor knew as Furlong.

Pendle struggled to her feet and rushed over to help them, but the patient's swinging feet caught the officer in the stomach. The policewoman bent double but maintained her balance. Rage showed red on her chubby face.

Procter cowered in a corner, sucking in deep breaths and massaging his bruised temples as he watched the riot.

"She's growling. She's growling," said the other porter, older than his colleague, and struggling to keep a hold of the wildcat. He was called Wilson.

Procter dragged himself to his feet and ran a shaky hand through his greying hair, which had lost its neatness and style during the attack. "Halo...Halo...Haloperidol," he said. His blood was up and fury bubbled in his chest. He shouted at the nurse. "Ten milligrams of Haloperidol! Now!"

The nurse had been watching from the safety of the corridor, but rushed into the room on the doctor's orders. Procter didn't know her name. She was new. Very pretty. He leered as she drew the sedative into the syringe. Procter shook his head, casting any lurid thoughts aside: this wasn't the time. He regained his anger as he turned towards the madwoman.

Forced back onto the examination table, the woman's arms were pinned down by Furlong and Wilson, with Pendle pressing her considerable weight across her legs.

You're so fat, thought Procter, staring at the police constable.

"What were you doing?" Pendle asked him through gritted teeth.

"Getting a blood sample," said the doctor. He snatched the syringe from the terrified nurse and said, "Shut the door."

A crowd had gathered to watch, and after the nurse closed the door they craned their necks to view through the portal window.

Procter approached the patient, and he smiled. *Right then you little slag*, he thought, needle in hand like a knife.

"Don't you hurt her, doctor," said Pendle.

Shut up, fat cow, he said to himself, and then, "No, this won't hurt a bit." He swung the syringe in an arc from above his head in a stabbing motion.

The patient stiffened. Procter jabbed the needle through the bandages on her forearms, driving it directly into a bite mark left by one of the dogs. Her face creased in pain.

Feeling her body relax, her captors eased their grip on the patient.

Her eyes snapped open. She tore her right arm free of Wilson's grip and punched him in the face. He staggered backwards, blood spilling from his nose.

The doctor backed against the wall. He threw up his arms to shield his face.

He watched as the policewoman and Furlong struggled against the girl's incredible strength. She grabbed the back of Furlong's neck and tossed him, all seventeen stone of him, head first into a cabinet.

Before she could release herself from Pendle's grip, the bloody-nosed Wilson slammed into the patient's flank. She gasped, the wind knocked out of her. Wilson held her from behind. He wrapped his arms around her waist in a desperate embrace. She elbowed him in the head, but he refused to let go.

Procter sensed his confidence return. She was under control. "Another 20 milligrams, nurse," he said.

"But doctor—"

He scowled at the nurse. "Another 20 milligrams." He saw the fear in her blue eyes. He saw how lovely she was and how her mouth gaped. He saw how glorious she would look on her back, her legs spread for him. Desire fluttered in his belly.

Furlong had regained his balance, and folded his arms around the girl's shoulders.

She was clamped.

Grinning, Procter took the syringe from the nurse, letting his finger trail across the smooth skin on the back on her hand. Then he searched out more flesh.

He took his time, gazing occasionally into the madwoman's burning eyes, watching her teeth as they snapped at her captors.

I bet you're a beauty in bed, he thought as he hitched the blue hospital gown over the woman's thigh. He jabbed the needle into the leg and stroked the skin.

I could kiss it if you'd like, he thought.

24

He was so stiff it hurt.

The girl's struggles weakened. Procter kept caressing her thigh.

He'd administered three times the recommended dosage of the sedative, but she wasn't completely calm. Such an amount would knock out a strong, healthy man.

What was she?

What kind of blood ran through her veins that she was so protective of it?

He prepared the vacutainers that would contain the bitch's blood. He stared at the nurse. She looked terrified. Procter grinned at her and winked.

CHAPTER 6.
HERETIC.

MICHAEL surveyed his arcade. He chose a football game, selecting to be England against the machine's Germany.

Behind him, the clinking of glass signalled his father was pouring himself another brandy. *Drink yourself blind, you old fool*, thought Michael, *You've nothing left to celebrate.*

The crowd in the machine cheered as Michael wove a cartoon David Beckham through the German defence and cracked the ball into the top left-hand corner. The screen flashed: GOAL – ENGLAND 1 GERMANY 0, as the animated soccer stars kissed and hugged.

But Michael's mind wasn't on the action.

"I don't want you to talk to me like that in the presence of others," said his father, the voice slurred and bitter. Michael ignored the old man, but his father said, "Did you hear me?"

Michael spun round, letting the Germans glide through an unmarshalled defence to equalise. His father wavered behind the bar, his thick white hair matted on his scalp, his face cragged and lined like dried out leaves. He looked twice his sixty-two years. He looked like he should be dead.

Michael said, "Why won't you prosecute? Even if it isn't her." He creased his brow and stared at his father. "But I think it is. And you do too."

His father gulped at the brandy, spilling some over his chin.

"It's over now." The old man's voice stumbled as if the words were tripwires. "I don't want to do anything else. It's done."

"It's not done. You only say that because if it is her, you know you've failed."

Sir Adam slammed the glass on the bar, brandy spouting onto the varnished wood.

"Failed? Failed what? What do you know of what I did or didn't do? How do you know how I feel?"

"You're babbling, father. Look at you." Michael stepped to the billiard table and hopped up to sit on the edge, feet dangling like a schoolboy's over a wall. "You look like you should be selling Big Issue at Monument station."

Drink dribbled from his father's mouth. Michael shook his head in disgust. "You should be proud. You did something no other Templeton ever did: you won the war. But for some stupid reason, you're ashamed. And all I remember since then is *this*." Michael wafted an arm at the drunk at the bar.

"I made a mistake."

"Then undo it. Kill the bitch."

The old man hurled the brandy glass. Michael ducked as the tumbler shot past him and smithereened against the wall. He raised his head to see a fire in his father's eyes. The tendons at the old man's neck tightened and his face flushed.

"Never ever say that. Ever, ever again. Never call her that."

"What's the matter with you?" Michael could feel his heart pulsing. He'd never seen his father like this. For a moment he felt fear grab at his balls. But it faded like a Polaroid and made him feel good about his father's fate.

The older man looked away, as if ashamed of his outburst. He padded the bar with his hand, seeking out the glass he'd shattered against the wall. He spoke, but the heat in his voice had been doused. "I don't want her mentioned. Don't want anything done. It's over. There's just her. She's the last of them. She can do no harm."

"There may be others. She could breed."

"There's no one else." Sir Adam cast the idea away with a flap of his hand. "All gone."

"Then..." Michael thought long about this. Should he speak of what had been whispered in cabals? Discuss what had been wish-listed by the new Templeton blood? He considered it like a heretic would consider before declaring a deviation of faith, knowing his words could mean a burning at the stake. "Why don't we use her blood and be what *we* were?"

The fury returned to Sir Adam's eyes. Michael saw the animal that lay dormant in his father, in him, in his family, rage in the old man's stare. Sir Adam's lips quivered as if unsure how to unleash the words. Instead, a gush of air whooshed from his lungs, and he staggered from behind the bar, making his way to the door.

He turned to face his son. "I cannot believe...I cannot believe..." His voice was a hiss, like air from a punctured tyre. "I would rather die. I would rather see you dead."

Michael jerked as the door slammed. A smile eased across his face as he listened to his father's footsteps echo through the corridors of the house that would soon be his.

CHAPTER 7.
LITTLE BIRD.

WALLACE Furlong had a bump the size of a billiard ball on his head. He dabbed it with his thumb and hissed at the pain in his skull.

She was a tough little bird, he thought as he walked along the empty corridor towards the lab.

The porter looked down at the yellow box containing the girl's blood samples.

Steel in your veins, Little Bird.

A father of three girls, a grandfather of four, Wallace admired a stand-up-for-herself type of woman. He'd always encouraged his daughters to be bold, be brave, be proud. Maybe it was the lack of a son that had seen him play-fight with his angels, take them to football matches, urge them to climb trees and get into scrapes against the good sense of their mother. But they turned out fine, those girls. One was an MP, another a doctor, and the youngest was making a name for herself on the London stage.

Wallace glowed as he thought of them, a warmth in his chest as he turned the corner, his footsteps echoing in the emptiness.

Not bad for a hospital porter and a nurse, he thought.

At first he'd been scared to manhandle the little bird in the examination room. He was a building of a man and could've snapped her body in two if he'd wanted to. That's what he guessed when he first saw the girl. But when she tossed him clean over the bed and sent him crashing against the cupboard, any notion that she was fragile left his mind.

She was a fighter, and he admired her for that.

He reached the lab door. Through the frosted glass, darkness. He fished for the bundle of keys in his pockets, looking up and down the corridor as he did so.

It was quiet and still. The smell of chemicals flooded his nostrils, and he shivered.

"Don't be silly. Nothing to be afraid of."

But he didn't like coming up here at night. So many terrors can lurk in the silence. Noise is better, noise is safer. Maybe growing up with eight brothers and sisters, raising his daughters, then the grandchildren, made him crave sound. He never liked the quiet.

Wallace pushed the key into the lock. A soft *phut-phut-phut* noise broke the silence. It sounded like bullets fired through a silencer. Getting louder.

He looked left down the corridor.

The keys dropped from his shaking hand.

"Damn." Bending his massive frame, he picked them off the floor.

Something caught his eye. To the right.

The little bird in blue raced towards him, her black hair sailing out behind her like a vampire's cape.

CHAPTER 8.
A TIME TO KILL.

THE monster lurked as night crept through the streets to swallow houses crammed together like teeth.

This was one of the areas untouched by the bulldozer and the town planners. A glut of modern estates and tower blocks had sprouted over the past few years, replacing these grim terraced jungles that reeked of misery.

He cowered in the dark, his frame protected against the spiteful December wind by a thick Red Army overcoat. He filched it from the body of a Soviet soldier in Afghanistan the previous Christmas after slitting the youth's throat.

A woolen hat was pulled low over his face, shrouding his eyes in shadow.

He listened. Nothing to break the silence but his breathing and the whistling wind.

Time to kill.

He slid his hand beneath the dead Russian's overcoat and sunk it into the inside pocket. It rested on the Skorpion M61 submachine gun. The weapon was cool to the touch. A beauty. His favourite.

Measuring 10.6 inches with its wire butt folded, and weighing just over four pounds with a 20-round magazine in place, the Skorpion was perfect for concealment. Perfect for killing. The 7.65mm chamber released 840 rounds a minute.

Three years before the Red Brigade used a Skorpion to kill Aldo Moro. In September 1977, eight months before the Italian statesman fell, assassins armed with a Skorpion tried to murder Iran's Princess Ashraf on the French Riviera. Police raiding the Paris hideout of Carlos the Jackal in 1975 found a Skorpion.

He added the killing of Martin Greenacre in Wallsend, Newcastle to that list.

He checked his watch. It was ten-twenty-six. The others would be doing the same. An army was on the move. Scattered throughout the British Isles, in cities, in towns, in villages, marching alone but as one.

The house was close, a hundred-and-fifty yards. He glanced across the street and through a window. A man stood, waving his arms. He was shouting, though his voice was muffled. The Skorpion-carrier kept staring as he passed other windows, each showing a vignette of life in this grim suburb. A shudder ran through him. *Thank God I'll soon be soon be free of grey old England*, he thought.

The time again. Shit. Ten-thirty. Late. Not like him. He hurried his steps. Some of the targets would be dead. Maybe his five comrades here in the north-east had already emptied their magazines.

He jogged the last few yards, crossing the road towards the door of number 51. He drew out the Skorpion as he reached the house and paused at the front step. The light was on. Violins whined from the house. Classical music. He hated classical stuff.

Funny to hear posh music in a dump like this, he thought.

He tugged the woolen hat over his face then glanced up and down the street through the eyeholes in the balaclava.

He rapped on the door with the barrel of the Skorpion.

If the man came to the door, he'd let him have it. If it was the woman, he'd force his way in. The child would be asleep, so that was all right.

The target here was the man; just the man. The kid and the wife were Greenacres, too, but for some reason he wasn't to bother with them. Actually, "keep them alive" was the order. All the other Greenacres in the fucking country were dying tonight: men, women, and children. But not this child, not this woman. He shrugged. So fucking what? If that's what the moneyman wanted, who was he to question five grand a kill?

From inside, feet pattered downstairs. He stepped back into the road and held the gun out at head height, knuckles turning white as his finger tensed on the trigger.

The door opened by itself onto a narrow hallway.

For a second he was confused, mind spinning, heart lurching.

His gaze dropped.

He gawped at the tiny girl with half-moon eyes and crow-black hair. She was four, maybe five. She wore a pink dressing gown over Sindy-patterned pyjamas. She craned her neck to stare up at the man who had come to kill her father.

CHAPTER 9.
THRILLS AND SPILLS.

HEXHAM GENERAL HOSPITAL – AUGUST 6, 1999

WALLACE Furlong skidded along the shiny floor like a seventeen-stone ice hockey puck.

Little Bird had smacked into his shoulder and sent him sprawling down the corridor.

He was stunned by her power as he sat in a heap against a wall ten yards away from where she crouched over the yellow box.

How could something as tiny as her do that to a man like me?

Wallace knew he was almost an entire human heavier than her. But still she forced him back like a twig in a storm.

He struggled to his feet.

"What're you doing, girlie?"

Little Bird ripped at the box and emptied the blood-filled vacutainers on the floor. They cracked, and red liquid oozed onto the linoleum.

"What're you doing, little birdie? Why are you doing this?"

Wallace felt her terror, knew she was scared. If she wasn't scared, she wouldn't be acting in this way. He wanted to know. He could help her, maybe.

He risked a step.

She thrust forward on all fours, and snarled, snapping her head from side to side.

Wallace held his breath.

It was not a snarl a human would make. It was guttural. Like an animal. A proper, dangerous animal.

Wallace moved back against the wall.

Little Bird turned back to her spilt blood. Grabbing the yellow box, she started mashing it into the glass and blood on the floor. Fragments of cardboard tore away from the box and mixed with the blood. Glass particles cut into the linoleum.

The girl picked up the keys and tried two in the lab door's lock with no luck.

She lobbed the keys to Wallace, who flinched as they fell in an arc into his hands.

With one hand on the handle, she lent against the door. She looked at Wallace and smiled, before stepping back and slamming her shoulder against the wood and the glass.

The girl flew into the lab as if a huge force had dragged her into the room. Glass and splinters erupted from the demolished door as an alarm squealed its warning, a red light at the far end of the corridor flashing deliriously.

Wallace started to whimper.

He took a few steps forward.

Little Bird stepped into the corridor. She held a bottle in her hand. Opening the container, she poured its clear contents over the yellow box and blood and glass on the floor. The mixture hissed. Plumes of smoke rose from the linoleum filling the air with the smell of burning flesh.

Wallace covered his nose. The odour made him sick, and he fell to his knees. Little Bird stood over the chemical reaction and watched her blood sample die.

So intent was she on ensuring no droplet survived, she failed to see the security guards hurtle around the corner.

Wallace spotted them.

"Little Bird," he said.

She glanced at him.

"You'd better run away, Little Bird," he said, indicating the point of danger with his eyes.

The girl turned to look.

The porter expected her to sprint in his direction. He would pretend to make a grab for her legs, but would let her get past. He didn't want her caught, his Little Bird. Didn't want this wild beauty trapped, even though she'd scared the skin off his bones.

But she didn't come to him.

She went the other way.

"No, no." Wallace could see her flesh through the slit at the back of her blue gown as she ran towards the men. Her hair wrapped itself around the air, and Wallace wished it would turn into wings and take her to freedom.

But it didn't, and she kept on running to them and they ran to her.

They ran and ran and ran, and crashed into each other in a scattering of bodies.

CHAPTER 10.
REPRESENTATION.

HEXHAM POLICE STATION – AUGUST 7, 1999

IT WAS almost one a.m. when Ellis Cole arrived. He was tired after fucking the girl. His muscles were tight from forcing his body into awkward positions in the Rover's cramped back seat. Her perfume and sweat haunted his nostrils, and her taste loitered in his mouth. In his head, he could hear the sounds she made. He liked the sounds best of all. He relaxed and drew out a smile for the constable at the desk.

Cole was buzzed through. Sergeant Ken Travis waited for him on the other side of the security door with a mug of tea steaming in his hand.

"I could do with one of those, Ken," said Cole, gesturing towards the drink.

"I'll get you one." Travis turned and headed down the corridor. "Couldn't get you at home, Ellis. Thought you were duty solicitor tonight."

Cole, following Travis, sharpened his tone. "I had my mobile. You can always get me on my mobile." The sergeant had no business knowing where he spent his evenings, or what he spent them doing. The tiredness swept over him again, and he wanted to get this done so he could go home and sleep the girl out of his system. "What's the story?"

Travis told him as they stood outside the door marked INTERVIEW ROOM.

Cole chuckled. "She pissed in your car."

"Left Pendle at the hospital with her. Had to bring it back here, clean the bugger out. Stinks of disinfectant now. Don't know what's worse, bleach or piss."

Cole shook his head and chuckled as he opened the door and entered the room. "Pissed in your car."

"She might do the same in your briefcase if you leave it open, Ellis. Very territorial, she said. Like a dog. I'll go and get her."

Cole sat down in one of the two plastic chairs facing each other over a Formica desk. He took his jacket off, draped it on his chair, and shouted, "And bring the tea."

Pissed in your car.

Cole thought that was funny. It was good, too. The girl had to be mental or something. It could help in mitigation.

He took an A4 pad from his briefcase and placed it on the desk. He plucked a pen from his jacket pocket, laid it on the pad. Cole cupped his face in his hands. He pushed his fingers through his thinning hair and sighed.

Get it sorted, go home.

He glanced at the briefcase, open like a coffin on the desk.

She might do the same in your briefcase.

He smiled, shut the case, and slid it under the desk.

He sat up in his chair as the footsteps approached. Cole put on his official mask: friendly but serious, concerned but no-nonsense.

The door opened and she stepped in ahead of Travis.

Cole's belly did a somersault. His heart bumped against his breast. The hairs on his nape stiffened, and it felt as if cold water were rushing through his veins.

"This is Mr Ellis Cole," Travis told the girl. "He's a solicitor."

Please don't let her recognise me, thought Cole. He knew he should stand as she entered, but his legs weren't playing. *She won't recognise me*, he thought. *She won't.*

Travis followed her into the room and pulled the chair out for her to sit. The policeman placed a mug of tea on the desk in front of Cole. The steam rising from the drink and into his face broke the solicitor's trance.

"Looks like you need that," said Travis and shut the door behind him.

She was as delicious as Cole remembered. Rough round the edges, perhaps – more as nature intended. No make up tonight, and a bruise cradling her eye. The usually shiny hair was matted, and tendrils snaked over her ivory-smooth face. The rest of her too, like that; soft and white. Cole had seen. In his head he made the blue smock she wore disappear. And the bandages wrapped around her forearms turned into gold bangles. His erection pressed against his pants. He shifted in the plastic chair, and coughed.

He picked up the pen and stared at his pad.

"I'm Ellis Cole. I'm a solicitor here in Hexham. Since you did not indicate to investigating officers that you have representation, I've been asked to attend." Cole looked up from his blank sheet. "Are you happy for me to attend?"

She tilted her head. Strands of hair brushed against her shoulder. She swept locks of hair from her face, unveiling those pit-deep eyes, reddish-brown.

"If you have representation, I can contact them," said Cole. "If you'd like to –"

"I want to go home."

He'd seen her so many times. Seen so much of her. But it was the first time Cole had heard her voice. It was sharp. But a softness lurked there somewhere. Cole imagined that when she was in the mood, her voice sounded like being brushed with silk.

"What about your name?"

"Laura Greenacre. I want to go home."

He scribbled on his pad and licked his lips. "I don't think I can do that right now, Laura."

Laura.

It felt like a sweet on his tongue. "If you're tired, you can sleep. We'll do this tomorrow." He glanced at his watch – one-fifteen a.m. – and said, "I mean later today; the seventh. I lose track of time."

She sighed and slumped in her chair.

Cole continued. "You've been arrested and the allegations made against you are quite serious." He reeled off what Travis had told him: "Trespassing. Resisting arrest. Wounding with intent, maybe – that's quite serious. Criminal damage. And, um, urinating, um, in, um..."

"I pissed in the car," she said. "Marking my territory. It's like I own it, now, that car."

She scanned the room.

Cole touched his briefcase, safely under the table, with his foot.

Please don't piss here. Please don't.

"Ma...marking your territory. Is that what you were doing at Templeton Hall? Could you tell me why you were there?"

"What's going to happen now?"

"Well, the officers will need to interview you. They may charge you overnight – if you're up to talking, that is – then, later this morning you'll appear at the local magistrates' court."

"Can't I go home?" The sweetness he guessed was in her voice appeared. Little girl lost. Puppy dog eyes. Yes, yes, yes.

I'll take you home, if you beg and beg and beg.

"I'm afraid it's –"

"How long can they keep me here?"

"No one can be detained for more than twenty-four hours without being charged."

"Twenty-four hours?"

"But they're likely, very likely, to...to either charge you or let you go in the next couple of hours. They should let you home for a change of clothes. You'll be on police bail."

Laura leaned forward and he liked her face close to his face. Her odour teased his nostrils. She narrowed her eyes. He imagined her glistening and sticky and eyes half-closed.

She said, "If they don't let me go, I'll do it myself. I'll get out of here. I will do something they've never seen before."

Currents flashed through his groin.

Do something they've never seen before? Oh yes. Do something to me I've never seen before. Do things to me and I'll do things to you.

She pushed back in her seat. "I will, you know."

"I'm sure. Can we get back to–"

"By the way."

He looked up at her. She leaned in again. Not aggressive this time. Flirty. Eyes half-closed as before, but half-closed like Cole imagined and wanted. She rested her chin on her knuckle and smiled with one side of her mouth.

Asking for it, he thought.

She said, "You think I don't know."

His skin tingled, and heat rushed into his cheeks.

"But I do," she said, and wagged a finger at his nose. "I've seen you, and we both know where, you naughty boy."

CHAPTER 11.
SAD OLD SOAK.

Templeton Hall, near Hexham — August 7, 1999

THE creatures stalking Sir Adam Templeton across the moors of his nightmares were not wolves, but that's how his sleeping brain labelled them. They were creatures fused by his sub-conscious, a sub-conscious saturated in history and guilt and brandy.

The primary hunter was female. Her face was human, but her body a mix of canine and equine: a thick pelt like a wolf; hooves like a horse.

She may have been the only one chasing him, or there could have been thousands. He couldn't tell in his nightmare. But when he glanced over his shoulder at the pack it was her face he saw, pale as the moon. Her night-coloured hair swept back over her head, down her furred back, and formed the creature's whipping, swiping tail.

She gained on him with every bound.

It was the rumble in his ears and the trembling of the earth that made him fear a pack was on his heels. Hooves thundered, louder, louder, until his screams were drowned by a sound like war drums; a sound that called for his death.

He burst out of his nightmare and sat upright in the bed. Sweat oozed from his pores. He gasped, heart racing. He dropped his face into his hands and calmed himself, before struggling out of bed.

Sir Adam tottered towards the en suite bathroom and clicked on the light. He groaned, head throbbing, stomach spewing a watery heat up into his throat. His heart still knocked against his ribcage. He poured himself a glass of water and gulped it down, gazing at his reflection in the mirror as he drank.

This is what I am, the real me: not the patriarch of a noble family, but a sad old soak.

The speech he gave a few hours ago at the launch ceremony was given through a mask. All about the pride and the passion and the determination and the commitment. He and his business partners wanted this venture to succeed so their pockets would swell so much they wouldn't be able to walk straight. If hundreds of jobs were created in the process, good; but in the same breath, if hundreds of hopes had to be squandered for his fortune to balloon, let it be.

A mask. Everything was a mask. His life, outside his head and these walls, had been a mask for twenty years.

"I want to spend more time in my constituency" was his reason for leaving the Government in 1985. "I need to focus on business ventures," the lie he told when he stood down from Parliament two years later.

Constituency. Business ventures. Masks. Masks to hide the truth about Sir Adam Templeton and the Templeton family, and the atrocity he committed in their name. It gnawed at him, made him weak, made him sick, made him lonely, turned him on to booze, the booze saying, "Come slow dance with me in oblivion, baby. It's so much better than the real world." It was. Getting drunk helped. Until sobriety came along to spoil the party and switch on the lights, like an angry parent returning home to find their teenager had invited friends round for a bash.

He poured himself another glass of water. Switching off the light, he shuffled into the bedroom. He sat on the edge of his bed and sipped the water. His mouth felt less like gravel, more like damp newspaper.

He looked at the clock radio's digital face: 3.32 a.m..

Tomorrow at breakfast he'd pull on the mask again. A few family members stayed the night at Templeton Hall, including some of Michael's hooligan cousins. Sir Adam, as head of the clan, would be expected to perform.

He thought about the girl and it made his bowels chill. If she appeared in court her name would be publicised. The family would know. Not everything, of course. Not the truth of that night. But

42

they'd know it wasn't finished. They'd know the past – the long, long distant past – had returned.

Why, he wondered?

To haunt?

"He thinks the past's come back to haunt him," Michael had tried to say earlier.

He placed the glass of water on the bedside table and slid beneath the duvet. Sir Adam Templeton closed his eyes to search again for the dream of wolves. He would risk being run down by the pack to see her face.

Sleep tugged him in. His sub-conscious flared. Thoughts, memories, images flickered. A spark ignited something deep in his mind. His eyes snapped open, and a chill spread over him.

The past had not come back to haunt. The past had come back to kill.

CHAPTER 12.
MURDER.

THE killer brushed the girl aside and marched into the hallway.

For a laugh, he considered saying, "Is your Daddy home, sweetie? I've come to kill him." But better to get it over with. This wasn't a forest in Rhodesia or a mountain pass in Afghanistan where you could kill anyone, take your time about it, and no one would give a shit. This was England. Someone hears gunfire in England, they poke their nose into places where it'll get blown off. No need for that. Get the job done, and get out.

His senses sharpened: Ahead of him, an open door – the kitchen; the shape of the sink unit in the dark. The hallway lit by a lamp standing on a small table at the bottom of the staircase. Music drifting from behind the closed door to his right. Patterned wallpaper – cheap. Thick carpet, like grass beneath his feet. A fusty odour, the smell you get from a dog. Coats draped on hooks.

He threw a glance at the girl, just to check. She was curled up into a ball at the bottom of the stairs. She gazed towards the kitchen door and the darkness beyond. He turned to look in the same direction. The wolf's yellow eyes locked on him from the kitch –

Jesus Christ almighty!

The gun came up.

The wolf growled. The wolf pounced.

The man yelled. He pressed the trigger.

Bullets smacked into the wolf. But not a wolf like any he'd seen. As big as a fucking lion. Black fur bursting red as the Skorpion spat its load. Blood spraying as the creature leaped. It yelped in mid-air, bullets tearing its body.

The child screeched. The wolf crashed at the killer's feet. The impact made the floor shudder. The girl fell silent. The man stared down at his kill, his heart thumping, and his eyes blinking like a camera shutter. They were fixed on the carcass. He should be checking on the kid. His brain raced through all its compartments, seeking a name for the dead animal. But the man had never seen anything like this. Fear for his comrades made his stomach knot.

What if they weren't as quick?

The moneyman warned them to be on their guard. Some of the guys laughed, thinking: we've seen everything there is to be seen.

Not this –

The man screamed as pain seared the back of his neck. He clawed at the attacker. It was the fucking child. He should've checked on her.

"Get off, you little bitch."

Wrapped around his shoulders, her sharp little teeth were buried in his throat. She growled, ripping through the wool of the balaclava and into his skin. He spun, reaching over to grab at the child. He clutched a handful of hair. He yanked the child over his shoulder. The flesh at his neck tore away, blood spitting on his cheeks. He slammed the child to the floor next to the –

Jesus Christ!

The killer staggered backwards towards the front door. Camera-shutter eyes again. Focusing on the naked man, his body mauled by the Skorpion's power. Where was the fucking animal? Did he see a fucking animal?

The shooter shook his head.

Focus. Focus. You're seeing it. You're dreaming it. It was an animal. A colossal fucking animal. Or was it still really an animal and his mind was seeing a man?

He wanted to be sick. His body was a furnace beneath the overcoat. His head was spinning. A sob broke his stare.

The girl looked up. Tears spilled down her cheeks. Her mouth, snarling, full of black wool and red meat.

The murderer staggered backwards out of the front door, and raised his weapon.

He aimed at the child's head.

CHAPTER 13.
MASK.

HE could never sleep when they danced in his mind. He endeavoured to resist the waves that washed through his body, and would declare this before God on The Day Of Reckoning when forced to defend his actions. But like all the others who faced those waves, he was a useless Canute.

He'd seen a film once, *Village Of The Damned*, about alien children taking over a place called Midwich. They were defeated by brave George Sanders, whose character built a brick wall in his mind to block the kids' psychic power. He tried the same trick to hold back his urges. But he was not George Sanders, and this was not a Fifties sci-fi film with a satisfying conclusion (not a happy one, since George Sanders dies, sacrificing himself for the sake of humanity).

So after digging out his gear and stuffing it into his old school satchel, he sneaked out of the house.

Dawn hinted its return as he strolled through the town. He glanced at his watch. It was gone four in the morning. He sucked in a deep breath, blew it out hard, to calm himself. He'd have to be quick. He stared up at the blue-black sky. His legs trembled as he turned into the High Street.

I need it so badly, he thought. So badly it suffocated him. He drowned in his needs, and to breathe again there had to be an unleashing, a gasp, an intake of oxygen. And that came about through his actions.

He felt better on seeing the car. It was a Ford Fiesta. A-registration. No alarm system. But tinted windows.

He smirked. Nice touch. The idiot wastes money on trendy additions when the cash could have been spent on making sure the car wasn't taken without the owner's consent.

He slid the screwdriver between the car door and its frame, and it clicked open. He threw the satchel across to the passenger seat. He settled behind the steering wheel and cracked open the ignition panel.

"I should've been a car thief," he said. "Well, technically I *am* a car thief. But with a little extra thrown in."

He got it going and drove for only five minutes before he spotted one. She strolled beside a high wall. Overhanging branches thick with evergreen leaves draped her in shadow.

But I can seeeee you.

Watching her walk, he stripped off his T-shirt and trousers, and kicked off his slip-on shoes. He reached for the satchel and took out the mask and the protective suit. He tugged the mask down over his head and then spat some threads of wool out his mouth. He slipped on the protective suit. Eyes fixed on the woman, he gathered his clothes and stuffed them into the school bag.

The Fiesta struck her at ten miles-per-hour, but it was enough to fling her against the wall. She cracked her head on the stonework and crumpled to the pavement.

He slammed the brakes, hit neutral, and leaped out of the car. He was panting, adrenalin cascading through his body. The woman groaned. He dragged her to the car and tossed her into the passenger seat.

His erection dangled in the loose suit as he trotted around to the driver's side.

Hitting the road again, he glanced across at her. Early to mid-twenties. She wore a nurse's tunic beneath her denim jacket. Blood trickled from her scalp, matting in her short brown hair. He thought he should apologise later for the contusion. But he had to have her like this: wounded; slightly broken. It was a shame, but they'd never come without being injured, knocked out cold.

He couldn't help it if a woman danced in his head.

What could he say? *Sorry, but I have to answer when it calls. Or I'll* drown. I'll suffocate. It's terrible that feeling of struggling for air, you see. It's like dying. And what I'm going to do to you, that's like living.

No. She'd be all right.

Well, he thought after a moment, *not really*.

CHAPTER 14.
LOOKING TO THE FUTURE.

TEMPLETON HALL — 9 A.M., AUGUST 7

MICHAEL ducked under the yellow plastic tape marked POLICE: DO NOT ENTER that hemmed off the woods.

Forensic officers in white overalls and hoods lurked among the beeches. They reminded Michael of those government bad guys in ET: The Extra Terrestrial, searching for the little alien, trampling on citizens' privacy.

Wedges of sunlight sliced through the covering of trees, bleaching areas of undergrowth. Michael's eyes roved the thicket for blood. Three officers squatted in a circle. They'd found something. Michael knew the dogs — what was left of them — had been removed the previous night. But bits and pieces remained or these white overalled bastards wouldn't be wasting their time. He stepped forward, feet crunching on dead leaves.

"Hey."

Michael stopped and turned towards the voice. Ross Andersson swaggered across the gravel drive that separated the woods from the lawn.

"Morbid curiosity got you out of bed, Templeton?" he said.

Sweat trickled from beneath Ross's curly blond hair and glistened on his brow. His pink shirt – the one he wore last night for the party – hung creased from his pants. The young man drank from a jug of orange juice.

"Just keeping an eye on things." Michael dipped under the tape and crossed to his cousin.

"Good man." Ross slurped from the jug. "Can't have the pigs thinking they're running the show, can we?"

Michael grabbed the jug from Ross's hand. He gulped down some juice. It was refreshing, and broke a thirst he didn't realise he had.

Ross took the jug, then gestured towards the woods. "What exactly kicked off last night, Michael? There was all kinds of bollocks said at breakfast."

Michael turned to see three forensic officers chatting at the plastic barrier. A fourth came out of the woods carrying a plastic bag containing what appeared to be dirt. He took it to a police van parked on the drive. Michael creased his brow, wondering what was in the bag.

He turned back to Ross and told him what had happened in the woods, and mentioned the argument he had with his father.

Ross said, "Shit. She was a Greenacre? You think that's possible?"

"Yes, I do. It's one of them. Everything's so fucking obvious. The dogs. The girl. Everything. She killed the fucking dogs. Or what she turned *into* killed the fucking dogs."

"You actually believe all this stuff? The old stories about the family."

Michael glared at his cousin. "Don't you?"

Ross shrugged. "Can't say I do. Thought it was a bit of silly fun."

Michael felt the blood pumping in his ears.

"But living in London, you know, out of the heartland and stuff. Don't really feel I'm a Templeton," said Ross, raising the jug to his mouth for another slurp of juice.

Michael shoved him. Ross staggered backwards, dropping the jug. It smashed on the gravel, juice sloshing on the drive.

Ross gawped up at Michael. "What the fuck you do that for?"

Michael said, "You're a Templeton like me. Like the rest of us. Your mother's a Templeton. It's in her like it's in Dad. Like it's in me, and in you. It's in all of us."

Ross got to his feet and brushed himself down. "No need to push, though. Don't get all family-minded all of a sudden."

"Can't you see, Ross? Can't you see how strong we can be?"

"We are strong. We're fucking richer than God."

"Not like that. Not powerful in monetary terms. Physically powerful. We could run the world. There must be hundreds of us. Imagine it. We'd be un-fucking-stoppable."

Ross stared at him, and Michael paused. He realised that he was preaching; sounding like a TV evangelist. He calmed down, let his head clear.

Ross said, "I don't understand."

Michael picked up a piece of shattered glass, remains of the jug, from the gravel. "If we are what our history tells us we once were, we can be that again, surely. All we have to do is re-ignite that in ourselves. Switch it on again."

Ross shook his head. "Switch what on?"

Michael ran a hand through his hair and tugged at his ponytail. He said, "If we, once upon a time, could do what she can do, and then someone decided we shouldn't do it anymore, it doesn't mean it's dead in us. It's dormant, Ross. Like a volcano."

"Waiting to explode, yeah? But don't I remember stuff like 'pure blood' and 'uncontaminated genes' and all that bollocks?"

"Yes, okay, the gene pool may be polluted – or maybe only *di*luted. But it's still in us. All we need is pure blood."

"Are you suggesting I fuck my sister? Didn't the Greenacres do stuff like that? The fucking freaks. All that in-breeding shit. Mountain man crap."

"No, no, you twat. *Her* pure blood. The Greenacre bitch."

"*Her* blood? If she *is* a Greenacre."

"She is. I know."

"So what are you saying? Transfusion?"

Michael shrugged. He wasn't sure. A few ideas swirled around in his head.

Ross said, "This is weird science, Michael. I'm a stockbroker, not a fucking biologist. And you make corporate videos, so you're hardly qualified."

"Maybe. But isn't it worth trying? She's here, mate. A real-life, man-eating, shape-shifting bitch of the Greenacre clan. All our legends living in this girl."

Ross's eyes roved the woods and Michael watched him, almost seeing his brain rolling this over and over. Michael fingered the glass

51

shard in his hand, its edges cutting into his palm. *Cool and sharp, like we could be*, he thought.

He said, "If she's pure blood, and if she's hot, we could shag her. All the Templeton males."

Ross's face stretched into a smile. "Yes. I like that. That, my man, sounds like fun."

Michael scowled. He said, "Fun, sure. But it wouldn't be fucking. It would be breeding."

Michael walked from the gravel drive and onto the lawn. He'd let this stew in Ross's head. His cousin would spread the idea like a plague among the others. Meanwhile, Michael had another sickness to cure.

CHAPTER 15.
SOMETHING'S COOKING.

BACON sizzled on the grill, fried eggs spat oil from the frying pan, beans bubbled thick in the saucepan: if God had another crack at the Grand Plan he'd make the kitchen in Templeton Hall His Eden.

Thorn's plate brimmed with a breakfast that would strike fear into a nutritionist. Three sausages, two rashers of bacon, two fried eggs, beans, two slices of black pudding, kidneys, and fried bread. The aroma made him salivate.

"Mrs Garvey, you are the finest cook in the world," he said, chewing on a mouthful, "And by far the prettiest."

The grey-haired cook giggled as she flipped over an egg in the frying pan. "Young Mr Thorn, I am old enough to be you're mother. And I'm very happily married, thank you very much."

"I've told you before," said Thorn, dunking a piece of fried bread in the soft yoke of an egg, "leave him, and marry me. I'm running out of patience."

"You have plenty of young ladies after you, I'm sure. Time you found yourself a girlfriend." Mrs Garvey put a plate containing a smaller version of Thorn's breakfast on a tray for the waitresses to take upstairs.

"But I only want you, Mrs Garvey." Thorn feigned tears. "You're breaking my heart. I can't live without you or your amazing breakfasts."

Mrs Garvey giggled again, her cheeks rosy from the heat in the kitchen. She sat at the pine table and poured tea from a pot into a

Newcastle United mug. She switched on a radio.

"Let's have some music," she said, "or you'll have me all hot and bothered."

Thorn readied his response, but the news headlines interrupted his retort. The masked rapist had claimed his fourth victim.

Mrs Garvey gasped and put a hand over her mouth. Thorn noticed the redness drain from the woman's cheeks. He gathered the last piece of sausage, black pudding, and egg onto his fork and put them into his mouth.

"So terrible. Poor, poor girl." She looked up at Thorn. He couldn't tell if it was the shimmer in her glasses or the tears beneath her lids that made her eyes appear moist. "They'll catch him soon, won't they, Mr Thorn?"

The rapist had struck four times. Twice in Hexham, last night's attack being the second; once in Newcastle; and once in Ponteland, where Northumbria Police HQ was based. A senior detective described the attack to Thorn as being "right outside our fucking front door".

Mrs Garvey sobbed. "I just think of Louise. I couldn't bear it... dreadful."

Thorn rose from his stool at the breakfast counter. He crossed to the table and switched off the radio. He put a hand on the cook's shoulder and felt her shiver. "It'll be okay," he said. "We'll get him. You shouldn't worry about your daughter. The chances—"

She turned a wrinkle-lined face towards Thorn. "I worry for all daughters, Sergeant Thorn."

A chill rinsed his insides.

Sophie, he thought. He shook the dread away.

He thanked Mrs Garvey for the feast and said he'd see her tomorrow.

"Same time, same place, same chat-up lines," she said, forcing humour into her voice.

Thorn left the kitchen and headed upstairs to Sir Adam Templeton's room.

He passed through the dining room where the Templeton clan was ploughing through Mrs Garvey's breakfast. They didn't notice him as they babbled, probably about last night. As far as Thorn knew, they hadn't been told. Their imaginations must have been working overtime.

Thorn nodded at the ashen-faced Finch and Norton who were

going off duty. The pair hadn't slept, stayed up with him all night talking through what had happened.

Reaching Templeton's door on the second floor, Thorn halted. From inside the room came a shuffling. Like the scurrying of rats. He knocked. More shuffling. The rats scattering.

"Come in."

Thorn entered and found Templeton cross-legged on the bed. He was in his dressing gown. He held on to his forearm, the flesh going white as he cut off the blood supply. Thorn's eyes scanned the letters and photographs and newspaper cuttings that littered the room.

Templeton said, "John…it's a mess." He stumbled off the bed and gathered a pile of papers from the floor. But they spilled through his arms. "Oh dear."

Thorn saw blood trickle from the man's forearm and he said, "What've you been doing, sir?"

Templeton glanced at the sliver of blood. He looked at Thorn. "It's not what you think. No, no. Not drugs. Not that it's any of your business."

"Your well-being is my business."

"Yes, thank you, but I was taking out, not putting in." He kneeled beside the bed and picked something from the mound of litter at his feet. Standing, he held out the glass tube. "Taking a blood sample, you see."

The container was half-filled. Thorn wrinkled his nose. *Don't ask*, he told himself. But he had to. "Why?"

"For the doctor. He needed a sample."

"Shouldn't he be doing that himself? I didn't realise it was a DIY procedure."

"That's enough, John." He dropped the tube into the pocket of his dressing gown and rubbed the pinprick on his forearm. "Give me ten minutes to shower and shave, then we'll go."

"Am I allowed to ask where we're going?"

Templeton skewered him with a look.

Thorn raised his hands in surrender.

"I'm sorry, John," said Templeton, turning his gaze to the chaos on the floor. "It's been a stressful few hours. Didn't sleep too well. Of course you need to know where we're going." Templeton gazed up at him and said, "We're going to court."

CHAPTER 16.
GIRL TROUBLE.

"LOOK at this dust." Elena McIntyre swiped a finger across the light switch. She held up the black-tipped finger. "Shows a lack of care and attention."

"Elena, sit down and have some coffee," said Hannah, chewing on her toast.

"We're fine. You shouldn't fuss," said Chloe, joining Hannah at the breakfast table.

"It's my job to worry." Elena gave the kitchen a quick scan. "I am your duenna."

The girls at the table laughed, and Hannah mimicked, "I am your duenna." Crumbs fell from her lips as she chuckled.

A smile stretched the crow's feet at the corners of Elena's eyes and she crossed to the table, dragging a chair out to sit with Hannah and Chloe.

She said it to all her girls – "I am your duenna" – though she knew most of them had no idea what it meant. She'd read it in The Collector by John Fowles years ago. She looked the word up in a dictionary and claimed it as a catchphrase.

"Oh, we shouldn't be laughing." Elena sighed as the coffee's odour calmed her. She sipped at the drink. She looked up at the ceiling and said, "Poor girl."

"She'll be all right," said Chloe through the hair clips in her teeth as she bundled her blonde hair on top of her head. "She must've got drunk, got lost, that's all. Happens all the time." She took the clips from her mouth and grappled the tresses into place.

"Sure it'll be okay," said Hannah. "Laura may be weird, but they like weirdness these days. But what had she drunk? What was she doing there? She was naked. It said so on the radio."

Elena felt her legs quiver under the table. She locked eyes with Looney Tunes' Tasmanian devil, glued to the fridge by its magnetic backside. She wanted to change the subject. She knew why Laura was at Templeton Hall, but had no idea why she'd been so stupid as to get caught. Turning to Hannah and Chloe, she said, "Where's that Alison girl this morning?"

"Playing away from home again," said Hannah, pasting marmalade on another slice of toast. "Went down to Foundation after finishing her shift last night. Pulled some soldier."

"All very sweet," said Chloe. "They were at school together. She only goes out with guys who were at school with her." She rained Rice Krispies into a bowl and showered them with milk. The cereal crackled and snapped.

Elena said, "She should be careful. You all should. This maniac. Did you hear it on the radio this morning? Another girl in Hexham."

"We're okay, Elena," said Hannah. "There are four of us. He's probably a pathetic, inadequate little perv who's terrified of women. Same as half the population."

Chloe laughed and Elena scowled as she saw milk dribble from the blonde girl's mouth.

Elena said, "Not with your mouth open," and then realised what she'd said was about to be twisted. And, inevitably, Hannah and Chloe started to laugh. Elena said, "You're dreadful." She got up. "Dirty, dirty minds. I should send you to a nunnery. You're nothing but trouble, you lot." She checked her watch. It was ten-thirty. "I'm going to scurry that girl along."

Elena left the kitchen and headed for the stairs. She took one step but the voice stopped her.

"Will I do?"

Elena raised her eyes. Laura stood at the top of the first flight in a blue trouser suit and white satin top. Her hair was tied back in a ponytail. She'd got back from the police station in Hexham at seven a.m. and gone straight to bed. And now Sleeping Beauty had just woken, as lovely as ever. Something melted in Elena's breast, the something that holds back tears and makes hearts cold. Her eyes were wet, and she sniffed. She said, "You will."

Laura said, "Thank you," and smiled as she walked down the stairs.

Elena hugged her. "You smell gorgeous, too."

Laura chuckled.

Elena said, "What were you thinking?"

"It's all right."

Elena pulled away, and looked at Laura. "It's not, is it. How can it be all right? They will know it's you. *He* will know it's you."

"Let him know. Let his blood run cold."

Elena brushed the bruise under Laura's eye. "That's what you get for fighting."

Laura blushed and looked away, a smile on her lips.

A car horn blared outside.

Elena said, "Cab's here," and she grabbed her coat from a hook near the front door. She looked at Laura for a moment. The girl was pale. Elena felt sadness well up in her breast, and she said, "Why don't you run, Laura? You don't have to do this."

Laura's face tightened. "Hunted things run. I'm not a hunted thing."

★ ★ ★

Ellis Cole's mouth dropped open when she walked into court. She looked – he skewed his head and watched her – delicate, fragile, precious. Cole actually swooned, and he never swooned. He lusted, yes. But swooned? No, no, no. Swooning was for softies; lusting was for, well: lusting was for blokes. And when he saw Laura Greenacre dance at Bliss on Saturday night, it was lust he felt; the feeling Ellis Cole liked best.

She sat next to him and looked at him.

A woman's voice boomed. "Court rise." Cole stood and looked over at Gail Taylor, the clerk to the justice. There was scraping and shuffling as those present got to their feet.

Taylor said, "Next case is Laura Greenacre," and she looked down her sharp nose at Cole and his client.

Cole thought, *Don't you do the high and mighty with me, cow – I've seen you in the buff too. I've had you.*

Taylor read out the charges, and in his head Cole stripped her,

58

pushing aside the promise of Laura Greenacre to replace it with the actuality of Gail Taylor.

She was a mountain of a woman, a Mother Earth of nooks and crannies, crevices where fingers could delve and discover.

Her full-moon face flushed now like it flushed when she bucked and barked on top of him last Christmas.

In Cole's head Taylor was astride him, on the storeroom floor, his hands mauling her heavy breasts, her curly brown hair bouncing about her face as the rest of her bounced on Cole's sweaty body, the stench of sex thick in his nostrils.

And you loved *it,* he thought as Taylor sat down. *You* wanted *me. I'll give you another big package next Christmas. Just what you want.*

The Crown Prosecution Service solicitor stood and spoke, snapping Cole from his rapture like a dog tugged back on its leash. Cole glanced at the Greenacre woman in her prim and proper mask. She was still, like something frozen. Only her nostrils moved. They flared as if she were sniffing the air. She wasn't even blinking.

She's delicious, he thought, *I'll have —*

The CPS solicitor's words, reeling off the charges, crashed through the haze in his head and Cole jumped to his feet.

He said, "Excuse me, forgive me, but —"

"Mr Cole," said Gail Taylor, looking like a schoolteacher about to whip some discipline into a misbehaving student.

"Mr Cole," the chairman of the bench echoed, glaring at the solicitor over the gold-rimmed half-moon glasses perched on his stub of a nose.

Cole felt heat creep up his body and the hairs at his nape pricked as all eyes in the courtroom glared at him.

"I apologise to the court. But what Mrs Kelly" – he glanced across at the Medusa from CPS trying to turn him into stone with her stare – "has told the court comes as a complete surprise to the defence. We, I, my client, we were not aware that the trespass charge had been dropped."

Cole heard shuffling at the rear of the court. He noticed the chairman's gaze lift to the back of the room. Cole sneaked a look at his client. Her head was jolting from side to side as she sniffed the air.

Cole continued, "So I ask that the rest of the charges be dropp —"

The oak table pitched. His notes were tossed to the floor. Cole threw an arm up to protect himself. Laura Greenacre was up, snarling.

Cole staggered, raised voices in the court, the chairman turning red, shouting.

Laura lunged for the back of the court. Three security men, built as if purposely bred for heavy work, lumbered after her.

Reporters, solicitors, suspects, crime victims leaped from their seats. Gasps and shouts echoed as the three giants grabbed at the girl. Cole leaned against the wall, loosened his tie, saw her struggle, growl, hurl one of her attackers aside. The other two struggled to hold on to her.

Cole scanned the court. People huddled like safety-in-numbers antelope massing to avoid a lion attack. Cole glimpsed a face shielded behind Sergeant John Thorn. The face of Sir Adam Templeton, his eyes locked on the snarling, struggling Laura Greenacre. And his eyes, unlike the others that gawped at the girl, held no fear.

CHAPTER 17.
THE LAW OF THE JUNGLE.

MICHAEL huddled in a corner of the pub. It stank of tobacco and sweat and booze. He swigged from a bottle of Budweiser. Trying to avoid eye contact with a trio who were playing pool, he stared down at the table-top, which had been used as a visitors' book. Names had been scrawled into the wood. Declarations of love, declarations of hate, accusations of sexual deviancy, claims of adultery.

Shouts alerted Michael that another game of pool was done, and he raised his gaze. The victor waved his cue in the air like a gladiator celebrating a kill. Then he chucked his weapon on the table. Michael's heart flipped as the pole clattered off the baize to the tiled floor. He glanced at the landlord behind the bar, fat face buried in the Evening Chronicle's sports section.

The trio left the pub, their howls dying away as they headed to another drinking den, no doubt. Michael sighed. Why meet here for fuck's sake? This hovel where pondlife get pissed on watered-down beer. *The fucker's trying to get* me *killed*, he thought.

Showered by the glare from an angled wallwasher light, the bulb grimed in dust, Michael swigged at the Budweiser then checked his watch. He glanced around the pub. The walls, once cream he guessed, were as black as a smoker's lungs and plaster cracked and peeled away. Plain cornices were draped in cobwebs. Fag butts peppered the tiled floor.

Michael looked over at the landlord and said, "Can we have some music?"

The landlord dragged his eyes from the sports pages and glared at Michael. "You can sing if you like, but you're likely to get a beating," said the man.

Michael almost stood to leave but the front door opened and Richie Jarvis swaggered into the pub. He shot a glance at Michael then he strolled to the bar where the landlord pulled him a pint of something yellowish-brown.

Jarvis sat opposite Michael and said, "Got the gear, man?"

"What? Here? You want it here?"

"Put it on the fucking table."

Michael fished into his coat pocket and brought out the plastic bag. He placed it on the table and Jarvis gathered it, and the pills it contained, in his tattooed fist.

"Price has gone up," said Jarvis, stuffing the Ecstasy tablets into the chest pocket of his denim jacket.

"You what?"

"Five grand." Jarvis gulped half his drink.

"You can fuck off. Two. That's it."

Jarvis lit a Benson and Hedges and puffed smoke into Michael's face. Michael waved the fog away and coughed.

"You said the dogs were caged," said Jarvis, sucking on the fag.

"Copper let them out. They're dead now."

"Yeah, and I saw what killed them."

The hackles spiked on Michael's nape.

Jarvis said, "That's why I want five. Fucking danger money, man. What the fuck kind of dog is that you keep?"

"Dog? What did you see?"

"Fucking huge. Like a wolf. Bigger. Just a black streak. Saw it smack into one of the rotties. Cut the fucking dog to pieces."

Michael guessed that Jarvis would have been high when he came to Templeton Hall last night to kill the old man. His drug-addled brain could have warped what the thug saw in the darkness.

Fucking huge. Like a wolf.

Michael said, "Were you stoned?"

"Fuck off." Jarvis supped at the beer then sucked on the fag, eyes still fixed on Michael.

Michael bumped the arguments to and fro in his head.

Like a wolf. Bigger.

Jarvis had seen something. It had to be her. She really was real, then.

"Okay," said Michael, "I'll give you three-five."

"Four-five."

"Four."

"Four grand? Aye, four grand." Jarvis stubbed the cigarette into the table, then jabbed a finger at Michael. "But not at the fucking house. Not with that dog on the loose."

Michael nodded. He swigged from the bottle of beer. His mind was miles from here. Brimming with dreams of power and glory and bloodletting.

Jarvis emptied his beer glass and made a smacking sound with his lips. "Your round, man."

Michael stood. "Get your own booze, Jarvis." He headed for the door and fresh air beyond.

Jarvis said, "Hey, what kind of dog was that? Special breed?"

Michael stopped and looked round at Jarvis. "Special breed, yes," he said. "Been in the family for centuries."

★ ★ ★

"Oh no, not again."

Thorn turned to the voice. It was Sergeant Ken Travis standing at the door of the courtroom. Travis marched into the court, followed by a stumpy female officer. Thorn watched them rush to the mass of bodies in the aisle.

Laura Greenacre snarled and spat, eyes narrowed, hair loosened and spraying about. If she broke free from the men grappling her, she'd kill the man huddled behind the Thorn.

People spilled out of the courtroom, herded by the black-cloaked ushers. The magistrates had already abandoned their post, and only Ellis Cole and a middle-aged blonde woman remained at the front end of the court.

Laura Greenacre's arm snapped free. Thorn stepped back, pushing Sir Adam with him. Thorn said, "We'd better leave."

"No, wait," said Sir Adam.

"I really think we should go," said Thorn.

The woman's free hand latched on to a security guard's throat. Thorn gasped as she picked the guy up off his feet and tossed him against the benches. Travis grasped at the arm. He was shaken like a rag, but managed to hold on.

63

The woman's face was reddening, veins bulging at her throat and temples, nostrils flaring, skin stretching.

Thorn saw a flash of black as the stumpy female officer's baton arced for the wild woman's head.

Thorn shut his eyes as –

THWACK!

– bone and baton collided. Laura Greenacre flopped into the arms of the security guards, hair a black veil across her face.

"Take her down to the cells," said Travis, swiping a forearm across his gleaming brow. He turned to the female PC, who puffed air into her lungs. "Well done, Susan. You all right?"

Thorn saw PC Susan nod as one of the security men swept Laura Greenacre up in his arms and carried her through a door behind the magistrates' bench. The blonde woman and Cole went to follow.

Sir Adam said, "Elena."

Thorn's heart flipped as Templeton left his side and marched towards the woman. She turned.

"Sir Adam," said Thorn, reaching out to stop his charge.

The woman was in her fifties, blonde hair cropped short to frame an attractive face. Her thin painted lips formed a scowl beneath her button nose, and Thorn could feel the chill from her cold blue eyes.

"Elena," said Sir Adam again and stopped two yards short of the woman.

Thorn came to his shoulder and looked from one to the other. Knight and ice queen locked in a Mexican standoff. Broken when Templeton fished into his jacket pocket and brought out a brown envelope. He held it out the woman. Her gaze dropped to the envelope, then back to Templeton's grey eyes.

"Please give this to Laura," he said.

Thorn watched the woman's facial muscles dance beneath make-up and skin as she clenched her jaw. She snatched the letter then slapped Sir Adam across the face.

Thorn pulled Templeton away.

"It's all right, John," said Sir Adam. "It's all right."

Thorn watched the woman. She crumpled the envelope and stuffed it into her handbag. Her mouth arched. Tears spilled down her cheeks. She said, "You deserve more than a slap across the cheeks, Adam Templeton." She sniffed back the tears. "But that's all I have the power to do."

CHAPTER 18.
QUESTIONS.

DARK clouds bruised the sky as Thorn guided the Saab 9-3 Aero out of Hexham.

With a price tag nearing twenty-seven grand, it was beyond Thorn's modest bank balance. So driving Sir Adam Templeton on little errands was a perk in this machine. For larger functions, they would take a Merc. Thorn in the back with his charge, a hired driver at the wheel. But the Saab was Thorn's to tease around the roads. Bach's Mass in B Minor drifted on low-volume from the CD system. The whiff of flowers wafted from the air freshener dangling from the rear view mirror. Traffic choked the roads. Laura Greenacre danced in Thorn's head.

He said, "Why did you drop the charges, sir?"

Templeton's elbow rested on the window frame. He gazed at the world, or maybe dreamed of another. He turned to his bodyguard and said, "I can do whatever I want, John. But that's the problem, I suppose." His gaze returned to the window.

"I can't understand. If she'd have got free I think she may have killed you."

Thorn thought he heard Templeton chuckle, then the older man said, "She has a passion."

"She looked crazy, if you ask me. How d'you know her?"

Templeton sighed. "She's a dream I once had."

Thorn furrowed his brow. What kind of gibberish was that? "She's a dream you had?"

"Civilization robs us of so many things. Instincts like her instincts. Passion like her passion. Wildness like her wildness."

"I think I should know about her."

"You don't need to know a thing about her, John. It's not relevant to your job."

"I think she's a threat. That makes it relevant."

Templeton turned to look at the bodyguard. Thorn glanced at him before returning his gaze to the road ahead. "You do mostly what I tell you to do, don't you?"

Thorn nodded. "Everything. Within the boundaries."

"Then I'm going to tell you to look after her."

Thorn's head snapped round to look at Templeton. A horn blared. Thorn, eyes front again, veered the steering wheel left, back into lane.

Templeton laughed. "Now you're trying to kill me."

"Is *she* trying to kill you?"

Templeton held up his hand. "Whatever Laura Greenacre does to me, do not blame her. There is a reason why she does what she does. I'm asking you as a police officer to accept that. I'm asking you as a friend to look out for her."

Thorn shook his head, then Templeton said, "How's Sophie?"

Clever bastard, thought Thorn. Slamming the brakes on a horde of questions by raising Thorn's favourite subject.

Thorn said, "She's fine."

"When was the last time you saw her?"

"Couple of weeks ago."

"You miss her?"

"Like I can't believe. I feel like crying sometimes."

"Then cry."

"I do."

"How old is she?"

"Seven in November."

"Your wife —"

"Ex-wife. Very ex-wife."

"Yes. She shouldn't have taken her so far away."

"It's only Edinburgh. That's what she says."

"Well, I suppose that's true. But a child needs its father."

"If that father's a good father." Guilt knotted Thorn's stomach. He squeezed his eyes shut for a moment as a memory came into his mind:

Sophie's fourth birthday. She's dressed as a fairy princess: pink tutu, white wings, tiara, and a wand. She's huddled on the couch, pain in that pretty face. Thorn comes in saying, "Kiss for Dad, birthday girl?" Jane carries paper plates spattered in birthday cake crumbs to the kitchen, and says in a whisper, "You bastard," as Thorn's stomach knots. He goes to Sophie, still on the couch, her face flashing blue in the glare of the TV screen. "Hey, little lady. Did you like your present? Don't I get a kiss?" Sophie looks at him. It's the saddest thing he's ever seen and all that made him strong melts away, and he is weak and fragile and broken. Sophie leaps from the couch. She tramps through to the kitchen to her mother. She weeps into her mother's tummy, saying, "It was my birthday. You said you'd come. You didn't come."

Thorn shook his head. Purged the flashback. He shuddered, then said, "And I wish I'd been a good father."

"So do I, John," said Templeton.

Silence held their burdens. Two fathers whose children were lost to them.

CHAPTER 19.
BE THERE.

COLE said, "You are so, so, so lucky. So lucky." He jabbed a finger at her. "I cannot believe what you did in there. Cannot believe."

Laura Greenacre sat in the corner of this grey room buried in the bowels of the court building. Her hair was loose and long over her shoulders.

Like it was on Saturday, thought Cole, *when you swung around that pole; when you peeled off that blue dress; when you wiggled your hips –*

"Damn it," he said, slapping the desk. He held out his hands and looked at them, trying to rid his mind of Laura the pole dancer and focus, as he should, on Laura the client. He said, "Any idea why Sir Adam Templeton would drop the charges?"

She fixed him with those autumn-coloured eyes. Her top lip curled to give him a peek at the teeth. "I don't know. I couldn't explain," she said. She looked across to Elena McIntyre, who leaned against the door.

Cole said, "I'm going to have a word with the magistrates and the clerk to the justices. Find out what's going on." He gave her a smile, and pointed at her. "Don't go running off, now."

He waited, but she didn't smile back.

★ ★ ★

Laura said, "Why d'you think he did that?"

Elena shook her head as she crossed to Laura. She crouched before the younger woman, reaching out to brush the hair back from Laura's face.

Elena said, "I thought you were going to change."

Laura shook her head.

"You shouldn't have done that. You lost control."

"No I didn't,' said Laura. "If I'd lost control they'd all be dead."

Elena stood up. She plucked the crumpled letter from her handbag. "He gave me this. For you."

Laura took the envelope and stared at it as if it were an artefact, brittle with age, burning with secrets. She said, "I can't open it," and held it out.

Elena took it and tore it open. Inside was a postcard showing a picture of Hadrian's Wall. She read the scrawl on the reverse:

Laura,

I deserve the fate you intend for me. I have things I must tell you, things I must give you before I die — and I do deserve to die; I deserve to be punished for my terrible crimes. The man I trust more than any other is John Thorn. He's my police bodyguard. I've not told him anything of what you are or why you have come. But I've told him to look out for you after you do what you have to do. I've told him not to blame you. People will come after you, so go to Thorn and he'll help you because I've asked him. Meet me here, where this picture was taken. Tonight. 9pm. My ancestors built this wall. Our ancestors. All I ask of you is that my blood be spilled on the stones that hold their sweat. Be there.

Adam

Elena shivered, reading the note again. She gave it to Laura and watched her eyes slide over the words. Laura's mouth opened and her eyes narrowed as she trawled the words for hidden meaning.

When she was finished, Laura said, "He wants me to kill him."

"It's a trap. You're not going."

"Of course, I'm going."

"You're not. He aims to kill you."

"But he says he deserves to die."

"He would say that, wouldn't he. He does deserve to die for what he did."

"What does he want to show me? And why would he mention this Thorn man?"

"It's a trap, Laura. You can't go."

Laura got up. "I came here to do what he wants me to do, Elena. If it's a trap, I'll sniff it out."

"He's clever."

"He may have brains," she said, tucking the postcard into her jacket pocket. "But I have instincts."

Laura crossed to the door. She tugged at the handle. It was locked. Glancing over her shoulder, she said, "I'm going to give him what he wants." She tore the handle from the door. Pine cracked as metal was ripped from its gut. Splinters rained from the rendered wood. Holding the broken handle, Laura turned to face Elena. "I'm going to eat him alive."

CHAPTER 20.
BRIDGES.

MY city is a city of bridges, thought Michael. The first was Pont Aelius, cast across the Tyne by the Romans in 120AD to link their forces north and south of the water; the last will be the Millennium Eye Bridge, which would be raised in the year 2000 to wink at ships sailing up the river.

Gazing right from the balcony of his Quayside flat, Michael Templeton could see the Tyne Bridge span the clouded sky. Beyond its giant bow stood the High Level Bridge, opened by Queen Victoria in 1849.

From Pont Aelius to the Millennium Eye: spanning history. Just what Michael dreamed of doing. But he wouldn't be using steel and timber and concrete. The foundation, structure, and span of Michael Templeton's bridge would be blood.

He went inside, the reek of the river lingering in his nostrils as he slumped into the leather couch and opened a file out on his lap. Commissioned by his father and the old man's business associates to produce a video encouraging companies to invest in their planned retail park, he'd been writing since lunchtime. But initial power-words such as "initiative", "regeneration", "skillful", "thriving" had devolved into doodles.

He slammed the file shut and hurled it into the armchair. He popped a video into the VCR and sprawled on the couch.

Michael watched himself on the TV screen. He saw himself sitting naked on the edge of his bed. The blonde head bobbed at his crotch.

Watching himself being sucked, he rubbed his privates. His on-screen self glanced up at the hidden camera coiled into the cornice. He smiled at the camera, at himself watching himself. And he smiled back at the screen, chuckled, and stroked himself.

DZZZZZ!

He tumbled from the couch and scrambled for the remote control, hitting the STOP button.

DZZZZZ!

He hooked the receiver from the wall, gasped, "Yeah?"

"It's me, Templeton. You sound knackered. You got a girl up there? Buzz me in, let me have a go."

Ross came up and made a quick search of the flat before chucking the file discarded by Michael on the floor and sitting in the armchair. He smacked the rolled up newspaper against the arm of the chair.

Ross said, "Where's the girl?"

"No girl. Just tired, man."

"Seen the rag?" Ross held up the tube in his hand.

Michael shook his head. "Why?"

Ross lobbed the paper over and it unfurled into Michael's lap.

KILL THIS DEVIL DOG blared the white-on-black block letters. Michael scanned the three-par splash beneath an image of a snarling Bull Mastiff. A dog like this had mauled a five-year-old girl in Byker.

"Page seven," said Ross.

Michael flipped the pages. He felt the rage rise up in his breast.

The headline screamed: VICTIM'S PLEA FOR ACCUSED, the sub-deck below: Disorder In The Court.

"A former government minister pleaded for clemency in the case of a woman found trespassing on his land," said Michael, reading the story. He continued, adding his own flourish here and there: "Sir Adam stupid-fucking-bastard Templeton, former Minister of State in the Northern Ireland Office, and high-profile businessman, and full-time twat – " He tossed the paper aside. "What is this wank? What the hell is he up to?"

Ross picked up the paper and read. "Says she threw a security guard against the wall. Fuck me. In court. That's serious." He laughed.

Michael said, "He's lost it, he's going mad in his old age."

"Why would he do that if she's supposed to be who she is?"

"Fucking idiot. I warned him. They'll let her go, you know."

"Says he dropped the trespass charge."

Michael said, "We've got to get her."

"What? You still want to do this?"

"You didn't mention it to the others did you? What I said?"

Ross's face flushed. He shook his head. "'Course not. What d'you think I am?"

Michael sat on the couch and grinned. "A liar and a cheat, Andersson. What did they say?"

Ross puffed out his cheeks and said, "I didn't...I told you...I wouldn't..."

Michael's grin faded. "What did they say?"

Shrugging, his cousin said, "Some of them thought...cool. Some of the others thought it was nuts. But they liked the idea at its fundamental level. The fundamental level being they'd get to have sex with this Greenacre girl." He shook his head and tutted. "I don't think everyone believes the, you know, stories."

Michael gazed to his balcony, to the thick clouds that clogged the sky. "They will," he said. "They will when I make it happen."

"Yeah, but how? If we try to catch her...well...if it's true, you know, that she can change...she'll fucking rip us apart."

"I want her to change, Ross." Michael turned to glare at his cousin, a smile snaking across his lips. "I'm going to make her bite me."

CHAPTER 21.
BOYS' TOYS.

ELLIS Cole stroked the Saab and said, "Bet this has got pulling power."

"It does all right," said Thorn, leaning against the car park wall as he watched Cole admire the car.

"I bet."

A drizzle had coated the Saab as Thorn returned to Hexham after dropping Templeton at the Hall.

"She rides like a dream, I'm sure" said the solicitor, gliding a hand over the car's slick roof. He turned to Thorn, plucked a handkerchief from his pocket and wiped his hands. "You interested in my client, Johnny? Hot stuff, don't you think?"

"Don't talk about her like that, Ellis. She's your client."

Cole swatted the protest away with his handkerchief before stuffing the cloth into his pocket. "We're boys together. Nothing wrong in that."

"Okay, so what's her story?"

"Ahhh." The solicitor wagged a finger. "I'll talk to you about her curves. I'll talk to you about her smell, her great legs and what lies between. But I'll not discuss matters that could breach client–solicitor confidentiality."

"Come on, Cole. You're not consorting with the enemy here. Templeton's dropped the charges."

Cole hummed and wrinkled his nose.

Thorn said, "So you don't know why she did what she did?"

Cole shook his head and leaned on the Saab.

"Don't lean on the car," said Thorn.

Cole straightened, tucked his hands in his pockets. He said, "Maybe he's her sugar-daddy." He gazed out across Hexham. "Lucky fucker. What's he told you?"

Thorn paused. He decided to hold on to what Templeton told him.

Whatever Laura Greenacre does to me, do not blame her. There is a reason why she does what she does. I'm asking you as a police officer to accept that. I'm asking you as a friend to look out for her.

Thorn shook his head. "What else d'you know about her, Ellis?"

Cole glared at him.

Thorn rolled his eyes. "Okay, anything that won't breach confidentiality, you tosser."

Cole told him what Laura Greenacre did for a living. He leered over the idea of her dancing at Bliss. He said, "Maybe we should visit her one Saturday night. Get her to dance for us, eh?"

"Not my scene."

"Hey, come on. We're both single."

"I'm not single. I'm divorced."

"It's just a bit of fun."

"You think the girls enjoy it?"

Cole shrugged. "They must do. Or they wouldn't do it. And anyway, can any of us say we enjoy what we do? I can't. So, how about it?"

"How about what?"

"You and me hitting the Bigg Market one Saturday night. Pulling a slapper or two. How long's it been since you pulled, John?"

Thorn strode towards the Saab.

"Touchy subject, eh?" said Cole.

Thorn twisted to face the solicitor. "I don't like you thinking about her like a piece of meat, Ellis." He tugged open the car door. "Just make sure you do your job and look after her interests."

Guiding the car out of the car park and into traffic, Thorn wondered,

Why should I be the one to do that? Why should I look out for this girl?

CHAPTER 22.
OPPORTUNITY KNOCKS.

MICHAEL stomped into Templeton Hall.

The house was built in four acres of land by Sir William Templeton in 1658, welcoming guests through its Palladian frontage. The hall was all symmetry and proportion, all angles and uniform. Like the dynasty who had lived within its walls these past three hundred years. No rough edges.

Until now.

Michael entered the hallway where marble busts of Roman emperors skirted the walls. Red-faced, heavy-lunged, he halted, watched by these killer kings.

"Father." His voice echoed in the empty house. "Where are you?"

Footfalls on the curved staircase behind him. Michael turned and glared up at his father.

Sir Adam said, "What is it?" He wore a Barbour jacket, walking boots, and a flat cap.

Michael bounded up the stairs and his father stopped in his tracks. Michael said, "Why did you speak up for her? Why did you drop the charges?"

For a moment both were frozen like the marble emperors. The father brushed passed his son and strolled down stairs.

Michael said, "Where are you going? Don't just turn your back on me." He started after his father. "Where are you going?"

"Out, Michael. I'm going out."

"Out where?"

"As if you cared."

"I do care. How dare you say I don't care." He reached his father and smacked a hand on the old man's shoulder.

Sir Adam turned to face his son, and said, "I don't know if it was me who made you like you are. It may have been losing your mother, I don't know. I'm sorry if things haven't been as they should."

"You don't sound sorry to me."

They stared at each other, then the older Templeton turned and walked into the hallway.

Michael said, "Tell me where you're going. Is Thorn going with you?"

"I'm going to the Wall. To walk for a while. To think. Thorn won't be coming. Goodbye, Michael."

The front door slammed and threw an echo through the hall.

Michael's eyes were fixed on the gloom below.

From his coat pocket he took out his mobile phone.

Clicking the Address Book he punched the letter "J". It scanned down to the name he sought. Pressing the CALL button, he raised the phone to his ear and gazed at one of the portraits lining the staircase.

Perched on a black stallion, Sir Edward Templeton (1803–1865) wore hunter's red. He glared down his nose at Michael, who sneered at his ancestor.

★ ★ ★

Michael slumped on the edge of his bed in Templeton Hall. Adrenalin pumped through him, filling his heart. His legs trembled, his stomach knotted, his head swam. He thought he would be sick; he thought he would faint.

Emotions warred within him: his father would soon be dead; he would claim his heritage; and a monster would be unleashed.

A memory filtered through the chaos of his thoughts:

Michael Adam David Templeton, brave little soldier, sat on his bed in his best suit and black tie, still wondering why mummy had decided to live with Jesus and not with them. Perhaps she liked Jesus more than she liked him. Perhaps that's why she always cried, her face so grey and thin. Perhaps the little packets of floury stuff Michael found in her purse one day when digging for money was a present from Jesus. Jesus must have loved more than they did to give her such gifts.

An hour before in the churchyard, strangers and family, all dressed in black, wept as the large wooden box was lowered into the hole in the ground. Was that his mother in that box? Was that her special carriage, that shiny thing in which he could see his image?

They had returned to Templeton Hall in a convoy of black cars.

Women crouched and called him a brave little man and he liked their smell. Men towered and patted him on the head and he hated their smiles.

Then his father told him in a quiet voice to go up to his room. A few minutes later the door opened and Father, a tall man with long black hair, came into Michael's room.

"Your mother's gone now," said Father. "It's you and me. And we're very, very special. Did you know that? Very special."

RAT-TAT-TAT-TAT.

Michael flinched. What was that noise at the door?

RAT-TAT-TAT-TAT.

Michael's eyes flitted from bedroom door to Father's face. His father reeled off the tale, deaf to the *RAT-TAT-TAT-TAT*. The rattling sound, someone knocking, someone insistent, drowned out Father's voice.

RAT-TAT-TAT-TAT.

Michael threw himself from the bed. He shouted for the noise to stop.

RAT-TAT-TAT-TAT...

★ ★ ★

Michael woke with a start, his breathing rapid and his heart thumping. The memory scattered.

RAT-TAT-TAT-TAT.

"Who...who's there?"

"It's John Thorn," said the voice outside the bedroom door.

"Okay, okay, come in. It's open."

Thorn was pale, his eyes wide. "Where's your father?" he said, pushing into the room.

"I...I was asleep." Michael blinked, swept back his thick black hair.

"Your father. Where is he?"

"I don't..." Michael steadied himself, reeled in his emotions. He said, "I have no idea, John. You look like a ghost. Is there a reason to be concerned?"

"There is. I'm not with him. He..." The policeman cut off.

"What? What were you going to say?"

"Nothing. I've got to find him, Michael."

Michael paused, and that pause, he hoped, would eat into his father's life. Then he said, "Would you be my bodyguard, John?"

"What?"

"If I paid you. If I hired you."

"I'm not for hire. It isn't a private agreement. The taxpayer pays me."

"I'd double your salary."

The cop clenched his jaw and his dark eyes narrowed. "Tell me where your dad's gone, you little shit."

"I don't know." Michael stiffened. Thorn was intimidating. "Don't talk to me like that. Help."

"Help? What do you mean 'help'?"

"I mean you're the help. The staff. Don't talk to me like that."

Thorn leaned into Michael and said, "Where is he?"

Michael cursed himself for being a coward. He gritted his teeth and thought, *When I'm a monster, I'll come looking for you, Mr Thorn.*

He cowered as Thorn pushed his chest out and scowled. It's all right to tell him, thought Michael. It'll be too late by now. And if I don't tell him, and the old man's dead, then this fucking gorilla will blame me. Michael said, "I don't know for sure, John, but he said something about going to the Wall. You've been to the Wall with him. I don't know."

Thorn bolted out of the bedroom. Michael puffed out a breath and wiped sweat off his brow. He was shivering. He glanced at his watch. Too late to save him. It was done, his father was dust.

Thorn would have to drive like an idiot to get there in time.

CHAPTER 23.
FINISQUE AB
ORIGINE PENDET.

ADAM Templeton rested at the edge of the Empire. The sun sank behind the horizon. Gloom blanketed the rugged landscape.

"Are you here?" he said. "I wish I could smell you. I wish I had your instincts. Your mother's instincts."

A groan from the dark. He spun to face the noise, his pulse pumping in his head. Too late to change your mind now, he thought, too late to turn coward. He pictured himself begging for his life, and it made his guts go cold.

Then he thought, *No. I'll not babble like an old woman. I'll grit my teeth and let her tear me apart. I will.*

But it was useless, this fake courage: horror had him by the throat. His bladder sapped and he thought he would piss his pants like some geriatric. Nausea swept over him and he put a hand on the cold stone. The Wall steadied him.

The border between life and death. No matter how brave we think we are as we prepare to cross that frontier, we still shit our pants, he thought.

He sunk to the grass, back against the Wall. He leaned his head against the stone that was carried here by order of the Emperor Hadrian in 122AD to stifle guerilla raids by the northern Picts.

This Wall marked the edge of the Roman Empire.

Sir Adam dwelled on its history, and it calmed him:

Aulus Platorius Nepos supervised the building of Hadrian's Wall, and it snaked 74 miles west to east, from Pont Aelius to Bowness on the Solway Firth. It stood five metres high when Roman guards gazed north from its parapets. Almost 2000 years later, the finest examples were only one metre from the ground.

Growing impatient, he said, "Don't make me wait like this, Laura. I want to see you. I want to look at you when you change. I want to smell your breath and see your teeth."

Twigs cracked in thickets to his left, and he jerked. He got up and scanned the wilderness. He said, "I have things to tell you. Things to show you to make you understand. You know there's no one here with me. You know it's not a trick."

A shuffling in the shadows to his right. He looked around, gasped. His legs almost buckled. His tongue was dry. He was trying to control his breathing, but he was hitching air sharply into his lungs. He said, "You know, a Roman named Manilius wrote that from the moment of birth we begin to die."

His head snapped from side to side to catch the attack. He was shaking, the terror unbearable. His body was in flight mode, but something held him there; something deep inside that demanded he face his responsibilities. He said, "It wasn't true in my case, Laura. I started to dic twenty years ago."

Bleating beyond the Wall as sheep sensed predators.

"Manilius said the end hangs from the beginning."

Something scrabbling through undergrowth to the north, beyond the Wall. "That was the beginning wasn't it, Laura." He peered towards the noise. "And this is my end."

Leaning across the wall, squinting to see through gloom, Sir Adam searched for his killer. Something running up behind him, trampling the ground –

It sounded like hooves hammering the earth, louder, louder...the hunter gaining on its prey.

Grasping for a last breath, Sir Adam turned, he cried out. The moon glistened on steel, blinding him for a moment. A shadow loomed, the earth trembled. He screamed as the face of the beast appeared out of the murk, its teeth bared, snarling with fury, claws slashing the air.

Sir Adam raised his arms across his face, eyes wide, his mouth in a soundless scream. Hot breath hit his face, a sour stench saturated his nostrils. He saw the blade and his bladder gave out.

He said, "Oh, no, not this, not th – " and the steel punched him in the stomach, and the beast slammed against him, pressing him to the Wall. Sir Adam hissed, he spluttered into the monster's face, and the monster laughed.

He clutched at the beast, his fingers sinking into biceps. Pain surged from his gut to his chest, his insides shifting and tearing. He craned his neck, stared at the moon, and wailed. His throat clogged. His legs buckled. He felt life seep away and he reached out for it, but it was gone.

* * *

Thorn raced the five miles from Templeton Hall to Corbridge along the B6305.

The Saab's horn blared to warn other traffic, and its headlights sliced the gloom.

Michael's words echoed in Thorn's head.

You've been there with him.

Thorn never thought Templeton was a spiritual man. Church visits were for show at Christmas and Easter. But when they coursed the Northumbrian wilds, Thorn was sure he saw Sir Adam smile; he could almost smell his charge's contentment.

The sergeant would trudge after Sir Adam after they'd parked at the Roman remains of Corstopitum, HQ for troops guarding the eastern section of the Wall. As they lumbered the three miles north to Hadrian's barricade, Templeton would speak about the Wall, its builders, its history. This is what made him the happiest, thought Thorn.

Corbridge, where the Romans camped in 81AD and cut into the land a road that would lead to Scotland; where King Ethelred I of Northumbria was murdered in 796; where the Viking Regnald thrashed the combined forces of Northumbria and the Franks in 918; where King John pillaged in the thirteenth century, searching for a treasure never unearthed.

Blood and intrigue.

Not much changes, thought Thorn. If Templeton died, Thorn would face an internal inquiry at police HQ. He should fear for his career. But he pushed that concern to the back of his mind.

Got to get to him, he thought. *He's going to get himself killed.* Irish terror groups had failed (if they'd ever tried; it was the 1980s when Sir Adam was in government, so it was possible), but a strange pole dancer may well succeed.

Skidding the Saab to a halt, he saw Templeton's battered Mini in the corner of a car park. Fear clutched Thorn's heart.

CHAPTER 24.
GUTS.

RICHIE Jarvis slit his victim from stomach to sternum.

Templeton gurgled blood, convulsing as a bulge of intestine dropped out of the tear in his belly.

The stench struck at Jarvis and he turned to retch, bloody knife clenched in his fist. He glared again at the jerking body at his feet.

"Die, you fuck."

But he didn't. The fuck sat up. The strain on his abdomen spilling his insides out. Blueish-white intestines looped out of Templeton's rendered gut.

Jarvis grimaced and covered his nose and mouth with a hand caked in his victim's blood. Templeton glared at his killer, mouth an "O", eyes bugged out like a cartoon lunatic. He rasped, and Jarvis flinched.

Black blood sprayed from Templeton's mouth. He slumped on his back, body arching like a stretching bow.

Jarvis moaned as the older man's sphincter muscle quit. Shit mixed with blood in the air. The body flopped.

Holding his breath, Jarvis rushed to the carcass. Kneeling, knife in hand, he rifled through the pockets of the Barbour jacket. Jarvis's heart rained blows on his ribcage.

Got to be something worth nicking, he thought.

He fished out a Jiffy bag, thick with something. More cash to add to the four grand he'd make for this job? Fingering the envelope, he found himself relaxing, Templeton's carcass oozing blood and gas at his feet. Jarvis was stunned to find he had an erection.

Hey, killing makes me horny.

He chuckled, and then he stopped, and froze, his insides growing cold.

A cracking noise in thickets the other side of the Wall had him backing away, knife in one hand, envelope in the other.

Come on, he thought, bravado returning, *come on and try it.* He'd killed once, he could do it again. Easy. He had a taste for it, now. He gritted his teeth, tensed his muscles, waited for whoever it was out there. He thought, *I'm going to slice you —*

Then the blackest demon that only nightmares could forge erupted from the undergrowth, and whatever bravado Jarvis had mustered melted away.

He screamed, and he knew what the thing was: it had come from hell to kill him like it killed the dogs at Templeton Hall that night.

From thirty yards away, its yellow eyes fixed on Jarvis, and Jarvis felt death's fingers curl around his throat.

From twenty yards away, its fangs snapped at Jarvis, and Jarvis felt piss trickle down his leg.

From ten yards away, its claws, curved into hooves, churned up the earth and Jarvis screamed and turned and bolted, his legs pumping like pistons.

Prayers babbling, Jarvis ran and didn't look back as thunder drummed in his ears, and the earth trembled under his feet.

★ ★ ★

The scream gave Thorn a jolt.

He slammed the accelerator and the Saab bumped through the field, throwing up dirt from its wheels as it sliced through the grassland.

Hedgerows loomed in the headlights, and Thorn eased his foot off the speed pedal.

Then he floored it.

The Saab roared and crashed through the hawthorn, twigs rattling and scratching the paintwork as the car tore the hedge apart.

Trapped in the headlights, a woman crouched over a piece of meat.

Panic leached through Thorn's veins. He hammered the brakes and the car's wheels locked, ripping up chunks of earth.

The girl looked up, eyes glinting in the headlights.

Thorn pulled out his Browning and leapt out of the car.

He aimed the gun at her and said, "Get away from him."

His finger twitched at the trigger. Sweat soaked his palms, and he thought the gun would slip from his grasp.

"I said, get away from him."

She rose and stepped away from the corpse. She was dressed in a white T-shirt and cream combat pants. Her feet were bare. She flicked hair from her face and said, "It wasn't me."

He glanced at the dead body. "Jesus Christ. What have you done?" Tears in Thorn's voice, seeing Templeton's guts sagging out. Steam rose from the remains and the stench reached the sergeant as he moved forward.

He fixed on the woman, gun still pointing at her head. He said, "What have you done?"

"I told you. I didn't do it. It was the same guy I…I saw on the grounds last night."

"What?" Thorn's eyes flitted from Laura Greenacre to Sir Adam Templeton.

She said, "There was someone else there last night. The dogs were chasing him. And he did this." She gestured towards Templeton's body.

Thorn's forearms tensed. His knuckles felt as if they were bursting through his skin. He said, "Stay still."

"You're John Thorn," she said.

Thorn listened to his rapid breathing. *Calm down, son,* he thought. "I am," he said.

"I'm Laura – "

"I know who you are."

"All right, grumpy."

"Grumpy?"

"And you don't have to point that thing at me. I'm not going anywhere. I mean, I could if I wanted to, and you couldn't do anything about it. But I'm not. So, you can put it down."

"I won't, if you don't mind."

She shrugged, unconcerned by the Browning's barrel five yards from her chest.

Holding the gun with his right hand, Thorn dug in his jacket pocket for the mobile phone.

She said, "Who are you calling?"

"Ambulance –"

"Too late, I think."

" – and police."

She frowned. "I didn't do this." Thorn noticed the swelling beneath her left eye.

She fingered the bruise and said, "You gave me this. D'you remember?"

"It was an accident," he said, then thought, *What the fuck am I apologising for?*

"I know. You're not the type to hit a woman, are you? Or to shoot a woman."

"I will if I have to."

"No you won't. If I ran away, you wouldn't pull the trigger."

"Try me."

"Another time, maybe."

His gaze dropped to the phone and he punched in 999, and then –

It was like a horse had kicked him in the chest. Huffing breath from his lungs. Phone and gun flipped from his grasp. He was hurled through the air. Face muffled in thick black hair. Feet kicking empty space.

Thorn gasped as the ground smacked into his back, the weight on his chest crushing him into the grass.

He opened his eyes and groaned, finding himself shrouded in darkness and staring up at a bruised-eyed angel, her mouth moments from his, her pupils gaping to swallow him whole. Pores rippled in her flesh to flood his nostrils with her scent.

She'd locked his arms above his head, pressing against him. Laura Greenacre's contours melted into his body. He felt the swell of her breasts against his chest. Her thighs were warm, clasped around his waist. Swirling hair draped to curtain their faces.

It stirred in his abdomen and snaked downwards to rouse his penis. She said, "My, what a big boy you are."

Thorn shut his eyes to fight the heat rising in him. He jerked to push her away. She didn't budge. Her strength astounded him and he opened his eyes to look at her face again.

Her lips stretched into a smile, raising dimples, narrowing her eyes. She said, "Don't be embarrassed. It's natural. You shouldn't be ashamed of nature."

"Can you let me go?" He was too comfortable, she on him, her touch delicious.

Laura shook her head, her hair tickling his face. "No. Don't trust you yet. That bastard over there made out I should, but then I'd never trust him."

"Why'd you come to the hall last night? Has he done something to you?"

She said nothing. She got up on her knees, her legs either side of Thorn's thighs, and brushed hair back from her face.

He leaned up on his elbows and gazed up at her, saying, "He told me to look after you."

"I don't think I need looking after."

"But why would he say that?" He glanced at the corpse. He felt ashamed: *I should cover the body,* he thought, *not let it lie in the elements like that.*

He got to his feet and took off his jacket. Squinting at the carcass he thought of covering the wounds below Templeton's chest. Yeah, make it easy for yourself, Johnny. So you don't have to look. He draped the jacket over Templeton's face and chest. He looked down at the body for a moment, and sadness made his heart heavy. He turned to Laura, still kneeling on the grass, her back arched, her face to the moon.

He said, "What did he do to make you hate him? And why, if you hated him so much, did he express nothing but concern about your welfare?"

Her nostrils flared as she breathed long and hard. Then she looked over at Thorn and said, "I think I will trust you, Mr Thorn. And if you *are* part of some game, well, it doesn't matter." She got to her feet and went over to where Thorn stood near Templeton's remains. With the body lying between them, she stared at the sergeant and said, "Because I'll just eat you up and spit you out."

Thorn glared at her. He said, "Why did you go to Templeton Hall? Why were you running around naked?"

"The naked bit will have to wait. But I was there to get revenge."

Thorn arched an eyebrow. "Revenge for what?"

Laura lowered her gaze to the covered carcass. Steam still rose from the spilled intestines. She sniffed. "Meat," she said, as if to herself. "So hungry." Her eyes glazed over and she swayed.

Thorn looked for the gun. It was ten feet away. "Tell me why," he said, thinking how far he'd get before she pounced.

Still gazing at the meat, Laura said, "Because Adam Templeton killed my family."

PART TWO.

PACK ANIMALS.

CHAPTER 25.
FIGHT OR FLIGHT.

LAURA had lurked in the shadows for an hour before Templeton arrived. She sniffed the air, scanned the landscape, and waited.

When he came, he came alone and he babbled:

"I wish I had your instincts," he said. "Your mother's instincts."

She flinched and thought, *Why did you say that? You want to upset me? Are you trying to get me riled? You don't have to, you bastard; I'll kill you cold. You don't need to make me hot and angry.*

He tottered about and called again. Urging her to unleash herself. Promising to tell her things, show her things... "to make you understand."

Understand what?

And then he'd said, "I started to die twenty years ago."

She kicked off her trainers, tore off her T-shirt, dragged down her pants.

She crouched on all fours, head lashing from side to side. She growled and flexed her muscles, and from deep inside her, deep in her belly, heat flourished and shuttled through her body.

Laura shuddered. This was ecstasy, always ecstasy: the rapture of the primal.

Her skin tingled and her sex throbbed, as adrenalin flooded her heart.

Through the bliss of change, an odour disturbed her senses: a scent she knew.

She stopped transforming, freezing in a form that was half human, half wolf: eyes yellow, teeth sharp, skin pale, face thrust out in a half-muzzle.

Laura stayed still, like any predator stalking prey. She watched the man, whose odour she'd recognised, rush towards Templeton. She watched him sink a knife into Templeton's gut, and slice the older man open.

The stench of raw meat filled the air.

The killer bent down to the body and rummaged through Templeton's pockets.

Laura snarled, and snapped her teeth, and let the change start up again. She transformed and...

...she burst from the shadows snaring the figure in her sights.

Her mouth livid with juices, her muzzle scenting fear and meat. The prey saw her and showed his terror. He backed away, carefully. She prowled him, haunches up, head down, ready to spring.

The prey galloped. It screamed.

The sour reek of fear in her nostrils.

She let it flee into the darkness and turned her attention to the dead flesh. She sniffed the body and its spillage, and she recognised death.

She bolted back into the shadows.

Sprawled on twigs and leaves, her tongue lolling from lethal jaws, the creature melted into curves of flesh...

...and Laura lay there for a moment, breathing deeply to relax her stretched muscles, tendons, nerves, and organs.

Pulling on the T-shirt and pants, she rushed back to Templeton's body.

Bastard, bastard, bastard, she thought. Then someone shouted, "Get away from him."

* * *

Templeton's bodyguard reversed the car through the breach in the hedge. He parked the Saab in the shadow of an oak tree.

"Stay there," he said, jabbing a finger at Laura.

"What if I don't?"

"I'll tell the police what you told me. Then they have motive."

Bastard, she thought, watching him trot the hundred yards to where Templeton lay, *how dare you have a nice bum.*

He was sweet, really. Thorn had insisted she wore the Burberry coat he kept in the car. Slumped in the back seat, she pulled the coat around her. She could smell him on the garment, and she liked his odour.

"You could fit two of me in this," she told herself. The empty sleeves made it look as if her hands had been chopped off. She glanced down her body. The hem of the jacket hung to her knees.

Laura glanced down at her feet and said, "Shit." She looked for Thorn. He stood against the night, staring down at Templeton's carcass.

She had to tell him.

Laura grabbed the door handle. Sirens wailed in the distance. The sky flashed blue.

"Shit." She snuggled up against the far door, feet up on the seat. Bare feet. "Shit."

She watched from the darkness as three police cars and an ambulance rocked across the field from the west. They cut their engines and wails about a hundred yards from Thorn. Their lights still splashed against the night.

"Shit again." Laura stared down at her feet and wiggled her toes.

CHAPTER 26.
AUNT RUTH.

MICHAEL crouched at the edge of the pool and washed his hands in the tinted water. He splashed water on his chest, his shoulders, his face. He stood and looked over the pool. The spotlights hanging from the rafters cast a shimmer on the water's surface. Chlorine wafted in the air as Michael sucked in deep breaths to calm the tension in his muscles.

Beyond the glass and steel of the pool area, night pressed in on Templeton Hall. Out there in the darkness his father, hopefully, lay dead.

Michael glanced to the far side of the pool area. Ross Andersson, Peter Straker, and Josh Reaney were slumped on wicker chairs, sleeping off a day of drinking in Newcastle. They'd left soon after Michael spoke to Ross that morning. Michael turned down the invitation. They had returned drunk and smelling of Indian food an hour ago.

Michael slipped out of his shorts. He looked down at his tanned body, damp and shiny in the glow of the spotlights. Sliding a hand down his stomach, through his pubic hair, he grabbed his penis, and pissed into the swimming pool.

Just marking my territory, he thought, *I'll make a great monster.*

Sucking in a breath, locking it in his lungs, Michael dived into the pool, slicing through the surface into the thick silence below.

Arms pointing the way, legs kicking in short, sharp stabs, he swam. The world below was clear blue. The world above warped and blurred.

The only sound, his limbs thudding against water.

Adrenalin pumped through his veins, hammering his heart, and his lungs tightened, desperate for oxygen. Nausea made his head spin and his limbs felt heavy.

He pushed up and burst through the surface, grabbing the edge of the pool. He sucked in air, gasping as his lungs fed their hunger. He wiped a hand over his face, flicked his head back to throw damp hair over his shoulders. He rested his elbows on the edge of the pool.

She stood next to his sleeping cousins.

He said, "Hello, Aunt Ruth."

Fifty-seven and still fuckable, thought Michael. *Will you crouch in front of me and say that I'm a brave little man, and let me smell your scent up close like you did when my mother died? Will you do that now my father's gone?*

She was in her evening gown after a meal with business associates, her shoulders and upper chest bare and golden. The rippling water reflected on her skin. Her face was contoured, but the years had accentuated her looks.

She said, "Why was I not told about the dogs? About the girl?" Her voice rippled with anger.

"We – my father thought it best not to spoil the occasion."

Ruth clutched the back of the whicker chair where Ross snoozed. She shook it. Ross jolted from sleep and fell to the floor. He groaned as Ruth dragged the chair to the edge of the pool and sat facing Michael.

Ross said, "Mother," and then he curled into a ball and went back to sleep.

"I read the papers, Michael," said Ruth. She crossed her legs. Michael heard the swish of nylon at her thighs. He could stare up her dress if he wanted to, but fixed on her face instead.

He said, "I'm sure he would've told you, Aunt Ruth."

"Where is he?"

"He went out."

"Is he upset?"

"Well, I..."

She leaned forward. Her perfume came to him. She said, "Is he upset, Michael?"

He nodded. "Seemed troubled. Didn't say much. Just bolted."

"Was the bodyguard with him?"

Michael nodded again.

Ruth's eyes scanned the rafters and she said, "A little bitch survived, then."

"Looks like it." Since she was not watching him, Michael chanced a look at her legs. His stare moved upwards to the hem of her dress.

"Michael."

He quickly looked up at her face. Ruth's frown told him she knew where his eyes were going.

She said, "The dogs."

"What about the dogs?"

"It said in the paper that three dogs were killed. How 'killed' were they?"

"Very 'killed' according to Thorn. He found the remains."

"It's her, then. No question."

"Shall we kill her?"

Her eyes narrowed. "We'll speak to your father. We'd all hoped you and" – she glanced over at her son, prone on the floor, and the other two cousins napping in the chairs – "this new generation would be free of this curse. But it seems not." She stood and stared down at Michael. "If she's here to cause trouble, we'll have to do something. When did you expect your father?"

Michael shrugged. *In the next life*, he thought.

Ruth said, "It's almost eleven."

"I'm sure he won't be long."

"All right. I'll see him in the morning." She turned to leave the pool area.

Michael pushed himself out of the water and the splashing made Ruth twist round.

He smiled as her eyes slid from his face, down his torso, to his crotch.

Her face was cold. She locked eyes with her nephew and said, "You're my brother's son, Michael." She turned her back and walked towards the door. Without turning, she said, "And still a boy to me."

CHAPTER 27.
THE BILL.

DETECTIVE Chief Superintendent Lorraine Denton stood, arms folded, near the Rover. Beside her in shirtsleeves, his tie pulled down his chest, was Sergeant John Thorn. Head bowed, the tall, usually so handsome, officer looked drawn.

She said, "You all right, sergeant?"

His head snapped back as if he'd been roused from sleep. "Yes...yes, Ma'am...okay...thanks."

She turned away and watched the action. "We'll chat in a while."

Thorn made the call at ten-thirty p.m. Corbridge was a sub-station, not continuously manned. Officers from the principal station in Hexham rushed here with an ambulance in tow. Before Denton and her detectives, forensic teams, and pathologist arrived half-an-hour later, only the police surgeon was allowed near Sir Adam Templeton's body. The surgeon certified death and took a body temperature to guess – and it was always a guess – when Templeton died.

Phosphorescent tape skirted the scene of crime. A path had been cut from the emergency services' vehicles to the where the body fell. The Yellow Brick Road to Oz, the *only* permissible route. The area crawled with SOCOs searching for evidence. These civilian scenes-of-crime officers are trained at the national centre near Durham. Dressed in sterile overalls, over-shoes, gloves and hoods, they always reminded Denton of invading aliens.

Photos and videotape of the crime scene were already on their way to the Incident Room at Hexham. Templeton's remains had been slipped into a polythene body bag and taken to hospital for a post-mortem examination. Denton guessed from the damage that the ex-MP had been the victim of a vicious knife attack.

Denton's eyes ranged the scene. Glare from the vehicles' headlights painted the darkness. She said, "The hedge over there," and nodded towards the gap in the hawthorn, "you say you did that?"

"I did, yes," said Thorn.

"Where's your car now, sergeant?"

"I moved it, uh, over there." He pointed. Denton squinted and saw the outline of the vehicle sheltered beneath an oak.

"Why did you move your car, sergeant?"

"Um...I..."

Denton turned to face him. His eyes were glazed. Strands of hair hung over his brow.

"I don't know," he said, "I just thought I'd get it out of your way."

"You shouldn't have done that."

"I know. I'm sorry, Ma'am."

"Seems you shouldn't have done a lot of things, sergeant."

A little fire ignited in his eyes, and he said, "What does that mean?"

"Are you not seconded – apologies – *were* you not seconded to Sir Adam Templeton as his police bodyguard?"

Thorn nodded, his forehead creased.

"Then why did you leave your post?"

"He said he didn't want me tonight –"

"But you're here."

"Yes, but he said earlier that he didn't need me, so I went home."

"Home?"

"My home."

He was flustered. Her short jabs hurting.

"And that's where?"

"Jesmond."

"Then?"

Thorn puffed out a breath and ran a hand through his hair. He said, "I thought, under the circumstances –"

"What circumstances?"

Denton saw his jaw muscles tense. He glared at the chief super. *You always look so grim, don't you,* she thought.

He said, "Circumstances surrounding the incident at Templeton Hall involving the woman we found."

"And the dogs."

"Yes, and the dogs – under those circumstances I thought I should be with Sir Adam."

"So you had a guilty conscience."

"Maybe…you could say that."

"At your apparent dereliction of duty."

He came to life saying, "Hang on a fucking minute."

"Pardon me, Sergeant Thorn?"

He mumbled an apology, but Denton didn't care. She said, "This girl found wandering on Templeton Hall grounds last night did not have Sir Adam's well-being in mind. Wouldn't you say?"

"He dropped the charges."

"Why did he do that, do you think? Did he tell you?"

Thorn shook his head.

Liar, thought Denton. *Go on, keep digging a hole for yourself, my boy.* "I hear there was an incident at court, too."

He nodded.

She said, "Could you describe to me what happened?"

"I'm assuming you know what happened, Ma'am."

"You're not doing yourself any favours, Sergeant Thorn."

He looked at her and said, "Will anything I do or say count in my favour, now? My charge is dead, and for a protection officer that's the ultimate failure. My future's pretty bleak at the moment, so forgive me if I'm a little unhelpful. And to compound things –"

"Compound things, Sergeant Thorn?"

"Yes, compound things: to compound things, I happened to be quite fond of Sir Adam Templeton. I may have lost my career, but I've also lost a good friend."

He looked away, across the dark, rough landscape and beyond the Wall; past the rim of civilisation. Denton looked at him and saw he was doomed. She was about to say something when someone called out to her. She turned and saw an overalled detective vaulting the Wall.

She said, "What have you got, Mark?"

Detective Constable Mark Bailey had a polythene bag in his gloved hand. He held up the bag and said, "In the undergrowth over there," gesturing with his head, "and they look pretty new to me. Haven't been there long. And the insides are warm."

Denton glanced at Thorn. He was still looking away. She shook her head, and turned her attention to the polythene bag and the trainers inside it.

CHAPTER 28.
LOST CAUSE.

LAURA bowed her head and started to pick her nails. Her heart felt heavy. Grief had punched a hole in her belly. The sadness welled in her eyes and she sniffed back the tears. Everything was lost; her reason for being stolen from her by a stranger with a knife. She was surprised how miserable she felt. *Shouldn't I be elated that he's dead?* she thought

"Are you all right?" Thorn glanced across at her and then turned his attention back to the road. The car hummed along the A69 heading for Newcastle. Headlights scalpeled the night as the Saab streaked at over ninety miles per hour. Laura heard the engine noise drop as Thorn drew his foot off the accelerator. Sixty. Three cars whooshed past in the outside lane. "Laura, tell me what's the matter."

"Nothing."

It was nothing, too. Like a big void, eating away at her. Seeing herself thrown back into the life she had lived up until June. It would be worse, now, because she knew who she was, and *what* she was. She knew why she was here, and why those who loved her weren't around anymore.

He said, "Is it your family? How did they die, Laura? You say he killed them. Why would he do that? Do want to talk about it?"

No thank you, she thought.

She should have kept her mouth shut. Not told him. But he was Templeton's bodyguard, and he liked the old man. Thought the bastard was wonderful, no doubt. And she wanted him to know the truth about Sir Adam.

What d'you think of your Mr Wonderful now, Mr Thorn? Head in a spin, is it? In a bit of trouble 'cause you couldn't look after him?

She said, "Are you in trouble?"

His hands crushed the steering wheel, making the muscles in his forearms bulge. She traced his profile. A heavy brow shielding dark eyes. Thin sharp nose over lips that were fixed in a frown.

She wondered what he looked like when he smiled.

Laura flared her nostrils and smelled him. His sweat made her tingle. It seeped out of perforations in the body spray and deodorant. No aftershave. Just the soft sweetness of a moisturising balm.

She wondered what he smelled like when he was fucking, and her skin goosepimpled.

"Don't worry about me," he said.

"But you worried about me."

"It was nothing."

"Motive, you said. It could've given me a motive, that he killed my family."

He turned to face her and she saw the scowl, the grim eyes, the angled chin, she saw them full on. He said, "Did he kill them?" He looked back to the road. A siren wailed. The eastern sky flashed blue as the fire engine whined. It streaked past them. Thorn's eyes followed the red blur as it shot by his window.

"It doesn't matter anymore if he did or not," said Laura. She tugged at the jacket's lapels, tucking herself into it.

He said, "You cold?"

She shook her head.

"Tell me if you're cold."

She wrinkled her nose and said, "Why are you being so nice to me?" Her voice was accusing. She toned it down. "I mean...I've got you into a lot of trouble, I think."

"Maybe. I'll be fine. Tell me about Templeton. If you're telling the truth −"

She lashed out and struck the dashboard. The cop flinched. She said, "I am telling the truth. Why would I lie?"

She sunk into her seat, arms folded across her chest.

Thorn said, "If he − when he killed your family, why didn't you go to the police?"

"Because I was four."

"What about relatives? Didn't they −"

"I was the last, okay?" Then wanting this to end said, "Have you got a girlfriend?"

"Divorced and no girlfriend," he said, then, obviously *not* wanting this to end, "What d'you mean by 'the last'? I don't understand."

She didn't say anything. She thought, *Let's leave it at that, then. What you don't know won't kill you.* But then without thinking she said, "What you don't know won't kill you." She threw her hands to her face. She said, "I just want to be left alone," face buried in hands. "I'm sorry I fucked things up for you, but it's over. There's nothing left for me anymore. I'm sorry."

The words tumbled out.

She said, "I came here to kill him, to kill your boss, 'cause he killed my family. What would you do?" She looked up at Thorn. "Would you do the same thing?"

He said nothing. He drove.

She said, "You would, wouldn't you?"

Thorn shrugged. "I couldn't tell you. When it happened, maybe. Straight after. But twenty years down the line." He shook his head. "Don't know."

"What if you'd *lost* those twenty years?"

"What d'you mean by that?"

She thought for a moment, then said, "I don't mean anything." She stamped her bare feet into the rubber mat at the base of her seat. "It's over. It's done. I didn't kill him."

"The police don't think that. They found your trainers."

The first thing he said when he sneaked back to the car was, "They found your fucking trainers." They were lead weights on a net being used to trap her. "And they found your dress at Templeton Hall."

"They found *me* at Templeton Hall. Well, you did." She brushed her cheek below the bruise.

It was quiet between them; she listened to the engine hum, and it calmed her.

It didn't matter, really, that they found her trainers. So what? She could disappear. This wasn't home; nowhere was home.

One thing though: the guy who killed Templeton had seen her in her wolf shape — twice: here and at Templeton Hall the previous night. And no one who'd seen her like that had survived. Maybe she could hunt him down, kill him. It would give her something to do while she — Laura glanced at Thorn — hung around to see what happened here.

You know more than you need to know, she thought, looking at Thorn.

Soon he'd want to know about the Templetons and the Greenacres. About everything. How much could she let him know without killing him, too? She thought about that, and about other things to do with John Thorn; things she hadn't done with men in a long time.

CHAPTER 29.
CHECKLIST.

"THIS is wrong. It has to be."

The killer shook his head to say no, it wasn't wrong, and he grimaced as the wound on his neck thrust nails into his brain. He hissed at the pain and lay a hand on his throat. The bite had been washed with iodine and dressed. A brownish-yellow hoop tinged the skin around the bandage.

"The girl," said the killer. *Little bitch*, he thought as he touched the dressing, "and the..." He was going to say "man." It was certainly a man *after* it died. He said, "...and the father."

Adam Templeton shot him a look. His lower lip trembled and his cheeks turned red.

"I'm guessing he was the father," said the killer, "but there were two of them in the house. Him and the girl."

"It's wrong," said Templeton, eyes back on the sheet of A4. "The woman. Where was the woman?"

"There was no fucking woman. I told you."

"Did you check the house?"

The killer shook his head and said, "The shouting would've brought her out of hiding."

The paymaster checked his list again. His brow furrowed. He traced a finger down the ladder of names. He was shaking his head. "You've killed one too many." Templeton's forehead was glossed in sweat. He hitched in breath after breath.

He's going to have a cardiac, thought the mercenary. He gazed around the library. If the man collapsed he'd bail out, taking a few goodies with him. But there were only books. Shelf upon shelf upon shelf, skirting the room, their fusty smell saturating the atmosphere.

Templeton said, "Who went to Barret Street?"

The mercenary's brain clicked over the operation, the meeting in the old barn at the far end of Templeton Hall grounds, the names tacked to the map. He said, "Klaus Markus."

"Then Markus messed up. There's four dead at that address. There were only three in the house." Templeton jumped to his feet and tossed away the list. He ran a hand through his black hair. "He's killed too many."

"Jesus Christ, Templeton." The killer was pissed off. He wanted his money. Wanted this man out of his life. "What's one more? Thirty-three people, man. What's one more?"

Templeton thrust a finger in the mercenary's face. "Thirty-two. That was the contract. Thirty-two. The woman and the child were not to be harmed."

Fury rose in the mercenary's breast. He sprang to his feet and glared down from his six-feet-six at the politician. "The child is alive. The woman wasn't there. I want my fucking money."

Templeton swallowed. "You'll take half. You messed up."

The soldier growled and whipped a knife from the sheath tied next to his ribs. Templeton didn't have time to move, and the blade pressed into his throat.

The mercenary said, "The head lives on for a minute after decapitation. I'll take you by the hair and show you your headless body, Templeton. You can watch it writhe until life leaves your brain. My money."

Templeton's eyes flickered from blade to a point beyond the killer's right arm. The soldier backed away then glanced over his shoulder. The boy framed in the doorway was about seven or eight. He wore an *Empire Strikes Back* T-shirt. His weapon was aimed at the mercenary's heart.

The boy said, "Put down your weapon, or I'll kill you with my light-sabre, Vadar. The Force is strong in me."

The soldier-of-fortune chuckled. "You're Luke Skywalker, are you?"

The boy nodded. He flicked a switch on his light-sabre and the tube hummed, glared green. The boy swished the weapon about.

The mercenary turned to face him. Holding out the knife, he said, "You want to fight with me?" He looked back at Templeton and said, "What d'you say? Shall I fight the kid?" The politician's face was white. A clicking sound came from his throat. The mercenary smiled and said, "Should I kill him and feed you his heart?"

Templeton said, "Take the money. It's in the briefcase, under the desk."

Knife held out, eyes watching man and boy, the soldier crossed to the desk and picked up the briefcase from underneath. He put it down on the desk and flipped it open. His balls tingled. His stomach knotted. His heart beat faster. Crisp notes. Almost two hundred grand. He licked his lips. Flipped the briefcase shut and grabbed it by the handle.

Templeton stood in the doorway, arms around his Luke Skywalker. "Get out," he said to the mercenary. "Through the back."

As the killer left the library with his money, Templeton told him, "I never want to see or hear from you again."

The mercenary smiled, and then another voice made him laugh out loud:

The little Luke Skywalker saying, "I never want to see or hear from you again, Vadar."

CHAPTER 30.
THE BOOK.

RICHIE Jarvis put the Yale into the lock and pushed open the door. Once inside, he leaned against the door, and tried to steady his breathing. Panic had made him cold and clammy, and he wanted a cool place to chill out with a smoke. His throat was like sandpaper; he was desperate for a beer.

Come on, he told himself, *calm down, man, calm down. you're home. You're safe.*

Jarvis smelled curry and weed. Leigh must have got a takeaway to comfort her while he was out, the fat cow, and then smoked his dope.

"Bitch," he said, "nicking my gear."

He marched into the living room and snapped on the lights. The remains of her rogan josh stained a plate on the coffee table. Three empty bottles of Rolling Rock stood around the plate. The remains of three joints — three fucking joints — were in the ashtray, along with dozens of fag ends; *his* fucking fags, again. A Rizzla packet was open on the table. A cigarette, slit up the middle for its tobacco, balanced on the lip of the ashtray. The cellophane that was wrapped around his dope had been rolled up into a ball — an *empty* ball.

"Bitch." If she'd been down here, fat arse slumped on the sofa, he'd have kicked her about. But she was upstairs, so he couldn't be bothered, now. Anyway, he'd kick her out tomorrow. He wasn't sharing the cash with her, the useless slag; he could upgrade with the money he'd make of this Templeton job.

He went into the kitchen and, ignoring the tower of dirty plates in the sink, fished in his trouser pocket for the key to the cellar door. *His* cellar. He unlocked the door and went in, locking the door behind him.

He put the light on and breathed in the fusty atmosphere as he walked down the stone stairs. The plaster walls were glossed with condensation and in places the pink paint cracked and peeled.

A fridge in the corner hummed. Jarvis opened it. The gear was still inside. Leigh hadn't broken in and stolen his good stash; she just got her hands on the crap he kept under the sink.

He pulled out a wooden chair from beneath the Formica table at the centre of the cellar. He took off his jacket and hung it on the back of the chair, and then noticed the sticky bloodstain on his shirt. He took the garment off, chucked it in the corner, reminded himself to burn it later.

His body prickled with goosepimples as the chill of the cellar crawled over his flesh. He shivered and sat at the table. Taking the Jiffy bag from one inside coat pocket, the knife from the other, he laid the items on the Formica. He gazed at each in turn.

He sliced open the envelope with the knife, then threw the weapon in the shirt's direction. It clanked against the floor, and slid under the fridge.

I'll get it later, he thought.

Jarvis spilled the contents of the Jiffy bag onto the table and said, "Bollocks."

No cash. Papers, that's all. Photographs. A diary.

He rifled through the material. There were letters, the writing a scrawl, but it didn't really matter how bad the handwriting was, Jarvis couldn't read it anyway.

The photos, though, were interesting: a man – Jesus, it was Templeton – and a woman on a beach.

Templeton was young in this picture. Long black hair, bushy sideburns. The woman was a cracker, dark-hair, tits looked great in that bikini. Jarvis got an erection.

He turned the picture and saw what he guessed was a date. He couldn't read letters, but he knew numbers.

The writing was a word, which he couldn't understand, and then "1974." He smiled and said, "That's when I were born. Good man, Richie, lad."

He looked at the photograph again and wondered if the woman was Templeton's wife. He tried to remember the wedding picture he'd seen on the mantelpiece at Templeton Hall. His only visit, labouring for a builder who was renovating the house nine months earlier. His memory was blurred. The bride's face wouldn't come to his head. Too much drink and drugs, he smiled to himself.

He threw the picture aside and looked at the others. More of Templeton and the woman. Then he came across a picture of a baby, swaddled in red. It had a grimace on its face like it was about to shit. Its hair was pitch black. It was only a few weeks old.

Jarvis said, "You were an ugly little bastard, Michael."

He cast the picture aside and picked up the book. It was small and thick, almost like the bible that man outside the pub had last weekend. The man tried to save Richie, said Christ was his saviour. It was night-time, and fuck knows what the man was doing out late on a Saturday. Richie, pissed and high, headbutted him and stole a few quid from his pocket. The man said, "The Lord loves you," as Richie ran away.

This book had a blue cover, and there was a name written on the front in gold letters. He sniffed the book. It smelled damp. He flicked through the pages and the words were just a mess to him, but the book fell open at the back cover.

Buried into a groove cut into the cardboard was a vial half-filled with blood. He pulled the glass tube out of its bed and held it up in front of his wrinkled nose.

"What the fuck?"

He put the tube of blood back into the slot in the cover.

He flipped through the book to the first page. There was a picture glued to the page. It was that Templeton man, again, with a little girl, dark hair, smiling, about three years old. Words had been written underneath it in black felt tip pen. Jarvis squinted, as if that was going to help him read the words.

Whatever they said, he guessed the book, and the photos, and everything else in the padded envelope was worth a lot of money. He started thinking of numbers again. He thought of the four grand Michael was going to pay him, then he put another zero at the end of that number, and then another one for luck.

CHAPTER 31.
NATURE.

DROPPING her off a few hours earlier, he'd said, "I think we should maybe go for a drink, you know, talk about this. I don't know. What do you think? I think we should."

She smiled at him, at his fumblings, and said okay, she would, that was probably a good idea, she'd like to dot every "i" and cross every "t" before deciding what to do.

And he said, "Deciding what to do?" with his eyebrows raised, and she said, "Yes, a girl in trouble's got to have options."

He was good looking, and there was a grim charm to him. She could see the pain in his eyes. He said he was divorced. Maybe that was the source of the hurt. She didn't want to know too much about him, not if she'd have to kill him.

Laura brushed her damp hair. Her skin, washed of grime and sweat, tingled from the hot shower. Sitting on the edge of her bed wearing a dressing gown, she watched her reflection.

So this is what they see, she thought. At last, this is me.

When Elena found her in that Manchester club, Laura had no idea of who she was. An animal without self-awareness, that's all. An animal that could gaze at its reflection and not realise that it was its own eyes that gazed back.

She had no memory of the first four years of her life. That night Templeton slaughtered her family had wiped it all away. But Elena re-awakened the memory, made it like this mirror in her bedroom.

She looked at her reflection and saw the child she was, felt the rage she felt, tasted the blood she swallowed. Even then she could make fangs. But only at the age of eleven did her true abilities become apparent. More than blood, more than growing, Laura started to shift her shape. And it terrified her.

She was twelve and her foster mother took her to the park. She told Laura about growing up, about becoming a woman. She said, *It happens to every girl, it happened to me, to my mother, to your mother, too, and it was nothing to be scared of.*

But it was something to be scared of, because the woman didn't tell her everything.

She didn't say anything about bones crunching, nerves twisting, muscles tearing; nothing about gums being pierced by sharp teeth, and hands curled into claws, and skin ripped by coarse fur.

Laura didn't want to mention these things; she didn't want to be a crybaby. So she ran away. Again and again and again. Over the years, she harnessed her skills, controlled them, and by fourteen she could will herself, painlessly, to change shape.

Change shape and kill.

She sighed as she watched herself in the mirror.

To kill, she thought, moisturising her face. It was so easy, killing. She shrugged. Well, so what? Life's about survival. If I have to kill to survive, nature won't condemn me for it. Nature positively encouraged it.

Laura stood and slipped off the dressing gown and put on a fading pink T-shirt from the pile of clothes on the wicker chair. Sliding beneath her duvet, she thought how easy it would be to kill Templeton's killer.

How easy would it be to kill John Thorn?

Remember how easy it's always been, she thought, drifting into sleep. And as her mind slipped away, a memory was freed.

★ ★ ★

MORGAN HILL HOUSE, BIRMINGHAM – NOVEMBER 25, 1992

Laura sensed the tension when he swaggered into the canteen or TV room. The girls cowered whenever he was around. She didn't care, though; couldn't give a shit as long as she was left alone.

She was in the toilets, and something whimpered in one of the cubicles. Laura pushed open the door and curled up in there was a matchstick of a girl with pale blue eyes, damp with tears. She was no more than thirteen, and Laura thought her name was Mary or Marian.

Laura said, "What's the matter?" like she didn't want to know.

The girl said, "Colin raped me."

Laura looked at the Mary girl. Her suffering touched something in Laura, but at the time Laura said, "What do you want me to do about it?"

Two hours later, Laura sat on the windowsill of the TV room looking out of the window. She stared at the moon, which she liked doing. She thought about the Mary girl, weak, fragile, broken, and thought about the girl's life after she left this place. She'd always be like that, wouldn't she: men abusing her, making her cry.

I'm not like that, she thought, *I'll never be like that: pathetic and useless.*

Rain pebbled the windows. Laura watched it drip on the glass. She sniffed something, a familiar odour, and she turned.

Colin said, "Hello, girls," standing there with his hands on his hips. "Shall I sit here?" and he sat next to a girl about fourteen, a new girl. The other girls moved away, and the new girl tried to do the same but Colin grabbed her arm and said, "You don't want to do that, you know. You want to be nice to me and I'll be nice to you."

The girl trembled, glanced around, but the others ignored her; they were playing pool, cards, table tennis, anything to avoid looking at her and feeling guilty that they did nothing – what could they do? – to stop this bastard from hurting her.

Laura glanced at the clock above the door. It was nine-thirty, half-an-hour until lights out. She stood and strolled over to the couch. Leaning towards Colin, she said, "Is she playing hard to get? Don't worry, not all of us do," and she walked away.

She could feel his eyes drill into her back as she sauntered for the door, swaying her hips as she went. She knew she had him.

Walking along the corridor to her room, Laura thought how badly the weak would cope if the world became wild. The Mary girl, and the new girl in there, and Colin, too: they were all weak and all they would be if the world became wild was prey.

It was ten-to-midnight. She lay on the bed in the dim-lit room, a table lamp's forty-watt bulb holding back the dark. She heard the key in the lock. The door opened and closed. A croaky voice said, "Laura, Laura, look who's coming."

Colin stood in the room, a smile revealing his fag-stained teeth. Laura smelled his festering breath, the sweat on his skin, the blood throbbing through his veins.

He sat on the bed and the springs creaked under his weight.

He said, "You're a surprise package. I thought you were hard and cold, a bit of a bitch, unappreciative of what I can give you."

She said, "Well, you were wrong. You can give me plenty."

He licked his lips, the tongue flicking out of his mouth and over his lips like a slug.

He said, "That's a nice nightie," looking her up and down.

Laura looked down at herself. It was only a T-shirt, but she said, "Do you like it? I wore it for you."

"Little slag, eh. That's nice. Wanting it so much." He got up and unbuttoned his shirt, and his fat stomach, the colour of lard, flopped into view. "I can make you very happy, Laura."

Laura leaned forward, her black hair tumbling over her face.

His eyes went wide and he said, "You're fucking hot, you are," and he took off his trousers. "Are you going to be good for me, or bad, eh?"

Laura looked him up and down and tried not to retch. He was a slab of fat, that was all: a pale and pasty chunk of grease. Trying to add some promise into her voice, she said, "I'm going to be awful. A real bitch."

★ ★ ★

Colin tried to avoid loners with cold eyes, girls like Laura Greenacre.

He wasn't worried about being reported. They wouldn't dare; too scared. But even if they did, who would believe a little thief over a man of his standing? Church-going family man, scoutmaster, former kindly school caretaker; he was a stalwart, a pillar.

No, he wasn't concerned about a gossip. But the loners, the cold-eyed ones, they could fight back: bite him, scratch him, bruise him. If he was badly hurt, he'd have to report to sick bay, and then there would be paperwork, an inquiry, questions: "How did you manage to get a bite mark on your inside leg, Mr Pavin?"

Best leave the Laura Greenacres of this world alone, unless they come begging for it.

And here she was, begging for it. She was gorgeous, all right; looked a bit grown-up for him, but still...if it was being offered on a plate.

She was crouching on the bed, and he could see the shadows down her nightdress. He stood in his Y-fronts, hands on his hips, belly quivering. He said, "What are you going to do to me, you little bitch?"

"I'm going to eat you alive."

"Eat me alive, eh."

"Yes, every last morsel."

"There's a lot of me."

"I've got big teeth and a big appetite."

"Have you, now. You like to be slapped around, Laura?" he said, grabbing her chin. She whipped her head from side to side, her long dark hair slashing the gloom. Colin said, "I like slapping my bitch around, you see. You're going to get slapped around, whether you like it or not. And you will like it."

He pushed her face away, and turned round. He pushed down his underpants, and wobbled his fat bottom. "Like my arse, little bitch? Ha ha ha," and he turned around, naked. He said, "So eat me, then," and pushed out his groin.

Laura was smiling, baring her teeth, white, white teeth in the grey, grey light. Colin looked at her and thought he saw something different in her, and a chill leached into his intestines.

He furrowed his brow, looked at Laura, and Laura snarled, and for a moment he thought he liked it and laughed; but she was really snarling, a guttural snarling.

He thought, then, that he would maybe leave her because she was weird, but then he thought, *She's fucking horny and I'm horny,* but then her eyes became yellow with black slits and he took a step back.

Colin blinked and blinked and blinked; the room was too dark for him to see everything, but he could see most of it, and it was terrible.

He tried to cry out, and a tearing noise filled his ears and the nightdress, shredded, fluttered to the floor, Colin watching the pieces flutter; then his eyes lifted and his bowels seemed heavy and full of ice water. And he stared at where Laura was, and knew that he should be seeing warm, creamy flesh, not this coarse, black fur. His mouth opened in a scream and his face stretched out in horror. He knew he should be seeing soft, gentle hands reaching for his groin, not claws slashing at his balls.

His abdomen felt as if it was on fire. He screamed and his belly hissed, and he tried to stop his insides falling out.

He staggered back and said, "Laura," but it wasn't Laura, it was colossal and dangerous and showed sharp, white fangs, and moved menacingly towards him.

Colin trembled, fell to his knees, shat himself, tried to push his guts back into his body and cried because he couldn't and because it hurt so much.

The smell of his own muck filled his nostrils and the great, black thing loomed over him, and he looked up at it and said, "Laura?" and the thing fell on him and Colin screamed and heard himself being eaten alive.

CHAPTER 32.
BLESSINGS.

MICHAEL watched the dawn break bloody from the drawing room window.

He closed his eyes, fatigue pressing down on him. He'd only been in bed for an hour when Thorn arrived, pale and dark eyed. The policeman said, "I'm really sorry, Michael, this is my fault, but your father's been..." Thorn hesitated, and Michael tried not to show his excitement. Come on Thorn, he was thinking, tell me: my father's been...injured?...in an accident?...murdered?

And Thorn said, "...attacked, killed."

Michael turned his head away and spluttered. He felt Thorn's hand on his shoulder, Thorn saying, "I'm so sorry. It's my fault. I'd understand if you wanted to make an official complaint. I've been derelict in my duty."

Forcing out the tears, Michael said, "No. It's all right, John. I understand. He told you not to go with him, didn't he. It's that girl, you know."

Thorn's eyes were wide, and his mouth dropped open as if he was about to say something, but he didn't. He dropped his gaze, shook his head, and said he was sorry again. After Thorn left, Michael made a fist and said, "Yes."

The police arrived at two-thirty a.m. and Michael feigned grief again. He didn't bother going back to bed after they left. He was buzzing, the adrenalin coursing through him. But as the hours passed, fatigue started to overwhelm him. He sipped at the black coffee Mrs Garvey brewed when she arrived at five a.m., and it helped fight off the exhaustion.

The door opened and he heard the click of heels cross the panelled floorboards. He looked over his shoulder. She was already in mourning colours. Her platinum blonde hair was bundled back into a bun. Red eyes betrayed her tears. She had been there with Michael when the police told him of his father's murder. Then she went back to her room to tell Skipp, her husband, into whose shoulder she bawled, no doubt.

He should have sliced an onion in the kitchens and made himself cry. He showed no grief at all, nothing. *I'll put it down to shock*, he thought.

Ruth slipped an arm around his waist and he responded by draping his arm over her shoulders. She smelled of soap and hairspray.

His aunt said, "She'll be made to pay for this, won't she?"

Michael said, "You think it was her? They said he'd been stabbed. She would have...I don't know, not her style."

"She's in there somewhere, Michael. The police mentioned her. They think she's involved somehow. I think she's involved."

"Yes. I'm sure you're right." The need for sleep faded. "You mentioned last night the need take action, do something."

"Yes." Ruth slipped away from him and turned her back. "I'll leave that to you. You're master of this house, now." She turned to face him and said, "Did he tell you why he was going out last night?"

Michael lowered his gaze. He shook his head. "Just said he was going out. I thought his bodyguard was with him, but he wasn't. Gave him the night off. He was here, apologising, blaming himself."

Ruth shook her head. Michael saw her anger. He didn't want the blame for this shifted to an incompetent police protection officer. He wanted Laura Greenacre held responsible. He said, "Dad seemed troubled since the incident with the dogs."

"He knew it was her, didn't he."

"He did, yes." Then he twisted the knife a little further into Laura Greenacre. "He was convinced she was going to kill him."

Ruth nodded.

He said, "Can't blame her, I suppose."

He heard Ruth's gasp and she came to him and slapped his face. She was crying and her lips quivered.

She said, "He did that for you. Don't you ever excuse her. *Them*. Do you think it was easy for him? To slaughter women and children? He was never a callous man, Michael. Not like you. That, you got from your mother. Everything he did, he did for the family."

"I know," he said, rubbing his cheek.

"Take something from him, Michael. Take his warmth and his kindness and his pain. Take his pride in the Templeton name and his sense of history."

"Don't worry, Aunt Ruth." Michael turned away. "I'll take it all."

CHAPTER 33.
THE BLUES.

DENTON glared at Thorn and said, "What do you mean 'we', sergeant?"

Thorn looked at her. Her eyes were narrow, her brow creased. She was wearing blue, a cold blue. Her hands gripped the back of the chair, and she was leaning forward, fixing him with her stare. He said, "I mean it's something that needs looking into. The Greenacre girl says she saw someone at Templeton Hall the other night. That someone may be the person we're looking for."

"There's that 'we' again. You're not part of this investigation, sergeant, I hope you realise that."

He shuffled in the chair. "I realise," he said.

"And as for lines of inquiry," she said, turning to gaze out of her window, "they all seem to come to a dead end at Laura Greenacre's door." She was quiet for a moment, then she shot a look at Thorn and said, "Wouldn't you say so?"

He would say so, but wasn't going to, not here in front of Denton.

But she didn't let it go. Slipping into her chair, she said, "Not infatuated with this Greenacre girl, are we, Sergeant Thorn?"

Thorn felt the heat rise in his cheeks. He said, "Sir Adam Templeton

119

was good to me, and I was of fond of him. If I thought for one moment that Laura Greenacre killed him, you'd have to put me on a leash, Ma'am, because I'd go beyond the law to bring her to justice."

She looked at him, then said, "Maybe it's good that you're not part of the investigation. We couldn't have a police officer going 'Death Wish' on us, could we." She leaned forward, elbows on the desk. "We found trainers, and they are going to be her trainers, and her footprints. She's nailed, sergeant."

"I think he gave her a letter at court yesterday morning."

Denton's wrinkled her nose. "What letter?"

"Sir Adam asked her to meet him at Hadrian's Wall."

She pressed back into her chair, her body stiffening. "You didn't tell me this."

"Last night was upsetting. It slipped my mind."

"Slipped your mind. What did it say, this letter?"

"I've no idea. He didn't tell me."

"We're they having an affair?"

"I..." He hesitated. The thought made him feel sick. He said, "I can't say, but I doubt it. I was with Sir Adam twenty-four-seven – "

"Not quite twenty-four-seven."

He grimaced, but let it go, then said, "He certainly knew her. Why else give her this letter. You don't give a stranger a letter. You don't drop the charges against a stranger."

Denton thought for a moment. "What do you think happened to those dogs?"

"I really don't know. They were torn apart. It was like some animal, a very considerable animal, had got to them."

"She was there, this girl. But she wasn't hurt. She was naked, but wasn't hurt." Denton shook her head. "Naked. Why was she naked? Maybe she and Templeton were having sex in the trees. The dogs got free – "

"Templeton was in the house. They were all in the house. I was with them when the alarms went off. I ordered the dogs be released."

Denton dropped her gaze to the desk and shuffled some papers that didn't need shuffling. She said, "We'll wait 'til we get the science back. Forensics will put her at Hadrian's Wall, forensics will link her to Templeton's murder, forensics will tell us what killed those dogs."

"What about the man she says she saw at the Hall, the man she – " He stopped. He almost said, "She saw last night at the Wall."

Denton shot him a look and said, "She what? 'The man she' what?"

Thorn said the words slowly. "The man she claims was running through the trees the night the dogs were killed."

Denton focused on him for a moment, and he felt her eyes press into him. Then she looked away and said, "Thank you for insights, Sergeant Thorn. But I didn't ask you here to discuss the case." She looked at him and said, "I'll need your I.D., your gun, and your weapons permit."

Thorn knew this was coming, but it still flustered him. He felt the pace of his pulse increase, and the blood flush his cheeks.

Denton said, "You're suspended, on full pay, pending an internal investigation into your conduct. You'll get all the details in an official letter from the assistant chief constable. You can also expect a complaint from Michael Templeton. That'll bring in the Police Complaints Authority."

"That's great, thank you for that."

"We don't do sarcasm here. I don't find it amusing. I'm rubbish at amusing, you know that. That's why they call me 'Smiler'. It's ironic. I *do* do irony."

★ ★ ★

Laura hooked her knee around the pole. She grabbed the aluminum shaft with both hands. Throwing her head from side to side so that her hair flared about her shoulders and face, she slid down the pole. She leaned backwards, arms stretched out, then spun around, and down, until she was sat on the stage, the metal between her crossed legs.

She brushed her hair from her face and looked at Elena, who was sitting at a table scribbling in a ledger. Laura said, "I'm going to have to leave."

Elena raised her eyes from the book and placed the pen on the table.

Laura said, "The police will come looking for me."

Elena got up, crossed to the stage, and sat on the edge. Laura uncoiled herself from the metal pole and slid across the floorboards to join Elena. She leaned into the older woman.

Laura said, "I left my shoes."

"Oh, my God."

"Just like Cinderella."

"Oh, Laura."

"So I've got to leave."

Elena bit her bottom lip. Her brow furrowed and Laura sensed tears in the narrowed eyes. She said, "I don't want to lose you; I've only just found you."

"I've only just found myself, Elena."

"We should be together, you know. We're all that's left. *You're* all that's left."

"You still count yourself a Greenacre, then?"

"I was never a Greenacre. That was the problem, wasn't it." There was bitterness in her voice. "I only fell in love with a Greenacre. I could never be one. They'd never allow it."

Laura said, "Why have you been so kind to me if they treated you so badly?"

Elena looked at Laura. "You're still family. Richard was your uncle, and he loved you. If he loved you, I love you." She turned away, looked out over the club. "It was your father. He hated me. Hated his brother for marrying outside the tribe."

Laura said nothing. She gazed at Elena, saw the pain creased into her face.

Elena said, "I was in London when I heard of all those killings. I knew it was Templeton's doing. But what could I do? Some bimbo, an ex-stripper. Who'd believe me with a story like that? I came up here two years later. Visited Richard's grave." She gasped, as if the memory physically hurt her. "I went to the archives and read the papers, saw the names. It mentioned you. Sole survivor, they said." Elena brushed Laura's cheek with her finger and smiled. "I thought of looking for you."

"Why didn't you?"

"Who was I to you? I'd never known you. I'd been forced to leave before you were born." She furrowed her brow and said, "I prayed the scientists hadn't got a hold of you. Experimenting on you."

"I was all right. I got really careful. Sometimes I want to change – like in the hospital with that bastard of a doctor. But if I did, and killed all those people, everyone would know. I'd have been seen. I'd be hunted. I don't want to be hunted."

"I know." She paused a moment, then said, "I never believed in fate, but that night in Manchester: it was written in the stars, I'm sure of it. When I saw you throw that man over the balcony –"

Laura smiled at the recollection.

Elena said, "And then I saw the birthmark." She touched the back of Laura's shoulder. "It was unreal. But I should have left you."

"Why? I had nothing 'til you came along. I was no one. I didn't know who I was, what I was, I didn't know where my powers had come from."

"Maybe it was better that way. I brought it all back."

"You gave me a reason to live."

"And a reason to kill."

"To avenge. To avenge all of them. Richard, too. That's what you wanted, wasn't it, Elena? You knew I'd kill for you?"

"And look where it's got me. I'm about to lose you, now."

"I'll let you know where I am. But we've got to be careful. The cops'll come looking for you, asking questions."

They were quiet for a minute.

Then Laura said, "Do I remind you of Richard?"

"Oh, yes," said Elena. She took a handkerchief from her pocket and blew her nose. "You're the same blood, aren't you. The Greenacre tribe. You were more than uncle and niece. You were pure blood. More than I could ever offer if I'd been able to..." She hesitated, her jaw clenched. Then she spat out the words, "...breed for them." Elena sighed, and then said, "Where will you go?"

Laura leaned into her and wrapped her arms around Elena's shoulders. "I don't know. I don't know where's safe, now. They'll never leave me alone unless they find that man who killed Templeton. And they won't do that. They want me, Thorn said so." She pulled away and jumped off the stage. "I think I'll maybe go find him myself, you know. Give them his head on a plate."

They looked at each other, and Laura saw the wetness in Elena's eyes. She started to move towards her, to hug her, but a great thumping at the doors made her flinch.

Laura said, "What's that?"

"Sounds like the cavalry," said Elena, heading towards the entrance.

CHAPTER 34.
FIAT PUNTO.

THORN entered the grounds through the farm gate at the rear of the estate. The wooden barrier was cloaked by greenery and led out into a narrow, private lane.

He shut the gate, then went back to the car, but stopped and stared up at the house, monolithic against the moody sky. His shoulders slumped, and he felt a burden in his chest. Leaving would be difficult. The months here had not been what he would describe as happy, but Thorn had developed an affinity for both the hall and its master; a respect he didn't have for the heir.

Thorn guided the car past the farm buildings, empty since Adam Templeton had failed to find the same enthusiasm his father had for agriculture. The elements gladly took on what Sir Adam had rejected, and the buildings were rusted and battered by all that nature could hurl at them. Work was done on the interiors a few months ago, but it was cowboy stuff – shoddy and cheap.

He parked at the back of the house and entered through the servants' entrance. The odour of cooking wafted from the kitchen, Mrs Garvey at her duties. Thorn licked his lips and his stomach rumbled. He'd miss the nonsense moments shared with Mrs Garvey; he'd definitely miss her cholesterol-laden breakfasts. He'd drop by on his way out to say his farewells.

Thorn's room was bare. White walls, single bed, bedside table and lamp, wardrobe, and an en-suite bathroom. Thorn had never meant it to be a home from home; somewhere to put his head down when he was required at the house, that's all.

He took some shirts and trousers from the wardrobe and packed them into a sports bag. He gathered up a dozen CDs and an unopened biography of Darwin. He emptied the bedside table's drawers of underwear and socks, and as he dug out the garments he touched something cold.

He pulled out the gun. It was a twin of the standard issue Browning he left on Denton's desk that morning. An illegitimate twin. It was a "you-never-know" weapon, as a former protection squad officer had once referred to unlicensed guns.

("You never know when you'll need one, John.")

Thorn found a box of bullets buried under his underwear. He chucked the box, along with a handful of clothes, into the holdall.

A knock at the door startled him. He twisted, gun aimed at the door.

"John. Can I come in?"

He slipped the gun under the clothes in the bag and said, "Yes, Michael, come in."

Michael Templeton's eyes were cradled by shadows, and he frowned.

A wave of sympathy flooded Thorn's heart. He said, "Stupid question, but how do you feel this morning? Did you get any sleep after I left?"

"Not really. Police came. Questions, you know."

Thorn nodded. He said, "I should have been with him."

Michael waved the admission away and sat on the bed next Thorn's sports bag. He stared at the bag then picked up a CD from the pile scattered on top of the clothes.

Thorn looked at the bag and then looked at Michael, and held his breath for a few seconds.

Studying the CD, Michael wrinkled his nose. "Bach?" he said, as if he'd found a copy of Razzle in a bishop's bible, "A bit old-fashioned."

Thorn shrugged. "I like him," he said, taking the CD from Michael and tossing it into the bag. He zipped the bag up and put it on the floor.

"You don't need to leave, you know," said Michael.

Thorn smelled his own sweat. He rubbed the back of his neck. He wanted to grab the sports bag and go home. He said, "I'm suspended from duty. They're investigating the incident. My involvement, or lack of involvement."

"Don't blame yourself. Not your fault. He was unpredictable of late.

Especially after that girl..." Michael bit his lower lip, and then said, "Do they think it's her?"

Thorn shook his head. "I don't know. They'll want to question her. But...I don't think it was."

"You don't? Why not?"

"Whoever killed your father was strong. The wound...I'm sorry."

"It's all right. I know. It was bad."

Thorn said, "I just don't think it was her."

"She's strong. Stronger than you think."

Thorn remembered how easily Laura had overcome him last night. He narrowed his eyes and thought about that. Michael was right: she had strength. Maybe she was lying; manipulating him.

Thorn grabbed the sports bag by the handles and swung it over his shoulder. "I'd better get moving. I need to talk to the Police Federation. I think I'm in trouble over this."

"Not with me, you're not. I want you to stay, John."

"How do you mean?"

"I'll give you a job. I know we've had our differences, you and I, but I trust you. How about Director of Security? How does that sound? We'll need protecting. Dad may have only been the first."

"The first? You're suggesting a vendetta? Are you in danger?"

"I don't know. Possibly."

Thorn thought about Laura's claim that Sir Adam had killed her family. Could there have been another survivor? Could Michael be right about a vendetta? Thorn shook his head, casting the doubts from his head.

"Thanks for your offer, Michael. But I can't. Not now. I want to see how this investigation pans out. If it goes against me, and the offer's still open, perhaps I'll take you up on it." He went to the door.

Michael said, "It won't be. It's a one-time only job offer."

Thorn turned to look at Michael. The young man was scowling. They stared at each other for a few seconds, then Thorn said, "I'll say goodbye."

After a tearful Mrs Garvey hugged him to the point of suffocation, Thorn went to the car. He switched on the engine and glanced in the rear view mirror.

The yellow Fiat Punto rumbled down the route Thorn had taken half-an-hour earlier.

Thorn twisted in his seat. He squinted, trying to register the vehicle and the face behind its steering wheel. Thorn knew everyone who had access to Templeton Hall, through the front or rear gates. Only close family, staff, and tradesmen used the back road, and Thorn recognised every face, every vehicle.

Not this one.

He made a mental note of the registration number.

The Punto stopped about thirty yards behind Thorn's car. The driver stepped out. A lean, pale, ruffian in his mid-thirties. Trouble, if I ever saw it, thought Thorn. The stranger carried a thick Jiffy bag under one heavily tattooed arm. He looked across at Thorn and the men stared at each other for a few moments, until the newcomer dropped his gaze and crossed the gravel towards the back door.

Thorn switched off the engine and stepped out of the car. He said, "Can I help you?"

The stranger turned to face him. For a second Thorn saw fear in the man's face. The man said, "No, you can't."

"Do you have business here? My name's John Thorn. I'm a police officer. Can I ask you your name?"

The stranger stopped. He darted a look towards the Fiat Punto. Thorn saw the flight instinct flare in the man's face. Thorn got ready to run, bring him down.

The back door opened and Michael Templeton stepped out of the house. The stranger looked at him. Thorn followed his gaze. Michael's face lost its colour, and his eyes went wide. His throat moved as if words were trapped in his larynx. Michael was obviously nervous of this man, and this triggered Thorn's protective nature.

"Get inside, Michael," Thorn said, eyes fixed on the stranger.

Michael said, "No, it's all right."

Thorn stopped and looked at the young Templeton. "Do you know this guy?"

Michael seemed to relax, the tension dropped from his shoulders, and he said, "These things don't concern you any more, John."

Thorn frowned at Michael, then shot a look at the stranger. The man smirked, rubbed his unshaven chin, and said, "They don't concern you."

CHAPTER 35.
PRESSURE.

MICHAEL paced the kitchen and said, "What the fuck d'you think you're doing?" He stopped and glared at Jarvis. "You fucking demented special needs fuckwit. Thorn saw you. He's a fucking copper."

His father's killer leaned against a worktop where Mrs Garvey had been gutting fish for lunch. The briny odour hung in the room and the stench, or maybe it was the look on Jarvis's face, filled Michael's throat with hot liquid.

Jarvis glanced at the stainless steel fridge. "Any beer in there?" He crossed to the fridge, opened the door and dipped his head inside. "Fuck all," he said, shutting the fridge door.

"What do you want, Jarvis?"

"Where's my cash?"

"You'll get it. I told you. And I told you never to come here."

Jarvis grinned. His front two teeth were missing. Michael never noticed during their previous meetings. Jarvis had never smiled before, and never reeked of this kind of cockiness.

Michael said, "I'll get you the money. I said so, didn't I?" His anger faded, and in its place came a sense of fear. Was it being in the company of the man who, hours before, had killed his father? It couldn't be guilt. That feeling was alien to Michael. Conscience was something the weak-willed had to bear. He said, "And after you get paid, I don't want to see you again, Jarvis."

Jarvis said, "The price went up."

"You bastard – "

Jarvis' tossed the padded envelope on the worktop. Michael stared at it, creased his brow, then shrugged. "What's that? Fucking Christmas present?"

"Something you're going to be very interested in, Michael. Have a look, and if you like what you see it'll cost you a little bit extra to take it off my hands."

"How much extra?"

"'Bout twenty-grand extra."

CHAPTER 36.
UNSOLVED CRIMES.

KEN Travis sat in an armchair staring at the blank television screen. It was as if he was drawing pictures from his head and transplanting them onto the TV.

"It was awful, John. So much blood. So many dead. Women and children." He shook his head. "Never seen anything like it. The magnitude. Killed at the same time. Same way."

"How were they killed?" said Thorn, leaning forward in the chair with his elbows resting on his knees.

"Shot, all shot. They reckoned the killers were professionals. They never found them, never found out why. Unsolved crimes, all of them. Terrible."

Thorn studied the sergeant. Travis's eyes were distant, the bloodshed witnessed twenty years previous fixed in his mind. Thorn said, "Any names you remember?"

"Names?" Travis wrinkled his nose. "The ones I went to were called Ashley. Two men, a woman and..." he paused and dropped his gaze "... three kids. Who'd kill children in that way?" He raised his face to stare at Thorn. "Why children, John?"

Thorn said nothing. He felt as if he'd been gutted. Doubt crept over him again. Should he ask if there were Greenacres among the dead? How, if at all, was this Ashley family related to Laura? Then he said, "What do you make of the Greenacre girl, Ken?"

Thorn thought he saw Travis's pupils flare. Travis looked towards the clock on the mantelpiece. He said, "The dancer? I don't know. Why do you ask? What's she got to do with the killings?"

"I was just asking. You had her in the car after we found her at the Hall."

Travis shuffled. His cheeks went red. "Oh yes. I'm sorry about what's happened. Heard they were investigating. Not freelancing are you, John?"

"Just being nosey. You know, once a cop..."

"Hmmm." Travis got up. "I'd better get going. Criminals to catch and all that."

"Yes, sure." Thorn stood. "How are things developing on the masked rapist?"

Travis mumbled, shook his head. He grabbed the remote control laying on the coffee table and used it to switch on the television. "Not much. Nothing really. Another unsolved one, eh," he said, channel surfing.

Thorn watched him for a moment before reaching into his trouser pocket. "Could you do me a favour, Ken?"

CHAPTER 37.
HELPING WITH INQUIRIES.

DENTON said, "Where were you last night between eight o'clock and eleven o'clock, Miss Greenacre?"

"Snuggled up in bed with my teddy."

"Anyone able to confirm this?"

"Apart from my teddy, no. I sleep alone. I only *fuck* with other people."

Laura heard Ellis Cole, sitting next to her in the interview room, gasp. Her eyes held Lorraine Denton. The detective's face was pale and sharp and cold.

"Do you own a pair of trainers, Miss Greenacre?"

"They are a vital fashion accessory. Among the young."

Eyes on Laura, Denton leaned back and reached behind her chair.

Laura tried to be cool and arrogant, but fear chewed at her insides. It was rooted there originally when Denton, two detectives, and four uniformed officers stomped into Bliss that morning.

Elena's protests about warrants and rights were brushed away, Denton saying they were only seeking Miss Greenacre's help, and they would be ever so grateful, and possibly able to do something about the assault charges she faced after the incident at the hospital.

Denton lifted the polythene bag containing Laura's trainers onto the table. A detective constable whose name Laura didn't know said, "For the benefit of the tape, Detective Chief Superintendent Denton is showing a pair of trainers found at the scene."

"Are these yours, Miss Greenacre?" said Denton, head tilted.

Laura said, "No, they're not mine. Too cheap."

Denton ignored her, and said, "They were found in some undergrowth, twenty yards from Sir Adam Templeton's body. How did they get there, do you think?"

"They walked?"

Ellis Cole, leaning forward with his hands flat on the table, said, "Mrs Denton. Could I clarify: My client is not under arrest, is she?"

Denton's eyes stayed on Laura. "She is not under arrest."

"Then she can leave of her own free will. At any time. Am I correct?"

Still staring at Laura, Denton said, "You are correct, Mr Cole."

Cole stood. "Then I suggest we put a stop to this nonsense."

Denton said, "Will your client be willing to provide a DNA sample so we can eliminate her from our enquiries?" She stroked the polythene bag as if it were a cat that had caught a troublesome mouse. "If these trainers are not Miss Greenacre's, then we can move on. Is she willing to provide a sample?"

Laura jumped to her feet and said, "No she is not," and then strode towards the door, Cole on her heels.

Denton's voice stopped them. "You do understand that Miss Greenacre's refusal to comply allows us to assume she has something to hide. And if need be, we will get a court order requiring her to give a DNA sample. Do you have something to hide, Miss Greenacre?"

Laura smiled at Denton. She thought, *More than you know*. Her swagger seemed to unnerve the detective. Denton's face cracked, her forehead furrowing.

Laura turned and left the room. She strolled through the corridors. Cole walked behind her, and Laura knew he was looking at her backside. She didn't care. She focused on appearing confident and unconcerned; because inside she felt wretched and fragile

CHAPTER 38.
A DEATH FORETOLD.

MICHAEL sat on a leather chair in the office of Charles Groom of Groom, Hurley, and Finch, the Templeton family lawyers. His thoughts remained in the kitchen at Templeton Hall where he'd unravelled the package brought by Jarvis. Spreading its contents – photocopied notes and pictures – on the worktop where the cook had earlier been gutting fish, Michael read, and soon empathised with the salmon. The words, the images – grainy in presentation, clear in context – were like blades tearing at his insides.

Jarvis said, "Twenty thousand, or they go to the girl."

The details had shaken Michael's world. They were, to him, worth far more than twenty-grand, which he would happily part with to keep them secret.

The sun's rays sliced through the blinds on the window behind Charles Groom. The window gazed out across the Tyne to Gateshead.

The smells of leather, varnish, and perfume made Michael dizzy as he now considered what Jarvis had shown him.

"Michael." A hand brushed his forearm. "Michael."

It was Ruth. She was sitting next to him in an identical red leather chair.

"Yes. I'm sorry," he said, turning to face the lawyer. Charles Groom wore a blue pinstripe suit, pink shirt and blue silk tie. His thinning black hair was greased back over his skull. Rolls of skin cradled his eyes, and his chin had doubled itself near his reddened throat.

Groom said, "As I was explaining, Sir Adam contacted me two days ago regarding his will."

Michael wanted to scream. First Jarvis, now Groom. Messengers bearing bad tidings. And with Thorn refusing to be drawn into the fold, it was turning into a rotten day for news.

"The specifics don't change," said Groom.

Michael blew air from his puffed cheeks.

Ruth said, "What do you mean the specifics?"

The solicitor said, "I mean arrangements made for" – Groom paused, perched a pair of spectacles on his nose, and glanced at the papers in front of him – "the son, Michael Adam David Templeton; the sister, Ruth Elizabeth Templeton-Andersson –"

Michael said, "We are *here*, Charles. Can you refer to us in the first person. Not like you're talking about someone else."

Ruth put a hand on his arm and said his name. He leaned back, put a hand to his brow and said, "Okay. I'm sorry. Go on."

Groom said, "Do you need some water, Mr Templeton?"

Michael scowled and said, "Go on."

"Fine," said Groom. He cleared his throat and dropped his gaze to the details once more. "The amendment comes in the form of a one-hundred-thousand-pounds covenant to a named party –"

"A named party?" Michael's blood thumped in his head. His skin itched and his nerves twinged. He was trembling and couldn't control himself. "The bastard. The fucking bastard."

Ruth said, "Michael," her voice containing a sharp edge.

Michael said, "Who is this named party?"

"I am not at liberty to say," said Groom.

Michael gawped. He had words, but they got lost in his throat.

Ruth said, "Why not?"

The solicitor dabbed his forehead with a handkerchief. "Sir Adam's request."

"It's Laura Greenacre, isn't it," said Michael.

"What?" said his aunt.

Michael glowered at Groom and said, "It's her, isn't it."

The solicitor said, "I am not at liberty to say."

Michael stood and went over to a glass-fronted cabinet stacked with legal tomes. He saw Laura Greenacre's face in his own reflection. He balled his hands into fists, digging nails into his palms. His throat was dry and his Adam's apple bobbed. This day was getting worse and worse.

Then Groom said, "There's one more thing," and Michael almost

135

screamed; but he clenched his teeth, contained his rage. The solicitor said, "As you know, Sir Adam had made arrangements for his own funeral several years ago."

Ruth said, "He's changed them as well?" irritation in her voice.

"The specifics remain –"

Michael whirled around. "Fuck the specifics. Just tell us."

Ruth and Groom stared at him for a moment before the lawyer dipped into his papers, and said, "The guests."

"What about the guests?" Ruth's voice trembled. *What next?*, it asked. *What other twist has my brother thrown into this tale?*

"There has been an addition. Two, in fact."

Michael sneered at him, saying, "Are you at liberty to say?"

"Indeed," said Groom. "One is a Detective Sergeant John Thorn, the other, a Laura Greenacre."

Ruth gasped and Michael said, "No fucking way."

"I'm afraid there's nothing you can do," said Groom, "and the requests have been delivered today by courier, in accordance with your father's wishes. It's all very legal."

Michael said, "Cunt."

★ ★ ★

An accident outside the city's Central Station stifled their departure from Newcastle. Michael's hands tightened on the Shogun's steering wheel. Beside him, Ruth, her mascara wet, cried black tears. The wind whipped exhaust fumes from the crawling traffic through the 4x4's half-open window. Michael coughed and rolled up the window. He was thinking, *Why? Why has everything gone wrong?*

Ruth said, "It's guilt. Adam's conscience got the better of him. He's paying her off. Compensating her for what happened." She glanced at Michael. "Do you think?"

"It must be," said Michael, lying. He had to think about Jarvis's envelope, those letters, documents, and images. They threatened everything. And now the will, and the funeral. He shook his head. He thought, *Jarvis is going to have to go.*

The traffic crept forward and he gently pressed the accelerator.

Ruth said, "I can't bear the thought of her at the funeral."

Michael shrugged, trying to pretend it was all right. "If it's what he wanted, we have to abide by his wishes."

136

"He's dead. What difference would it make?"

"If father wanted her there, I want her there."

"How can you say that? He changed the arrangements that night after she was caught on the grounds. That means he knew he was going to die. He knew she was here to kill him. And he seems to thank her for it by changing his will. Now you're saying —"

"I'm saying that he knew what he was doing."

The traffic inched forward. Up ahead, a policeman directed cars around a mass of flashing blue lights.

Ruth said, "I don't understand what you mean."

"Don't worry. It'll soon be finished." He smiled as the gridlock evaporated and the Shogun hummed through its gears. "Father saw that it was time I took over the business. He couldn't carry on the fight, so he hands over the gauntlet to me. Inviting Laura Greenacre to the funeral, naming her in the will, makes her believe the war is over. She'll be vulnerable; in the lion's den; then we pounce."

She made a face and said, "Sounds a bit convoluted."

He shrugged and said, "That's my father for you"

The road was clear. He shifted gears, pressed on the accelerator, and the Shogun raced clear of the traffic. Laura Greenacre was about to become extinct. Then the Templetons, Michael at their helm, could be what they once were: kings of beasts.

CHAPTER 39.
INFORMATION.

DENTON sat at the head of the conference table in Hexham Police Station. It was five p.m. and she saw a few of the detectives in the room glancing at their watches. She was tempted to tell them to leave. Denton suffered no one who gave anything less than body and soul. A life beyond the job was, in her eyes, a sign of weakness. It was like that for her father, it was like that for her.

She said, "You have something better to do DC Bailey?" Bailey jerked and slipped his hand under the table, hiding his watch from the DCS. "The day is not done, ladies and gentlemen," said Denton, her gaze moving from officer to officer, her expectations and demands clear to all. "DI Williams, would you enlighten us."

Nathan Williams cleared his throat. He said, "We cross ref'd Laura Greenacre in HOLMES. In 1992 she's named as sole witness to the killing of a care worker at the Morgan Hill House young offenders unit in Birmingham. Colin Pavin was found butchered – I think that's the only word – in Greenacre's room at the unit where she'd been interred for an assault charge. She was discovered in an emotional state and failed to give any details of who – or what – had been responsible." He looked around the table. "It was believed to have been a large – very large – animal. Window was open."

"Like the dogs at Templeton Hall," said Detective Sergeant Carenza Drew, her brow furrowed as she digested the information.

"Continue, DI Williams," said Denton.

"An attempted armed robbery at an Esso service station in Chester in 1995. Barry Finch and Leon Maguire, two upstanding members of the community..."

The detectives chuckled. Denton frowned, allowed them their moment, then told Williams to continue.

Williams, from his notes, said, "Finch and Maguire forced themselves into the service station at one a.m. on April 24th armed with a sawn-off. Security cameras recorded the actual break-in, but once they got past the doors, Finch disabled the cameras. No more visuals. At one-twenty-three a.m. the distressed cashier called 999. Officers attended to discover Finch and Maguire to be no more. Literally, it seems: they'd been torn to shreds." He looked up from his notes. "The cashier was one Laura Greenacre."

DC Bailey said, "Three people ripped apart in her presence. But she can't have been directly responsible." He shrugged. "Does she have a pet tiger we don't know about?"

DS Drew said, "And she was there when the dogs were killed. One incident, okay; second time it happens" – she rotated her hand – "it's dubious, and you're starting to think; third time: she's got to be involved. Got to be."

"DS Murray," said Denton, "Takes us back."

Greg Murray scratched his mustache and said, "Laura Greenacre had an unsettled childhood. From the age of four she was in care, moved from foster home to foster home. Garnered a few convictions during her teenage years."

"She has a tendency towards violence, though," said Denton.

"Without nailing her for Pavin and the garage robbers, nothing to suggest she'd kill. There's an assault, though," said Murray. He flicked through his notebook. "On a Chris Farnham. Boyfriend, we think. She inflicted serious lacerations to his back and buttocks."

"A knife?" said Denton, sitting up.

Murray glanced up at the DSC. "The doctor who treated Farnham described the wounds as caused by, um, claws."

The silence bubbled. Denton's gaze drifted around the table. They were considering impossible things.

★ ★ ★

Dr Lawrence Procter looked down his long nose at the card Thorn held between thumb and forefinger.

"That's not proper identification. It's a business card," said the doctor. "I read the evening paper, Mr Thorn. I understand you to be suspended, therefore I am not required to discuss anything with you."

"I'm working for the family in a private capacity," said Thorn.

They were standing at the hospital's reception desk. Thorn could smell disinfectant and it made him nauseous. Or maybe it was Procter who made him sick.

The doctor leaned on the reception desk looking over some paperwork. "I still don't have to talk to you," he said. Thorn noticed the bruising at the doctor's temples. "And if you persist I shall have no option but to complain to your superiors. I'm sure they would be interested in your activities, Mr Thorn."

"I'm only asking."

Procter raised his eyes from the documents and glared at Thorn. "I'm only telling. Now, if you'll excuse me, I have patients." Procter turned and marched through a set of double doors.

Thorn watched him and felt the need to chase after him, grab him by the lapels, and punch him on the nose. But Laura had already given him a going over. Procter treated her when she attended the hospital following the incident at Templeton Hall. She still faced charges of assaulting the doctor. Thorn had hoped that Procter would talk about the incident, provide some insight, maybe. But the doctor's arrogance and rudeness surprised Thorn.

"Excuse me?" said a voice.

Thorn turned and the nurse smiled. Her eyes flitted about the reception area, as if talking to Thorn was the wrong thing to do. Thorn crossed to her and introduced himself.

"I know," she said, her voice almost a whisper. "You're the bodyguard. I read about you."

Thorn chuckled. "You too, eh?" It seemed everyone was aware of his activities. It would make a lesser man paranoid, he thought.

She said, "You're asking about that girl?"

Thorn nodded. "I am." He felt a tinge of excitement. The nurse's conspiratorial air had him hooked. He knew it may be nothing, but any fragment of detail was to be treasured.

She said, "The police didn't question me. Dr Procter" – she looked around, her eyes wide, her shoulders hunched – "told me I wasn't needed."

"Why would he say that?"

She stopped looking around, and focused on Thorn. She smiled and said, "Would you like to buy me a cup of coffee and a doughnut?"

★ ★ ★

DS Carenza Drew hooked a loose strand of hair behind her ear and said, "As DS Murray explained, Laura Greenacre has been in care since the age of four. This was because her parents, Martin and Joyce Greenacre, died. All the details, you'll find in the paperwork I provided."

A rustle of pages. Drew waited for her colleagues to sift through the information, then she continued:

"You'll see that on the date specified in the report, thirty-three victims – men, women, and kids – were shot in their homes. These killings occurred throughout Britain on the same night. Martin Greenacre was shot at his home in Wallsend. Joyce was killed at the home of some relatives, who were also murdered. Although there's no proof, the thinking is that everyone who died were members of the same family."

DI Williams said, "This is like The Godfather. You know, when Michael Corleone's at his son's christening, and he sends hitmen out to kill off his enemies." He wrinkled his nose. "Does this happen in real life?"

DS Drew said, "It's all very weird. There was nothing much in the papers about it. Official records are hard to come by. All the murders are unsolved and could be re-issued to cold case units at any stage. We should maybe look at that" – she looked at Denton – "what with the advanced scientific capabilities we have these days. They may be solvable." Denton's gaze was fixed on the notes. Drew said, "Anyway, the only survivor was Laura Greenacre."

Drew glanced at Denton to indicate she had finished. Denton nodded and closed her report. She said, "Laura Greenacre seems to find herself in awkward situations. I think we should question her again: over the deaths of the care worker, and the two service station robbers. I'm sure she has quite a story to tell."

Thorn watched the nurse – her name was Julia – chew on a doughnut. She licked the sugar from her lips. She sipped her coffee and swished it around her mouth to discard any crumbs. The girl was in her twenties, blonde and pretty, with wide green eyes.

Thorn said, "Why would you tell me this?"

Julia said, "I don't have a vendetta, don't think that. But I don't feel I owe him anything. He's a creep. He tries it on because he thinks he has the right to. Rejection makes him angry. He touched me once." She lowered her head and blushed. "On my breast."

"Did you report him?"

"I did not."

"You should have. He has no right."

"He's a doctor. Well-respected. Highly-regarded. I'm just a D-grade nurse."

"But what he did to Laura. You said he took blood without consent. The high-level of haloperidol."

The nurse shrugged, tore a piece from the doughnut and popped it into her mouth. "They protect their own. Who would you believe?"

Thorn held her gaze for a moment, then said, "You."

She smiled and averted her eyes. "That's kind of you. You're just saying that."

"What was Laura Greenacre like?"

The nurse's eyes widened, and she gasped. "God, she was strong. I've never seen anything like it, really. It was scary in there. I mean Wallace Furlong, he's one of the health service assistants, he's a big guy, you know. She just pulled him right across the bed. Like he was a" – she shook her head, looking for the word – "pillow."

"Could I speak to him, do you think?"

Again she shrugged. "I suppose. The police questioned him yesterday morning. He says it took seven security guys to take her down after she destroyed the blood samples. She was just chucking these guys around." She made throwing gestures with her hands. She took up her coffee again and sipped, licking her lips.

Thorn remembered Laura's strength at Hadrian's Wall.

The nurse's brow furrowed and Thorn said, "What is it?"

The nurse shook her head. "It's something Wallace said. Probably nothing, really. I mean she was wild."

"Tell me." He leaned across the table.

"Well," she said, "Wallace told me that she growled."

"Growled?"

"Yeah. Growled. Not like, you know..." She growled into Thorn's face and he gave a little smile. "Not like that, jokey. Wallace said it was a real guttural growl, like a proper wild animal – a big dog." She picked at the doughnut. "Or a wolf."

CHAPTER 40.
THE REQUEST.

ELENA said, "You can't be thinking of going?"

"Why not," said Laura, looking at the black card. She read the words, embossed into the card in gold, again:

You are requested to attend a tribute to Sir Adam James Charles Templeton at Templeton Hall, Hexham, Northumberland.

It was in two days, on the 10th.

Laura said, "Doesn't say how old he was or when he died."

"So what?"

Laura shrugged. "He must've had them done well in advance."

They were in Laura's room. An empty suitcase was open on the bed. Elena had answered the door to the courier, and then she brought the black envelope up to Laura's room.

Laura stared at the card. She creased her brow. Was this some kind of joke? Was it Templeton who did this before he died, or was it Michael who was responsible? If so, why did he want her at his father's funeral? "I mean, they hate me," she said.

"You thought they did," said Elena. "Seems Sir Adam Templeton got himself a little bit of human kindness in his later years. Maybe he felt guilty about what he did."

Laura looked up. "Who killed him? Who was the guy? He was there the first night I was at Templeton Hall, Elena. He was running away from the dogs."

Elena shrugged. "He might be there at the funeral as well."

"That's why I should go."

"What? No, that's not what I meant. Laura, that's madness. It's a lion's den. Everyone who hates you, all the Templeton family, they'll be there."

Laura grinned. "Yes."

Elena said, "Please don't go," and then went to the wardrobe, opened it and started filing through clothes. "If you want some help packing, let's do it now, together."

Laura put her hands on her hips. "Now you *want* me to leave."

Elena looked at her, her face creased with tears. "Oh, Laura, no. No I don't, my darling. I want you to be safe." She came to Laura and hugged her, then pulled away to look into Laura's eyes. "But I'd rather you leave Newcastle than go to Templeton's funeral. It's a trap. They mean to finish what they started twenty years ago. And I couldn't bear that, Laura, I couldn't bear it again."

Elena started to cry.

Laura stroked her hair and said, "It'll be all right."

"It won't be. You know it won't be. How can it be all right?"

"I'll think about it, then."

Elena shot her a look and said, "No, don't think about it. Promise me you won't go. Ask that policeman, if you're seeing him tonight, ask him what he thinks. He'll know. He knew Sir Adam."

Laura thought about Thorn. She should've said no to his request. She shouldn't be going out for a drink with a strange man a day after his employer's been killed and she's the prime suspect. She shook her head and said, "It's all a bit mad, isn't it."

She wanted to go to this funeral, for the hell of it. She knew it was a stupid thing to do, but Laura was intrigued. She wouldn't tell Thorn. He would react like Elena. He would tell Laura not to go, that it was a trap.

Elena said, "Do you like him, this man?"

"Which man?"

"The man you're thinking about, now, your eyes all glazed over, staring at the wall."

Laura huffed, took an armful of clothes out of the wardrobe and dropped them on the suitcase.

"You haven't been out on a date since we met," said Elena.

Laura scowled. "It's not a date. He's not in the mood for a date, and neither am I. This is honestly just a chat. I'll see if I can't get anything out of him about Templeton. He's got all the insider stuff, hasn't he."

"Maybe he's going to the funeral. I mean, he was the bodyguard."

"Yes," said Laura, "maybe he is."

"My bet is the place'll be crawling with police."

"Most likely."

"All out to get you."

Laura gasped. "Elena, they're not out to get me."

"They arrested you today."

"They didn't arrest me, I was 'helping them with their inquiries', that's all."

"But they will arrest you."

Laura started sorting through the pile of clothes. "What do you mean?"

"When they match those trainers to your feet, young lady." They looked at each other. Then Elena arched her eyebrows, threw out her arms, and said, "Please, Laura, can't you see how stupid this is? If you must leave here, then leave, but don't put me through any more anguish by going to Templeton Hall."

CHAPTER 41.
ON THE PROWL.

THE girl danced in his head. She called to him, her voice echoing along the caverns of his mind. The voice urged him to her, demanding her own violation.

The masked man pressed his forehead against the steering wheel of the stolen Vectra and squeezed his eyes shut. He sweated and trembled and babbled. The girl still tempted him with her voice and her dance and he knew he would have to answer her call.

Sitting up straight, breathing deeply, he opened his eyes and scanned the Bigg Market.

The meat market bustled.

Young men swaggered. Egos swollen by alcohol; testosterone levels volcanic; voices raised and peppered with curses – the human male's mating call, drawing attention, showing off.

Young women swayed. Bodies squeezed into tubes of material; flesh goose pimpling in the cool night air; voices raised and peppered with curses – the human female's mating call, drawing attention, showing off.

He ground his teeth and moaned, eyeing a girl in a red dress. *Why do they ask for it?* he thought. *Why do they force me to do such things?*

He watched as two men started fighting. Fists and feet flew with the curses. The masked man tensed, gripping the steering wheel. The fighters charged at each other, throwing punches and kicks that all missed. From inside the Vectra he could hear their shouts. A crowd gathered to watch the brawl.

The masked man switched on the engine. He glanced across the square to Bliss. The club's red neon name flickered above the archway. Two bouncers stood at the wrought iron gates, laughing at the brawlers.

He eased the Vectra off the pavement and steered the car into the shadows of Pudding Lane. He parked on the pavement, car and driver huddled in shadows. In his rear view mirror he watched Bliss's stage door and waited for its dancing girls.

Perhaps he'd go in and see them. He liked watching them sway and strip and tease with their smiles and their breasts and their legs and –

He gasped, putting a hand to his mouth. This was the most difficult time. The hours before he pulled on the mask, took off his clothes, put on the protective suit, and dragged one into the car. The minutes would crawl by, and he felt himself suffocating. By the time he was ready, his desperation resulted in brutality beyond what he had in mind. But it didn't matter, the anguish he inflicted – as long as he felt human again.

He regulated his breathing, opened the window an inch to let in some air, and focused on the Bigg Market again. The fight was over, both men hauled away by their friends. Three girls with barely a wisp on their bodies were shouting at each other.

He glanced in his mirror. The dancers were arriving, two of them giggling together, coming down the lane. He hunkered down, watched them in the rear view mirror. Sweat poured down his face, and plastered the shirt to his back.

A desire grew in his mind, an urge he pictured as decay eating into a carcass. It was monstrous – he gritted his teeth, he trembled, he whined – and beautiful.

CHAPTER 42.
NAKED.

THEY sat at a table on the balcony at Casa on the Quayside. Laura watched the ribbon of moonlight shimmer on the Tyne. She glanced across the table at Thorn and she liked him: the look of him, the smell of him, the way his narrow eyes flitted about.

She said, "Are you waiting for someone else?"

"What?"

"The way you keep looking around."

He sipped from the bottled beer. "Keeping an eye out, that's all."

"Don't worry about it. I can see them coming from miles off."

He looked at her for a moment and said, "I went to the hospital today."

"Oh. I hope it's cleared up by now."

He tried to push a smile on his face, but he was tense and the gesture looked more like a grimace.

Thorn said, "I spoke to the nurse and the porter. They told me –" She shuffled in her seat and he hesitated, then said, "What's the matter?"

"These questions," she said.

"Someone's got to ask them. Isn't it best that it's someone who..."

Laura looked at him, arched an eyebrow, and said, "'Someone who' what?"

He took a breath, then said, "Who sympathises. Who tends to believe – for God knows what reason – your story. Who wants to help you, if he can."

"Thanks. You're a trooper."

He shrugged. "Please. Hold back on the gratitude."

Laura rested her gaze on the river. She thought about the invitation to Templeton's "tribute". She'd decided not to tell Thorn; he'd advise her not to go.

Thorn leaned his elbows on the table. "The nurse and the porter said you were powerful. I know that you're weirdly strong."

She darted him a look. "Weirdly strong?"

"Unusually strong. Where does that come from? And don't tell me you squat and deadlift twice a week."

Laura shrugged and said, "I must get it from my parents, then. We inherit what we have from our parents, don't we; and our parents' parents. It's all in the blood, Johnny. Anyway" – she leaned forward, tilted her head – "are you going to Templeton's funeral?"

"Why do you ask?"

"Asking, that's all. Questions."

"I won't be going. The Police Federation has advised me against it. I'm suspended from duty as a result of his death. Some of the family may not be overwhelmed at my presence. Best not." He narrowed his eyes. "Why?"

"Nothing." Laura leaned back in her chair, moved on by saying, "What about the guy who killed Templeton? Any ideas?"

"No. It's not something that interests the police at the moment. They're really into you as a suspect."

She thought, *I've got to find him; I've got to know who he was and why he killed Templeton.*

Thorn said, "Why were you naked that night?"

"Wouldn't you like to know?"

"Yes, I would."

She shrugged, gave him a smile.

He sighed, drank some beer, and said, "What killed those dogs, then?"

She fixed him with a stare. No one had shared her secret. Only Elena knew what Laura was, what she could do to her body, what she became with a little effort. Could she ever consider sharing that life with someone else, someone who wasn't family? Everyone who'd seen that other side of her was dead. An ex-boyfriend was the only one who survived seeing any of that real animal in her. She was only thirteen, and Chris Farnham pushed his luck. He was sixteen and thought he could slap her about. She showed him her yellow eyes, she flicked out her claws and gouged flesh and blood from his body, but she stopped herself from a full transformation. *I was scared*, she thought, *scared of what I could be. Count yourself lucky, Christopher Farnham. And maybe I'm scared now, too. Scared of showing myself, scared of giving myself away, scared of handing myself over to someone else.*

She said, "I don't know. Maybe you should try to find that guy who killed Templeton, the same guy who was there that night I was naked. Maybe he'll be able to answer your questions. This is like an interrogation. I feel I'm under scrutiny, here."

"You are. I'm scrutinising you very carefully."

She saw a little smile in his eyes, and she made her eyes smile back. "Are you, now?"

"I am. You're very interesting. You're intriguing."

"Yes, I am, aren't I."

"And I just want to know." He leaned back and drank, then said, "What am I going to do? I'm not going to arrest you, am I? I've got no authority. I'm not going running to Denton. She wouldn't believe me anyway, and she quite likes the idea of me getting kicked off the force."

"Why's that? What's not to like in you, dear Johnny?"

"She doesn't like men."

Laura folded her arms. "She doesn't think much of women, either. That's the impression I got."

"She's ambitious, and she's scared of anyone who could threaten those aspirations. She wants to run the police force, then the country, then the world. Cold, hard woman, Lorraine Denton."

They were silent for a moment, and then Thorn said, "Do you mind taking your clothes off?"

She fluttered her eyelashes and said, "Can't you wait 'til we get home?"

He pulled his gaze away, trying to hide the smile and the blush in his cheeks. He said, "I mean the dancing."

"It's a job."

"Don't you feel exploited?"

"I get fifteen quid a dance. I dance seven to ten times a night. I leave with money in my pocket. They leave with an empty wallet."

Laura sipped her wine. She looked at the moon, new and fat and white. Its glow sent shivers through her body.

Thorn said, "Are you cold? Do you need your coat?" and he reached for his jacket that hung on the back of his chair.

She said, "No, I'm warm enough. I don't need anything."

He leaned back and looked at her.

"You look serious, Johnny," she said.

He nodded and said, "I think we should talk about Templeton."

★ ★ ★

"It's a family thing," she said as they strolled past Central Station. Taxis lined the entrance waiting for passengers and revellers. A group of girls giggled and staggered out of The Lounge and crossed the road towards the station.

"I really need to know, Laura."

"Why do you need to know?"

"They will ask me. And if they're to believe that you didn't kill him, you need to tell me —" He hesitated, then said, "As much as you can."

"If they ask you, don't tell them. I'm not going to tell them. It's motive. It's crazy."

"Why did he kill your family? I can't believe he would —"

"Oh, your sweet, dull old Sir Adam. Kind to children and animals. Don't you believe it, Johnny. He was as ruthless as his..."

"As what? As ruthless as what, Laura?"

"His family. That's what they are: ruthless, ambitious, cruel."

"What about your family? What did they do that was so terrible in his eyes that he tries to wipe you out?"

She was quiet for a moment, and then she said, "We lived our lives, that's all."

Thorn shrugged. "Okay, you don't want to tell me. But they'll find out, you know. They'll pop your name into the computer and it'll come up. Everything. They've probably done it already."

"I don't care. I won't be here."

"You can't leave."

She heard the hitch in his voice, and said, "Why can't I leave?"

They crossed the road towards the Centre for Life science museum. Laura stared at the glass-fronted building. Thorn still had not answered her question. So she pushed him, enjoying the discomfort she sensed in him. Liking the fact that he liked her. Hating the fact that she liked him. The confusion of emotions tingled her to the quick.

He said, "I don't know why you can't leave. I thought this was

152

home, that's all. Thought this was where you were born, that you were here to stay."

"With all of this hanging over me? There's no peace for me here. No peace for me anywhere." Laura stopped and he stopped, and they looked at each other. She swept a stray strand of hair from her face and hooked it behind her ear. She said, "Where are your family from?"

"They farm up in Northumberland. Have done for generations."

"Happy you became a policeman?"

"They...they were surprised. My younger brother runs the farm, now."

"You love them?"

"What?"

"Love them. Your family. Do you love your family?"

"Of course I do."

She said, "I loved mine, too."

She walked on and he walked up to her. She smelled him. The blood was rushing through his veins. She could sniff out the heat in his body. His odour saturated her nostrils and filled her lungs. She tingled all over, and itched at the spot that so often needed scratching.

Nature's such a bitch, she thought, licking her lips.

CHAPTER 43.
RAID.

AN hour later Laura swigged a Pepsi at the bar in Bliss. She tapped her foot to the music. She watched Chloe up on the stage. Chloe, wearing a silver bikini and silver platform heels, writhed around the pole. She teased the guys leaning on the front of the stage, plucking at the bikini's strings. They'd not have to wait long.

Laura glanced around the club. Half a dozen lads were swilling from four pitchers of beer at a corner table. They whooped at Chloe. They shouted, "Get 'em off." Jed the bouncer went up their table and smiled. He pressed his hands down in a "calm down" signal, and the lads toasted him.

Just wait a bit and she will get 'em off, thought Laura.

Men in pairs, in threes huddled at the tables, lone men were pressed into the corners. Laura made out shapes, and made out smells: sweat and aftershave and beer and fags.

She thought about Thorn and felt warm, but that warmth was rapidly replaced by a heavy feeling in her breast. She couldn't think about him that way: there was nothing in this for her; there was nothing in this for him. These momentary crushes occasionally brushed at her heart, but they were always swept away by reality.

I can never be happy, she thought, *I can never be normal.* The weight of it pushed up and she felt the tears well, but she held them back when a voice behind her said, "How was your date with the copper? Didn't bring him here, did you?"

It was Alison.

Laura said, "It wasn't a date. How was your soldier?"

Alison smiled. "Rough," she said.

"You seeing him again?"

"Oh no. He was at school with me. I didn't go out with him at school so – "

"You thought he should have a try."

"Yes. Why not. He was a bit of a weed at school. Not anymore." She perched on a stool next to Laura, whipped her dark hair behind her shoulder and said, "Are you dancing tonight?"

"No, not tonight. I'm taking a few days off. How 'bout you?"

"Yeah. I'm on the late shift, here 'til half-three. So you're okay?"

"I'm okay."

"So..." Alison hesitated, dropped her gaze and peeled the corner off a beer mat, "what were you actually doing there, Laura?"

"Where?"

"You know. That Hall place. Where that Lord guy lived."

Laura paused, glanced at Chloe who was topless on the stage, and said, "I went to a party. It got a bit wild."

"Right. And you were in court."

"Yes. It was in evening paper."

"I don't read the papers. Can't be bothered."

"Yeah, well."

"Yeah," said Alison, "so what happened?"

"Nothing. I got off."

"Cool. So they're not doing you for his murder, then."

"I hope not."

"Was he a customer? Did he come see you dance or something?"

A scuffle broke out near the door. Jed and Coyle, the other bouncer, tried to fend off a few – shit, thought, Laura, getting up – cops, and she said, "Police."

Alison stood up, craned her neck and said, "What's going on?"

Four uniformed officers pushed their way past the bouncers. Lorraine Denton and another detective Laura recognised came in. Denton waved at the DJ. Elena came out of the back and marched towards the police. The music switched off. The lads in the corner started to complain. Laura watched as the men in the club scurried into the corners like cockroaches.

"Can we have the lights on?" said Denton.

"No we can't," said Elena, in her face. "What's going on here? You have no right – "

Denton sneered at Elena and said, "Yes I do, so get out of my face, you old tart."

Laura saw Elena stiffen. *Don't hit her*, thought Laura, *please don't hit her*.

Denton stepped forward, saw Laura at the bar. Denton pointed at Laura, and gestured to the uniformed officers. The lads were on their feet, whooping, shouting at Denton to "get 'em off". Chloe stood on the stage, covering her breasts.

Alison, next to Laura, said, "I think they want to talk to you," and she moved away, saying, "I'll leave you to it."

Denton and two of the uniforms came up to her, and Denton said, "I'd like you to come to the station, Miss Greenacre."

"Why?"

"We have a few more questions we'd like you to answer."

"What if I don't know the answers?"

Denton grimaced. "We'd like you to try."

Elena said, "She doesn't have to come with you."

Denton said, "PC Morris, ask this woman behind me to move away or I'll close her nasty little strip joint."

The PC moved Elena away and Elena said, "I'm fully licensed. You can't close me down. Just you try it."

Denton ignored her and said to Laura, "Are you coming? Or will I have to arrest you?"

"Can you arrest me?"

"Yes I can."

"I want a lawyer, then."

"Well," said Denton, looking towards a darkened corner, "I see Ellis Cole, your legal representative, is here already." The corner was empty. Denton smiled. "He *was* there a minute a go. Seems to have slithered away with the rest of the creeps."

Laura said, "You scare them off, Lorraine."

★ ★ ★

"I thought she was going to be okay, I honestly did," said Chloe, taking her make-up off. She tilted her head this way, that way, studying herself in the theatrical mirror.

Alison sat next to her, applying her make-up. "She's weird, you know."

"Yeah, but she's sweet, though. She's kind in a…gruff kind of way."

"Do you really think she killed this Lord guy?"

Chloe said, "He wasn't a Lord, he was a knight."

"Well, whatever, but what do you think?"

"I think it's all a misunderstanding. She was" – Chloe tugged her hair into a pony tail – "at a party, got herself caught up in some nonsense – drunk, pills, maybe – wandered around naked and got to the nice big house, got caught."

Alison looked at her and leaned across. In a whisper she said, "They say three guard dogs were ripped apart. Blood and guts everywhere."

Chloe ignored her. She didn't want to know; didn't want to think about the remains of animals and Laura naked among them. She wanted Laura to be Laura again: her pal, her housemate, her agony aunt. They weren't close, not friends, but Chloe felt she could trust Laura with anything: she wouldn't laugh, she wouldn't betray, she wouldn't turn her back. She remembered this from only days after Laura had arrived:

Chloe sobbing on the stairs, make-up streaming black down her cheeks. Craig had come home and she was shivering with excitement.

She'd gone over to his flat with a key she'd snared. It hung from a hook near the front door. The last time she'd been there, saying goodbye to Craig before he went to the rig, Chloe had snaked an arm out while she was kissing him, and flipped the spare key off the hook.

Dressed to thrill, her stomach swarming with nerves, Chloe went to Craig's place, eager to surprise him, eager to slip off the fur coat and watch his eyes gape and his mouth open.

She sneaked in, heard noises, felt her chest tighten, the sweat break out on her back. She said, "Craig," and stormed through to the bedroom. Craig rolled off the woman. His face was red and sweaty. He scowled at Chloe, called her a bitch and said, "Get out," the other woman yelping, asking Chloe, "Who the fuck are you?" and asking Craig, "Who the fuck is that, Craig?"

Wrapped in her fur coat, sitting on the stairs at home, she cried. She didn't hear Laura come up behind her and sit one stair up from her. Laura said, "If it's a man, don't bother, 'cause he doesn't."

Chloe turned round. Laura, in T-shirt and combats, leaned forward, elbows on knees. Laura wore a scornful look. She said, "What did he do?"

Chloe told her. Laura sighed and said, "If that's it, don't cry over it. He's not crying, is he. He's laughing, probably. You laugh at him. Go round town saying he had a small willy, saying he was crap in bed. Tell his mates he had gay porn in the toilet. Anything, anything that makes you smile." Laura got up, looked down at Chloe and said, "If that's it, honestly – forget it."

Alison, rolling on the lipstick, leaning forward into the mirror, said, "That's maybe why they've arrested her tonight: the dogs; or perhaps they've got her on the Lord."

"He wasn't a Lord."

"Yeah, I know." Alison stood up, studied herself in the mirror. She was in her underwear. "Who shall I be tonight?"

Ten minutes later Chloe poked her head out of Bliss's stage door. It led out into an alley that dropped down from the havoc of the Bigg Market through to the bustle of Neville Street where Central Station stood. The lane was unlit. The Fleet Street pub was shut at this time of night. No printers smoked outside the back door of Thomson House where the Evening Chronicle and The Journal were produced. Four cars were hoisted onto the pavement on the opposite side of the lane. Any through-traffic would find it difficult to get by without clipping a wing mirror or scraping a back door.

Chloe thought, *Where are you when I need you, Laura?* They always walked to the station together, picking up a taxi at the rank. Chloe looked at her watch. It was one-thirty a.m. She could hear the Bigg Market behind her, buzzing. The night was still alive. But this passageway that danced with shadows, that protected dark corners, made Chloe's blood chill.

She stepped out into the lane, tugged her jacket around her, and started walking. Her breath steamed out. Her heart bumped against her breast. She shivered as sweat dampened her back.

She said to herself, "It'll be fine. Less than two hundred yards. Grow up, Chloe."

She strode past the first vehicle, a Ford van. Glancing left, she saw that Thomson House's back door was shut. It was dark inside. She gritted her teeth. She thought, *Wish those printer's were out having a fag, flirting with me, making lewd comments, laughing and jok –*

It punched the wind out of her, tossed her across the road, slammed her against the wall. Panting, she turned. The middle car, a Vectra; its door flung open.

He was lunging out of the car, masked and wearing white overalls.

She tried to scream, seeing him in those clothes and that mask she'd read about in the papers, knowing what he was and why he wanted her.

He ran towards her and she got up, flung her arms up, opened her throat to make the loudest noise on earth. He punched her in the mouth and pain jolted through her face; stars burst before her eyes.

Chloe moaned, tried to pull away, felt the pain in her head as he tugged her by the hair. She said, "No," but it didn't sound like a word to her. Something wet and warm in her mouth made it difficult to make words.

He pushed her into the car saying, "Get in, get in, it's all right," but Chloe again tried to say, "No," and pressed her hands against the doorframe, her legs weak, her bladder cold, her stomach rolling.

"Yes," said the masked man, "yes," and smashed her head against the door. Her head filled with lights, pain, faces, noise. Everything was blurred. Chloe heard herself moan, felt herself flop into the car, and she fell into darkness.

PART THREE.

BLOODLINE.

CHAPTER 44.
DESPERATE STRAITS.

DENTON reeled off Laura's past: Pavin, the guys at the garage, even Chris Farnham.

Laura stared at her all the time, not giving away her thunderous heartbeat, the sweat trickling down the back of her neck, her parched throat, the butterflies swarming in her stomach.

Denton, placing the sheet of paper on the desk between them, brushing it flat as if it were expensive silk, said, "What am I to make of all that, Laura?"

"I don't know, make a stew, make a curry, make a quilt. Do you sew, or is that a bit too girlie for you?"

"Being silly won't help. You're in trouble."

"No I'm not. I haven't done anything. What does all that mean?" she said, gesturing at the sheet of paper. "It only says I was there. How could I do such things? Look at me. I'm only a girl."

Denton frowned. She dropped her gaze, raised it again to Laura and said, "Advances in DNA technology will allow us to reassess evidence from all these cases."

"Bully for you, Lorraine."

"What do you think it'll say about what killed Colin Pavin? What ripped out his" – she picked up the sheet, narrowed her eyes

– "genitals, his stomach and intestines, gouged these terrifying wounds in his chest."

Laura put her elbows on the desk. She glanced across at the duty solicitor. The woman was pale and looked tired. Cole hadn't been available. He was probably too drunk or too embarrassed after Denton spotted him at the club.

Laura looked at Denton, tilted her head, and said, "Do you honestly believe that I did that?"

Denton shrugged.

"And would I," said Laura, "be able to disarm, and dismember, two armed robbers? I was terrified. Really shitting it. These guy charge in with guns, shouting, swearing, saying they're going to kill me if I don't do what they say." Laura leaned back, ran a hand through her hair. "Even if I had done those things, wouldn't it be self-defence?"

"I don't know. Did you do these things?"

Laura ignored her and said, "Do you know that Colin Pavin raped girls at Morgan Hill House? Had a little harem going. No one ever did anything about that, did nothing to protect those girls."

"Is that what you did, Laura? Take it upon yourself to protect them? Are you a bit of a vigilante?"

Laura folded her arms. "You haven't got anything." She looked at the solicitor and said, "Tell her she hasn't got anything."

The solicitor said, "Well, you – "

"I'll tell her myself." Laura leaned towards Denton again and said, "You haven't got anything."

Denton glanced around the interview room. Laura said, "For the benefit of the tape, DCS Denton is checking out the colour scheme in the interview room. She like this shade of drab."

Detective Constable Bailey huffed, and his cheeks went red. He said, "That's enough. Don't talk to the tape. Don't say that. That's what I say."

Laura rolled her eyes.

Denton said, "We've got quite a lot, you know, Laura. We've got your trainers."

"Who says they're mine?"

"I think the DNA'll say they're yours. What will you do then?"

Laura shrugged. "Get another pair?" Laura smiled. She was enjoying herself. Then something stung at her senses. She sniffed the air casually. She narrowed her eyes. *That's familiar,* she thought, *that's really familiar.*

Denton said, "I think this is a good time to take a break," and she got up.

Bailey stood. He said, "For the benefit of the tape. DCS Denton and DC Bailey are leaving." He nodded at the constable standing at the back of the interview room.

"Think about things," said Denton to Laura. "We'll give you fifteen minutes to have a chat with Miss Penney here." The detectives left.

Miss Penney, the solicitor, turned to the constable and said, "Could we have some coffee, do you think?"

The constable said he'd sort it out, and crossed to the door.

Laura leaped out of her chair, the chair tossed across the room. Miss Penney, startled, stood up, backed away. The constable stopped, turned to look at Laura, hand on his belt ready to go for his baton.

Laura sniffed the air, nostrils flaring, head moving from side to side.

The constable asked her to sit down. Laura ignored him so he asked Miss Penney, "Tell your client to sit down." Miss Penney asked her, but Laura ignored her.

She drew the air into her nostrils, let the odours saturate the tiny hairs inside her nose, shut her eyes to reel through the smells she had filed away over the years, then said, "Why's Chloe here? I want to know why Chloe's here? She's hurt. She's hurt."

★ ★ ★

Thorn paced the reception area. He rubbed his face, the sharp growth of hair prickling his hand. Thorn hadn't shaved in two days; he'd barely slept, and that consideration brought a yawn.

"Tired, sergeant?"

He turned, blinked, saw Detective Superintendent Tim Foreshawe stride through the door. Thorn looked up at the cheesestring and said, "Been a busy few days, sir."

"I hear."

Two other detectives scuttled behind Foreshawe: a woman with freckles and glasses who Thorn had seen before but couldn't name, and a lad in a grey suit who looked about twelve. Thorn nodded at them as they passed. The desk sergeant clicked them through the security door. Foreshawe let his two companions pass and then turned to Thorn, saying, "Of course. You're not one of us anymore, are you."

Thorn glowered at Foreshawe as the senior officer, sending out whoops of laughter, slammed the security door behind him.

Thorn's anger quelled. He looked at his watch. It was closing on two-thirty a.m. He felt the darkness press down on him. He thought, *What the hell's happening to me? My life's breaking apart, disintegrating.*

Perhaps this was the culmination of fifteen years of drive and ambition; the end times for his career.

His goals had already cost him his marriage. If he could, he would do things differently, fight to save his relationship with Jane: he would have come home on time, he would turn up to birthdays and anniversaries, he would not fall asleep when they had guests, he would go out with Jane and Sophie on sunny Saturday mornings.

Sophie. The thought of her brought pain to his breast. His legs felt weak, so he sat down on one of the plastic chairs lining the wall.

"You all right?" said the desk sergeant.

Thorn nodded and waved a hand at him. He dropped his face into his hands. *Yes, this is it,* he thought. Final punishment for his greed, his selfishness, his single-mindedness; the last kick in the balls for his ego.

The career he'd valued above everything finally taken away from him.

He said to himself, "You deserve it, John. You deserve it all. Idiot."

"What's that?" said the desk sergeant.

"Nothing," said Thorn. "Thinking out loud, that's all."

"I don't know if she'll be down, you know."

"I'll wait a bit longer."

The desk sergeant turned round, reacting to a noise behind him. "Think she's coming. I can smell the fire when she breathes." He chuckled.

Denton walked through the door, her cheeks red, her eyes narrow with anger. She came to Thorn and folded her arms, and said, "What is it?"

He stood. "I've come to see what's going on with the Greenacre girl."

"Why? How did you know she was here? Not listening to police frequencies, I hope."

"Her boss at the club rang me. Said you'd arrested her."

"She's not under arrest. Yet. She will be, though."

"She will?"

"Absolutely. Why are you still hanging around? You're like a fourth-former chasing after a sixth-year girl."

"Am I?"

"Do you have a crush on this woman, Thorn?"

"I'm interested in her well-being. I'm connected to her through Adam Templeton. I'm trying to find out why she's here."

"A private investigation, eh? You need accreditation for that. Don't step on our toes and, oh, if you do find anything, do tell us – if you fail to, I'll have you arrested."

He thought about Templeton killing Laura's family. Staring at Denton, Thorn considered telling the detective about that allegation. But he knew the investigator would regard it as a motive for murder.

The letter Templeton handed to Elena McIntyre at the court clearly indicated he had no ill will towards Laura, and he specifically told Thorn to keep an eye out for her. Should he tell Denton about that? Again, the letter would place Laura at the scene.

Denton said, "Do you know anything about this girl, Sergeant Thorn?"

"No more than you do, I'm sure."

"Well I know quite a bit."

Denton told Thorn about Colin Pavin, the robbery at the garage in Chester, and Chris Farnham. The fog surrounding Laura Greenacre thickened again. He was no closer to the truth. She said that Laura's family had been killed twenty years ago. Thorn flinched, and hoped Denton didn't spot the gesture.

She said, "We're trying to trace Farnham. He was a bad lad, and he's got a record. Low level stuff: shoplifting, joyriding, general thuggery."

"Sounds like a charmer. I'm sure he'll make an ideal witness: trustworthy, reliable."

Denton grinned. "Just like Laura Greenacre, then."

Thorn said, "I saw someone up at Templeton Hall earlier."

"How astute of you."

"I've seen him before, know the face."

She shook her head, flustered. "What's this got to do anything?"

"Michael Templeton got very defensive when I challenged this guy. Told me it was none of my business."

"Maybe it wasn't."

"Laura Greenacre claims there was someone else there the night we found her at Templeton Hall, and she – " He stopped himself. He almost said that Laura had seen someone kill Templeton, and she claimed it was the same man she'd seen at the Hall.

166

"What?" said Denton.

"She said there was someone else there that night, that's all."

"And?"

"And this guy, he drove a Fiat Punto..." He hesitated.

Thorn had no idea where he was going with this. He felt dazed, tired. Denton noticed. She raised her eyebrows and said, "Your powers are waning. You've lost that cold calculation that made you stand out as a young detective constable. Do something positive with your time away, sergeant. Re-acquire that steel. You can maybe use it again if you're cleared of any wrong-doing." She walked away, then looked over her shoulder at Thorn. "If," she said.

CHAPTER 45.
VICTIM.

CHLOE said, "He raped me."

Laura put a hand on Chloe's head, brushed her hair. It was wet and greasy. Chloe wept, her body shaking. She was sitting on an examining table. She wore a blue hospital tunic.

She said, "They've taken samples. Get his DNA. Catch him like that, with science. The policewoman, she said they'll get him for sure."

"Yeah," said Laura, "he'll be caught." She thought about Pavin, about eating him and him still alive; about tearing away the flesh he'd used all those times to abuse the girls at Morgan Hill House.

"I was thinking. I wish Laura were here. We always walk home together, don't we? Ever since you came, anyway. Before you came, I waited for the others, but that made it a long day, you know."

"I know," said Laura, putting her hands on Chloe's knees.

"I should've waited. Waited those couple of extra hours for Hannah and Alison, walked to the taxi rank with them. But I was tired, wanted my bed."

"Yes. It's all right."

Chloe's face was streaked with mascara. Her skin was pale. A cut whipped across her forehead. It had been stitched. Her lips were sore with wounds. There was blood on her chin. Chloe said, "It's not all right, really. I feel terrible. I feel like I want to die. This'll be with me forever, Laura. Him being inside me. Always be there, won't it."

Laura went to stroke her cheek, but Chloe flinched.

"Sorry," said Chloe, "but it hurts. He really bust me up, didn't he. Won't be able to work for while, make money, pay the rent."

"Elena'll look after you. She won't charge you rent. You'll be back working soon."

"I don't know. I'm not sure I want to again."

"You don't have to. But whatever you want to do, it'll be okay."

"I think I'll go home, you know. Back to Nottingham."

"Think about that when you get better."

"Will I get better, Laura?"

"Yes. 'Course you will."

Chloe said, "I don't know. Look at the state of me. I'm twenty-two, take my clothes off for a living. It's not promising, is it?"

"Elena's done all right out of it."

"Elena's really clever. She was always really clever."

"Yeah, you are too. The girls said Bliss wouldn't have won the quiz league three times in a row without your brains."

It almost got a smile out of Chloe; but it came out as a grimace in the end

"I don't know," said Chloe, "Nottingham sounds like the best place right now, that's all. And if you're going, there's not much point in staying."

"You were here before I arrived. You were okay, then."

"Yeah, I know. It's just...you going, it makes me think about stuff. It all started with that Craig thing, you know. And now this happening. I just want to go away, to hide...see my mum."

Chloe started to cry again. Laura hugged her. She started to smell things – a chaos of odours. She pulled away and said, "Do the others know yet? Elena, Hannah, Alison?"

"No. I asked the police to call Elena. I've only just got here, really. He threw me out of the car somewhere, I don't know. Police came. It's all quite blurry apart from the – " She buried her face in her hands, shuddering as she cried again.

Laura grabbed Chloe's arms and shook her. "I'll get him for you."

Chloe looked up and said, "What?"

"I'll get him. I can get him if you let me do something."

"Do what?"

"Don't tell anybody about this."

"What? What are you talking about? How can you get him?"

"Have you washed yet?"

169

Chloe shook her head. "Washed? No, they told me not to."

"I need to smell you."

Chloe's mouth dropped open. Laura could see the blood from the wounds inflicted by the rapist when he punched Chloe. Teeth were missing and her tongue was a deep pink from the blood that seeped from her gums.

Chloe said, "You want to..."

She let the sentence drop away. Laura finished it for her: "Smell you."

Laura looked down at Chloe's lap. She could feel Chloe tremble. Laura looked up into her friend's eyes and said, "Do you want me to?"

CHAPTER 46.
DOUBTING DENTON.

"WE'LL nail her for everything," said Denton, "all of it: assault, trespass, murder."

She sipped at her coffee, stared out of the window. The car park was well lit and even from up here, she could see Thorn trudge back to towards his car. He got into the vehicle and drove away, plunging into the darkness.

That's where you're headed, thought Denton.

Bailey, sitting opposite her, said, "Do you think Templeton killed Greenacre's family?"

Denton snapped a look at him. "What makes you say that?"

He shrugged. "Thinking, that's all. It would make sense. Her killing him, taking revenge for what he did to her family."

Denton said, "Sir Adam Templeton was an MP, a government minister. Why would he have dozens of people killed?" She thought for a moment and said, "We should look at links between the families. Go back a few years."

Bailey took a notebook from his shirt's breast pocket and wrote something.

"If that is the case," said Denton, "then Greenacre's got motive. That'd be good. It would make things easier."

Denton came to sit down, took another sip of her coffee. She looked at her watch. It was almost three-fifteen a.m., and another eighteen hour day slipping towards its close. She thought about Colin Pavin, the men in the Chester garage, and Chris Farnham. "What I'd like," she said, "would be to close those other cases she's linked to."

"Pavin and the robbers were torn apart, Ma'am. It's difficult to imagine anything human doing that. From the records, they seem like animal killings."

"Could have been a knife, Mark. She used a knife on Templeton. Maybe she had a bit more time to spend on Pavin and those lads. She was really able to go to work, tearing them apart."

"If we track Chris Farnham, he'll shed some light on her methods. If she used a knife on him. The report said claws but," Bailey shrugged, "that can't be possible."

"Maybe the police got it wrong with those cases. Maybe they misjudged the evidence, weren't up to it. They could have made mistakes. Had they looked closely, I'm sure they could've linked the Pavin murder and the garage killings to Greenacre."

"Do you think they'll ever be solved, Ma'am?"

Denton stood up and said, "We'll solve them, DC Bailey."

"We will?"

Four murders solved by one chief super: that would line me up for assistant chief constable, thought Denton.

Her spirits rose. Facing Foreshawe earlier enraged her. She was on her way down to see Thorn, and perhaps, in hindsight, that was a stupid decision. The sergeant had asked for her, and she should've refused to speak to him.

My ego taking over, she thought. Wanting to knock the man while he was down; seeing him squirm; enjoying his fall from grace.

Foolish of you, Lorraine, she said to herself. And maybe crossing paths with Foreshawe while making her way to the front desk to see Thorn was fate's way of scolding her.

"Tim," she said, blushing as he bounded up the stairs towards her.

"Lorraine. Still no home to go to, I see" – they stopped, faced each other half way up the stairs, Foreshawe's two minions halting a few steps down – "I understand we have another victim of my rapist upstairs."

"Still giving you the runaround is he, Tim?"

He narrowed his eyes. "I hear you're having a few problems with some cheap little stripper. Can't nail a bimbo for a big murder can you, Lorraine?"

"I'm actually not too far from nailing her for four murders, Tim, three of which have been unsolved for quite a few years."

Foreshawe let his gaze move down her body, then it came back up to her face. "Still biting off more than you can chew. Why don't you sort the one murder out, first?"

"Well, at least I am sorting it out. At least I have a suspect. Do you have any suspects, Tim? Anyway, must head off. Very busy."

Trembling, Denton scurried downstairs, her cheeks filling with blood. Behind her she heard Foreshawe say, "I had her fifteen years ago."

Denton finished her coffee. She thought about Foreshawe. His derision had started to chisel away at her confidence. Thorn's mystery man popped into her mind. She scorned the sergeant when he mentioned the stranger at Templeton Hall. But Denton knew that he was being a good cop: picking up on any detail, however meaningless it seemed.

She bit her lip, gazing out into the darkness again.

She was a good cop too, and knew this couldn't be ignored. The visitor to Templeton Hall was probably an innocent man, but his presence there had to be clarified; he had to be dotted and crossed, eliminated from Denton's inquiries.

Thorn's sighting gnawed at her, gouging a crevice of doubt into Denton's self-belief.

CHAPTER 47.
SECRETS.

LAURA said, "Why didn't you tell me?"

Thorn shook his head, kept his eyes on the road. His eyelids looked like they were being drawn down like shades. His eyes were red-rimmed and his complexion pallid. She thought he was falling asleep, so she punched him in the arm.

"Hey," he said, jerking the steering wheel, causing the Saab to slice the white lines. They were on the A696 headed south east towards Newcastle. It was five-thirty a.m., the dawn leaking into the eastern sky.

"Answer me," said Laura, glaring at him. He rubbed his arm, focused on the road. She said, "You looked like you need to sleep for a year."

"An hour would do me."

"So?"

"So what?"

"This man, this guy you saw at the Hall. Why didn't you tell me?"

"I didn't think it was important. It's not vital I tell you anything, anyway. We're not Morse and Lewis, are we. We're not a team."

That was like a punch in her guts, but she didn't show too much. She said, "The least you could've done is think up a female detective for me," folded her arms, and stared straight ahead.

He sighed. "You know what I mean."

"No, I don't know what you mean."

"I told the police, I've let them know. That's the most important thing. I don't even know if it is important. It's — it's a detail, that's all. And Denton didn't seem that thrilled. But she'll check it out, I'm sure of it."

"He could be the same man I saw, the man who killed Templeton."

"He could be. He could *not* be. Why would he be visiting Michael?"

"Perhaps Michael wanted his father dead. To inherit the fortune. The guy was a hitman."

Thorn huffed. "That's madness."

"Oh, and is there anything that's sane about this situation?"

He didn't say anything.

"Maybe Michael's gay," she said after a few moments, "and he's embarrassed."

Thorn shrugged. "He was protective of the guy. But Michael isn't gay. I've seen him with women. He's a dog."

"Is he, now?" She thought about Michael and the history of their families, the blood that bound them, a line stretching back to before the rise of Rome.

"He is."

"Are you a dog, Johnny?"

"No, I'm obviously a pussycat. That's Denton's opinion, anyway. She thinks I'm taken by you."

Laura felt her cheeks go red. "Taken?"

"Yes. Isn't that silly."

She sniffed the sweat that had broken out on the back of his neck, the blood that had drained into his face. She grinned and said, "Completely silly."

Silence fell. She watched, making sure he wouldn't fall asleep. She had to nudge him a couple of times.

He said, "Perhaps if you spoke to me, tell me something dramatic, that might keep me awake."

"All right," said Laura, "I know who the rapist is."

He jerked the wheel again. Laura grabbed for it, saying, "Watch out."

He straightened the car and said, "You know? How do you know?"

She thought about it, and breathed in. "Well," she said, "I've got a

175

really good sense of smell, you see."

Thorn huffed again and shook his head. Laura thought he was trying to say something, but he'd found the words hard to find. She told him about Chloe being attacked, but not about what she did to her friend in that room a few hours earlier. Laura looked into her lap and picked at her nails.

She said, "It's just something I can do."

Thorn didn't say anything. She glanced at him. His eyes were narrow. He was very still and he stared ahead as if he were looking at nothing.

★ ★ ★

She scooped her blonde hair out of her face and gave him a smile. "So," she said, leaning against the doorframe, "do you want to call me?"

Michael looked at her. He grinned, and walked towards her. She straightened and pouted, ready to fall into him and kiss him. Michael shoved her out into the corridor and slammed the door in her face.

Her heard her cry out and call him a bastard, and then she kicked the door. He yanked it open, said, "You do that again, you fucking bitch, and I'll have you fucking murdered and your fucking family murdered," and she recoiled, her face becoming grey, her mouth dropping open. He said, "Fuck off. You're nothing, okay. Some slag that opened her legs to my money, that's all. Fuck off back to your estate."

She went and he listened to her cry all the way to the lifts, then he shut the door.

He made a smoothie and drank it while watching himself have sex with the blonde. He fast-forwarded through them coming into the bedroom, taking each other's clothes off, to her sucking him and him between her thighs. He laughed at his own backside bobbing up and down, and her face, creased with desire. He looked at her face and smiled because he didn't remember her name.

He'd picked her up at Yates' wine bar after sending a bottle of champagne over to the table she shared with three of her friends. He would've brought all four back, and fucked them all, and filmed himself fucking them all if he'd had the will. But last night, he just didn't fancy it. One was enough. The contents of Jarvis's envelope had traumatised him; the details of his father's funeral had dazed him. Michael had too much on his mind to focus on four girls at once. He just wanted his oats, that's all, and she was the lucky one, the chosen. These bar pick-ups should be grateful, but they never were; they always wanted more.

What did that weeping bitch expect? His phone number? A date? These slags were so stupid. What made them think they were anything more than a shag?

He shook his head and watched himself come into her on the television screen.

Sometimes they came back, of course. Moaning, complaining, screaming that he'd betrayed them, used them. He'd ring 999, saying, "Hello, this is Michael Templeton, Sir Adam Templeton's son, I have a security breach," and a bunch of serious police with serious weaponry would turn up at the flat, arrest the girl, interrogate her for hours about any Irish Republican links she or her family might have, then send her home weeping and confused.

"Stupid cow," he said, switching off the tape.

The phone buzzed. Michael sighed. He got up, ready to threaten the girl. He picked up the receiver, opened his mouth, then heard Ross say, "I've just got myself a date with this tasty young blonde who's been left broken-hearted by some unscrupulous cad. Wouldn't be you, by any chance?"

"Of course it was me, dickhead."

Ross came up, dumped himself on the sofa, and planted his feet on the glass-top coffee table. He picked up a magazine, flicked through it, and then as an afterthought said, "How are you bearing up, mate?"

"I'm really pissed off."

Ross tossed the magazine aside. "Yeah, yeah, totally understandable."

"I'm pissed off that she's been invited to the funeral."

"Yeah, yeah, mum told me. Outrageous. How does that happen, then?"

"But," said Michael, gazing out of the window across the Tyne, "you have to look for positives in adversity."

"That's true, that's true. What do you mean?"

He turned to face Ross and said, "If she's going to be there, I think we should use this as an opportunity to get her."

"Get her?"

"Yes. Get her. And somehow..." He trailed off.

Ross said, "'Somehow' what?"

"Somehow get her to infect me, Ross."

Ross shook his head, his face creased with confusion. "Infect? Are you still going on about that transfusion stuff? Using her blood?"

"Not transfusion, I'm going to make her bite me."

"Bite you."

"Yes. Make her change into that werewolf shape of hers, and bite me, infect me, mix her juices with my blood, re-activate my genes, the genes with all the information that's needed to change me into what she is."

Ross stood up. "Michael, I know your upset what with your dad dying. And this kind of emotional trauma can have an affect – "

"I'm not mad, Ross. It'll work."

"She killed your father, she may kill – "

"Laura Greenacre didn't kill my father."

Ross hesitated, slanted his head to one side, arched an eyebrow. "She didn't?"

Michael said, "I did."

Ross's mouth fell open. His lower jaw moved up and down and he looked like a goldfish. His cheeks were white and his eyes wide.

Michael finished off his smoothie. "I didn't physically commit murder, I paid someone." He shook his head. "You pay peanuts, you get monkeys."

Michael knew he'd been stupid hiring Richie Jarvis to do the job. Jarvis was his dealer, a local gangster. Michael asked him a few months ago, "Can you get someone killed?" and Jarvis said, "I'd do it myself for cash."

And that was it: killed for cash. To Michael it seemed cheap, and if anything went wrong, who'd believe Jarvis? The cops would love to nail him for murder: that's Jarvis off the streets for twenty years.

But Michael knew he should have hired properly and got professionals to do the job. He shook his head and hissed. "Why was I so stupid?" he said.

"Stupid?" said Ross, his jaw still doing that goldfish thing.

"Yes. Hiring a cheap street thug. Stupid. He's now blackmailing me."

"Blackmailing?"

"So I'll have to have him put down as well."

The goldfish spoke again. "You killed your dad, you killed...Sir Adam Templeton."

"*Had* him killed, Ross, *had* him killed."

"That's the same as 'killed', Michael."

Michael flapped his hand. "So what?"

"They'll still do you for murder − I don't believe this, I don't − "

Michael grabbed Ross by the throat, pushed him against the wall. He smelled stale booze on Ross's breath. Michael said, "They won't do me for anything. They'll never find out. The only man who knows, he's going to be put down. Anyone else who knows" − he whacked Ross's head against the wall − "can either be with me or be against me. If they're against me" − he gave Ross's head another shove, and it cracked against the wall − "that's fine, because they'll go the same way as my old father and his assassin."

He let Ross go and walked away, standing in front of the window again to gaze out over the river.

Michael said, "So it's your call, Ross. Live or die. I don't care if you're family or not. Blood's not really thicker than water."

Ross coughed. "I don't have much choice, do I."

"No, not really. But if you're with me, you won't regret it. You'll be stronger than you've ever been, hornier than you've ever been."

"What are you going to do about this guy who...you got to kill your father?"

"I've hired someone who can do the job right. An old friend of the family."

"Am I allowed to ask who, or is that dangerous knowledge, too?"

Michael smiled, and he unearthed a memory. "It's Darth Vadar," he said.

CHAPTER 48.
RICHIE JARVIS.

A CONSTANT beep-beep-beep, like a cardiac monitor.

I'm all right, he thought, *that noise means I'm still alive; my heart's still beating.* He relaxed and stayed in sleep, listening to that beep-beep-beep, the sound of life.

Still that beep-beep-beep...he stirred, trying shift away from the noise, looking for deep, dark silence where his sleep could be smooth and constant...but that beep-bee-beep was insistent.

Thorn sat up in bed. He was in his shirt and trousers. He felt sweaty, exhausted. He rubbed his eyes, yawned, reached out and pressed the OFF button on the clock radio. The heart monitor sound stopped. He glanced at the time on the clock radio. It was eleven-fifteen a.m., and Thorn said, "Shit," throwing his legs off the bed.

He went through to the living room. He sat on the sofa, grabbed the phone, and dialled. It rang and it rang. "Come on, come on," he said, eyes scanning the living room. The walls were white, no photographs, no paintings, no ornaments hanging from them. He tapped his foot on the polished wooden floor, waiting for the phone to be picked up. "Come on," he said again.

Someone answered and said, "Hello."

"Jane, it's me."

He heard a breath, then silence.

He said, "Are you there?"

"I'm here, John."

"I — is she there?"

"Ten o'clock, we said."

"Yes, I know. I'm sorry, I got — " He stopped. How many times had he used that same excuse? I got held up; I worked late; We had a meeting.

"Same old lame old excuses," she said, a note of joy in her voice.

"It's not. Jane, I've been really good with this. You know I have. This is just the once, that's all. Is she there?"

"She was really upset. But then, you do that to her, don't you?"

He crushed a cushion in his fist. "Don't say that, please."

"It's true, though. How many times have you let her down in the past?"

"That's really unfair." The gloom pressed down on him. His shoulders slumped. "I miss her so much and I'd — I tried to make life good for you both. We had a nice house, a nice life, she had — "

"She didn't have a father, John."

"Yes she had, she always had a father."

"Not one who was there. Who turned up at birthdays, who took her to the park."

He shook his head. "We shouldn't be having this conversation."

"No we shouldn't," said Jane, "and we wouldn't be having it had you phoned at ten as arranged. She cried, John, she cried."

It tore at him like claws. He grabbed a handful of hair and clenched his teeth. He despised himself at that moment, the hate swelling up from his breast, leaching out through his pores to wrap around him.

"Where is she, Jane, please," he said.

"She's gone out."

"Out? Out where? With who?"

Jane took another breath, and paused.

He said, "Who?" and he could feel the heat prick his skin, a sweat breaking out on his back.

"I've met someone."

Thorn rubbed his chest. Jane had been single since she'd left him. Or at least that's what Thorn thought. She'd never mentioned a boyfriend, but that's how Thorn liked it: he didn't want to know. He knew he'd feel like this and he hated feeling like this.

"Who is he?"

That breath again. It was like an omen, a warning of bad news to come. She said, "He's Sophie's teacher."

"Teacher?"

"Yes. We're friends, that's all."

"Friends?"

"Yes. We haven't – anyway, it's none of your business."

"It is if it affects Sophie, it is my business."

"It doesn't affect her. She likes him, he's good to her."

"Good to her?" The rage bloomed in his breast.

"He's taken her to see cricket."

"Cricket? There's no cricket in Scotland."

"Yes there is, John, don't be ridiculous."

"You let a stranger take her – "

"He's not a stranger. She's knows him better than she ever knew you."

It felt like his heart had frozen. He listened to her breathe. Years ago that sound would make him swoon, would bring tears into his eyes, would make him say, "I love you, Jane, I love you."

She said, "I shouldn't have said that."

"You did."

"I know, I'm...sorry."

"Are you?"

"Yes. I don't want this to be difficult. She adores you, John, and I want you in her life. But please try to *be* in her life."

"I do, it's just – you know what's happened, you've seen the news."

She sighed. "I know, it sounds terrible."

"I'm being investigated."

"I'm sorry about that, and I'm sorry he died. Have they caught anyone?"

"No, not yet."

"All right. I know it must be hard for you, but" – she hesitated, made a tutting noise – "I don't give a shit. Sophie's my priority, and she should be yours. I'm sure this is all very traumatic for you, but the small matter of ringing your daughter at a designated time should not slip your mind. It doesn't matter what's going on in your life."

She was right and he told her she was right, and then he said, "I'll ring her later."

"No. Ring me tomorrow, and we'll make arrangements."

"Tomorrow. Why? Why can't I ring her later?"

"We're going out later, John. Me, Sophie, and...and Luke."

His name was like a bad taste. *I didn't want to know*, thought Thorn,

I didn't want to know, and then he said, "I don't want to know, you know."

"Know what?"

"About your love life."

"I know."

Jane said she had to go, and he promised to ring tomorrow. He put the phone down and sagged into the sofa. He wanted to sleep, to drop away into that quiet darkness for a good ten hours.

The phone rang and he flinched.

He answered it and it was Ken Travis.

Thorn said, "You sound like you're in a cave."

"I'm out, that's all. I put that number plate through the computer for you, and I got a name. It's a name I know."

"Is it a name I'd know?"

"Richie Jarvis."

"It *is* a name I know. Dealer. Low-level violence, kickings, beatings. General good-for-nothing piece of shit. Thanks, Ken. You okay? You sound weary."

"I *am* weary, but aren't we all."

They said goodbye. Thorn dialled a number and voice said, "Northumbria Police, how can I help."

Thorn said, "Detective Chief Superintendent Lorraine Denton, please."

★ ★ ★

Jarvis said, "So where's my twenty-grand?"

"Do you think I'd walk into a cesspit like this with twenty-grand?" said Michael leaning over his bottle of beer.

"When do I fucking get it then?"

Michael leaned back. He glanced round the pub. The same guys who were playing pool during his previous visit were at the table again. The place still stank, and it was grimy and menacing. He pulled his gaze away from the pool-players, not wanting to make eye contact with them.

He said, "You're not getting twenty-grand, Jarvis."

Jarvis grimaced, showed his yellow teeth. "You give me twenty-grand or..." He trailed off. His face was going red.

"Or what?"

Michael thought about the envelope, what he'd seen, the chill seeping through his veins when he saw what the content meant, the iciness in his bladder. He felt like someone had smacked him, and he'd recoiled. But then he'd looked at Jarvis, and Jarvis looked confused, his eyes flitting from the envelope's contents to Michael's face.

He took a drink of beer, then took a shot. "You don't even know what's in that envelope, Jarvis."

Jarvis was trembling. His hands had rolled into fists.

Michael said, "I remember when you came over, did that work on the farmhouses at the Hall. It slipped my mind, but when I saw you a couple of days ago in the kitchen, all those pictures and diaries and letters spilled out, you were trying to gauge my reaction, it came back to me. Do you remember? You had to get your little helper to read and sign the contract, said you'd sprained your hand doing the work, said he'd have to read and sign." Michael leaned forward and grinned. "You can't read, Jarvis, so you've got no clue what's in that envelope."

"There's pictures, pictures of your fucking dad," said Jarvis, spit showering the table, "pictures of him and a woman who's not your mother – I saw her, I saw her wedding picture. That wasn't the same woman."

Michael shrugged. "So what. My father was fucking around. Who gives a shit?"

"Papers would. MP and all."

"Old news. He's dead, now. No one'll give a shit."

"Maybe the cops'll like to know about it, then. How I got it. How I knew your dad was going to be up there that night."

"You'll confess to murder? You couldn't cope with that long a sentence."

"I'll make a fucking deal, sonny. Nail you. Take you down with me."

"They don't make deals with scum like you, Jarvis."

"Oh aye, we'll fucking see about that." He leaned back in his seat, grabbed the pint, and finished it. Bitter spilled down his chin. He slammed the glass down. "Give me the four grand for the job, and we'll forget the rest."

Michael shook his head. "Price has dropped. Two grand."

Jarvis leaped to his feet, grabbed the pint glass, shattered it again the table and pressed it into Michael's throat. "Give me my money you little shite; I want my fucking money. I almost got killed doing that job for you, almost got killed by some fucking great big animal – twice I almost got killed by it."

Michael tried to say he would get Jarvis's money, but he couldn't. His throat was dry, his heart racing. From the corner of his eye, Michael saw the landlord stride over. He thought the man would grab Jarvis and toss him out of the pub. But he stood at the table, lit a cigarette, and said, "Richie, man, put him down. I can do without any more blood in this place."

Michael whimpered. Jarvis put the glass down and said, "I'll be at the funeral tomorrow. Have my money ready. Four grand." He stormed out.

Michael, trembling, picked up he beer bottle to drink but the landlord swiped it from his hand.

The landlord said, "You fuck off, son, or I'll have some of the lads give you a kicking. We don't want strangers in our pub."

Michael got to his feet, stumbled out of the pub, and felt nauseous when the fresh air hit him. He watched Jarvis stride away. He looked at his watch. It was one p.m. A police car screeched to a halt next to Jarvis. A red Mondeo pulled up behind it. Men leaped out of the cars, uniformed and suited.

Jarvis tried to sprint away, but a uniform – his hat tumbling off – lunged at his legs, rugby-tackling him to the pavement.

Michael stepped back against the wall of the pub. He cowered, staying still, hoping they'd not see him. Jarvis yelped and struggled as the policemen pushed him into the back of the Mondeo.

CHAPTER 49.
BACK TO THE SCENE.

HE LIKED to go back and reminisce.

Returning to the scene, he would play out the action again. He could see it in his mind; every moment reeled off as if it were a film. It made him feel strong. He would think about the incident carefully, regard every moment and would criticise himself if he thought anything wasn't up to standard.

Sitting in a KFC on the Bigg Market, he glanced across at the police gathered outside Bliss. He had a baseball cap pulled low over his face, and the collar turned up on his jacket. If any officer happened to glance across, they wouldn't notice him.

He bit into the chicken. The woman who ran Bliss was standing outside the club. She was speaking to Foreshawe, the man in charge of the rape inquiry. Foreshawe was tall and lean and his blonde hair was whipped back across his skull to hide his baldness. The woman was short and slim and pretty for her age. He thought about her for a moment, then dismissed her.

You could have any woman you want, he thought, *and at the moment you prefer the younger ones.*

He reached over to the next table and nabbed the copy of the Evening Chronicle discarded by the previous occupants. He expected to see something on the front page, but it was dominated by Adam Templeton's murder. He scowled, popping a chip into his mouth. He flipped over the page, thinking: page three, at least.

He made a little growling noise when he saw that there was nothing on page three, either; or on page five; or seven; or –

There it was. The lead on page nine: WOMAN RAPED NEAR DANCE CLUB, screamed the headline; *Masked monster claims fifth victim*, the sub-deck said.

Monster, he thought, *I'm not a monster*. He was angry, his hands rolled into fists. He understood why they called him a rapist, but he was not a monster.

Bloody newspapers. Always sensationalising everything. What's a monster? What defines a monster? They're bloody stupid, journalists.

He glanced towards the club again, and over to the alley where he got her. That's where the paper's rear entrance was. He could sneak down there, under the tape marked POLICE: DO NOT CROSS, and try to get into the building, lambast the editor for using such stupid words.

"Monster. What does 'monster' mean?" he'd say.

Don't be ridiculous, he thought. *Stay where you are and eat your chicken. It doesn't matter what they call you. Don't get caught, that's all.*

He knew how difficult it was to get away with things, these days. Science had made it hard for the criminal. But his needs were great, and it wasn't as if he could switch this on and off. Dangerous or not, he had to continue.

He thought about the girl and the way she tried to scream. He thought about her flesh, cold and smooth. Her face was a mask of blood, the wound on her forehead leaking terribly. She wasn't nice to look at under those circumstances, but he had to go ahead with things. He couldn't stop. He couldn't say, "That blood on your face really puts me off, so I'm going to let you go."

After grabbing her, he drove east along Westgate Road, then took a right past the general hospital. The attack took place near St Nicholas's Cemetery, where he tossed her out of the Vectra. He drove across the river and dumped the Vectra in a Gateshead alleyway, a half-mile walk from where he'd parked his car.

He watched as Foreshawe ducked under the yellow tape and disappeared into the club. The woman who owned the place was still outside. She folded her arms across her chest as if she was cold. She was looking around, her gaze drifting up and down the Bigg Market, not really looking at anything.

Eyeing her, he wondered when his desires would rage again. He could, if he was careful, take another one from the club. They were ready made, really: whores who were used to flaunting themselves.

He popped the last piece of chicken into his mouth and smacked his lips. Maybe he could grab the one who'd been causing all the trouble; the one who made all that nuisance at the court; the one they suspected of murdering Adam Templeton; the one he had already touched.

CHAPTER 50.
BAD MEN.

DC MARK Bailey said, "What were you doing at Templeton Hall on the night of August the sixth?"

"I wasn't at Templeton Hall on whatever night of whatever night, man," said Jarvis.

"You weren't? Are you sure?"

"Yes, I'm sure.

"So where were you, Mr Jarvis?"

"I was shacked up in bed with my lass."

"Would she be able to confirm that?"

"She'd better."

"And if we phone your home, now, will she be there?"

Jarvis folded his arms. "No, man. I kicked her out. She was a useless fat cow. I don't know where she is."

"That's convenient."

"Not really, is it? She could tell you what I was doing to her that night if I knew where she was."

Bailey looked down at his notes. Jarvis stared at the detective's partner. He smiled at her and said, "What's your name again, pet?"

"Detective Sergeant Drew," she said.

"Oh, aye. Slipped my mind. You married? Shacked up with someone?"

She ignored his question and said, "What were you doing at Templeton Hall on August the eighth, Mr Jarvis?"

"August the eighth, now."

"That's right."

"You mean yesterday, then, DS Drew."

"I mean yesterday, yes."

Jarvis thought for a moment. He shot a glance at his brief. The solicitor looked about twelve and not really up to this kind of stuff. The lad was scribbling stuff on his pad, anyway, not paying much attention to the interview. Jarvis said, "Finishing off your homework, lad?"

The brief looked up.

"You paying attention to this torture?" said Jarvis.

"I don't think you're being tortured, Mr Jarvis," said the solicitor.

Drew said, "So, Mr Jarvis. Yesterday. You at the Hall. Would you like to tell us?"

"I don't have to, do I?" he said, looking at the brief.

The brief said he didn't have to, not at all.

Jarvis looked up at the ceiling. It was cracked and peeling and it made him feel at home. He said, "I was paying my respects to young Michael Templeton. I knew the family, did some work up there a few months back."

Bailey asked, "Have you supplied drugs to any member of the Templeton family?"

Jarvis sat up. "I've never supplied drugs in my life."

"You been convicted of supplying drugs, Richie," said Bailey.

"That was a fucking miscarriage of justice."

"Three times," said Bailey.

Jarvis leaned forward. "*Three* fucking miscarriages of justice."

Drew said, "What kind of drugs have you sold to Michael Templeton, Mr Jarvis?"

"Hey, I've told you. Nowt. No drugs. Never."

Jarvis's heart raced. He was sweating and finding it hard to breathe. His mind rolled over and over. He wanted to say what had happened, that Michael had hired him. But he knew he'd go down for it and there was no way he was spending ten, twelve, fifteen years in prison.

He thought about that animal he saw: it killed the dogs at Templeton Hall the first night he'd gone over there to try to kill Michael's dad, then the following night it chased him at the Wall after he gutted the old man.

Michael told him he must have been stoned. He was stoned, but that monster wasn't a hallucination; wasn't a product of the weed Jarvis had smoked.

He looked at Bailey, then he looked at Drew and he thought about telling them about the monster. But they wouldn't believe him. It would sound like drugs talk to them, as well. Jarvis started to tingle, his skin prickling. His left leg started to shake.

That fucking envelope, he thought. I'm going to burn it when I get out of here. I'm going to get my cash off Michael, and get out of Newcastle for a few months. Or for good.

Drew said, "What if we get a warrant, Mr Jarvis. Have a poke round your house. What would we find, there?"

The panic pressed on Jarvis's chest. He could barely suck in breath. *That's it*, he thought. *I'm out of here.*

★ ★ ★

Ray Craig had his feet up on the varnished oak desk. "No light-sabres this time?" he said.

Michael glared at the man's feet. They were huge, his heavy shoes caked in mud. "No, I'm not a kid anymore."

"No, you're not. All grown up, now, and the new owner of Templeton Hall. Not Luke Skywalker, anymore."

"Certainly not."

Craig pulled his feet off the table. "Last time I was here, you told me that you never wanted to see or hear from me again."

"It was eighteen years ago. Things change."

Craig shrugged. "Not much changes. Not really."

"You threatened to kill me."

"Yes, I remember. He wouldn't pay me."

"Would you have killed me?"

"What do you think?"

Michael looked at him. The memory of that day came back. Craig had aged. His hair was grey, his skin lined, but he was still a powerful and intimidating figure. No less of a threat than he was all those years ago.

Craig sniffed, and looked around. "This place still stinks of old books. Aren't you going to clear them away now the old man's gone?"

"Maybe," said Michael, and then, "I don't think you would've killed me."

Craig raised his eyebrows. "You don't?"

Michael shook his head.

Craig shrugged. "Well, we'll never know, will we?" He sat up, placed his hands on the table. "However, games aside, why do I get a call from Michael Templeton with inquiries about finishing a job I started almost twenty years ago?"

"How'd you like to make another hundred and sixty grand?"

Craig whistled. "The price for thirty-two hits is higher than that today, lad."

"It's not thirty-two, it's two."

"Two." Craig nodded. He leaned back in his chair, and furrowed his brow. "How'd you find me, Michael?"

"Found a number in one of dad's old books. Rang it, this man goes, 'How the fuck did you get this number, and what do you want?'"

Craig chuckled and nodded. "That's Brent, for you."

"I said I was looking for you, he asked why, and I said I had a job for you. He took some details and told me, 'Don't ring this fucking number again.' A few hours later, he rang back, said he'd got in touch with you and" – Michael shrugged, gestured towards Craig – "here you are, sat in my father's chair."

Craig slapped the chair's arms and said, "And very comfy it is, too." He stood up and Michael's gaze followed his height upwards. Michael rubbed the back of his neck. Craig said, "After I did that job, I went into hiding for a good ten years. There wasn't much publicity about the killings. No families to rant and rave, demanding the killers are brought to justice. I guess the bodies were scooted away, buried without much pomp. No one linked them except for the authorities; and I knew they were sniffing around. Some old fighting pals of mine warned me to keep my head down. Special services were on my arse. First Gulf War, I popped up again. Took a gamble."

"What happened?"

"Nothing. It went fine. Made some money. No one mentioned the killings. Since then I've been around the world and back again and – "

The door opened, and Michael turned to see Ruth step into the library. She froze. Michael looked back to Craig. The mercenary was smiling. Ruth strode towards them and said, "What is this man doing here?"

"You've not aged a bit," said Craig, "still as gorgeous as ever."

Ruth said, "Michael, what's he doing here?"

Michael looked from Ruth to Craig. Their eyes were fixed on each other. Craig's smile gave away more than Ruth hoped it would.

Michael said, "He's here to finish what he started, Aunt Ruth."

"Yes, Aunt Ruth," said Craig, "I'm here to pick up from where I left off."

Ruth stabbed a look at Michael. "Are you mad?"

"No, I'm not. I'm sorting things out." He took her by the arm and said to Craig, "Excuse us for a moment," then guided Ruth to the window.

Michael told her something and he felt her tremble and had to hold her so that she wouldn't fall. She raised a hand to her brow, and then placed it on her breast. All the colour leached from her cheeks. She shook her head saying the word, "No," over and over. She walked out of the library, appearing unsteady on her feet.

"Very nice lady, your aunt," said Craig after she'd gone.

"Did you sleep with her, Ray?"

Craig nodded. "Oh, yes. Most definitely."

"What did Uncle Skipp make of that?"

"What could he make of that? What was he going to do about it? If I want to sleep with a man's wife, I'll fucking sleep with a man's wife."

Michael envied him his power. *I'll have this kind of power, soon,* he thought. *Power to do anything to anyone. Physical power.*

Craig said, "So, 'finishing what I started', you said. What does that mean? Who are the two targets?"

Michael took out two cardboard files from the desk drawer and handed them to Craig. He looked at the name on the first and said, "Richie Jarvis." He shrugged and said, "All right." Then he looked at the other file and seemed to stare at Laura Greenacre's name for a long time. He raised his gaze to Michael and pulled his shirt collar away from his throat. Michael saw the crisscross of scars on the man's neck. Craig said, "She did this to me, the little bitch. I've waited a long time to put her down."

* * *

Things had got out of hand. It was time to cut and run. He didn't even care about the money that much. He would try to scare Michael Templeton into paying him, but if it proved too difficult, he'd say sod it and get on a plane.

Maybe Germany. Like the lads from Auf Wiedersehen, Pet. He'd get a job on the building sites. That should be easy. He'd done labouring before, and that's how he met Michael: doing that work on the farmhouses, the old barns at the back of Templeton Hall.

Hands in pockets, head down, Jarvis scurried through the streets. He'd got a bus back to Newcastle, then to North Shields, and that gave him time to think. Jarvis really needed a lot of time to think. His brain was fuzzed with dope so he couldn't always focus. A long bus ride allowed him to concentrate and make sure he got things right.

And he knew what was right.

He should have said he had no idea when Michael asked him if he knew how to get someone killed. He should have shrugged when Michael asked him if he knew any hard nuts who'd take someone out for a few grand. He should have said no when Michael asked him to do the job.

Well, he shouldn't have offered to do it in the first place.

Richie shook his head, cursed himself: always wanting to be the big man.

He turned into his street. A group of kids skulked on the corner, smoking. One of them said, "Hey, Richie, got some weed?"

Jarvis shook his head and kept walking, telling the kids he'd have some tomorrow.

He was fucked. He wanted to put his head down. He'd nap for a couple of hours, then pack a bag. He'd get over to the airport, see if he could get away cheap. He shuddered. Life was too short for this kind of bollocks.

He scanned the street. He saw a car. A memory nudged. He narrowed his eyes. Had he seen it somewhere before? The thought slipped away, faded into the haze in his head.

He fished out his front door key, started to open his door. He heard the car door open behind him. A sweat broke out on his back. He knew something was wrong. He pushed open the front door, said, "No," and looked over his shoulder.

The man shoulder charged Jarvis into the house.

CHAPTER 51.
THE LIST.

"THORN was right," said DC Bailey, "Jarvis was at Templeton Hall yesterday. Says he was paying his respects to Michael Templeton."

Denton made a face. "Jarvis paying respects to anyone, let alone Michael Templeton, is a ludicrous concept."

"He denied he was up there selling dope."

"He would, wouldn't he." She was looking out of the window of her office. The late afternoon sky was the colour of slate. Not what you'd expect in August. *Where's my summer gone?* thought Denton, *I haven't finished with it yet.* She cursed Thorn. He'd been right about Jarvis, that the scumbag had his fingers in this pie. She didn't know how; she didn't know how deeply. But the fact he was linked at all irritated Denton. "It's a pain in the backside," she said.

"Do you think he's got something to do with this?" said DC Bailey.

"Richie Jarvis has got something to do with everything. That's my problem."

Denton ground her teeth. She thought about meeting Foreshawe on the stairs. His words came back to her.

Still biting off more than you can chew. Why don't you sort the one murder out, first?

She scrunched up a piece of paper into a ball, digging her nails into it, imagining it to be Foreshawe's flesh.

She said, "I thought we were so close this morning, Mark."

"I think we are."

She looked at the DC. "I thought we were going to solve four killings in one go."

He shrugged. "It's not impossible."

She thought about Foreshawe's dig and said, "Maybe we should sort the one murder out, first."

"Once we get the DNA, we can nail Laura Greenacre to the scene."

"You think she killed Templeton?"

"I thought she was our prime suspect, Ma'am."

"She is. Doesn't mean she killed him though."

He canted his head to one side and said, "Are you thinking Jarvis?"

"I'm thinking we should get a search warrant, poke around Jarvis's hovel."

"Okay. A warrant should be straightforward."

"We're bound to find something. Drugs paraphernalia. Weapons. Something to charge the bastard with, get him out of our hair."

"Do we think he's a suspect in the murder?"

Denton creased her brow. "Damn Thorn. Poking his nose into my business." She sighed. "I'm afraid we have to consider Jarvis a suspect. He's now officially on the list. Until we get the DNA back on those trainers. Then we'll have enough to pin this on that Greenacre girl. My gut tells me she did it."

"I'm sure your gut is right, Ma'am."

She looked at him and said, "Do you still see Tanya?"

Bailey blushed, dropped his gaze. "We're...actually we're talking again. Trying to...patch things up."

Denton nodded. "I see." She thought for a moment and then said, "That's good, Mark. I'm pleased for you."

Someone rapped on the door and Denton said, "Come in."

A civilian worker entered and handed Denton an A4 envelope.

"What's this?" said Denton.

The woman said, "It's a list of guests for Sir Adam Templeton's funeral. The assistant chief constable asked for it to be circulated among senior officers. Security reasons."

Denton nodded and the woman left. Denton slid the piece of paper out of the envelope. She looked at the sheet and her eyes opened wide. She said, "How the hell does that happen?"

CHAPTER 52.
MONSTER.

THORN mule-kicked the door shut. He had a handful of Jarvis's T-shirt, shoving the drug dealer into the house.

Jarvis's face has lost its colour. His eyes were wide, his mouth opening and closing. Thorn was bigger, stronger, and Jarvis felt weak in his grip.

Thorn pushed Jarvis against a door. The dealer's head jerked, smacked against the door. His eyes rolled back, and for a moment Thorn thought the guy had been knocked out. Then Jarvis groaned.

Thorn shook him and said, "Why were you up at the Hall, Jarvis?"

"Who the fuck are − " Jarvis hesitated.

"You know me, Jarvis. You saw me up there. I saw you. You and your pal, Michael Templeton."

Jarvis struggled, said, "Let me go, bastard," but Thorn was too strong.

Jarvis tried to headbutt Thorn, but Thorn leaned back. He said, "You piss me off, Jarvis, and I'll do you some serious damage."

"You can't do that, you're a copper."

"I'm not a copper. I'm a copper who's been temporarily kicked off the force. That's the worst kind." He shoved Jarvis, and Jarvis crashed through the door. Thorn followed him into the kitchen. It stank of stale food. Cartons of takeaways were piled on the sink. A piece of pizza lay on the table. There was a knife next to it. Thorn said, "Good to see you take pride in your home, scumbag."

Jarvis leaned against the table. His eyes flitted about. He was trying to find an escape route.

Thorn said, "Don't think about it. You're staying put 'til I say."

Jarvis snatched the knife, lunged at Thorn. Thorn stepped aside, grabbed Jarvis's knife arm, twisted. Jarvis yelped, dropped the knife. Thorn pushed him away and tutted.

Jarvis said, "I'll have you for police brutality."

"I've told you: it doesn't count."

Jarvis jabbed a finger at him. "You're Templeton's bodyguard." A nervous smile twitched on his face. "You fucked up, didn't you, man."

Thorn clenched his fists. "I just told you, Jarvis: it wouldn't be police brutality if I beat the shit out of you, so don't push it."

"What do you want?"

"I want to know why you were at Templeton Hall, and don't give me that crap about paying your respects to Michael: you think sympathy's a new dance drug."

"Ha, ha, you're not funny."

"No, I'm not. I'm not funny at all." He glared at Jarvis. "What were you doing there?"

Jarvis stared back. He was trembling.

Thorn said, "We're not going anywhere 'til you tell me something I find vaguely interesting. If I don't find it vaguely interesting, you've got a house-guest on your hands – and we won't be going out much."

Jarvis groaned, rolled his head. He looked like he was going to cry. He said, "What do you expect me to say, man?"

"The truth is always good in my experience. Maybe you should try it."

Jarvis shook his head. "This is mad, like. Mad."

"What's mad?"

"It's all gone wrong."

Thorn stepped forward. Jarvis flinched. Thorn said, "What's gone wrong?"

Jarvis looked at Thorn. The dealer's eyes were wide, red-rimmed. His face was stretched with fear. It seemed as if he was about to beg. "There's this fucking monster on the loose, man," he said. "Fucking huge thing, like a..." He trailed off, glanced away as if he was looking for the word. Then, looking at Thorn again, he said, "Werewolf."

Thorn opened his mouth to say something, but nothing came out.

Jarvis, holding up his hands, said, "I know it sounds mad, but I'm telling the truth, man. This thing, it was..."

"Where have you seen it, Jarvis?"

"I...I...I want cash, man."

"Cash?"

"I need to get away."

"Get away from what?"

"The cops, everything."

"The" – Thorn checked himself before saying the word – "werewolf?"

"Don't take the piss, man. I'm serious. It's about seven-feet tall. Teeth like knives. Yellow eyes. Great big thing. Pissed myself."

Thorn narrowed his eyes. "You were at Templeton Hall the night the dogs were killed, weren't you."

Jarvis opened his mouth.

Thorn said, "And when Adam Templeton was murdered." He stepped towards Jarvis. "Was it you, Richie? Did you kill Adam Templeton?"

Jarvis, shaking his head, said, "I...I...it wasn't us, man. Oh no. You can't pin that on me, it was – I only – no way. That monster. It was that monster that did it."

"Templeton was gutted. Stabbed to death." Thorn glanced at the knife on the floor. He bent down, picked it up. "If I was to turn this place upside down, would I find that knife?"

Jarvis was trembling. His cheeks had turned scarlet. Sweat trickled from his hairline. Thorn pounced. He pressed Jarvis against the sink. Takeaway cartons toppled to the floor. Thorn pressed the knife into Jarvis's throat. Jarvis whimpered. Thorn felt the man's legs buckle, and he had to hold him up.

Thorn said, "It was you, you little bastard. You're going down for life."

"It weren't me, man, it weren't me. It were Michael, he did it, he killed his dad, I'm telling you. It were Michael Templeton. I've got some stuff. Downstairs. Give me some cash and you can have it. I'll show you, I'll show you, man. Pictures, letters, diaries and stuff. About Templeton."

★ ★ ★

The headlights sliced the gloom.

Craig watched the lorry rumble along the track towards the old barn. It carried nine men, all former elite services' operatives: The British SAS and SBS; the U.S. Special Forces; GSG9 from the old West Germany; the French Foreign Legion. They were all guns for hire. They'd seen action all over the world, as members of their country's armed forces and as mercenaries. Two of them – the German, Klaus Markus, and Craig's ex-SAS colleague, Steve Lloyd, had been there twenty years ago when Sir Adam Templeton hired him.

He rubbed the scars on his neck, recalling that night.

No mistakes this time, he thought. Two targets, that was all. Two targets, and ten guns to take them out.

The lorry's headlights showered Craig with its beams. He used the light to check his list. Top of the list, Markus. He was part of the GSG9 team sent to Mogadishu, in Somalia, in 1997 to rescue 86 Germans hijacked by The Red Army Faction. Then Lloyd, his ex-SAS buddy, George Murphy, and SBS men, Pete Cleaver and Harry McKay. Next came three American Special Forces guys: Morton Stick, Jerry Bahrman, and Phil Page. Luc Broos, a Foreign Legion veteran who'd seen action in Zaire in 1978 when 4,000 FNLC rebels murdered and raped Europeans in the Kolwezi region. France sent its Foreign Legion, eighty of them. Broos and his colleagues rescued 3,000, killed 300 FNLC insurgents, and captured a haul of weapons and ammo.

These men were elite troops. No one could stand in their way.

The truck rumbled into the barn. The headlights were killed and it fell into darkness. The rear door dropped open and Markus leaped out. He was wide and tall, his grin showing perfect white teeth.

"Do the job right this time, eh, Craig?" he said.

Craig smiled at him. "Yes, we do it right."

They unloaded the truck. Small arms, mostly. Half an hour later, beers and fags shared out, the group sat on old farm machinery listening to Craig.

"So, why so many guys for two kills?" said Bahrman, looking around.

"This is a good number," said Craig.

Bahrman shrugged. "Well, I guess I'm not paying."

"No, you're getting paid."

"I am, Craig, and that's good. But I want to know what I'm getting paid for."

Craig stared at the American. "You're getting paid to kill two targets. That's what you're getting paid for."

Bahrman folded his arms, tilted his head to one side. "One guy could cope with two hits. I think we should know what we're dealing with, here."

Craig glanced at Markus, and the German shrugged.

"Twenty years ago," said Craig, "we were on a job in this part of the world. It was pretty straightforward. But I came across something that was not straightforward. I came across something I'd never seen before."

He told them what he saw in the house that night, the monster changing back into the man. He said, "I want to make sure, that's all."

Bahrman laughed, and the others looked at each other.

The American said, "Sounds like you'd been spending a little too much time on the Brown Ale they have up here, Craig."

Craig whipped the knife out of its sheath, flicked it across the ten yards that separated him from the American. Bahrman grimaced as the blade sank into his left arm. He stared at Craig, showing his teeth. He plucked the knife out of his arm and flexed his bicep. Blood spilled out of the wound. Bahrman's grimace turned into a smile, and he said, "Okay, Craig, I guess you're serious. I'll play along. But you gotta understand me, I can't let this" – he held up the knife – "go unchallenged."

Craig said, "We'll get the job done, Bahrman. Then if you want to thrash things out, I'll gladly thrash things out."

CHAPTER 53.
THE WORLD COMES
TUMBLING DOWN.

CHLOE slept and Laura stroked her hair. She sat on the bed next to her sleeping friend. Laura had stayed with her that night, Chloe too scared to be on her own after the attack.

Laura thought about Chloe's assailant. She had the man's scent filed away. If she could smell him again, she'd be able to match the odours.

And then kill him.

She narrowed her eyes, and thought about everyone she'd met recently.

It was someone she'd been close to.

She cursed herself. It was frustrating. It was like the man she hunted was behind a door. His was voice muffled, his identity indistinguishable. Laura was rattling at the handle, trying to get through. But the door wouldn't budge however hard she pulled and shoved and rammed her shoulder into it.

Laura shut her eyes and concentrated, trying to pry that door open, trying to focus on that voice.

Who the hell was he? He's someone *here*, someone I know, *now*.

Chloe whimpered and Laura opened her eyes. She stopped stroking her friend's hair.

The terror of Chloe's ordeal chilled Laura's insides. She shuddered, and thought about Morgan Hill House those years ago, the girl called Mary or Marian crying in the toilet saying, "Colin raped me."

The rage had flared in Laura's breast that day. The same rage flushed through her after Chloe's torment.

The memory of Pavin's death came to her. The rapist torn to shreds. He begged for his life, and he screamed not to be hurt.

Chloe's attacker would go the same way.

Eaten alive.

Laura got up from the bed and quietly left Chloe's room. She went into her own bedroom and looked at the case, still open, still waiting to be filled.

"When will I ever get away?" she said to herself.

She sat down, glanced around the room. This was not a girl's room: no posters on the wall, no bright colours, no dressing table covered in make-up. It was barren: a wardrobe, a table with a mirror leaning against the wall, a simple wooden chair, a single bed. But that was all Laura needed. It was more a home than she'd ever known.

She got up, filed through her clothes in the wardrobe.

Black dress, she thought, *black dress*.

But did it have to be black? She wouldn't be mourning Adam Templeton, would she? She'd be celebrating his demise. Sir Adam's family would attend a service at Newcastle crematorium in the early afternoon, before the invited guests – including Laura – gathered for the "tribute" in the evening.

Elena had warned her not to go. And Laura had no intention until last night and the attack on Chloe. Her instincts told her that Chloe's attacker would be at Templeton Hall that evening. If he were there, she had to go.

She pulled out a sky blue evening dress, pressed it against her body.

Thorn drifted into her mind and his presence was comforting. Apart from Elena, he was her only ally.

Guilt made her screw up her face: she hadn't told him she'd be going to Sir Adam's "tribute".

But, she thought, *he didn't tell me about seeing that guy visiting Michael at Templeton Hall.*

She wondered about the man Thorn saw: could he be Templeton's killer, the man she chased away, the man whose fear filled the air the night Templeton died?

Laura glanced at the suitcase.

She said, "You'll have to wait, I'm afraid," and tipped it shut with her foot.

Too much to do before leaving.

"Laura," said Elena from downstairs.

"I'm up here."

"Someone to see you."

Her heart skipped, her stomach fluttered. She threw the dress down on the bed and went out of her room.

HADRIAN'S WALL, NORTHUMBERLAND — 10.22 A.M.

What had Laura said?

Perhaps Michael wanted his father dead. To inherit the fortune. The guy was a hitman.

Thorn had huffed, saying it was madness.

Maybe it was.

It certainly shouldn't be taken as gospel coming from Jarvis. But the weight of it was pressing down on Thorn, and he was becoming less able to reject the idea.

He rubbed his eyes and yawned, then ran a hand over his chin. It was like sandpaper. He licked his lips, trying to moisten them, but he had no spit.

He stepped out of the car and stretched, breathing in the Northumberland air. He gazed across the Wall, to the hostile territories where the Northern Tribes dwelled. He remembered Sir Adam telling him stories about this place. Not much of the detail had stuck in Thorn's mind. Only the part about who built the Wall, and why.

Thorn wished he could climb over the Wall and disappear into what the Romans must've regarded as badlands.

He wasn't sure he could bear what he'd heard and seen at Jarvis's house.

The drug dealer had shown Thorn the contents of an envelope. He refused to say how he got the package, but the stuff it contained shook Thorn. It changed everything. Shattered the mirror of pretence that the Templetons had been staring into for decades.

He leaned on the car.

This truth would be devastating. He didn't know how to carry it, how to convey it; he didn't understand how damaging it would be.

He looked north again and thought of Sophie. Any half-decent father would get in his car and drive up to Edinburgh. He'd rap on the door and demand to see his daughter.

He huffed. That would go down a treat with Jane. And the family courts would just love him, wouldn't they.

"You're impulsive, temperamental, and on the verge of losing your job – of course you can have access to your daughter at all times, Mr Thorn."

He got back in the car and leaned back in the seat. He closed his eyes and felt sleep slide over him. Thorn had gone home after leaving Jarvis's house. His mind raced with what he'd seen. He tried to control the information, to file it away, but its ferocity made it impossible to leash.

He'd got back in his car and driven around, ended up here at around four a.m. where he'd stopped, fallen asleep.

Thorn came to with a start. He looked at the clock on the dashboard. It was ten thirty five a.m. Staring at the dials, a ridiculous thought – forged by his fatigued brain – popped up: this isn't even my car. He laughed out loud. The Saab was Sir Adam's, but it was Thorn who always drove it. Denton hadn't said anything when she took his I.D. and his weapon. Michael never said a word.

At least I get something out of this mess, he thought.

But how useful would a car be with everything else falling apart? Thorn's world was crumbling. *Maybe it's this Y2K thing they've been talking about,* he thought. When the millennium arrived in four months time, and the computer dials fail to recognise 0000, nothing will matter. Sophie, Jane, Laura, having a car, having a job, a house, none of it would be important. Everything would be chaos. It was only months away. He was starting early, that's all: his 0000 had already arrived.

Thorn thought for a moment. He leaned forward and opened the Saab's compartment. The "you-never-know" Browning was there.

Jarvis had asked for money: ten grand. Instead, Thorn would put the Browning in his mouth and in exchange for the envelope he'd promise not to pull the trigger.

He started the car and guided it out into the road.

He headed for Newcastle.

CHAPTER 54.
CREEP.

ELLIS Cole sat at the kitchen table, hands flat on the surface. Laura walked in and he said, "Hello, my lovely client."

She faltered, expecting – hoping for – someone else. So where was he, then? She'd not heard from him in ages. And what was this little creep doing here?

Elena, standing by the sink, said, "How's Chloe?"

"Ah, yes," said Cole, frowning, "terrible business. Is she, well, coping?"

Laura ignored him, looked at Elena and said, "She's asleep."

Cole said, "Has she thought along the lines of personal damages?"

Laura glared at him. "I'm sure that's what she's dreaming about right now: 'How much money am I going to make out of being raped, I wonder?' What do you think, Elena?"

"What I think is that Mr Cole should say what he needs to say and then leave. We've got things to do." Elena went to the door, and said to Laura, "I'll be with Chloe."

Laura waited until she heard Elena's footsteps on the stairs, then sat opposite Cole. He bent down and took a yellow pad out of his briefcase. He nudged the briefcase under his chair with his foot, glancing nervously at Laura.

"Still worried I'm going to piss in your case?"

He said nothing. He looked down at his pad, some notes scribbled there. Then he said, "You were questioned last night."

"I had a woman there, a duty solicitor."

"I understand that, but – "

"It's confidential, and you know it."

"But I'm your official legal representative."

Laura creased her brow. "I'm not beholden to you, to anyone."

"Beholden? No, you're not. But we made a verbal agreement that I'm to represent you in these matters."

"Don't bullshit me with jargon. Someone else sat with me, that's it. You weren't there last night. You were too pissed."

Cole grinded his teeth. "Tired," he said, "I was tired."

"Long night wanking over the dancing girls, Mr Cole."

He leered. "Call me, Ellis. Please."

"I don't want to call you anything." She got up, went to pour herself a glass of water. She leaned on the sink, drinking.

"Don't I get a coffee?" said Cole.

"Did Elena offer you a coffee?"

"No, she didn't."

She finished the water and put the glass in the sink. "There you are, then. It's Elena's house, she decides who gets coffee and who doesn't. You don't."

He scowled. "You should be more respectful. I'm trying to help you."

"No you're not. You're leering at me. Same as you leered at Chloe last night."

He tilted his head, looked at her. "That's what she's there for. That's what you're all there for." He let his eyes slip down Laura's body, then up again to fix on her face. "For my delectation. Where would girls like you, like Chloe, be without men like me?"

Laura lunged onto the table. She was on all fours. Her eyes were yellow. The colour seeped from Cole's face. His eyes bulged. He leaned back as far as he could. Laura pressed forward, her face in his face, and she hissed.

She said, "Chloe would be un-raped, Chloe would be at home with her family, Chloe would be safe."

Cole's chest went up and down. She could smell his stale breath. Last night's beer, she thought. Perfume on him too – only a hint, but it was there beneath the layers of sweat and soap and aftershave.

"Who was she?" said Laura, sliding off the table. "Did you have to pay?"

Cole stared at her as she moved away to stand at the door. He said, "Your eyes, what was that with your eyes? They were...they were like – "

She shot him a look, the human colour back in her eyes. "They were like nothing. They were angry, that's all. Very angry. You're imagining things. Like you imagined you were important. Like you imagined we liked you and creeps like you." She stared at him. She could smell his fear and his rage. He had no idea how to react: should he tremble or seethe? His sweat saturated the air. *If I'd shown him my teeth, he would've really pissed himself,* she thought.

Cole said, "You shouldn't underestimate me. I have influence, a lot of say in a lot of things."

"Bully for you."

He got up, packed his briefcase. "Girls like you, you take your clothes off, you act sexy for men, you dance, you smile, you tease – and you think men should walk by on the other side. You think you're untouchable when you're the most touchable women in the world."

"No touching. That's the rule."

Cole shook his head. "You've no idea. There's plenty of touching. Lots of it. But it's all in here" – he touched his temple – "and there's nothing you can do about it."

Laura's nostrils flared, her eyes narrowed. "You don't know what I can do."

"I think I do. I think you came here to kill Adam Templeton. And I think maybe you did. You've got a track record, Laura. I've checked you out. I'm your legal representative, so, obviously, I've got your best interests at heart. I want to know everything about you."

Laura raised an eyebrow. "Everything?"

He ignored her confidence. She knew he hated that. He said, "Men die when you're around. Die badly, from what I've learned."

"Maybe you should take that as a warning, then, and leave," she said, "before something nasty happens."

CHAPTER 55.
CONFESSIONS.

HE got to Jarvis's house at eleven-fifteen. He knocked and called Jarvis's name, but Jarvis didn't come to the door.

Thorn glanced around the street. A girl, fourteen or fifteen, pushed a buggy on the other side of the road. She was thin and fragile, her blonde hair tugged back into a tight ponytail. A fag drooped from her lips, the smoke wafting into the baby's face.

Further up the street, a couple of lads loitered. If they'd seen Thorn, they weren't showing it. He probably looked like another buyer; or maybe in this suit he looked like a heavy from another dealer. Perhaps that's why the lads weren't bothering with him. They had a swagger about them, but Thorn knew he could snap them like twigs if they hassled him.

And he was in a snappy mood.

He knocked again, bent down and shouted Jarvis's name through the letterbox.

"I've got some cash for you. I'll pay for the stuff, Richie. Five grand, yeah?"

He waited. If money didn't bring Jarvis to the door, nothing would; if money didn't bring Jarvis to the door, then he probably couldn't get to the door.

Thorn's stomach rolled. Nerves and hunger, he thought. Something was wrong here. He looked around. The teenage girl was chatting to the lads. One offered her something; she took it, pushing it under the baby in the buggy. She moved on.

Thorn walked down the street, away from the boys. At the end, he turned right, and then right again into the alley that backed up on to the terrace. Weeds crawled up the rear fences on both sides. A shopping trolley blocked Thorn's route. He nudged it out of the way, and it rolled into a gate.

The alley was littered with debris: cans and bottles, pizza boxes, takeaway cartons, he saw a few syringes, and some condoms, too. The lane smelled of decay. He moved down the path, counting down to Jarvis's house.

Thorn tore the back gate off its rusty hinges and rested it against the fence. He strode through the knee-high grass and weeds and up to the back door. It was ajar. Thorn froze. His policeman's paranoia switched into high gear. It was like a sixth sense, an intuition. A lot of the lads claimed it was a gift. But Thorn guessed it was a general attitude that copper's had: if it looked wrong, it was wrong.

And this looked wrong.

Jarvis's back door shouldn't be open.

Why not? thought Thorn. *Why shouldn't it be open?*

He shook his head, dismissing his own argument: it just shouldn't be.

He gently pushed the door open. He sneaked into the house. He wanted to call Jarvis's name. But if there was anyone else here, the last thing Thorn wanted was to make himself known. He crept into the kitchen, eyes flitting about the room. The door to the cellar was shut. Jarvis had led Thorn down there yesterday to show him the pictures and the letters. He'd let the drug dealer walk down a few steps first, before he followed.

"Try anything, Jarvis, I'll push you down the stairs and break your neck."

Jarvis hadn't tried anything. The man was shutting down. His defences were crumbling. There was nothing left, and it was clear to Thorn that he wanted to cleanse himself of everything, to confess. And Thorn was his priest.

He stepped further into the kitchen and the smell hit him. He recoiled, raised his hand to his nose.

It was shit.

Thorn's heart raced. A sweat broke out on his forehead. The

answer lay ahead, and he could see it, and he knew what it was. But he pretended he was far enough away not to see. He said, "Jarvis," knowing he wouldn't get an answer.

Thorn moved towards the kitchen door. He opened it, and the aroma of excrement was like a wave sweeping over him. He bent double, retched. Holding his breath, Thorn straightened. He looked towards the stairs.

Jarvis's feet were twelve inches off the floor. His naked legs were covered in his own dirt. His arms hung by his side, the hands clenched. Thorn noticed the thumbnails were tinted blue. Jarvis's head seemed swollen, as if the rope wrapped around his throat had pushed air into his skull. His tongue lolled like a slug over blue lips. His ears had a bluish hue. His wide, bulging eyes showed burst capillaries. Blood stained his lips and his nose. A piece of paper was tucked into the breast pocket of his shirt.

★ ★ ★

The letter in Jarvis's pocket was full of spelling mistakes. It said he killed Templeton, but it was Laura who put him up to it. Jarvis claimed she seduced him and they were lovers. Thorn shuddered. The thought made him sick. He shook it away and continued to read the letter. Jarvis made the allegation that was in the diaries and the letters he'd shown Thorn the day before.

Thorn folded the letter and tucked it into his jacket pocket. He opened the cupboard under the sink. Jarvis had taken the key to the cellar from this cupboard yesterday. Thorn trashed it, tossing cleaning fluids, dustpan and brush, cloths, a hammer, screwdrivers, crowbar, and bin bags on the kitchen floor. He found the key in a plastic sandwich box containing screws and nails.

Thorn went down into the cellar. It stank of cannabis. He opened the fridge. It wasn't switched on. Jarvis used it to store his drugs. Thorn saw the bags of weed on every shelf. He shut the door and slid his hand underneath the fridge. He'd seen Jarvis do that to retrieve the padded envelope.

Thorn cursed. His hand was too big. He got up and grabbed the fridge, gritted his teeth and pulled. It scraped the concrete floor. He tugged again, muscles straining. It jolted clear of its slot. Thorn dragged it away from the wall. He grunted and tossed it on its side. The door fell open. The drugs spilled out. Thorn ignored them, his eyes fixed on the cockroaches scuttling away from the light. He picked up the envelope and flicked it to clear away the spider.

Then he saw the blade.

A serrated kitchen knife with a red handle.

Thorn looked around for something to pick up the knife. He saw the drugs in their plastic bags. He kneeled, and rifled through the packages, throwing them about. He came across a fist of empty plastic bags wound up in an elastic band. He plucked a bag from the cluster and used it to pick up the knife. He put the knife in the polythene and knotted the bag.

He dangled the plastic bag in front of his face.

Was this the blade that killed Sir Adam?

Just odd that it was under the fridge. As if it had been slid there. And who would slide a knife under a fridge, under anything, unless they were trying to hide it? And why hide a knife?

Convinced he'd answered his own questions, he then looked at the envelope. He was going to burn it. He didn't know what good the knowledge within it would bring. None at all, he guessed; more pain, that was all.

He thought about it for a moment.

Did he have a right to make that decision? It wasn't his life, was it? He shook his head.

Up in the house the front door crashed open and everything apart from that splintering noise and what it meant for him dropped out of Thorn's mind.

★ ★ ★

"That should solve all their problems," said Michael. "It'll also solve quite a few of ours."

"What if the girl's arrested?" said Craig. "That's going to spoil our fun."

"My guess is she'll make it to tonight's fiasco. I think she's as intrigued as we were as to why my idiot father invited her over here. She'll lay low, keep out of the cops' way. And I would like to see her face when everything becomes apparent." Michael sat back, satisfied. He put his feet on the desk and cupped his hands behind his head. "Then, you can kill her, Craig. We'll tell the cops she'd come here to murder me, too, and they'll accept that. They're an accepting bunch when they get to dot their 'i's and cross their 't's."

Craig bit into his bacon sandwich. The men were eating their breakfasts in the truck. As far as anyone was concerned, they were providing the security for the evening's event.

The smell of bacon made the juices flow in Michael's mouth. His own plate was empty. He'd devoured the sandwich, his appetite intense after Craig returned from North Shields with news of Richie Jarvis's terrible suicide.

He was helped on his way, of course, old Richie; and Craig and Markus were a great encouragement in such circumstances.

They'd taken a note that was written by Michael, misspellings and all, and forced Jarvis to copy it out. He seemed unwilling, claiming that he couldn't write, Craig had said.

But when Markus put his .22-calibre Ruger Mark II with muzzle suppressor to Jarvis's head, the drug dealer discovered an amazing ability to write – or to copy writing, at least.

Craig folded the letter and popped it into Jarvis's shirt pocket. Markus climbed the stairs and leaned over the banister. He looped the rope around Jarvis's throat. He hoisted Jarvis off his feet. The dealer, panicking, kicked out. But his weak legs, his bare feet, made no impression against Craig's body.

The mercenary smiled as Jarvis lifted up. The dying man's face went red. His tongue hung out of his mouth. He croaked and kicked and tore at the rope. Capillaries in his eyes burst. Blood frothed in his mouth. A thread of blood trickled from his left nostril.

"Light as a feather," said Markus from above, tying the rope to the banister.

Jarvis shat himself. Craig laughed. He was used to smelling men's fear.

Michael lapped up the story of Jarvis's death. The bastard was finally out of the way. Again Michael chided himself for not getting Craig involved at the beginning. None of this would have happened. Craig would have sorted things that first night, and killed the Greenacre bitch as well.

After Craig and Markus had returned, and Craig had given Michael a re-run of Jarvis's suicide, Ruth had made the call.

Michael noticed the way Craig watched her. The mercenary's eyes fixed on Ruth as she swayed over to the phone. Michael thought he noted nostalgia in those eyes. As if they'd once seen more than they were seeing today. He smiled, thinking about the scandal it would cause: a City trader's respectable wife fucking some rough, crude beast. Michael wondered what his aunt was like when she was a bitch on all fours, and some great big dog like Craig was rutting her. He pondered this as Ruth called the police and claimed to have caught a terrible smell when she was strolling past a certain house in North Shields that morning.

"Like someone had" – she paused, and Michael thought it was effective – "died."

Michael, hands behind his head, feet up on the table, said, "Yes, everything's fine. It'll all be done by tonight. And then, the fun really begins."

CHAPTER 56.
LOOKING FOR LAURA.

THE reek of shit hit Denton. She flinched. She saw Bailey turn his head away. The two officers who battered down Jarvis's front door had stormed upstairs shouting, "Police, police." Uniforms spilled past Denton into the house. They shouted, "Police, police."

Denton said, "Get an ambulance, DC Bailey. Tell them there's no rush."

She moved into the house, a handkerchief covering her nose. She looked Jarvis up and down. He was naked from the waist down.

A uniformed sergeant came out of the kitchen. "Nothing in here, nothing out the back, Ma'am. Gates been taken off at the hinges, but we can't say if that's recent."

A woman PC, red-faced, stepped through from the kitchen. She said, "Down in the cellar. There's a fridge; it's overturned. Full of cannabis. Someone's ransacked it."

Denton said, "Get forensics down here, get a photographer."

The sergeant nodded and went out of the front door, followed by the PC.

Denton said, "Let's be careful ladies and gentlemen, this is a crime scene." She frowned. She hated to compromise a crime scene. She looked around. The stink of excrement was overwhelming.

Someone had ransacked the cellar. She glanced up at Jarvis. Got yourself murdered? she thought.

One of the battering ram cops was on the stairs, canting his head from side to side to study the knot at Jarvis's throat. He glanced up the stairs and said, "Anything, Mike?"

Mike, his voice muffled, said, "Eff-all. Seemed to live on nothing, our mate, Richie."

"Lived on drugs," said the battering ram cop. "May have died on them, too."

"Suicide, Ma'am?" said Bailey at Denton's shoulder.

She said, "No sign of a suicide note?"

"Jarvis couldn't read or write."

Denton nodded. Most of the officers were outside, at the front or rear of the house. They were hemming the scene off with yellow tape. Denton heard voices: locals poking their noses in.

"Get someone to ask the gathering vultures if they saw anything," she said to Bailey. He went outside. Denton stared up at Jarvis. *Is this your own work, laddie?* she thought. Denton didn't want it to be Jarvis's handiwork. She wanted Greenacre to be involved. Denton thought how she could implicate the girl in this apparent suicide. How could she link Greenacre to the ransacking of the cellar? The back of her neck prickled, and she turned away from Jarvis's corpse.

Don't go down that road, Lorraine, she thought, *there's no need to incriminate Laura Greenacre; she'll soon incriminate herself.* She made a fist and thought, *I just need those DNA results.*

Bailey came in and said, "A couple of lads say they saw a big guy, dark hair, grey suit, knocking on the door and shouting through the letterbox earlier."

"How much earlier?"

Bailey glanced at his notes. "They said, 'This morning, don't remember, we was stoned but you can't prove it'."

Denton bit her lip. Not Thorn, she thought. Surely not Thorn. What the hell was he doing here? She shook her head. He was digging his own grave and doing a grand job of it.

"What's the matter, Ma'am?" said Bailey, noticing her shake of the head.

"Nothing. Can you think who it would be?"

Bailey shrugged. "Michael Templeton?"

Not the answer Denton wanted.

"One of Jarvis's druggie customers?"

"In a grey suit?"

"Business types, Ma'am. They're into their dope. Just like your common-to-garden scum of the earth."

"Who else?"

"I can't think."

"How about Thorn?" she said.

Bailey frowned. "Why would he be here?"

"He saw Jarvis at Templeton Hall, put us on to him. I think Thorn thinks Jarvis was involved – or he wanted him to be involved so he could save that Greenacre girl's skin."

"Do you think he did this?" said Bailey, gesturing towards Jarvis.

She wanted to say, *Yes*. Wanted to say that Thorn had strung this good-for-nothing up. Had become executioner. A vigilante wiping out Newcastle's lowlifes. But pinning that on Thorn would be like getting Tim Foreshawe to like her again –

She gasped. Where did that come from?

"Ma'am, are you all right?" said Bailey.

She said, "Yes, fine, of course," and stepped past the DC into the fresh air. It hit her like that battering ram had hit the door, jolting her, making her stagger back a step. It swept away the particles of shit that soaked her nasal passage, her throat, her lungs. She scanned the street. Locals smoked and chattered behind the police line. They were mostly thin women who looked twenty years older than they were because of booze and drugs and beatings and too many children. A uniform was talking to two lads, probably the two lads who told Bailey they saw the grey suited man here earlier.

"What's going on?" said a woman, puffing on a fag, her face lined by too much sun, her hair bleached white. "Richie under arrest? Why can't you bastards leave him alone, he's not done nothing. Provides a service, gives the kids something to do."

She cackled, and her mates cackled with her.

Big joke, thought Denton, selling drugs to kids, turning kids into runners and later into dealers. The wail of an ambulance broke her thoughts. The locals looked to see it turn into the street.

"We won't be bothering him anymore," said Denton, and went back into the house.

★ ★ ★

217

The front door had crashed open. Thorn bounded up the cellar stairs. He'd thrown himself out of the backdoor.

Cops spilled into the kitchen, down into the cellar, shouting, "Police, police."

Thorn didn't look back. He ducked down, ran through the overgrown grass. He listened for a voice saying, "Stop, police," but the voice didn't come.

He darted through the back gate and down the alley. He expected to hear the sound of heavy boots tramping after him, calling for him to stop, but no one followed.

He slowed to a stroll, passing the junction, glancing down the road at the three police cars, their lights flashing. Some of the locals started to congregate. He saw the two lads he'd seen earlier crane their necks above the crowd to see what was going on.

Thorn kept walking, round to the next street where the Saab was parked.

Ten minutes later he was hammering his horn. "Come on, you bastards, come on," he said, but the traffic sludged the A1108 headed back to Newcastle. It was a twenty minute trip, for God's sake. "What the fuck's going on?"

He gasped for breath, then steadied himself. He rolled down the window. Cool air seeped into the car. He felt the sweat dry on his body.

No point losing it, he thought. *I'm no good to anyone if I lose it; get spotted; get arrested.* Arrested for what, he didn't know, but his fear, his paranoia had billowed over the past couple of days.

He had to get to Laura. Had to make a choice over this stuff. He glanced at the envelope on the passenger seat.

What am I going to do? he thought.

He didn't know, but he knew he wanted to take care of her, look out for her like Templeton had asked him to.

Whatever he decided to tell her, things would be better when he was with her.

The traffic trickled on. Thorn felt the tension rise in his body, but he kept it at bay. He contemplated the end of this; a conclusion to everything. *What will I do then?* he wondered. A part of him didn't want it to end, because at the moment he had Laura in his life: she was havoc, she was trouble, but he liked it. He liked her.

"You're a mess, John Thorn," he said to the rear view mirror, staring into his own eyes, seeing the bags cradling them, seeing the unshaven cheeks, and the tousled hair. "And you need a bath."

The traffic cleared. The cars stretched out. Thorn pressed on the accelerator. He shook his head and tutted. No indication of what had caused the delay. There never was. You get stuck in traffic on a motorway. The jam clears. You're driving on, looking for the reason you were sitting in your car for forty-five minutes. There never was a reason. Everything was random; everything was meaningless.

Fifteen minutes later he parked in Summerhill Terrace. He trotted up the hill, knocked on the door. No answer. He knocked again. A voice, trembling, said, "Who...who's that?"

He said who it was, and the door opened a crack. Chloe peered through. Her eyes were wide, her skin pale. She looked broken, and Thorn sagged when he saw her. He said it was him again and asked her if she was all right.

"Not really," she said.

"They'll catch him, you know."

"Laura said she'll catch him. She − "

That was another problem: Laura's one-woman posse. That terrible film, Dirty Weekend, slipped into his head; the woman on a revenge mission. He scurried it out of his mind and said, "Is she here, Chloe? I need to speak to her urgently."

Chloe shook her head, said Laura left around an hour ago.

Thorn said, "Do you know where she went?"

"She had a bag with her."

Thorn tensed. His insides seemed flushed with icy water. "Where... did she say?"

"Try Bliss."

* * *

Elena sat at the bar. The club was empty. It was gloomy; none of the lights were on. The only illumination was a strip of daylight slicing through a narrow window above the main door.

She liked it like this. She was at peace in the silence. Lost in her own head, her memories, her secrets.

She swigged from the bottle of Evian. *Tepid*, she thought, making a face. *I must tell Jimmy to look at that fridge when he comes in.* She looked at the clock above the bar. Jimmy would be here in an hour, getting the bar ready. The club would open its doors at eight p.m. and customers would begin to trickle in an hour later.

And Laura was on the rota to dance tonight. But that was unlikely. She was planning to go to Templeton Hall, to that do celebrating Sir Adam's life.

Sadness pressed down on her, and she sagged against the bar. Tears welled in her eyes. Laura: her last link to Richard, to the family who had loved her and loathed her. They tried to make Elena welcome, but their traditions prevented the Greenacres from embracing her fully. Laura was her way of being part of the family.

Elena sipped her water.

She thought about Laura leaving. It was inevitable. She had to, or be framed for killing Templeton. The police were fixed on her as a suspect. Only the real killer's capture could save Laura.

What will I do when you leave? she thought.

Elena had felt dislocated for years. She'd gone back to dancing in London after splitting from Richard. A couple of years later, she heard that Richard had been killed, murdered in his home. Ten years ago, at the age of forty-two, she brought the shell of a pub on the Bigg Market in Newcastle and transformed it into Bliss.

But she had continued to ponder her past.

And on a June night in Manchester, it came back to haunt her.

Elena travelled to find girls. She'd visit clubs across Britain. She was looking for ordinary girls who could dance. She'd ask them if they'd be interested in joining the Bliss family. Most times she got a polite, "no, I don't think so," often she was told to, "piss off, what d'you think I am? A prostitute?" but a few times she'd hear, "yeah, okay, I'll give that a go."

Two weeks after seeing her in the Manchester club tossing that man into the dance floor, Elena traced Laura. She lived in a flat in Salford. Elena called her and asked to meet. Laura said, "Why not," and they met in a Burger King in Manchester.

Sitting in the fast food restaurant, Elena said, "I knew it was you straight away."

Laura was devouring a Whopper with cheese. Elena had a coffee. Elena had said she knew Laura's family, and Laura said, "That's more than I ever did."

"Do you remember them killing your father?"

Laura stopped chewing. Her pupils flared. She gave a little shake of her head and said, "I don't remember," and looked at the burger in her hands.

Elena asked if she was all right.

Laura said, "The taste of meat."

"What about the taste of meat?"

Laura was still. She stared at the burger. She shook her head. She said, "Nothing," and carried on chewing.

Elena had leaned across the table, touched Laura's arm. Laura glanced at Elena's hand. Elena said, "I know that you can change."

Laura flinched, dropped the burger. Her face went pale. Her eyes went wide, and the pupils flared again. Elena thought she saw something black shift across Laura's eyes.

And then Elena said, "Have you hurt someone yet?"

Laura got up. She stomped away from the table and out of the door. Elena followed, calling the girl's name, saying, "It's all right. I understand. I know about it. I can help you."

Laura strode down the street. Elena trotted after her, calling her name. Laura could've raced away if she'd wanted to, and Elena knew that, but the younger woman was allowing Elena to gain on her, to keep her in view.

After two hundred yards, Laura stopped, turned. Elena was gasping, trying to keep up. She stopped and saw tears on Laura's cheeks. Elena said, "Don't worry," and put her arms around Laura. "Don't worry."

They went back to Laura's bedsit: one room and a toilet. The place smelled of decay. The paint peeled off the walls. The stove was caked in grime. The view from the window was the back of a grey building. Laura said she did odd jobs: stacked shelves, cleaned toilets, distributed flyers.

Laura said, "I don't have many friends. I just get through the day. There's a big chunk missing out of my life. I feel so lost. I feel like there's something I don't know."

"There's a lot you don't know."

"You know it, though. Will you tell me?"

Elena did tell her, and it made Laura wail. Elena held her and she trembled in the older woman's arms, weeping for what she'd lost and found again.

Laura pulled herself from Elena's embrace and said, "The taste of meat. What I said earlier. You remember?"

Elena nodded.

Laura said, "I attacked him. The man with the gun. I leapt on his back, chewed his throat. I remember doing that. I was four and didn't know what I was, but I knew to do that. Instinct."

They talked about the Greenacres. Elena told her about her family. Laura nodded, like she knew it all anyway. Maybe a mental dam had been breached allowing those lost memories to flood back into her mind.

Elena said, "Come home with me. You don't have to dance if you don't want to."

"I'd like to. Dance, I mean. Strip."

Elena smiled. "It's not called that anymore."

"Okay. But I want to. It'll feel – I don't know: good. Not to show myself off but to" – she shook her head, wrinkled her nose – "be me, I suppose."

★ ★ ★

And now you're leaving, thought Elena, leaning against the bar. She looked around the club. It had taken years to make Bliss a success. *Time and money*, thought Elena.

Laura was Elena's family, her link to Richard.

If she leaves then I leave too: sell-up, go with her, thought Elena. *If Laura* wants *me to. If Laura lets *me*.

"And she won't, I know she won't," she said, dropping her head into her hands.

The front door rattled and Elena looked up. She straightened on the stool. The door shook again, someone really yanking at the handle. Elena felt herself tighten. Where were the bloody bouncers when you needed them?

Someone shouted, "Laura, are you in there?" from outside, and the voice was familiar.

Getting off the stool, Elena said, "Who's that? I'll phone the police."

"I *am* the police."

"What do you want? Laura's not here."

"It's John Thorn. I have to see her. I have to tell her something."

It was Templeton's bodyguard. The one Laura liked. Elena thought for a moment.

Thorn said, "Are you still there? Is that you, Elena?"

"Yes," she said, and running towards the door said, "Hold on."

She let him in.

"You look dreadful," she said.

"Thanks. It's my new look."

He plonked himself down on one of the sofas that lined the walls. He ran a hand through his hair. He was handsome and the thought of him and Laura warmed Elena's breast.

"Where is she?" he said.

Laura had said not to tell Thorn she'd be going to Templeton Hall. Elena, hoping she wasn't blushing, said, "I don't know."

He looked at her. "You're lying; I know you're lying. I can tell."

Elena shook her head, took a step back, said, "I'm not, I'm not lying."

"I'm not going to hurt you, am I," he put his elbows on the table, rested his forehead in his hands. "I couldn't if I wanted to. I can barely lift my arms. I'm broken, Elena. Shattered." He looked at her. "But I've got to see Laura." He went into his pocket, took out a folded piece of paper. He tossed it on the table and said, "Have a look at that and if you're still not interested, I'll walk away and throw myself into the Tyne, put everyone out of their misery."

Elena picked up the paper, gingerly unfolded it. She read it. Her blood chilled. Cold sweat broke at her nape. She shuddered, looked at Thorn, looked back at the letter that said things about Laura and the Templetons and was signed by someone called Richie Jarvis.

"If you think that's scary," said Thorn, taking a padded envelope from his inside jacket pocket, and putting it on the table, "wait 'til you see this."

CHAPTER 57.
PICKING UP A SCENT.

TEMPLETON Hall was riddled with odours, and Laura opened her senses to all of them. They cascaded into her nostrils. She swished them around in her mind, like a wine connoisseur would with a fine Bordeaux, seeking out all the different flavours.

She stood on the gravel path that circled the hall. The front doors were open. Guests milled around in the hallway. Laura glanced left, through the tall windows of the drawing room. There, other guests chatted and drank and ate from the buffet. Their voices wafted out into the coolness and Laura let them pass over her, picking the odd one out: a word, a laugh, a curse, a name.

She sniffed again. She was looking for Michael. She'd confront him, see what this was about: why she'd been invited here by her enemy? Was it a trap as Elena warned? If it was, Laura was ready. She'd kill Michael, put an end to the war, and then disappear.

She'd left a bag full of her belongings in the woods behind her; the woods where she'd killed the dogs, and where Thorn found her naked. She pushed him out her mind. He'd be nothing after this was done; she couldn't keep thinking about him.

She'd finish things here, get changed, get away, never return.

She'd go back to her isolation, but at least this time she wouldn't be confused and frustrated. She knew who she was, thanks to Elena. She knew where she came from. There was no feeling of a lost past, a missing link.

Solitude would be perfect under those circumstances. The knowledge that everything was over. Her father, her mother, Uncle Richard, all of them avenged. Their centuries-old adversaries dead.

She brushed her hands over her stomach. The blue dress clung to her. She felt sexy and dangerous. She smiled at the thought: fucking and killing, that's all you're good for, girl.

She let the smile drop away.

Fucking and killing.

What more is there, anyway?

Nothing.

She strode towards the front doors. The voices grew louder. The odours grew stronger. Her skin tingled.

She stood in the doorway and the warmth of the house washed against her. Heads turned her way, eyes bulged, jaws dropped. She heard them whisper; she saw them frown. The hallway was clogged with guests. They lined the stairs. Laura had no idea who they were: family, she guessed; friends; politicians; businesspeople.

She stepped over the threshold. A few guests flinched. It was as if she'd broken a taboo. *Templetons,* thought Laura, *disgusted that a Greenacre has been allowed into this church of theirs.*

I'll piss in the beds and mark them as my territory.

A butler glided her way. He was tall and lean. He wore a frown and carried a silver tray full of champagne flutes. He stopped in front of Laura, nodded his head, and said, "Champagne, Miss."

Laura took one, said thanks, and moved away. She gazed around the hallway, up the staircase, left into the drawing room. Her heart raced. She felt light-headed. To be here, in the enemy's house, was unbelievable.

Her guard was down. A hand touched her bare arm. She spun round.

"You look good enough to eat," said Ellis Cole.

Laura looked him up and down. "So do you."

He flinched, not expecting what he thought was a compliment.

He said, "Surprised to see you here. Surely you weren't invited? There's not been some mistake, has there?"

"I wish there had been, then I wouldn't have had to see you again."

He leaned in. Laura wore heels, so Cole was a couple of inches shorter than her. She smelled the garlic on his breath. He said, "Stop flirting with me, you bitch. You shouldn't even be here. What will a jury make of it? You're a little tease."

She was about to make a scene by tossing Cole across the room when the door at the far end of the hallway opened. Three men in suits filed out. An odour tweaked her senses. She gave a little growl. The hairs of the back of her neck prickled.

Cole said, "You need a —"

But Laura walked away and lost the rest of his words. She was headed for that odour. It pulled her like magnets pull metals. She thrust the champagne flute into someone's hand.

Everything around her blurred: the figures, the voices, the hallway itself. Laura was fixed on the door in the far corner and the smell that wafted through it when the trio opened it and stepped through.

One of the men went upstairs. A second slipped into the drawing room. The third stood guard at the door they'd come through.

Laura zoned in on the door. Her glare fixed on that corner. Her eyes went animal. Her muscles tightened. She felt them ripple, shift, throb. She could smell chlorine. Her face started to swell, her muzzle push out.

Not yet, she thought, not yet.

The man's eyes opened wide and his mouth moved but Laura didn't hear the words that came out. He went to his belt, pulled out a baton. He raised it. Laura was on him. She swiped the baton away. She grabbed him by the throat, opened the door, forced him through, slammed the door behind her.

She snarled in the rapist's face.

★ ★ ★

Cole thought, Why doesn't she pounce on me like that? Little tart trying to make me jealous. Little slag.

He'd watched her advance on the man. Grab him, and push him into whatever room hid behind that door.

What was she going to do to him, the dirty little whore? *Whatever it is, I'll watch,* thought the lawyer.

Cole was disappointed when he arrived at Templeton Hall that evening. When the invitation had arrived a couple of days ago, he'd swelled with pride: *The Templetons must think I'm important*, he thought.

It turned out that most of the area's businessmen and women, lawyers, doctors, journalists, and anyone who had a professional qualification – and many who hadn't: the hall's handymen, labourers, gardeners, cooks – had been invited.

Even murder suspects and trespassers, he thought, thinking about Laura.

He hurried towards the door, gaze flitting about. The thrill of what he could be watching – participating in, if was lucky – was making him hard.

They were flirting, and she'd scurried away. A sure sign that a woman was horny and wanted the man she was toying with to follow. They'd sneak away to a private corner somewhere. He'd press her up against a wall and fill her, making her want more of him – that's what usually happened.

He'd tried to be professional with Laura, but it had been difficult. She was so sexy, so naughty. A bit of a handful, but hey…he'd soon have her on a leash.

And if he had to pay, like he eventually had to pay all the prettier ones, then he'd pay. These girls, they'd do anything for money.

Even scream, even bleed, even…well, let's say they'd do anything…

He got to the door, glanced behind him. He got the odd look, but most of the guests were ignoring him. Cole put his hand on the doorknob. He sniffed and then frowned.

That smells like a swimming pool, he thought.

Hey – a smile stretched his face – *maybe she's gone skinny-dipping.*

He opened the door and recoiled.

227

CHAPTER 58.
FAMILY MATTERS.

"YOU'VE got to tell me where she is," said Thorn.

Elena said no. "I promised Laura."

"It doesn't matter what you promised her, you can see this is important."

She darted a look in his direction. "My promise to Laura is important."

"This" – he jabbed at the contents of the envelope that were spilled on the table – "is more important."

"Laura's not been able to trust anyone before. All she's had in her life are broken promises. I won't do that. I just can't, Mr Thorn."

Thorn sat back in the sofa. He folded his arms. He stared at Elena. "Then she'll hear this from someone else. She'll hear it from someone who doesn't care about her." He leaned forward. "Michael knows, Elena. What if Michael tells her? What happens then?"

She looked away and frowned.

"It's important she hears this from someone who..." He hesitated, but then said, "Who cares for her, who loves her."

Elena looked at him. "Do you care for her?"

"Yes, I care for her. I don't know why, but I do."

"Laura's like that. You just want to love her. You don't know why sometimes. But it's easy for me to care, though."

"Is it? Why's that."

"I'm family, Mr Thorn. You don't seem surprised."

"Nothing surprises me about Laura anymore."

Elena raised an eyebrow. "We'll see."

"What does that mean?"

"Do you know anything about these families?" she said, fanning a hand over the papers, the photos, the journals on the table.

"The Templetons don't like the Greenacres."

"They're enemies."

"I guessed they weren't at the 'chatting-over-the-garden-fence' stage when Laura said that Adam Templeton murdered her family."

"Yes, he did. My husband was killed."

Thorn looked at her through narrowed eyes. "But you survived."

"I was separated from him at the time. I'm not really a Greenacre. I *married* a Greenacre."

"Wouldn't that make you a Greenacre?"

Elena shook her head. "That's not how it works."

She told him how it worked, and he said, "They *in*-breed?"

"It's not quite as awful as it sounds."

"What...what about Laura? Would she...if they were all still alive, would she have had to –? " He couldn't say the word.

"Families are enormous units, Mr Thorn. Don't tell me you know all your most distant cousins, your furthermost relatives?"

He shrugged. "Obviously not."

"Well, this is what it's like. The only difference is that the Greenacres *know* who their distant cousins are. And there's nothing illegal, nothing unhealthy, about marrying your cousin."

"You haven't seen my cousin."

She ignored his humour. She said, "Laura's the last, now."

"Could she" – he blushed – "you know: with someone who wasn't a Greenacre?"

"If she wanted to."

"About this war. You're claiming Templeton did kill the Greenacres."

"I know he did."

Thorn shook his head. "Why did he hate them?"

"Have you heard of the Etruscans?"

The front door opened. Jimmy came in. He saw Elena and Thorn. She said, "Go home, Jimmy. We won't be opening tonight. You'll get paid, but could you ring the others?"

"Is everything all right?" he said, eyes skipping from Elena to Thorn.

Thorn stared him down, and Elena said everything was fine.

Jimmy left. Thorn said, "The Etruscans."

★ ★ ★

Laura held him up against the wall. She bared her teeth. Her fingers dug into his neck. He was kicking, his face turning red, his mouth open and trying to suck air into his crushed throat.

The smell of chlorine from the swimming pool behind her made Laura feel dizzy. She ignored the nausea and focused on the rapist struggling in her grasp. She could hear the water lap behind her. Its reflection shimmered on the wall where Laura had the man pinned. The light from the pool's surface swam over the rapist's face. It made him appear nebulous.

Laura said, "You raped my friend. I'm going to rip you apart. I'm going to eat you while you're still alive."

The man gurgled. His eyes bulged. He kicked out at Laura. She didn't budge. Stared and snarled at him. Spit dribbled over his chin.

She dropped him. He thudded to the ground, his legs sprawled. He panted and rubbed his throat. He looked up at her, his mouth open. Laura loomed over him. Something moved in the corner of her vision. She sniffed a familiar odour. She whipped around.

Ellis Cole, peering around the doorframe, gasped.

Laura bared her teeth and moved on him. Cole stiffened. The colour drained from his face. His skin was like chalk.

Laura was ready to lunge, drag him into the corridor.

The sliding glass door behind her exploded. Glass sprayed over Laura. It stung her flesh. She threw her arms above her head and crouched.

She stayed down for a few seconds. The rapist coughed. She glanced at him. He'd been showered in glass. His face bled.

She looked at her arms. Tiny shards of glass were buried in the skin. Pinpricks of blood bubbled up from the wounds. She wiped the glass away. She plucked out the larger pieces. The wounds smarted. She touched her face and checked her hand and saw blood.

She glanced at the door. Cole had gone. She wondered what he'd seen.

She stood up, heard the water lap behind her. Laura turned. A man sat on a sun lounger at the other side of the swimming pool. He waved at Laura. She narrowed her eyes, fixing on him. She sniffed the air.

There was someone else in there, too. In hiding.

The poolhouse was made of glass, and the falling gloom outside made it difficult to see. She scanned the poolhouse but could only see the man at the far side of the pool.

The man said, "Hello, Greenacre bitch."

She knew it was Michael. She stepped through the shattered sliding door. The chlorine saturated her nostrils. She glanced down into the green-blue water. The rafters above reflected on the surface. She could see their shadows shimmer. She noticed another shadow among the rafters. It shifted slightly.

He's up there, she thought.

She tried to pick up his scent, but the chlorine was the prevailing odour and overwhelmed everything else.

She stared across at Michael. Fifty metres of water stretched out between them.

He stood up. "Nice of you to come," he said, his voice echoing around the poolhouse. "Sorry to disturb you over there. Seems you had a thing going with that guy."

"Nothing that can't wait," she said.

"Did you hurt yourself in that – uh – little accident with the door? I guess – although I can't see from here – that you're bleeding."

"A few scratches, that's all. Accidents happen."

"Yeah, they do." He glanced up at the rafters – just a glance, but Laura clocked it. Then he said, "Maybe you could jump in the pool, clean the wounds. You shouldn't really bleed in the water, but hey – who's worried about a little blood?"

"Yeah," said Laura, "who's worried about a little blood?"

"I'm sorry, I've not properly introduced myself. Although you may have guessed –"

"I've guessed."

"Good, that's good. You've got a nose on you. You can suss things out."

"I'm all right, yeah."

They were quiet. The water rippled.

Laura said, "What am I doing here?"

He shrugged. "You tell me."

"Your father invited me."

"Yes, he did. Why would he do that?"

"I don't know?"

"You weren't his...bitch, were you?"

"I'm no one's bitch."

"His whore, then."

She didn't say anything. She clenched her teeth. Her hands rolled into fists and her nails dug into her palms.

Michael said, "Like your mother." He was waiting for a reaction, but didn't get one. He said, "She was a whore, you know. A slut like all the Greenacre bitches. Bet you're one too, huh? Is that what you were up to with that guy over there? Giving up your cunt as easily as your mother gave up hers?"

His insults echoed off the glass and steel of the poolhouse. He kept hurling abuse. "My father messed up when he tried to wipe out your fucking diseased family. He left you, didn't he. For some reason, he didn't want you dead. I thought maybe he wanted to wait 'til you became mature, then use you as his bitch. Breed with a Greenacre whore and bring the Templetons back to life. Put some animal back into our family." He chuckled. "But now I know differently. I know the truth. But I don't care about the truth. Doesn't mean anything to me. So I'm going to finish what my father started."

He looked up at the rafters.

Laura followed his gaze.

She stared at the man aiming a rifle at her. He was tucked away in the shadows, pressed against the twilight sky that she could see through the glass ceiling.

Michael said, "Do it, Craig."

Laura dived. She heard the rifle pop. She hit the water. The bullet pinged off the tiled floor. Laura sliced the surface. Everything was muffled. She kicked, carving through the water like a dolphin. She headed for Michael, who was gesticulating at the shooter in the rafters.

Laura started to change, her eyes going first as they fixed on Michael as any predator's eyes would fix on prey.

★ ★ ★

232

When the bullet shattered the sliding glass and splintered into the tiled wall two yards from his nose, Cole shut the door and pressed himself against it.

After a few moments, he snuck another look. Laura wasn't there. He could hear voices. She'd stepped through the jagged remains of the sliding doors into the pool area.

Cole crept into the corridor where the man Laura was pinning up against the wall lay sprawled. It was a short corridor: from the door Cole came through, to the door at the far end marked CHANGING ROOMS, it was only ten feet. The back wall was tiled blue. The sliding doors on the left wall led to the pool area.

Cole squatted next to the man, and glanced towards the pool. Laura had her back to him. He let his gaze move down to her bottom. He gritted his teeth. Great backside; she was so fucking tasty. But sadly, this wasn't the time. She was talking to Michael Templeton, who lounged on the far side of the pool.

Cole looked at the man on the floor. His face was bleeding but he was conscious, and he stared back at the solicitor.

Cole said, "So you raped her friend. It was you. And all the other women, too." He shook his head. "Who'd have thought it? You, of all people."

The man stared at Cole and was afraid; the solicitor saw it in his eyes.

Cole, helping the man up, said, "Don't fret. Come on, let's get you cleaned up, and you can tell me all about it."

He started to lead the man towards the changing rooms. A bullet cracked into the tiles a few yards away. Cole ducked. He pushed the man towards the door.

He saw Laura dive into the pool.

He saw her shoot through the water.

He saw something happen to her under the surface.

Cole gasped. His guts turned cold.

He stared at the great black thing slicing through the water.

CHAPTER 59.
HISTORY LESSONS.

"THE Etruscans were a tribe who lived in Italy before the birth of Rome," said Elena.

Thorn thought, *More history lessons. Why does everyone give me history lessons?*

"They were a cultured people," said Elena, "and although they disappeared after Rome was founded, much of their influence can be seen in Roman culture."

"I see," said Thorn, resting his chin on his fist.

"The wolf, for example."

"The wolf."

"Yes. Sacred to Etruscans, central to Roman mythology. You know the story of Romulus and Remus, the orphans who founded Rome."

"Yes. Remind me."

"Suckled by a she-wolf."

"Of course. What's this got to do with Laura?"

Elena ignored him. She said, "Like Romulus and Remus, there were two Etruscan brothers. They were princes. They were also lycanthropes."

"Lycanthropes?"

"Men who can change into wolves. Werewolves."

Thorn arched his eyebrows. This was different to the history Sir Adam used to bore him with. Werewolves. *What next?* he thought. Vampires? Mummies? Jekyll and Hydes?

Elena said, "The brothers were proud of their Etruscan heritage, their wild streak, the animal in them. Their family had always been like this: true to their nature. But soon after the founding of Rome, one of the brothers wanted more power; he wanted to be part of the establishment. The Etruscans were slowly being assimilated into the Roman way of life. Etruscan kings ruled Rome for hundreds of years. So this brother, like many Etruscans, went Roman."

"Went Roman?"

"Yes. Denied his past. Denied what he was. Stopped shapeshifting. He married outside the family, and so did his descendants, and slowly, over generations, the blood was diluted. Until they just couldn't change anymore. They became the Templetons somewhere in history."

"And this is all true, is it? Lycanthropes."

Elena closed her eyes to shut him up. Then she looked at him again and said, "The other brother was furious at this betrayal of culture, of family. The brothers went to war. The one who went respectable, his offspring had the power of Rome behind them. The werewolves had to flee. Their culture was suppressed. Their history vilified. But wherever they went, they were hunted by their Roman cousins. They became the Greenacres. And the war between the families has been fought throughout history."

"They don't teach you that at school."

"Michael Templeton and Laura Greenacre are the last of the families."

Thorn narrowed his eyes. "Are you telling me that" – he shook his head as if wafting away the cobwebs that veiled his understanding of this story – "they're werewolves?"

"Laura's a werewolf. But Michael can't change, now. The Templetons forgot what they knew; they lost who they were."

He looked at her for a long time. Then he said, "You'll have to tell me where she is," his tone dismissing Elena's story.

Elena looked away. She chewed a fingernail. Her face was creased with worry. She looked at Thorn and said, "She's gone to Templeton Hall. She was invited to the post-funeral gathering."

For a moment, Thorn couldn't move. Then he leaped from the seat, tossing the table aside. Striding towards the door, he said, "Michael's going to tell her, and then he'll kill her."

★ ★ ★

235

Michael watched Laura cut through the water.

He saw things happen to her, her shape change. He thought it was the movement of the water playing tricks. But it wasn't the water; it was Laura.

He dress tore away. Her body bulged. Her long dark hair seemed to flood out over her body. Her head, her face unmade themselves. In seconds, he'd seen her change from Laura into a huge, powerful werewolf.

Michael's legs buckled.

That thing was scything through the water. It was heading straight for him. Michael looked up to the rafters. "Fucking kill it, Craig."

"I thought you wanted it to attack you."

Michael watched the creature torpedo towards him. He said, "I don't know. I'm shitting myself."

"Oh, fuck. What do you want me to do?"

The werewolf burst out of the pool. Water showered off its hide. It shook in the air like a dog shakes when it's wet. Michael was drenched by the spray. He staggered back and tripped into the lounger.

The animal fell towards him, its teeth bared, its eyes yellow, its claws displayed. "Don't," he said, throwing his hands up, "don't −"

The werewolf landed in front of Michael. Michael panted. The creature was colossal. It dropped to its haunches, ready to pounce.

"Oh, Jesus Christ," said Michael. He thought he'd piss himself. His cock shrivelled like a dried mushroom.

The werewolf drooled. Tendrils of saliva hung from its teeth.

Fucking hell, thought Michael, *those teeth are like fucking kitchen knives.*

He imagined them sinking into his flesh.

"Michael. Michael, what d'you want me to do?"

It was Craig. His voice echoed in the poolhouse. Michael's brain screamed for Craig to shoot this animal − fill the fucking thing with bullets, for fuck's sake − but if he could hold on for a few seconds, go through with it, suffer some pain, and then −

The werewolf sprang forward. Michael screamed. He threw up his arms. The werewolf was on him. Michael gasped. The smell of dog filled his nostrils. He screamed again. The bones in his arm cracked as the werewolf bit into it. The pain shot through Michael. Claws tore at his stomach. The werewolf crushed him into the lounger, and the lounger collapsed.

Michael's body went into panic mode. His bladder was about to burst. His sphincter muscle weakened. He kicked out, he screamed, he started to cry. They say your life flashes before you when you're about to die. It doesn't; you forget everything: who you were, who you are – everything.

Michael lost himself for a moment.

Then, things came back to him. He found the words he wanted to say and the strength to say them. "You can't kill me, Laura, you can't."

The werewolf's eyes widened. It stopped biting and tearing.

Michael stared into the yellow, animal eyes, and spoke to the Laura in them.

He said, "He's your father, Laura."

The werewolf growled. Steam hissed from its nostrils.

Michael smelled the beast's breath. He recoiled. He said, "My father, he's...he's your father. You can't kill me, Laura. You can't kill me, because I'm your brother."

The werewolf blinked.

Michael thought, *She's going to let me go, and then she'll be dead.*

The werewolf growled. Its eyes narrowed. It bit harder. Michael screamed. The pain tearing up his arm. His torso was shredded. He felt as if he'd been burned with boiling oil.

She was going to kill him.

"Shoot the fucking bitch," he said.

Craig fired. The silenced muzzle popped. A bullet pierced the werewolf's shoulder. Blood spurted from the wound. The bullet hit Michael in the neck. His throat filled with blood. He started to cough.

The werewolf leaped away, howling.

Michael rolled off the lounger. He groaned. He was in agony.

The werewolf hurtled towards the windows. Michael tried to say, "Kill it, kill it," but he spluttered blood. He felt faint. He watched Craig's bullets chase the werewolf.

Michael coughed. He sprayed blood into the water.

The windows shattered. The werewolf plunged into the night.

Someone shouted Michael's name. His vision blurred. He toppled into the pool and dropped into darkness.

CHAPTER 60.
DIRTY DEALS.

COLE said, "I can't believe it's you."

The masked rapist was panting. His face was lacerated from the shattered glass. His throat was already bruising after Laura had almost crushed the life out of him.

Cole had dragged him down a set of stairs to the changing rooms. The walls were lined with wooden benches and lockers. There were showers and a sauna. The reek of chlorine and soap clung to the air.

Cole said, "How did she find out?"

The masked rapist shook his head. Tears dribbled down his cheeks, running into the blood.

"Did you see what she did in the pool, how she changed?" said the solicitor.

The rapist shut his eyes. He shook his head again. He coughed and wheezed.

"Finding it hard to breathe?" said Cole, feigning concern. "What a shame. Must hurt. Your pride, too, I guess. Being thrashed by a girl. How does that feel?"

The man didn't answer. He was sitting on a bench, leaning against the lockers.

"I've never defended a rapist. That must be quite a challenge. The way you'd go about it, I guess, is to cast aspersions on the so-called victims. I mean" – he shrugged – "I know from experience that some women like it rough. We'd say, 'These women loved rough sex, Your

Honour'. Yes. That's what we'd say. We'd have them up in the witness box telling the world about their private affairs. It could be" – he looked away, pondering a trial – "fun."

"Don't hand me in."

Cole looked at the man and said, "What did you say?"

The rapist's voice was a croak, like he'd spoken the words through a voice box. He said again, "Don't hand me in, Ellis."

Cole tutted. "I don't know about that. It's my duty. Law Society'd be on my back if I didn't act truthfully and honestly in these matters. Police'd want a word, too, I guess. No. I'm a law-abiding citizen. A man of honour."

"I'll do anything. Please. My family."

Cole shrugged. "You should've thought about that before getting horny." He looked up at the ceiling, wondering what was happening above them in the poolhouse. He looked at the other man and said, "Are you sure you didn't see Laura Greenacre – a *naked* Laura Greenacre – change into, into, into something else?"

He was sure of what he'd seen. Laura Greenacre dived into the pool. She shed her dress. Her body changed shape. It grew, bulged, sprouted what seemed to be coarse black fur. He saw it, he was absolutely certain he'd seen it. But witness evidence was unreliable. He knew that from his experiences in court. Eyewitness testimony could be unravelled. The brain, under pressure, was erratic. It could play tricks. Detectives, solicitors, psychologists, they all knew that and would never depend on an onlooker's word alone.

I couldn't have seen what I saw, he thought.

The rapist said, "I wish the bitch'd change into a bug so I could stamp on her and crush her into the ground."

"Would you like to have her?"

"It's not like that. It's not who I'd like to have. It's – it's what I have to do to meet my needs. As long as she's pretty. I like to look at their pretty faces. They scream and beg, but they've enjoyed it. They enjoy sex like we do."

"Yes," said Cole, loosening his collar, feeling sweaty, "they do."

"I was doing what I had to do or I'd go mad."

Cole thought for a moment. Then he said, "She knows."

The rapist looked at him.

"Laura Greenacre knows. And so will that friend of hers. She said you raped her friend. I'm sure Laura will tell her. She'll say, 'I've found him and I'll hand him over to the police'."

The other man, still panting and wheezing, considered Cole's words. "What are you saying?" he said.

"You have to sort them out. Or they'll tell on you."

"I thought you were going to tell."

"Well, we can come to an arrangement, I'm sure."

"An arrangement?"

CHAPTER 61.
BATTLEGROUND.

KLAUS Markus, taking cover in the dense treeline that skirted the walls surrounding Templeton Hall, switched on the night goggles.

The world turned green.

He scanned left. The truck was reversed into the barn. Its headlights on full beam created a pool of light. Jerry Bahrman stood in the light.

"You'll be bait," said Craig that afternoon as they planned this wolf hunt.

Bahrman smiled, although it may have been a grimace. "What if I don't want to be bait?"

"If you don't want to be bait, you can pack up and fuck off back to Alabama or whatever sister-fucking State you come from."

"I'm from Washington. We don't fuck *our* sisters in Washington. We fuck *your* sisters."

Bahrman was bait. He didn't have a choice. He wanted the money, he wanted to kill, so he had to do as Craig said. They'd square up after this was done, but for now, Craig was boss.

The trap was laid. Bahrman was wired. He'd get the word from Markus that the target was approaching. Bahrman would open up with suppressed muzzle fire.

"It's aggressive, so won't be put off by a lone gunman," said Craig. "It'll come for you, Bahrman."

Once in the pool of light, the target would be easy prey for the rest of the team. Four men were waiting in the barn, two either side of the truck. The other three were concealed in the gloom beyond the illuminated Bahrman.

"It's a small kill zone," Craig had said, indicating the circle on the diagram that showed where Bahrman would be standing. "Get it in there quick, kill it quick. There are civilians in the Hall, remember that. All fire is suppressed muzzle. Sort your silencers out. We don't want panic. We want this done quietly, quickly."

"What do we do with the body?" said Steve Lloyd.

"Toss it in the truck," said Craig, "pack up, be on our way; we stop in the middle of nowhere, dig a hole, chuck the body in, cover it in lime, bury it and we're" – he slapped his hands together – "sorted."

Bahrman mimicked him with the hands and said, "What about my fee?"

"Wired to your accounts, as usual."

Wired to my account, thought Markus now, watching the darkness through his goggles. Building up that retirement fund. Not that he'd ever retire. He liked this too much. The planning; the hunting; the killing.

Once a soldier, always a soldier. You can't take that away from a man, even after he's left the forces.

He heard breaking glass in the distance. He tensed, tucked the Mauser SP 66 sniper's rifle to his shoulder. He flipped his goggles on to his forehead, and looked through the rifle's night-vision scope.

He held his breath.

What the fuck was that?

Craig had told him what to expect: "It's an animal, a fucking huge thing that can run on two legs and four. It's got speed, it's got power, it's" – he hesitated, creasing his brow – "it's a werewolf."

That's crazy, Markus had thought.

This *is crazy*, he was thinking now, staring down the scope.

It loped through the gloom. It was on four legs, its massive back haunches pushing forward. It was limping, favouring its right side.

Markus fixed the animal in the crosshairs.

He was sweating, breathing hard.

He said, "Target approaching. Get ready, Bahrman. It's dead ahead, hundred and fifty yards," and he heard Bahrman pant in his earpiece.

I could kill it myself, right now, thought Markus. *Why wait?*

He pressed the rifle to his shoulder. He licked his lips. The crosshairs settled on the creature's forehead. Markus steadied himself. His finger rested on the trigger.

The animal stopped moving. It lifted its head, craned its neck. It was sniffing the air. Markus had a clean shot into the chest. He fixed the crosshairs on the monster's heart.

The animal bolted left.

Markus pulled the trigger. The rifle recoiled.

"Fuck," he said, knowing he'd missed, "fuck."

Voices in his earpiece.

Markus, panting, looked through the scope, darted the scope around, the world a blur of green and black.

"Where the fuck is it?" he said.

"Markus," said Bahrman in his ear, "Markus, what the hell's going on, man?"

Markus fixed on Bahrman. The American was squatting. An easy target in the light.

Markus threw the scope around again, searching the darkness. A chaos of voices in his head, the men shouting for instruction.

Then a voice pressed through the cacophony, saying, "Jesus God! Jesus God!" and a roar in his ear made Markus flinch.

Silence.

Markus said, "Report, report," in a whisper.

A scream flooded his head. He jerked and tugged the earpiece out. The scream filled the night.

★ ★ ★

Adrenaline flushed Luc Broos's veins.

They were shouting in his ear. Markus had said, "Where the fuck is it?" and Bahrman wanted to know what the hell was going on, and the others were throwing their voices into the cauldron, too.

It was fucking chaos, and he tried to stay calm. He'd seen a lot, so this should be nothing special; no different.

The adrenaline pumping through his body was nothing more than a natural reaction; his body preparing to fight or fly.

Broos had been lying down, his rifle pointed towards Bahrman in the light. When the havoc started in his ear, he got into a crouching position. He moved his weapon around in the dark, trying to fix on whatever was coming.

They'd said it was an animal.

"But it doesn't matter what sort," said Craig that afternoon, "it can be killed, so kill it."

Broos stood up slowly.

Then something massive hit him in the back, throwing him forward, crushing the breath from his body.

The rifle slipped from his grip. He crashed to the ground. He gasped for air. Pain shot through his body.

Broken ribs, he thought.

He sat up. The earth trembled. Yellow eyes stared at him from the murk. A shape formed in the darkness, and became colossal and black, and the shape towered over him and showed its teeth and roared.

Broos screamed as the monster pounced. It buried its teeth into Broos's shoulder. The teeth cracked through bone, ripped through flesh, pierced Broos's lung. The pain was terrible. He shrieked as the air hissed out of his body.

★ ★ ★

"Everyone to Bahrman," said Markus, and crashed through the trees to join the American in the circle of light.

They all came out from under cover: Lloyd, Murphy, Stick, and McKay from the barn; Page, Cleaver, and –

"Broos," said Markus, "where's Broos?"

They huddled into a circle, back to back, so that all angles were covered.

Markus called out to Broos, but Broos didn't answer. That was the scream, thought Markus: one man down.

"Fuck, shit," said McKay.

"What the hell is it, Markus?" said Bahrman.

"It doesn't matter," said the German. "It's injured, so that means it can die."

"So can we," said Bahrman. "What's Craig got us into? I'll fucking kill him."

Markus's eyes scanned the darkness beyond their illuminated island. He stared over towards the hall. It loomed grey in the gloom. The light cast from the mansion's windows was too distant, too dim, to help them.

He said, "We have to get to the lorry."

No one moved. They listened to the darkness. The darkness was still and silent.

Markus said, "Bahrman, you go. We can cover you."

"No fucking way, man," said the American.

Harry McKay said, "I'll go. But keep a fucking eye on me, you bastards. Shoot anything that gets near me, I don't care if it's a fucking vole."

The Scotsman ducked down and started running the fifty yards to the lorry. He was caught in the headlights, a dark shape crouched low bobbing into the light.

McKay was ten yards from the truck. He straightened, a sign that he was confident. A black shape shot across the beams. It struck McKay, sweeping him away into the shadows.

The men swore. They fired into the darkness, their silenced weapons phut-phut-phutting. McKay screeched from the darkness The men stopped firing, and they froze. McKay screeched again. A tearing sound split the night. Markus grimaced.

A silence fell.

His voice a whisper, Markus said, "McKay?"

A ball-shaped object lobbed out of the dark towards them. They all jerked their weapons in its direction. Markus told them to hold their fire.

McKay's head fell near the huddle of men and rolled for a couple of yards. It settled upright, facing the mercenaries. The eyes were blank and wide. Blood seeped from the open mouth, covering the chin. The flesh at the throat was shredded. Veins and arteries hung like ribbons.

Markus had seen beheadings many times. He'd beheaded a man himself. No, not a man; a boy: a nineteen-year-old Russian conscript snared by the Mujahideen Markus had fought for in Afghanistan in the Eighties.

But this wasn't a beheading.

McKay's head had been ripped from his shoulders. Teeth marks punctured the skin at the temples where the jaws had fastened, then torn away.

The men stared at the head. The air steamed with their breath.

A knot of fear tightened in Markus's stomach. He couldn't take his eyes off McKay's face.

This animal, he thought, *is hunting us.*

CHAPTER 62.
TO THE RESCUE.

CRAIG reached into the darkening water and grabbed Michael's collar. He plucked the drowning man out of the pool and laid him on the tiles.

Michael's arm had almost been severed by the werewolf. Blood seeped from the wound. It swirled in the pool, turning the water red.

The bullethole in his throat also throbbed out blood. Craig checked and found that the bullet had lodged in Michael's neck. That could be a good thing. Craig had seen embedded bullets save lives: they acted as a plug to stop internal bleeding.

Michael coughed, then spluttered. Blood spat from his mouth. He looked pale. He opened his eyes and reached out to touch Craig's arm. "Get...Ross...take me...safe place..." he said, his voice a croak.

Craig said, "You need medical attention."

Michael gripped Craig's hefty forearm. He shook his head, his mouth shaping no, then he said, "Ross...safe place..."

Craig stood. He glanced at Michael. He was bleeding on the tiles. Craig looked over at the shattered window through which the werewolf had escaped. He hoped Markus had that thing dead in the back of the truck.

We want this done quietly, quickly.

That's what he told them.

He cursed. He should've killed it when he had the chance. When it stood in its human form – in its Laura Greenacre form – on the other side of the pool.

Craig had shattered the sliding glass doors with a bullet to get her attention. Then, when she stood there, he'd obeyed Michael's wishes.

"Just take a pot shot at her," Michael had said, "to make sure she gets into the water, to make sure she comes at me."

That's what Craig did.

He watched her sweep into the pool; watched her change from human to monster.

It was astonishing. Just like it was eighteen years ago when he saw her father change from beast to man. This was impossible, against nature. His mouth had dropped open, and he almost lost his footing in the rafters.

He should've ignored Michael and killed the werewolf when it burst out of the water; when it pounced; when it attacked.

But when he finally got the chance to kill it, he fucked it up; shot the bloody thing through the shoulder and hit Michael.

Then the animal was away, heading for the windows. It moved at an incredible speed and Craig's fire fell short.

The mercenary gazed out into the night.

I should've killed it when I had the chance, he thought.

He picked Michael up and carried him away.

★ ★ ★

Thorn, surviving on adrenalin, overtook three cars. Horns blared. Headlights flashed. Elena gasped.

She said, "What are you trying to do?"

He said, "Why the hell did she go to Templeton Hall? Why did she take up the invite? Do you think she knows?"

"No, she doesn't know."

"Then why?"

"She wanted to know what Templeton was up to."

"She will soon enough."

"She couldn't understand why she'd been invited to this thing tonight. Why he'd been forgiving. She wanted to know."

"We have to be the ones to tell her."

Elena shook her head. "It may drive her mad. Imagine: everything you believed, shattered. Your life a lie."

They were quiet for a few moments.

Then Elena said, "Do you think Michael will tell her?"

"I don't know. How will she react? To know that he's her brother."

"Oh my God," said Elena, bringing her hands to her face. "What would Richard say? What would Martin think? He lived his life thinking he was Laura's father. This is...heresy."

"Heresy?"

"It was bad enough that Richard married me, an outsider. But for a Templeton to father a Greenacre." She shook her head.

Thorn drove past Templeton Hall's main gate. "Shut and guarded. No way through," he said, casting a glance in the rear view mirror at the police car blocking the entrance. "There's a back road, unclassified."

He drove on, pressing the accelerator, gliding past traffic.

He felt ill, as if his life was coming to a close, but he sensed that this was something he had to do before dying. He felt that it would decide the fate of his soul.

CHAPTER 63.
HUNTED.

PHIL Page made it to the lorry; Steve Lloyd was seized by the werewolf. He was dragged away by a foot, screaming for his mates to help him. But they were punching the air as Page got the truck started. Lloyd didn't scream for long, and by the time he died Page was rolling the vehicle out of the barn.

The Americans, Bahrman and Stick, made a run for the truck. Markus called for them to wait. They ignored him.

The truck rumbled forward, throwing its beams beyond the men. Markus turned, watched the light stream across the ground.

Bahrman and Stick leaped on the lorry's running board, Stick on the driver's side. The other guys backed up, made room for the truck.

Markus scanned his surroundings. He swallowed and licked his lips. Where was that thing? The Brits, Cleaver and Murphy, stood at the periphery of the light. They were casting their eyes around. They were alert, tense.

Markus's stomach knotted. He squinted into the darkness behind them. He gasped, raised his rifle. In the green light of the night scope, the werewolf darted up behind Cleaver and Murphy.

Markus said, "Out of the way," and he fired at the monster.

Cleaver bent to the left, caught the bullet in the head. His brains sprayed over Murphy, who flinched.

Markus shouted Murphy's name and said, "No."

Bahrman and Stick leaped from the lorry and pointed their weapons at the Brits. But the Americans didn't have night vision so had no idea what was going on beyond the dead Cleaver and the terrified Murphy.

The werewolf leaped on Murphy's back. The man fell forward. They fell into the light. The monster pressed him face-first to the ground.

Bahrman and Stick shouted. They started firing. Silenced guns popped. Nozzles flashed in the dark. Markus cowered in the rain of bullets. Murphy screamed as the creature yanked him into the shadows.

The men fired. Murphy screamed again. The sound of tearing, and more intense screaming, made Markus cringe.

The screaming stopped, and when Markus raised his hand, the shooting also stopped; they were in silence – a terrifying, nerve-wracking silence – again.

After a few seconds, Bahrman said, "Markus, you prick, you killed Cleaver."

Page, in the truck, said, "I think we should get outta here while we still can."

Markus turned to look at the men.

Four of us left, he thought, *and I'm stuck with three Americans.* He took a step towards the truck.

The werewolf rammed into the side of the vehicle. The suspension creaked. The engine clanked. The truck tipped over on two wheels, and almost toppled on its side.

Markus staggered backwards, his mouth opening but no sound coming out. Bahrman yelled Page's name, but Page had been snatched from the cab by his arm.

The werewolf, dragging the screaming, struggling Page away, turned and glared at Markus. The German felt that knot of terror in his belly unravel and his insides turn soft, and he thought he would melt away in a pool of cold, liquid fear.

Bahrman shot at the monster, but he missed; the werewolf darted back into the darkness with Page in its jaws.

"Okay, Stick, we're getting outta here, now," said Bahrman, leaping into the truck. Stick joined him in the cab, and leaned out of the window.

He said, "Come on, German. You don't want to be hanging around here in the dark."

Markus's grip on his weapon tightened. He steeled himself, and the fear that had threatened to melt his guts seemed to dissolve.

He said, "You go. You don't get paid, but go if you're cowards."

Bahrman gave him the finger from the cab window and said, "Fuck you, Markus. And tell Craig, fuck him, as well," and he fired up the truck, driving it towards the rear gate.

Markus heard the truck's engine fade; he saw its lights dim.

He was left in darkness. The silence was dense, the night impenetrable.

"Okay, bitch," he said, "you think you can take me, come and get me."

He raised the Mauser to his shoulder. He peered through the night scope. The green world was still. He slowly turned one-hundred-and-eighty degrees. His breathing was sharp. Sweat poured down his back. His pulse drummed in his ears. He took in his surroundings in that eerie shade created by the night scope.

"Where the fuck is it?" he said.

A shape, dashing across the grounds. He gasped. He held it in the crosshairs. Was that it, at a distant? No, too small. He tracked it.

Shit, he thought.

A fox, out hunting rabbits under cover of darkness. He moved the rifle round, following the fox. He was going to kill it so he could say he'd killed something that night; some animal, at least.

The fox trotted towards the thick conifers that made the landscape black in Markus's night vision.

He moved the rifle to the left. Holding the fox in the crosshairs, Markus steadied himself. He was ready to fire.

He kept tracking the fox. The scope ranged after the vermin.

Markus started to press the trigger.

A great shape, all teeth and claws, filled his scope. Markus yelled. He fumbled the rifle. It dropped from his hands.

The werewolf pounced on him. Markus screamed and saw himself being torn apart.

★ ★ ★

The headlights blinded Thorn. He lifted his arm to cover his face. The truck rocked towards him over the bumpy ground. He was leaning on the wooden gate. The truck driver wasn't going to stop; he was going to crash through the fragile barrier and whatever else happened to be in his way.

Thorn looked over his shoulder at Elena, sitting in the Saab. He waved at her, gesturing that she reverse the car. She shrugged, *I can't drive.* Thorn said, "Drive the bloody thing."

Elena leaped into the driver's seat. He watched her switch on the engine. He turned and the truck's headlights swept over him. He gasped. He saw the driver's eyes. He saw the passenger aiming a gun. Thorn cowered. He leaped out of the way. The lorry smashed through the gate. The wood splintered. Timber rained on Thorn. The truck's tyres sprayed mud all over him.

The truck jerked and buckled, and for a moment Thorn thought it was going to fall on him and crush him. But the vehicle stayed upright. It turned left out of the gate. The back wheels threw up some more mud. The lorry sped away.

Elena, out of the car, said, "Are you all right?"

Thorn, covered in mud, got up and said he was fine.

"You've hurt your face," said Elena.

"What?" he said, bringing a hand to his cheek.

"Splinters of wood."

"I'm fine." He went to the opening where the gate had been. The crushed, splintered barrier crunched under his feet. He looked down at the remains. "I always said this could do with replacing."

A scream pierced the air.

"What was that?" said Elena.

Thorn started running towards the sound telling Elena to stay in the car. In the distance he could see the dark shape of Templeton Hall. It was a good three-quarters of a mile away.

He kept running. He wanted to call out; but if those guys in the truck had friends, they still might be around.

Thorn's foot clumped something heavy, and he tripped over.

"What the hell's that?" he said.

He got up. A familiar smell struck at his nostrils. He approached the shape. It was a body without a head. The smell was blood. Thorn cursed. He looked around, but it was too dark to see any distance.

A shape filled the night some fifty yards ahead of him. He froze, felt a chill creep down his backbone. Something huge was charging towards him. The gun was in the car.

He thought about Jarvis claiming to have seen a monster; he thought about Elena's crazy story about werewolves; and then he thought: Laura.

He said, "Laura," as the shape became apparent and seemed to melt in the darkness, and then out of that darkness the shape became Laura.

Thorn said her name again and went to her. She was naked. He took his jacket off. She fell into him, burying her face in his chest. He wrapped her up in his jacket. She was trembling and crying.

He said her name again, and she looked up at him. Her face was bloody and dirty. He saw her shoulder and it oozed blood.

"You've been shot," he said.

Tears smeared her blood-spattered face. She said, "Everything's wrecked, Johnny, everything's wrecked and I'm lost again."

PART FOUR.

A NEW WAR.

CHAPTER 64.
WEIRD SCIENCE.

DENTON said, "The science is wrong. Forensics must have got muddled. They'll have to do it again."

"They're insistent," said Detective Sergeant Carenza Drew.

"About what?"

"That they've got it right, Ma'am," said Drew.

Denton slammed the conference table. "Well, they haven't, have they?"

She looked at the silver-haired man in the blue suit. He was scribbling in a notebook. His tanned brow was furrowed. He doesn't look impressed, she thought. He probably thinks we're hicks from the provinces, incapable of running a proper investigation.

Perhaps he was right.

This whole thing had been a cock-up from start to finish. They'd failed to pin anything on Laura Greenacre. The evidence was piled up against her; but that one little piece that would have toppled the heap all over her seemed missing.

Denton wanted to go to Templeton Hall for the post-funeral gathering. She was ready to arrest Greenacre, cart her away in front of all those guests. But Michael Templeton only agreed to a low-level police presence; a few men in civilian garb to keep an eye out for trouble.

Denton shook her head and said, "I want the lab to test it all again; everything."

"That'll take time," said Drew. "Time we haven't got."

Denton glared at her. "When did you decide what time we have or haven't got, Sergeant Drew?"

"Ma'am, the results will be the same. I've spoken to them. I asked if they're sure the results are right. They're sure."

Denton looked at her notes. "But they say she's not human."

"Not completely," said Drew, "not completely wolf, either. A strange kind of species. A mix, a hybrid."

"This is impossible." Denton looked around the conference table at the detectives. "Does everyone agree it's impossible?"

The detectives mumbled and nodded; except for the silver-haired man who kept scribbling in his notebook.

Denton said, "Have we made tracks to find her yet?"

"Seems she's done a runner," said Detective Constable Mark Bailey.

"After the incident at the Hall, typically."

"Yes, Ma'am," said Bailey. "Along with John Thorn."

"That's his career over," said Denton.

"Yours isn't looking up, either."

They all turned. The silver-haired man was still scribbling. He spoke again, saying, "And I wouldn't be too hopeful for the rest of you." He looked up. "But that's not my concern. You and your...whatever pet-gone-bad you've got up here...you can wait, as far as I'm concerned. I've got seven dead mercenaries on the slab at the mortuary, all of them linked to Ray Craig, who, in turn, is wanted for murder in Britain, Australia, France, and South Africa."

Denton said, "There is a possibility – I'm sorry, I've not been made aware of your rank."

"My rank is 'Mr'," said the silver-haired man.

"All right. There is a possibility, Mr Keegan, that our pet-gone-bad did for your mercenaries. Isn't that a consideration?"

Keegan's nostrils flared. He said, "The Security Services are concerned only with knowing why these men were in the north-east, and where – if at all – does Ray Craig fit into all of this." He shuffled some papers. "I'm sure you've been made aware of the murders that occurred on the same night throughout Britain nearly twenty years ago. We suspect Ray Craig was involved."

"Why were those murders committed?" said Drew.

Keegan stared at Drew. He said, in a softer voice, "We're not clear. It's not really a concern. All we're concerned about is catching Ray Craig and these mercenaries. These men aren't legitimate freelance security personnel; these guys are soldiers for hire who will kill for money."

"Not any more they won't," said Bailey. "They're on the slab."

"Yes, son," said Keegan, the steel in his voice again, his gaze fixed on Bailey, "on the slab. But Craig's still out there, and Craig's a one-man army. If he's still in the north-east, just hope he'll never cross your path. He eats little provincial cops like you for tea."

CHAPTER 65.
INFECTED.

MICHAEL coughed up more blood. It was agony, like someone was pulling his insides out through his throat.

"I can't die," he said, "don't let me die."

The doctor said, "You're terribly ill, Mr Templeton. You have some form of virus, blood poisoning, even. It would be better if you'd agree to be taken to a hospital. We can provide – "

"I'm paying for you to look after me here. You look after me. Make me better."

"I – we – we don't know what's wrong with you, Mr Templeton. We need to carry out more tests, and those tests would be easier to conduct in a hospital."

Michael tried to sit up. The pain surged through him. He groaned. Sweat glued him to the bedsheets. He felt sick and weak, sicker and weaker than he'd ever felt. He couldn't eat or drink, so they fed him through tubes. They snaked from his body. They poured fluids into his poisoned veins.

This better be worth it, he thought.

The doctor said, "There are unusual things happening to your body. It – it seems to be altering." The doctor shook his head. He looked confused. He pressed a hand to his forehead. "I've not seen anything like it before, which is why I'd suggest you – "

"No hospitals. Staying here. Safe here."

"I don't understand why you feel safe here, Mr Templeton; you'd be much safer in a proper medical facility."

The door opened, someone came in, but Michael couldn't sit up to see.

"Is he still throwing a sickie, doc?"

It was Ross. Michael wanted to tell him to fuck off, but he was too weak. Instead, he stuck two fingers up in Ross's general direction.

The doctor said, "He's very ill, and I'm trying to persuade him to go to a hospital when he can be evaluated, kept under observation, treated."

Ross stood above Michael and said, "You look shit, mate."

"Thanks. Get rid of the quack."

The doctor said, "Excuse me, but – "

Ross said, "Sorry, doctor, family business. Thanks for your time. Come back soon," and he ushered the man out of the room.

Michael heard the door shut. Ross came back to his bedside, and pulled up a chair. He sat down and said, "This is all fucked up."

After the werewolf attack, Craig carried Michael from the poolhouse to a car. The mercenary went to find Ross and Ruth. They got Michael medical attention, then had him driven down to London. He was laid up at Ross Andersson's four-storey townhouse in Kensington. Doctors known to take backhanders had been given backhanders, and they treated Michael. The bite wound had broken his arm; it also infected his blood. The bullet was lodged in Michael's throat. He'd suffered severe lacerations to his torso.

"I think I'm getting stronger," said Michael.

"That's deluded. You can't sit up. You can't eat. What are we supposed to do if you die? What happens to the Greenacre bitch, then?"

"You'll have to go and kill her yourself, Ross."

"I'm not a fucking killer."

Michael laughed, the sound like an old car being cranked up. He coughed again, his head jerking forward.

"Jesus, man," said Ross, "I think the doctor's right, you know."

Michael ignored him and said, "Have the police been in touch?"

"Yeah, nosy bastards. Some woman. Denton. Wanted to know if we knew where you were. Mum spoke to her."

"Good. What did she say?"

"She was quite forceful, mum. Said you'd been under tremendous stress of late and that you'd decided to go away. She said she didn't know where but when you got in touch she'd be happy to let you know the police were asking after you."

"Are they after me in a bad way or just a 'helping us with our enquiries' way?"

Ross shrugged. He knew fuck all, as usual. He said, "I can't imagine you're a suspect. A suspect for what, anyway?"

"Have you got a phone on you?"

Ross took a mobile from his pocket and gave it to Michael. It was a struggle to dial the number, Michael's hands as weak as the rest of his body.

A voice said, "What?"

"Craig? It's me."

Static peppered the line.

Craig said, "Yeah."

"Where are you?"

"Stupid fucking question."

"Okay. Are you still in the UK?"

"Stupid fucking question again."

"Can you still help me?"

"All but two of my guys are dead. Those two have done a disappearing act on me."

"I know. At least you won't have to share the money, now."

Static again, Craig thinking. Then the mercenary said, "What do you want?"

"Do you know where the girl is?"

"I might be mad, but I'm not that mad. I'm not going near that thing."

"I didn't ask you to. I asked you if you knew where she was."

"I don't. I don't want to. She's dangerous."

"Not like you to be scared, Craig."

The static hissed.

Craig said, "Fear keeps you alive, Michael. Fear keeps you sharp. It's good to know what can kill you, then you can avoid it killing you. Only a fool walks into a hail of bullets and thinks he's a hero."

"Okay. But do you still want the cash?"

"I'm *having* the cash, son."

"Yes. After one last job. An easy one."

"Tell me."

"Get Elena McIntyre. Bring her here. That'll force Laura out of hiding. Then we'll kill them both."

CHAPTER 66.
ALL IS REVEALED.

EAGLE'S STONE FARM NEAR ALNWICK,
NORTHUMBERLAND – 11 A.M.

LAURA held up the vial of blood that had been tucked into the cover of Sir Adam Templeton's diary.

"What am I supposed to do with this?" she said.

Thorn said, "He wasn't sure you'd believe him, I think. He didn't want you to doubt. The blood's for testing against your DNA."

Laura shrugged. "Could be anyone's blood. Could be dog's blood, pig's blood, rat's blood, anything."

"I saw him take it. Walked in on him, thought he was shooting up."

Laura put the vial down. She looked at Thorn and said, "There's a lot you haven't told me."

"There's a lot *you* haven't told me."

They stared at each other for a few moments. Then Laura said, "Thank you for coming, saving me."

Thorn nodded.

"This is all so" – she hesitated, looking at the spread of photos, letters, journals on the table – "destructive. Everything I thought I was, everything I thought was right and true, is a lie. I'm my enemy's daughter."

"Can't that be a good thing? That you've found out the truth?"

263

"There are lines drawn in the sand that can't be un-drawn."

"What does that mean?"

"When Elena found me and told me who I was, where I came from, it re-awakened a lot of things; it made me remember things before my family were killed. That's something that I remember my father – who I *thought* was my father – saying: There are lines drawn in the sand that can't be un-drawn. Some enemies will always be enemies."

"I think you can just" – he made a wiping gesture with his hand – "scrub those lines away."

"How can I do that? He did kill my family. He is a mass murderer, Johnny."

"I know."

Thorn cast his eyes towards the quilt of fields that spread up beyond the farmhouse to the horizon. The caravan where they were sitting, where they'd slept for three nights, was tucked into the corner of a field on Peter Thorn's farm. Thorn's brother had welcomed them suspiciously. Thorn asked if the caravan was still there and could they stay in it for a few days. Peter said yes it was, and that they could.

"We used to play in it as kids," said Thorn to Laura as they walked towards the rusted old thing, its axles resting on concrete blocks. "It's been a stagecoach, a cave, a Roman chariot, a castle, a U.S. army fort. It's been everything."

"What is it now?"

"It's a safe place."

The caravan smelled old and damp but it was warm, and perfectly comfortable. Thorn slept sporadically on the narrow seats that bounded the rear end of the caravan. Laura took the tiny bedroom. They'd stopped at a 24-hour Tesco on the way up to Alnwick and brought enough provisions for a week.

The plan was that there was no plan. Laura wanted to leave but had "some business to sort" before she went. Thorn guessed it was to do with Chloe's attacker, or Michael Templeton. He didn't press it; there were other things he wanted to know.

He said they'd stay at the caravan for a few days, see what the police got up to, and then get Laura out of the country. Elena was already trying to sort transport: some dodgy fishing boat, perhaps, or a long-distance lorry driver willing to take live cargo.

Gazing towards the horizon Thorn said, "He's paid for that crime with his life."

"You're still trying to protect him."

He looked at her. "I'm not. I'm trying to let him rest. I'm trying to find a peace here, Laura. Some kind of accord to this...this war."

Laura picked up the photograph of a three-year-old girl and a young, handsome Adam Templeton. She was sitting on his knee. They were smiling, but his eyes showed apprehension, fear even. The words underneath, written in felt-tip pen, said, "My beautiful daughter, Laura, whom I shall love until the last."

"He *did* love you," said Thorn.

He thought about the contents of the blue journal: Sir Adam's account of his dangerous affair with Joyce Greenacre, a liaison that spanned fifteen years.

When it ended, Sir Adam's anger erupted and he started to plan the Greenacres' destruction. But even in his jealous rage, he could not see his lover and their daughter killed. He ordered the hired guns to spare the woman and child at Martin Greenacre's address. Unfortunately, that night, Joyce Greenacre visited family in Barret Street. She was murdered with three others.

"Ever since," wrote Sir Adam in the journal, "I have looked for you, Laura. I planned my own death and wished it to be at your hands."

Thorn looked at a picture of Templeton and a beautiful dark-haired woman – Joyce Greenacre, he guessed – on a beach. He showed the photo to Laura and said, "What do you want to do with these?"

"I don't know. I can't decide. It doesn't matter, really. They're only photos and words, they don't mean anything."

"They show you who you are."

She swiped the stuff off the table and said, "I know who I am."

Laura got up, turned her back on him. He went to stand behind her. He could smell her hair and her skin and their odours warmed him. He wanted to wrap her up in his arms, pull her to him. He put his hands on her shoulders. She was trembling. Thorn said her name. She pressed back into him and he enveloped her. She cried, then turned so her face was buried in his chest.

"Do you know who I am?" she said into his shirt.

He thought for a moment. The crazy stuff Elena said about werewolves.

What am I holding in my arms? he wondered.

"Do you?" she said, looking up at him. She was beautiful. Her face pale, no make-up, sharp features; her eyes tear-stained; her hair tugged back into a ponytail.

He knew, then, that he loved this girl who wasn't human.

"It doesn't matter," he said, "it doesn't matter if I know who you are."

"I want to show you, all the same."

She stepped from his embrace. She pulled the T-shirt over her head. Thorn flinched at the suddenness of her undressing, and something trilled in his belly. She cast the garment aside. He looked at her and she was more beautiful. The only blemish was the cruel, yellow-black bruise that stained her shoulder. The bullet that caused it had gone right through. The wound would heal in time, and she'd be perfect again.

Laura undid her jeans, slid them down her legs, and as she bent Thorn watched her breasts sway and he grew with that movement.

She stood in her underwear and let him gaze at her, and after a good time she said, "Are you ready?"

Thorn said that he was, lost himself in her, and made as if to move towards her. But something changed and he stopped with a gasp, and then cowered.

His stomach knotted and his veins piped ice cold fear into his heart. The hard passion that had risen in him shrank away.

CHAPTER 67.
BECOMING THE BEAST.

MICHAEL convulsed on the bed. He gasped for air. His body ached and he felt it swell and ripple. His skin stretched as if it was being filled with water. He tried to yell, tried to call for help, but his throat burned. He thrashed about. The tubes attached to him came loose. They flailed, spilling fluid over the bedroom floor. The machines keeping him alive bleeped. Pain beat through his head. He tried to force out a scream. Every muscle in his body flexed. Blood flushed his brain and oozed out of his nose.

Jesus Christ, I'm dying, he thought.

Can't breathe, can't breathe…no, no, God, no…that bitch, that bitch killed me…she –

He sat upright and screamed, all the tension pouring out of him. He screamed so loud his ears rang. The pain flooded out of his body. He felt strength fill him. An energy washed through him that he'd never experienced – not even when he was stoned.

Michael felt as if he could fly.

The door opened. Ross rushed in followed by a nurse

"Are you all right? What's going on, mate?" said Ross.

The nurse pushed past him. She tried to make Michael lie down. He brushed her away. She bent down to gather up the tubes.

"Oh, my Lord," she was saying, "oh, my Lord. We got to get doctor; we got to phone doctor now. Oh, my Lord – "

"Shut your mouth," said Michael.

The nurse froze, stared up at him.

Ross said, "What's up, man? You screamed the house down. There's blood." He pointed at the bed sheets. "From your nose."

The nurse got up, started to wipe Michael's face. He swatted her away.

She said, "Please, Mr Michael, let me – "

"Ross, get this fat foreign cow out of here before I fucking rip her apart."

Ross got rid of the nurse. She protested, said she'd have to ring the doctor. Ross told her if she did she'd be sacked and sent home to whatever fucking voodoo worshipping island she came from.

"All right, so what's up?" he said.

Michael took a long, deep breath. He said, "No wheezing, no pain – I've just been cured, Ross."

"Cured, man? How?"

He leapt from the bed. He ripped off his T-shirt. He checked himself out in the full-length mirror. The werewolf had gouged his flanks. The wounds whipped across his torso, from armpit to abdomen.

"But they're healing," he said. "Can you see? They don't smart like they did this morning. I can't feel a thing."

Ross cringed. "I guess they look a bit better."

Michael whacked his plaster-cast broken arm against a wardrobe. He smiled and said, "Nothing. No pain."

"Miracle cure."

"And look at this." Michael pulled the bandage from his throat. He slanted his head so Ross could see the bullet wound. The bruising had faded; the swelling had gone down. "That doesn't hurt, either. I could feel the bullet in there. Like a bone stuck in my throat. Now, there's nothing."

"You're back to normal."

Michael turned to look at his cousin. "I don't think I'm back to normal, Ross. I think the poison's taken hold."

Ross took a step back and Michael saw a flash of fear sweep across his eyes. "So...what...what do you mean, mate? You mean you're a – "

Michael lunged for him; Ross yelped and cowered.

Michael laughed. "You twat. Look at you like a girl, scared shitless."

"Bollocks. You surprised me, that's all. Made me jump."

"Not scared, then?"

"No. Scared of what?"

"Scared I'll change and eat you alive. Eat you while you're watching."

Ross looked Michael up and down. He swallowed, took a step back. The colour left his cheeks. He said, "All right, that scares me. Wouldn't it scare you? I bet it did scare you. When she was coming for you. When she was attacking you. Bet you pissed yourself."

Michael paused and dwelled on the memory of that night: Laura sweeping through the pool, transforming under the water, bursting through the surface, pouncing on him, sinking her teeth into his arm, tearing his flesh.

He said, "That's the kind of terror I'll instill in people, Ross. They'll fear me. They'll look at me with awe. They'll know that I'm their every nightmare." He looked at Ross. He watched his cousin digest that agenda then said, "Do you want to play, too? Do you want to be feared? Would you like those brash City fucks to cower before you, knowing how terrifying you could be if they pissed you off?"

"Yeah," said Ross, although not convincingly, "that'd be cool."

"Ross."

"Uh-huh."

"You don't have a choice, mate."

"I don't?"

"You're with me or against me. You're a Templeton or you're not. This is the age of monsters. I'm going to lead an army of wolf-men. We're going to be top dogs, Ross, and nothing, no one, is going to stop us."

Michael turned back to the mirror. He stretched out his arms and studied his reflection.

"Now," he said, furrowing his brow, "how the fuck do I change into a werewolf?"

CHAPTER 68.
LIVING WITNESS.

LAURA got dressed. She didn't look at Thorn. She was embarrassed and felt her skin redden. It wasn't because she'd been naked; it was because she'd revealed her animal self and let someone who'd seen it live.

People who witnessed this change usually died.

This was new to her. It felt like first sex — awkward and messy. She was self-conscious and insecure. They were conditions Laura had never experienced before.

Tying her hair into a ponytail again, she turned to look at him. He was sitting on the couch. His skin was pale and his eyes were blank. His shoulders moved up and down as he breathed steadily.

When she changed, her werewolf form filling the caravan, her head pressed against the ceiling, Thorn had recoiled. He moved away, his eyes fixed on her, his mouth open and his Adam's apple bobbing in his throat.

She watched him through her black pupils; she smelled him through her wide nostrils. He was small and puny to her. He would snap beneath her powerful frame. She could feel herself wanting to attack him. That animal urge to kill, to protect, was livid in her breast. But she tempered it and saw that he wasn't her enemy.

She softened and shrank and smoothed, and became Laura once more.

"So," she said, shrugging her shoulders, "how was it for you?"

His mouth opened but no words came out.

She shrugged. "Speechless, then. I guess that's better than dead."

She sat down. He shifted round so he was facing her. She looked at him. He still looked awed; scared, too, perhaps.

"Your first time, was it?" she said, trying to get a smile, a gesture – anything – out of him. "Mine, too. Awkward, isn't it."

Thorn said, "What did you mean, 'better than dead'?"

She made an "O" with her mouth, surprised that he'd said something. Then she said, "I meant that this isn't some kind of floor show. I don't go up to men and say, 'Hey, handsome, do you want to see the animal in me?' When I do what I just did, people die. They get eaten, Johnny."

Now he made an "O" with his mouth.

She said, "No one's ever seen me change like that and got away with it. I don't alter myself to amuse men, Johnny, I do it to protect myself."

"Why do you eat them?"

Laura shrugged. "I just do. It's that part of me. The animal."

"That's cannibalism."

"Only if I were human. I'm not really human. I'm a different thing altogether. I'm a lycanthrope. Just like my people were. And now" – she looked out of the window – "like Michael, too."

"Michael? I thought Michael couldn't – I mean...Elena said he couldn't."

"He can unless he's dead, and I don't think I did enough damage to kill him." She looked at Thorn again. "I bit him. I infected his blood. I planted my DNA, my ancient, lycanthropic DNA, into his veins. The formula for Michael to change is still in his make-up. It was just dormant, that's all. Diluted over generations. My bite's likely to re-activate that gene in him. He'll change. I think that's what he wanted all along."

"What? To be a werewolf?"

"Yes. He wanted me to attack him. He wanted me to infect him. And I did."

Thorn put his head in his hands. "I'm sorry if I appear irritated, confused, a bit pissed off, but this is all very crazy, and completely impossible."

"You're sticking to that, are you? After what you've just seen me do? D'you think it was a trick? Like a magician makes a tiger appear in cage, I make a seven-foot werewolf materialise in a caravan in

Northumberland. Is that how you're trying to explain this?"

"I have to try to explain it somehow, Laura. It defies everything. But everything defies everything this week. Is it something to do with the millennium? With Y2K?"

"You now think I'm some kind of computer bug. I thought you liked me."

He fixed her with a long, deep gaze. She felt it to her core and it made her tremble.

He said, "I adore you. You're spectacular. You make my heart skip – you make it stop and race at a thousand-beats-a-minute, too, but it mostly skips."

"Skips," she said, not knowing where her voice came from, but feeling it slide from somewhere warm and soft in her belly.

"But then I think, How can that be? It's surely sick of me to feel desire for..." He hesitated, narrowed his eyes as if thinking about the words.

Laura felt the weight of rejection in her breast. She knew it was impossible for them to be together, but she didn't want him to loathe her. She couldn't bear that.

Then he said, "...an animal."

She spluttered and tears spilled down her cheeks. But before she could rise and go from him, he clutched her hands and held them and said her name. And then he said her name again. And he said her name in a way that a man would never say an animal's name, only the name of something he loved.

CHAPTER 69.
NOWHERE TO HIDE.

ELLIS Cole had him by the balls. And to prove it, the bloody fool had ordered him here, to where the bitch lived. Nerves riddled his body. Fear coiled in his belly. She'd really scared him at Templeton Hall that night.

He'd spent a couple of days trying to recover from the wounds to his throat. The injuries were superficial, but they were difficult to explain. He told his wife that he got hurt during the confrontation at the Hall. He got caught up in it, he said, and there was nothing he could do. He was sketchy over what exactly went on, but he claimed it all happened quickly. Local media had reported "an incident" at Sir Adam Templeton's memorial, so at least that confirmed his story.

His wife scolded him, told him to be more careful, and said he should sue; but he said everything would be all right and all he needed were a few days rest.

At home he'd managed to look relaxed, like he was recuperating; but inside he was panicking. Dread gouged a pit in his stomach. His blood pressure must have been close to lethal. He knew his heartbeat was: he timed it at over a hundred-beats-a-minute that first morning. Every time the doorbell rang he came out in a cold sweat, fearing that Cole had gone back on his word and reported him to the police.

"You can trust me, of course," said Cole, "but that girl – she knows, and my guess is that sooner or later she'll tell the police."

The solicitor, leaning back in his leather chair, feet up on the desk, tutted and shook his head. It was the morning after the memorial event at Templeton Hall.

Cole had said, "It doesn't look good, does it."

"What can we do?"

"We may have some time. This girl, she's a suspect in Templeton's murder, obviously. The police are keen to nail her for it. My guess is they're out looking for her right now. She's not going to stroll into a police station and report you just yet."

"So I'll be all right, you think?"

Cole shook his head. "Not what I said, not what I said. There will come a time when she's arrested. And when that time comes, she'll be looking to deal, and this piece of information may be just what she needs to barter with."

"They won't believe her."

"No, but they'll want to make certain. They'll ask you to provide a DNA sample. The other girl, the one you attacked, could I.D. you."

"I wore a mask; I always wear a mask."

"Still, your smell, your voice, your shape. She could recognise you," said Cole. He leaned forward, elbows resting on the desk. "The papers say you wear a white boiler suit."

"It's a protective suit. Like forensics use. I'm not going to wear my own clothes. I don't want to leave anything incriminating behind, do I. A thread, a button, anything – they'll get you with a tiny bit of fiber these days."

"So once you'd got them in the car – "

"I'd knock them unconscious and drive them somewhere out-of-the-way. I'd put on the protective suit. The type worn by forensic officers. Then we'd..." He trailed off and looked away. His cheeks flushed. Thinking about it made his head hurt; made the whole process start again – made him frustrated.

"And the car you'd stolen?"

"Leave it with the keys in the ignition. It usually got stolen again, then the joyriders would conveniently destroy any evidence I left behind, plastering the car in their own DNA; or they'd burn it out."

Cole was thinking, stroking his upper lip with his forefinger.

"What do I need to do, Ellis?"

"I think," said Cole, "that what you need to do is go to the house –"

"House?"

"Where that girl you attacked lives; where Laura Greenacre lives."

"Oh."

"And" – he hesitated, folded his arms – "deal with the matter."

"Deal?"

"She'll tell on you, that girl you attacked. With her out of the way – "

"You're saying I should kill her?"

"Well," said Cole, shrugging, "I feel you must."

"But what about the others? There are others. They could identify me, too. I can't go back and kill them all. I'm not a murderer, Ellis."

Cole smiled. "You say that as if you've got some code of honour." He scowled. "You rape women. You're a shade above paedophiles and line dancers. I don't think killing's above you, old friend."

"I can't kill them all."

"This one'll do for a start. Maybe the others'll see that it's best to shut up. They'll guess it was you who killed her, and they won't want you visiting them again, will they? And anyway, it'll be difficult for the others to I.D. you – without a DNA sample, that is."

"I can't do this."

"Yes you can, and you will. You'll go there Saturday afternoon. No one about. Everyone in town, in the pub. It'll be fine."

"What if the Greenacre girl's there?"

"She won't be. She's out of action for a while, I think. I'd know. I'm a solicitor."

"If I get caught, will you get me off?"

"Of course I will. You're my client, now. And we've got that trust, that client-solicitor confidentiality thing."

Cole winked at him.

* * *

He'd lurked in the alleyway a few doors down from the house for half-an-hour. He peered up and down the street again. Cole had been right: Saturday afternoon was quiet.

He put his hand in his coat pocket and felt the hammer. The iron was cool on his sweaty fingers.

Fear chilled his blood. He couldn't believe he was going to kill a girl. They were to be enjoyed, women; their lovely faces studied as they stretched and creased with lust and terror.

Battering this one's pretty head was going to be difficult.

And whatever Cole had said about him being only a notch above child molesters, he was no killer.

He swallowed. Panic dried out his throat. He took in a few deep breaths, trying to slow his racing heart. He just couldn't make it slow down. His pulse thundered in his head.

He checked the street again. Cars zipped past the junction with Westmorland Road to the left, and up the hill he could see the sweep of traffic on Westgate Road. But the Terrace itself was still.

He slipped out of the alleyway, strolled towards the house.

A vehicle trundled up the street behind him.

Shit, he thought, and almost stopped and turned back.

But he decided to go ahead with his plan: all it took was a quick rap on the door; she'd answer and then he'd force her inside. No one would notice.

He kept walking. The vehicle's engine rumbled behind him.

He was ten yards from the house.

CHAPTER 70.
SITTING DUCKS.

SOMEONE knocked on the door and, coming down the stairs, Elena said, "I'll get it."

Chloe, sitting at the kitchen table staring into a cup of tea, was glad. She still had no desire to see anyone apart from close friends. Her stuff was packed, and she was ready to leave. The only thing that stopped her was that she wanted to say goodbye to Laura.

"Laura's gone away for a few days," Elena had said a couple of days ago. "She'll understand if you go. I'll give her your number and she will ring you."

"Where is she? What's happened?"

"It's just this business, you know."

"Did she kill that man?"

"She didn't. But the police think she did."

"Wouldn't it be better if she just went to see the police, explained things?"

"They've got her down as their main suspect, Chloe. They'll not let go until they've got her charged and convicted. They don't seem concerned with the truth."

"They should be trying to catch...that..." And she broke down again. Thinking about it made her cry, so she was crying a lot.

She hoped that going home to Nottingham would distance her from the attack, and the attacker.

"Do you think it'll make me forget what happened?" she said to Elena, and Elena said that if Chloe thought it would make her forget, then she should go home.

Her mother wanted her back. "We'll look after you here, darling," her mum had said, tears hitching her voice after Chloe had told her what happened. Her brothers wanted to bring some mates up to Newcastle to find the rapist.

Chloe said, "Have you told dad?" and her mum said that yes, she had, but she didn't tell Chloe how he'd reacted.

Her mum and dad had split up ten years ago. But they lived next door to each other on the estate and still got on okay. Dad had been furious when Chloe went off "to be a tart for the bloody Geordies."

"It's just a 'dad' thing," said mum, "doesn't want to think about his little girl grown up with a woman's body."

Elena, at the bottom of the stairs, said, "Are you expecting anybody, Chloe?"

Chloe said no, she wasn't.

"Maybe it's one of Alison's 'I-was-at-school-with-him' boyfriends," said Elena.

"Maybe."

"Where are Alison and Hannah?"

"Hannah's gone shopping. Alison didn't come home."

"Again," said Elena, and Chloe heard her open the door.

Elena yelled. Chloe sat up. The hairs on the back of her neck stood on end. A knot of fear tightened in her belly.

Elena, wide-eyed, her face pale, came to the kitchen door. She tossed a mobile phone into the kitchen and said, "Laura," in a whisper as a shadow loomed over her.

Chloe recoiled, tried to get up but her legs buckled and she fell.

Elena yelped as the man grabbed her round the waist and yanked her from the doorway.

Chloe scrambled to a corner and cowered.

Elena's voice was muffled and it faded off. A car door slammed. An engine revved. The car accelerated away.

Everything was quiet. Chloe whimpered, arms covering her head. She looked at the mobile phone under the table. She didn't move. She stared at the phone like it was a huge spider and if she moved, the spider would move and probably scuttle towards her and make her scream.

After a time – she didn't know how long, but a minute or two at least – she crawled over to the phone and looked at it. She pressed MENU and then PHONEBOOK, and scrawled down to "L".

The name was there, and Chloe held her breath. It was like finding treasure.

★ ★ ★

Holding her hands across the table, Thorn said, "Can you die?"

She squinted, put her head to one side and said, "What do you mean?"

"I mean…like films…silver bullets…I don't know, crucifixes, is it? I mean, what can kill you?"

"A gun, a knife, a road accident, cancer" – she paused and dropped her gaze to their knitted fingers – "a broken heart."

"That's the worst one."

"Yes, I heard. Been lucky so far. What about you?"

"I've suffered a few," he said, "but you get by. They're generally never fatal, not if you can get through the first week."

She sighed, smiling at him. "Who'd break your heart, Johnny? Who'd want not to be with you?"

"Plenty, I can tell you. I've been a fool. It's the work-life thing. I thought that if I could get promoted, get more money, I'd be able to provide a better life for those I loved, for Jane and Sophie. Doesn't happen like that. We don't want money. We want love. We want kindness. We want to be wanted and desired. We want to share. We want to live our dreams."

"What were your dreams?"

"I didn't have any. That was the problem. But I had obsessions – my work, mostly."

"I think she should've held on to you. I think you would've come through, in the end. And then it would've been wonderful, wouldn't it. *You* would've been wonderful. I think she'd like you, now."

He blushed, shook his head. "That's gone. I don't love Jane. I care for her; she's the mother of my child. But no, our wants are different."

"What do you want?"

He looked at her for a moment and said, "I want you."

They stared at each other, and they couldn't look away. He leaned forward and she leaned forward and they saw each other get closer and closer in the other's eyes. Their breaths swirled together in the inches between their lips.

A phone trilled.

Laura pulled away. She looked towards the ringing. She said, "That's the phone Elena gave me. It's for emergencies." She got up, strode across the caravan, rifled through her bag and found the phone.

"Elena?"

"It's — it's me," said a voice that was timid and tiny.

"Chloe?"

"Someone took Elena."

"What? Who?"

"I don't know. A man. I didn't see him. Grabbed her. She threw the phone, whispered your name. I found your number. Laura. Laura, I'm scared, and I don't know what to do."

"It's all right, it's all right, we'll come to you. Stay where you are. Is Alison or Hannah with you?"

Chloe panted.

Laura said, "Chloe, are you all right? Can you hear me? Where's Hannah? Where's Alison?"

Chloe continued to pant.

Laura said her name again, louder this time, then she said it a second time, shouting it, and she was about to shout it again when Chloe said, "He's here."

"Who's there, Chloe?"

"He's here. The man. He's standing in the kitchen and he's looking at me and seeing me speak to you. He's standing in the kitchen door."

Panic surged through Laura. She put a hand on her head and felt the sweat on her scalp.

She said, "Who's there? Who is he?"

"He's the man who raped me, Laura."

CHAPTER 71.
BETRAYAL.

CHEWING his nails, Cole sat in his office and stared at the phone.

He glanced up at the clock. Surely he'd be there by now; inside the house already, perhaps.

I've got to do it, he thought, got to do it and get in my car to be there when they arrive.

He picked up the phone, dialled, cleared his throat.

"Good afternoon, BBC North East and Cumbria," said a woman.

"Newsdesk," said Cole.

She put him through and he waited, every ring of the phone making him flinch.

"Newsroom," said another woman.

Ellis coughed, then said, "Right, my name's Ellis Cole, I'm a solicitor – and also an investigator – based at Hexham."

"Yes?"

"I've been looking into the recent terrible attacks on woman, here in Hexham and a few days ago in Newcastle."

"Okay."

"My investigations have unearthed a suspect."

"A suspect?"

"Yes, I know who it is. I know his identity, and I know that he is, in fact, attending the home of his last victim at this moment."

"What?"

"He's there, planning to do her serious harm. I am, of course, putting my career in jeopardy, here. I'm doing it to protect the women of Newcastle and Hexham."

"Have you phoned the police? Shouldn't we – "

"Of course I have," he said, thinking, shit, shit, why can't these local BBC people be like proper journalists? Phone the police? What's the matter with this woman? Sod the police. He was planning to be there with the BBC camera team when the masked rapist stepped out of Summerhill Terrace.

"Mr Cole, I don't understand – "

"You don't understand? What kind of bloody journalist are you? Get a camera team out there and be the first to get his face on film. Don't you want to beat the Chronicle and the Journal, for once? The papers always beat you to the real stories, don't they? I'm giving you a brilliant story on a plate. I'll be there in fifteen minutes. Make a name for yourself, will you?"

He slammed the phone down.

Should've phoned the papers, he thought. At least they're bloody proper journalists. They chase stories. Not like the rubbish BBC who expected stories to fall into their laps. Well, one hell of a tale just did.

He grabbed his jacket, left the office, and locked up.

I'm going to be a hero, he thought, getting into his car. The man who caught the Newcastle rapist. The man who protected Newcastle's women and girls. They'll all want to sleep with me.

Driving away from the car park, he wondered what the rapist would say. The bastard would try to claim that Cole had set him up, encouraged him to kill the girl; but no one would believe a pervert.

Cole would say, "Of course I knew the man, he was a stalwart member of the community; it's not a surprise that he'd try to pin the blame on someone else – and who better than a lawyer. My work isn't popular with everybody. There's always someone out there who wants to sully the reputation of a hard-working, highly-respected, fair-minded solicitor."

Everything would be good.

He pressed on the accelerator.

★ ★ ★

"What did they say?"

"They said they'll get somebody round there," said Thorn.

"Now?"

"Yes, Laura, now."

"Drive faster."

"I'm going very fast."

"Go very faster, then."

It was a forty-minute trip from Eagle's Stone Farm to Newcastle, but Thorn's driving could knock twenty minutes off the journey. They'd had to dump the Saab: every force in Britain was probably tracking it. Thorn had bought a Ford Mondeo for three hundred quid from a bloke in Alnwick.

Laura made him ring the police, so he dialled 999 and told them a woman was being attacked in Summerhill Terrace, Newcastle. The operator asked lots of questions. Thorn put on a frantic voice, indicating he didn't have time to answer her stupid queries; a woman was in danger, he said.

"Chloe said that someone took Elena," said Laura.

"The same guy who attacked Chloe?"

"I don't know."

"Is Chloe confused? Have we been set up?"

"No. No, she wouldn't do that to me. It was genuine."

"Are you sure?"

"I'm sure. She wouldn't."

"Then who'd take Elena?"

There was a few seconds of silence between them, then they glanced at each other and Laura said, "Michael."

"We should tell the police about that, too," said Thorn.

"We don't know where he's taken her."

"Doesn't matter. The police can find her."

"They haven't found us, have they," said Laura, "and we're hardly holed up in the hills."

"He's luring you out."

"He's going to get what he wants, then."

★ ★ ★

"You know who I am, don't you?" said the man.

Chloe did know. She didn't know how she knew, but she knew.

283

Maybe it was his shape, his eyes, his voice had certainly triggered something in her brain; but she knew. It was him.

She slid up slowly, her back pressed against the cupboard.

"Matters have come to a head," he said. "Circumstances beyond my control. The situation has become uncontainable. Where's your friend?"

Chloe, up on her feet, shook her head. She took a step towards the sink, her eyes fixed on the man. Her bladder felt heavy. The memory of him and the anguish he caused played over and over in her mind – and she couldn't make it go away.

She lunged for the sink, grabbed the bread knife, brandished it.

The man didn't move. She'd already tossed the mobile phone at him. It missed, clattering against the doorframe and breaking into pieces on the kitchen floor.

He said, "You can't do anything with that, Chloe. I can take it off you if I like, use it against you. What if I cut you up? How would you feel about that?"

Chloe trembled, her grip on the knife loosening. The handle felt slippery in her sweaty palm.

"I don't know how she knows," said the man, "but your friend knows. She knows who I am and what we did."

Chloe gasped. The "we did" made her recoil. *They* didn't do anything. He made it sound consensual; an act of unified passion.

"I don't know if she's told you yet, but even if she hasn't, I'm sure she's planning to. And anyway, you've seen me now, haven't you. And I can't have that, you see. I have a wife. Children. They're grown-up, but they're still my boys, you know."

Chloe felt cold. She shivered and started to cry. Her knife hand trembled. She didn't know how long she'd be able to hold on to the weapon. Her legs began to buckle. She tried to beg him not to hurt her, not to do the terrible things he did to her again. But she couldn't make words; she could only babble.

And he said, "Stop babbling. This is difficult for the both of us. I've never had to do this before. I'm not a monster, you know."

Chloe cried out.

He whipped out a hammer from his jacket and stepped towards her.

CHAPTER 72.
LOVE/HATE.

"YOU look at hot as ever, Ruth," he said.

"This is not the time. Do you have her?"

Craig said, "In the back of the van. Trussed up with nowhere to go. Reminds me: you liked a bit of trussing up didn't you – "

"That's enough, Mr Craig."

"Mr Craig, now, is it?"

"You're an employee, nothing more."

"I was an employee twenty years ago, Ruth. Didn't stop you messing with me. You still make me hard, you know." He rubbed his crotch. "Have a feel."

"No, thank you. I like them young."

Craig put a hand to his chest. "You break my heart."

Ruth glanced around the barn so she wouldn't have to look at Craig. She smelled the damp atmosphere. The van was parked in the doorway. It blotted out the light. She said, "When will I never see you again?"

"When I get paid."

"If I pay you now, will you go?"

Craig tutted. "Wish I could. But Michael's the man. He wants this tart delivered to London."

"I'll get someone to do that. I can do it myself."

"You couldn't. What if the cops stop you? What do you do then?"

"What do you do, Mr Craig?"

"I deal with it. I can handle problems, Ruth."

"So can I."

"Not this kind. Don't worry about it. I'll take this one down to Michael, wait around if he wants me, then I'll fuck off out of your life. You'll never see me again."

"You said that twenty years ago."

He shrugged. "I'm a heartbreaker, baby."

Ruth sighed, shook her head. "Anyone see you today?"

"There was another girl in the house. I guess she did."

"Then she'll phone the police, they'll put it out to the media. Greenacre will see it, hopefully. She'll be the only one to link the kidnapping to us."

"How will she know we've gone to London?"

"It doesn't matter. She'll work it out. It's best we have a few days. Michael isn't healthy, yet."

"How's he getting along?"

"I spoke to him earlier. He's much stronger."

"So...he's going to be...like her?"

"Like her but better. He's a Templeton. We're stronger, superior."

"You approve of what your nephew's doing?"

"It doesn't matter. I support him. He's family."

Craig smiled. "You have a soft spot for the lad, Ruth. You like 'em young."

She felt herself blush. Her jaw tightened and she turned away from Craig. "Get on the road, Craig. I hope this is the last time I'll ever see you."

"How about a goodbye kiss, then."

He grabbed her shoulder, and spun her around. He pulled her to him. She beat at his chest with her fists, but it was like beating at a sheer rock face. He pressed his mouth to hers. She smelled his sweat, his musky odour, and although she despised him, it made her flush. His tongue pushed into her mouth and her tongue flailed against it. His body was hard, and she was crushed into him. He loosened his hold, and she pushed away.

"You bastard," she said, "how dare you. I'll have Michael eat you alive for that, you disgusting pig."

Craig chuckled. "You loved it, Ruth. Like you loved it twenty years ago. You moaned about it back then, too. Moaned and moaned and said, 'Oh yes, you bastard, fuck me hard, you bastard.'"

He walked towards the van, still laughing.

Ruth looked around, saw a plank of wood. She grabbed it and swung it at Craig.

He swatted the strike away. Ruth lost her grip on the plank. She dropped it, and it clanked on the concrete floor.

Craig looked at her. She cowered, thinking he was going to come for her.

He said, "Maybe I won't leave after this is done. Maybe I'll ask Michael for a job. How about family security advisor? Then we can be *really* close, Ruth. All the time."

He turned away, chuckling, and climbed into the van.

★ ★ ★

"What the hell are you doing here?" said Foreshawe.

"I saw the address come up on the bulletins," said Denton. "It's Laura Greenacre's address. She lived here."

"Oh, yes: 'Lived'. That's past tense, isn't it? You always seem to operate in the past tense don't you, Lorraine? Always a bit late on the scene."

They were at the Westmorland Road end of Summerhill Terrace. Both had officers at the top end of the street, too, where the Terrace junctioned with Westgate Road.

"This is my investigation, Lorraine. My suspect's in that house. The address of his previous victim."

"The cases may be linked. I'm hanging around, Tim."

"Hang around, then; just don't stick your nose into my business."

"I wouldn't think of it – couldn't be sure what kind of dirt I'd smell in there."

"Meaning what?"

"Meaning, get on with it or your bloody suspect will have gone, and the victim'll sue you for being a prat."

DC Bailey said, "Excuse me, but can you two get a grip?"

Foreshawe and Denton glared at him. He swallowed hard and lost some colour in his cheeks. He darted glances from one to the other.

Foreshawe said, "Bailey."

"Sir?"

"You're right." Foreshawe turned, headed for his car and said, "See you up there," to Denton.

A detective, staring up towards the house, said, "Look at that, sir."

Foreshawe said, "What?" and Denton trotted up to join him.
They all stared up the street.
Denton said, "Oh, no."
Foreshawe said, "Shit."
The detective who'd alerted Foreshawe said, "It's a camera crew."

CHAPTER 73.
NEWSHOUNDS.

"AND my own personal investigation," Cole said to the camera, "led me to conclude that the man who has attacked five women in the Newcastle and Hexham areas would return to his latest victim."

"How did you come to that conclusion, Mr Cole?" said the local BBC reporter Karen Hughes, who thought she was Kate Adie – and probably guessed she could be after a story like this.

"Hard work. Diligence. Investigative skills acquired during these many years I've practiced law. I'm not just a – " He hesitated. He glanced up the street, then down the street, and saw them come. He said, "Who called the police?"

Karen looked around, said, "Come on, Phil," and she tottered away on her heels, followed by the cameraman.

Cole recognised Foreshawe step out of the silver Rover that stopped fifty yards away. Karen Hughes was already on to the detective, saying, "Mr Foreshawe, could you tell me if you were aware of the suspect – "

He brushed past her, glaring at Cole.

The reporter and her cameraman spotted Lorraine Denton. They ran towards her. Denton said, "Put that camera down, Karen."

"Miss Denton," said the reporter, "are you any closer to – "

Denton said, "If you film anything, you'll get into trouble. There's a suspect in that house and if you get it on film, your bosses will be charged with contempt."

Cole saw the reporter thinking. She gestured for the cameraman to drop his lens. Cole cursed. He said to Foreshawe, "How did you know about this?"

"Who are you?"

"Ellis Cole, I" – he thought for a moment – "I'm a solicitor, here to represent my client; to protect him from himself and from you, Mr Foreshawe."

"If there's an incident here, and you've not phoned the police, I'll have you hung, drawn and quartered, arsehole."

"Don't threaten me, mate."

"Fuck off," said Foreshawe, shoving past him, going to the door.

Cole turned towards Karen. The camera was aimed at him again.

★ ★ ★

Voices leaked into the house from outside.

"Who's that?" the man said to Chloe and Chloe shook her head. Then he said, "Are you expecting anyone? Friend? Laura Greenacre? Where is she, Chloe? Where's Laura Greenacre?"

Chloe shook her head. She still brandished the knife. The man stood a few yards away with his hammer. He looked panicked. His head snapped from side to side, towards the hallway then back to Chloe.

Chloe heard shouts. She heard feet tramping up and down the pavement. She couldn't hear all the words that were coming from outside but she was sure the word "police" was there somewhere.

And then the man said, "That sounds like police."

Chloe tensed. She found the strength to grip the knife again.

"Who were you speaking to on the phone when I came in?" he said. "Was that the police? Did you ring them? You shouldn't have done that."

He took a step towards her. Chloe whimpered, steadied herself against the sink, jabbed out the knife.

"I'll knock that out of your hand, Chloe. You don't have the strength; you don't have the guts to use it on me. You couldn't bear to stab anyone, could you? It's horrible, you know, when a blade penetrates flesh. You can't do that. You're too weak."

"Don't come any closer."

"A few swats with this," he said, swinging the hammer, "and you're dead. Then I can get out through the back, slip through the cordon, and I'm free. I'm going to kill you, and I'm going to get away with it. I never wanted to kill you, of course. I wanted you to be alive, to remember me, what we did together."

Chloe flinched. Her guts tangled with fear. She shivered, her body sweating coldly.

He said, "I'm not a murderer. It's not what I am. I only do what I have to do. It's like a thirst, and I quench it, you see."

Chloe cried.

He said, "Sorry," then lunged towards her and she screamed, thrusting out the knife.

The door crashed open.

The rapist swung his hammer.

Chloe recoiled.

The hammer struck her shoulder.

Bone cracked. Pain lashed through her chest. She screamed and stabbed out.

The man swung his hammer again. He grabbed her hair. He growled, called her a whore and a bitch.

Shouts filled the kitchen. Police rushed in.

Someone said, "Leave her alone, Travis."

The man hammered her head.

Pain exploded in her skull and everything went black.

CHAPTER 74.
WHEN ANIMALS ATTACK.

DENTON watched as two officers led Ken Travis out of the house. He was handcuffed and stared down at his feet. The officers ushered him towards a police car. Foreshawe came out of the house. His nose was in the air. He was grinning. He brushed his sleeve, adjusted his tie.

Bastard, thought Denton.

Karen Hughes and Phil the cameraman pushed forward, Karen saying, "Mr Foreshawe, Mr Foreshawe, could you tell us who he is? Could you tell us how you caught him?"

Cole, putting his arm up like a keen kid at school, said, "Excuse me, it was me – it was – I brought you – " but a policeman shepherded him away.

Foreshawe, chest out, gestured at the cops taking Travis to the car to stop. The cameraman swivelled to get a shot of Travis. The cameraman said, "Could you get in shot, Mr Foreshawe, so we can have him over your shoulder – yeah, that's grand, that's grand."

Foreshawe, in shot, said, "I can't say anything at the moment. The suspect's identity won't be disclosed while he's being questioned. If – and I stress 'if' because he is, at present, only a suspect – if we charge him, then his name will be made public through the court list."

"And tell us about the investigation, Mr Foreshawe, how you traced him here?"

"Hard work. Diligence. The expertise of my officers who've worked non-stop on this investigation for months. We got a tip-off, studied that information carefully, and made a decision that it was valid information. We've had a suspect in mind for weeks, but I cannot – at this time – reveal if he is the man we have arrested here today."

He was doing everything by the book – apart from allowing the BBC to film the suspect; apart from claiming he tracked him down to Summerhill Terrace; apart from boasting they'd been watching Travis.

Travis, Denton thought. How the hell does that happen? Decent, respectable officer; father-of-two, and a good husband.

We've all got masks; we've all got things to hide.

Put him in the car, thought Denton, watching Foreshawe drag out the interview so the cameraman could get decent shots of Travis. They wouldn't be allowed to use them until he was charged. But they were "in the can", and Karen Hughes and her cameraman could look forward to a pat on the back and perhaps a promotion.

Denton glanced around. Neighbours peeked out of their windows. Passers-by stopped and pointed. A couple of kids waved at the camera. A colossal animal crashed through the trees lining the opposite side of the road.

Screams pierced the air. People fled. The kids raced away. Denton's legs buckled. Foreshawe stumbled. The cameraman twisted towards the creature.

It was huge and black – wolf-like. It sprang from the trees and landed on top of the police car. The vehicle's roof buckled. The creature squatted there on powerful hind legs; legs that bent backwards like the legs of a horse, or a dog.

Denton panted. She pressed a hand to her breast. She felt herself go cold. She stepped back. She heard Cole scream behind her.

The cops holding Travis backed off. Travis's face stretched in horror. The creature leaped off the car. It crashed into Travis, swatting the two policemen aside.

Karen Hughes said, "Are you getting this? Jesus, Phil, are you getting this?"

Phil stumbled about, trying to film what was happening, trying not to get killed.

Foreshawe staggered away, his mouth open, his eyes wide and fixed on the great, black thing that grabbed Travis in its jaws.

Travis, hands cuffed behind his back, screamed and thrashed. The animal had him by the shoulder, and it dragged him towards the house.

Denton thought she was going to be sick. The animal's yellow eyes were on her, watching her, gauging her. Denton put out a hand. Foreshawe took her arm, steadied her.

Foreshawe said, "What is it?"

Screams shrilled, fading away as the passers-by fled.

The creature pulled a struggling, terrified Travis into the house.

Denton said, "I think – " She couldn't say it; found the words impossible. But then, hearing sounds of anguish and fear and killing coming from the house, she said, "I think it's her."

CHAPTER 75.
HERITAGE IN A SYRINGE.

IT WAS late afternoon by the time they got there. They were all in the living room drinking bottled beer, watching the early season football results rattle off the videprinter.

Michael stormed into the room and they all flinched.

"Fuck me, mate," said Peter Straker, "you look fucking good to think you were at death's door a few hours ago."

"I feel better than I've ever felt" – he pointed at the TV – "and switch that crap off."

Ross switched off the TV. They all looked at Michael. Their faces showed awe. These dozen young men, born into this great family, had grown up on the legends and myths of the Templetons. But they hadn't seen the truth in those stories. Not until today.

Josh Reaney said, "What happened?"

Michael said, "What happened is that I've got better, and in getting better I've improved, I've changed – I've gone back to our roots."

"So it worked then? Is that what you're saying?" said Peter.

"Yes, it worked."

"Everything they say about us, those legends, they're true?" said Josh.

"They're true," said Michael.

"I can vouch for that," said Ross, "'cause I've seen it."

"Seen it?" said one of the others, Ralph Cato.

Ross nodded. "Seen Michael change. Seen him be a werewolf, guys."

They pondered this, creasing brows and scratching chins, whispering and murmuring and shaking heads.

Ross left the room and after a few moments returned with a briefcase. He laid it on the coffee table in front of Michael. Michael crouched and said, "I went through fucking agony for the sake of this family. I put myself in the line of fire – in the line of teeth and claws and a great dribbling bitch, actually."

A few of the guys chuckled.

"I should expect you, every one of you, to go through what I did," he said, "but I've come up with a better way of giving you back your heritage."

Josh said, "What do you mean?"

"Yeah, giving us back our heritage," said Ralph, "you mean what, exactly?"

"I mean," said Michael, "giving you the power to change."

Josh looked at him. Then he said, "This really works, then?"

"This really works," said Ross. "I've told you, I've seen it."

Josh sneered at Ross. "So what about you? Are you going through with this?"

"Already have," said Ross.

"And how do you feel?"

"Feel fine, Josh."

"Where's the bite marks, then?"

"Josh," said Michael, opening the briefcase, "Ross doesn't have any bite marks. I said – you lot don't have to go through what I went through."

He twisted the briefcase round to show the men what was inside.

"Syringes," said Peter.

"Yeah," said Michael, "eleven of them – Ross has already got his dose. One for each of you."

Josh leaped out of his seat, spilling beer, saying, "Whoa, there."

"What's the problem, Josh?" said Michael.

Josh stared at the eleven syringes resting in the slots cut into the briefcase's foam inlay. Each syringe was full of blood. Josh said, "You're not sticking any of those into me, matey."

Michael said, "You've not usually got a problem about sticking needles in your arm."

"This won't give me a high. And I don't know what's in it."

"It's my blood. It's my changed DNA. It's our history – and I promise you, mate, it'll give you one hell of a high. Look at that" – he pressed his tracksuit pants around his erection – "been walking around with that all day – stiff as a poker – fuck anything, and then fuck it again."

They stared at his hard-on.

"Okay," said Ross, taking a syringe out of the briefcase, "who's first?" He looked at Josh but Josh shook his head. He looked at the others and they all stared at the needle.

Michael said, "You're all fucking cowards. You're not Templetons."

"We are," said Josh. "We are because we don't want to walk around like an animal, a werewolf. That's the whole point. Our heritage is human, Michael. We abandoned the wolf in us."

"That was a mistake," said Michael, "and it made us weak."

Josh shook his head. "No it didn't. It made us strong. It made us kings. It made us rich. It brought us power and gave us influence. We're from families who live in big houses, who sent us to private schools, who bought us flash cars for our eighteenth birthdays, who gave us jobs in daddy's firm and paid us a whacking great big salary so we can fuck about all day. I haven't done a day's work in my life. I like it like that. It gives me a purpose."

"I'm not asking you to work, Josh."

"I know, Michael. But all I'm saying is that it's our *human* attributes that have served us best. This" – he flapped a hand dismissively – "werewolf nonsense: it's for gypsies and travellers and council-house scum. That's what they are, that's what the Greenacres got out of this."

Michael glared at him, looked like he wanted to kill him; but then said, "Who's first?"

Peter stepped forward, rolled up his sleeve. Ross pushed the needle into his arm. The blood seeped into the vein. Peter said, "What'll happen to me? How long will it take?"

Michael said, "A few hours."

"I had mine ages ago," said Ross, "and I feel a little bit dizzy, that's all. Threw up a couple of times, but it's like a weak hangover."

"You won't go through what I went through," said Michael, as they lined up and rolled up their sleeves and then, one by one, moved past Ross.

The syringes plunged into skin; they were drained into bloodstreams.

"This blood you're getting is mine," said Michael, "so you won't have to be sickened and poisoned by that Greenacre shit like I was."

They looked at their arms where the blood had gone into them.

Michael glanced at Josh and said, "Are you coming along?"

"I don't think so."

"You don't think so?"

"No, I don't."

Michael narrowed his eyes. "That's really pissed me off."

"Well, you can do without me, can't you? It's not necessary, is it? You go ahead. You do what you want to do, and I'll stick to who I am."

"Not a Templeton, that's who you are."

Josh shrugged. "I'm a Reaney."

"You came from Templetons, though," said Michael. "You were lucky enough to be handed the genes. And now you're going to abandon them. You're just going to be what you are: a Reaney; a boring, useless, nobody when you could be a somebody."

"You talk bollocks, Michael."

"There's always one, isn't there."

"One what?"

"One traitor."

"I'm not a traitor," said Josh, putting his beer bottle down on top of the TV.

"Yes, you are. Betrayed us all. We were going to do this, every one of us. Thirteen of us together. But there's always one."

"I'm going," he said, grabbing his coat from a pile stacked on a chair, "'cause this is shit."

"Do you think this is shit?"

Michael tossed off his T-shirt and showed his lean, muscled torso. He made a bodybuilder pose, bringing his fists together at his abdomen, his elbows flaring outwards. The tendons in his neck corded. The muscles in his chest swelled. His arms bulged. His face went red and veins popped up on his temples. Blood trickled from his nostrils and from his tear ducts.

Josh took a step back. The others stared. Ross said, "Here we go."

And the werewolf Michael burst out of himself, opening up like a flower made of flesh, pushing his inside out and over his human shape.

They stumbled, trying to get out of the way. Ross said that it was all right, and not to be scared, because it was Michael.

But they huddled into the corners, their sleeves still rolled up, their skin still stinging from the needle pricks.

Josh cowered, his gaze moving up to follow the growing of the werewolf.

The werewolf growled and stared back.

Josh wailed and bolted for the door.

The werewolf roared and pounced.

The men watched Josh being ripped apart. They listened to the terrible sounds he made as he was being broken up. They flinched as the blood spattered them, and the pieces of Josh stuck to the walls and slid down, leaving trails of him behind.

CHAPTER 76.
DEALING WITH DEATH.

"YOU killed him."

"Dragged him into the house, killed him. Right there in front of Chloe. Did it for her. Left her the kill."

"And then?" said Thorn, eyes fixed on the road reaching out in front of him.

"Changed back into me, grabbed these combats and this T-shirt from the washing machine, hugged Chloe and told her I loved her — "

"Sorry," he said, interrupting, "what did she do?"

"She was in some kind of hypnotic state, I think. Very pale. Said nothing, just panted."

"Yes. Werewolves can have that affect on you. Especially when they bring you a kill. I used to have a cat who brought me dead mice." He hummed, and shook his head. "So you got out before they came in."

"I got out through the back. Leaped over the wall, into the alleyway, and down to you. No one saw me. No one would think. There were a lot of screams, lots of noise, everyone panicking. The cops were a bit shocked — "

"No, you don't say."

She glared at him. "Don't be sarcastic, Johnny." Looking back to the road, she said, "They weren't going to come into the house while I was there, were they. They didn't want to be heroes that much. Cole was there. Smelled his stinky arse."

"Cole?"

"Yeah. And a cameraman."

Thorn felt a jolt of panic punch into his heart. "A cameraman?"

"Yeah, 'fraid so."

"So you're on film."

"I think I am."

"Oh, shit."

"Yes. Shit. To think a few days ago I wouldn't let anyone see me as a werewolf unless I planned to kill them, now I'm pitching for my own TV show."

"They'll show it."

"I don't care, now. Everything's changed."

Thorn drove carefully, keeping to the speed limit. He glanced in the rear view mirror now and then, making sure they weren't being followed.

He said, "What's changed?"

They pulled into the road that ran behind Templeton Hall.

Laura said, "Templeton's dead. This secret war is over."

"Is it?"

"Yes. Once we get Elena back. Once I do Michael. That's it, then."

"And you'll be a celebrity. Hunted across the world."

He shook his head. He stopped at the rear entrance. The gate still lay torn and broken. He looked up towards the house. It seemed greyer, gloomier than he remembered it. He turned the car into the entrance and guided it up the track towards the farm buildings. He parked the Mondeo in the barn.

He looked at her and said, "A few days ago you wouldn't change when some creep doctor tried to take your blood; you held your nerve, fought back and didn't kill. Now, you're on telly, and you don't care."

"I do care, but there's nothing I can do about it."

They got out, looked towards the house.

He said, "Let's be careful, okay."

She frowned. "When have I ever been reckless?"

They sneaked up to the house.

The rear door that led to the kitchen was ajar.

Thorn shoved it open and poked his head round the door frame. Laura pushed past him and stomped along the corridor. He cursed, followed her, grabbing her arm.

"Hold on," he said, "they might be here."

"Good. I want them to be here." She turned away and stuck her nose in the air. "Smell that."

He sniffed. He licked his lips. Bacon.

They went along the corridor. They stopped at the door to the kitchen. They heard the sizzle of bacon. They smelled it and they drooled.

"Funny," said Laura, "seeing as I just ate."

Thorn was about to say something when he felt the cold steel of a shotgun barrel press against the back of his neck.

★ ★ ★

Denton sipped her white wine and said, "What did we see?"

Foreshawe stared into his pint. They were sitting at the bar of The Seven Stars in Ponteland. They'd been sitting there all afternoon, and the evening had started to sneak up on them – the bustle of a Saturday night threatened to disturb their thoughts.

Foreshawe, speaking into his beer, said, "I can still prove it was Travis. We've got DNA. He used a condom, but one of his victims, she managed to scratch him. She had some skin under one of her nails. Just a tiny, tiny shred. Enough, though. We can still have him."

"He's dead, Tim."

"But if it's him, and we – I – I almost got to him, I can still claim it, can't I. I mean, what happened to him was a freak thing. An act of God."

"I'm not sure God bears any responsibility for what killed Travis."

He wasn't listening. He said, "And Travis being one of our own, that'll send a signal that we don't protect dirty cops; we nail them like we nail any other bastard out there."

"I think," said Denton, "that what we saw today also killed those dogs at Templeton Hall. It must be – " She looked away, pondered her words. "It must be *some* kind of animal," she said. "One we don't know about, that's all. There are plenty of animals out there we don't know about, surely."

She thought about what Keegan had said.

"Pet-gone-bad."

"What?" said Foreshawe, coming out of his thoughts. He was looking at her and around at the bar as if he were seeing them sitting here for the first time. "What was that you said?"

302

"Pet-gone-bad. It's what Keegan, that guy from London, said. I think that's what *did* kill his mercenaries. I think that killed a lot of people."

"Travis. It killed Travis."

"Yes. Travis. I wish I could pin Templeton's death on it."

"You got someone for that?"

"We got Jarvis. We're pretty sure. Found a knife in his cellar. Templeton's blood on it." She shrugged. "Could've been planted, though. By Greenacre. By that animal."

"Have you got anything on her?"

"Assault. Criminal damage. That's all. She attacked the doctor and destroyed some blood samples. Thing is, we've got a complaint about that same doctor, now. Procter, his name was. Seems to have been a bit too hands-on with some of the nurses."

"That's sex crimes. That's me."

"Yes, Tim. That's you. You're welcome to it. It just came into the office, that's all. You're welcome to it all. I just want Greenacre."

"And the animal."

She looked at him. "Maybe."

"Are you going to hand the footage back to the Beeb?"

"We'll see. It's a bit too weird to go out on BBC North East and Cumbria. Scare a few farmers worried about their flocks. Karen Hughes's making a noise about it, though. Accusing us of censorship. She's got Ellis Cole on the case."

"So you think it's her, then?"

"Who's her?"

"Come on, Lorraine. Do you think Laura Greenacre's that animal we saw today? Do you believe in werewolves?"

She grinned. "Don't be ridiculous, Tim."

Her phone rang. It was Bailey. She listened, nodding, sipping at her wine, and finally said, "Thanks, Mark, that's something to go on," and put the phone down on the bar.

Foreshawe raised his chin, waiting for her to speak.

She drank, thought about something, and then said, "They found Thorn's Saab. Actually, it was registered to Adam Templeton. We can do Thorn for taking without consent."

"Is that all?"

"They found some papers in the back. Scrunched up. There was a letter."

"A letter?"

"Yes, very useful. Richie Jarvis's suicide note. He couldn't write, of course, but that's a trivial matter. Says that Laura Greenacre was his lover and she persuaded him to kill Templeton."

Foreshawe chuckled and sipped his beer. "That's bugger all."

"It's enough for me to hunt her down. Enough for me to never ever leave her alone." She took a drink, put the glass down empty. "It'll do me."

"What about Thorn?"

Denton shook her head. "He's doomed. He crossed over a long time ago to somewhere wild and lost. He's not coming back. He's not one of us anymore."

Denton gazed at the top shelf of spirits and thought which one she'd like to drink. She sensed Foreshawe's eyes on her, and she turned to look at him.

He said, "Will you sleep with me again, Lorraine?"

She thought about their time before, and played it through in her mind. It was good, some of it, but a lot of it was bad. After seeing it all, she said, "No."

★ ★ ★

"Mr Thorn," said the familiar voice behind him.

"Mrs Garvey," he said, turning away from the cold barrel at his neck. The cook stood there, shotgun pointed at Thorn's face. He guided the barrel away and said, "What are you doing here with that?"

"Oh, Mr Thorn," she said, lowering the weapon, "it's been terrible here since Sir Adam died, hasn't it. Deaths and violence and all kinds. It's been much worse since you left. I wish you could've stayed."

He took the gun from Mrs Garvey, gave it to Laura.

The cook's shoulders slumped. She started to cry and Thorn embraced her saying, "It's all right, Mrs Garvey, everything's going to be all right."

Ten minutes later they were in the kitchen. She made them bacon sandwiches and tea. "I was making myself a buttie," she said, "to get me going. Turned up this morning, there's no one here. They've all gone."

"When did Michael leave?" said Thorn, chewing his food. He didn't realise how hungry he was until he started on the sandwich. He hadn't eaten properly in days.

"He left that night, that terrible night when they said there was an animal loose in the grounds...and those soldiers, all of them killed, they say. That's when he left."

Laura's eyes met Thorn's for a moment.

Thorn looked at the cook again. He leaned forward, put a hand on her shoulder. "Do you know where he's gone, Mrs Garvey?"

"I think London. I came out to see what was going on – all the shouting and screaming. I heard young Mr Andersson, one of Michael's cousins, saying he was taking him to London."

Thorn felt Laura tense. She wanted to go. It was likely that Elena was on her way to London, too. Thorn shared her urge to get on the road, but he didn't want to abandon Mrs Garvey. They'd had a rapport, and he liked the cook.

"Is there anyone left here, now?"

The cook said, "Sir Adam's sister, Ruth, left a few hours ago. Said I should stay on until I heard different; said she'd keep paying my wages. There's a housekeeper and a couple of cleaners; a groundsman comes in twice a week to tend the gardens."

Mrs Garvey blew her nose.

"It's not like it was in Sir Adam's day," she said. "It was all so busy. Felt like a proper house. Like it was when my mother worked here. She was cook before me, you know. Her aunt was cook before her. Family tradition almost. Not anymore."

"It'll be all right," said Thorn, knowing that it probably wouldn't be.

Mrs Garvey knew that, too, and she said, "I can't see how. That Michael – even if he does come back, I don't think I could work for him. Such a rude, offensive young man. Spends most of his time in that flat of his in Newcastle, or in London, or somewhere with his cousins." She tutted. "The Templetons have lived here for centuries. Respectable and decent. Michael should continue that tradition, don't you think?"

Mrs Garvey looked at Thorn, then at Laura. Thorn noticed Laura's gaze drop away. He said, "Things change. And I'm sure he will, too."

CHAPTER 77.
HEAT.

"I'M concerned about my son," said Ruth.

"Ross'll be fine. He's got a temperature. He's thrashing about a bit. He's vomiting, but he'll be fine."

"Michael, I spoke to him earlier today. He told me the only symptom he had was mild dizziness. Now you're telling me his system's breaking down."

Michael said, "Of course it's breaking down – he's changing, Ruth. So are the others. They're all feeling the effects. But so did I. And much worse. I thought I was going to die, so let them feel a bit under the weather."

"I don't care about the others. I care about Ross."

Michael swatted her concerns away. "I tell you, he'll be fine. He'll be better, stronger, fitter – and hornier."

She turned away, folded her arms. They were in the living room where Ross had earlier injected Michael's blood into ten cousins; where Michael had butchered Josh Reaney; where they cleaned up the mess.

Ruth had noticed a "strange smell in here" when she walked in, but Michael dismissed her suggestion.

Ruth said, "I don't want to know if my son's horny or not."

Michael moved up behind her. She smelled of flowers, but he could smell other things, too, with his newly sharpened senses: he could smell her heat.

And it made him hard.

He put his hands on her waist.

She tensed.

Michael rested his chin on her shoulder. He gazed through the window at London's skyline.

"This 'new me,' I'm so randy," he said.

"You were always randy. Ever since your voice broke."

He pressed against her, and he was hard, and she gasped.

"See how randy I am, Ruth?"

"You're still my brother's son."

"I know. And that makes our coupling ideal. It's all the rage in the werewolf community, you know. That's how the Greenacres kept themselves pure."

She pulled away and turned to face him. Her cheeks and her neck were red. Her pupils were dilated.

Michael breathed her in. He said, "I can smell you, and you smell so hot. It's unbelievable that I can pick up a scent like that, now. I can't wait to fuck with this new power of mine. Why don't you let me fuck you, auntie? You can be the first."

He moved towards her. She trembled and turned around. He slid his hands under her arms, cupping her breasts. She gasped and he felt her weaken. He pulled her against him and his hardness pushed into her lower back. Michael drooled, his saliva oozing from his gums, over his chin, dripping onto Ruth's shoulder and neck.

"I'm going to have myself a harem," he said, "a family of bitches: you can be queen bitch, and my sister can be second bitch."

Ruth stepped away from him and made a noise that sounded like disappointment; like she wanted to be there being mauled by him, being spread and pounded, but what he said had forced her to reject his advances.

She said, "I thought you were going to kill her, Michael. I don't want her to be part of this. Wipe your mouth."

He mopped the drool with the hem of his T-shirt. Ruth's gaze dropped to his eight-pack abdomen, then quickly darted to his face again.

She said, "She's our enemy. I don't care if she is your father's daughter. That was a mistake. That can be wiped from history now that they're all dead. There's only her left, and she's got to die too."

"Can't I have my fun with her, first?"

"Kill her."

"But can't I just do her once?"

"Kill her."

"It had better be worth it."

Ruth ripped her blouse open. Buttons popped. She slid the garment off her shoulders. Michael grinned and growled. He came forward. She trembled and reached behind her to unclasp the bra. She tossed it aside. Her breasts moved. Michael drooled. He was on her and bent to lick and suck her breasts. She gasped and dug her nails into his shoulders.

Ruth, her voice a moan, said, "Kill her."

* * *

They got into London at ten p.m., but it took them another hour to find a hotel.

It was in Earl's Court, a cheap hotel in a road of cheap hotels. They got the only room left, a double. The room was on the ground floor. There was a portable TV on a chest of drawers. The mattress was hard. The shower trickled tepid water. The bedspread showed dolphins skimming waves. Thorn looked through the window. Lights from the first- and second-floor rooms illuminated the over-grown garden. Thorn drew the curtains.

She sat on the bed.

Thorn turned to her and said, "It'll do."

"'Course. We're not on honeymoon, are we?"

"No, we're not."

"Still, could you ring room service for some champagne and caviar?"

"I think you'll be lucky to get a shrivelled sandwich and a glass of water."

Thorn switched on the television. He got static. It buzzed like a swarm of bees. He started to fiddle with the aerial. Forms appeared on the screen, but nothing identifiable.

"Sod it," he said, and switched it off. "Just wanted to see the news. See if you were on."

"Think I will be?"

He shrugged, sitting on the bed.

"Sorry about this," he said, gesturing at the bed.

"It's all right. What are you sorry for? I'll be perfectly comfortable.

I'm sure you'll be happy in the bath."

He looked at her, then she smiled.

"You're turning red, Johnny."

"Yeah...anyway, we'll sort that out...I can make do with a chair..."

"We'll be all right."

"Yeah, yeah, I know."

He fidgeted and looked at his hands. He thought about Sophie. He'd called from his brother's house. Jane told him to the previous day, promised Sophie would be there to talk to him. She wasn't and Thorn got angry. *You promised,* he told Jane, and Jane said, *How many times did you promise things?* He felt rage flare in his breast. He hesitated, not wanting to fight with her over Sophie. The anger shrivelled, and he told Jane, calmly, that he thought she'd been unfair. She said that she was sorry, that something had come up, that she'd had to go to the doctor. Sophie was with a friend. He asked her why she went to the doctor, *was everything all right?* Jane breathed and a chill leached through his veins.

And Jane said, "I'm pregnant."

He was pulled from his thoughts by a warm, soft hand stroking the back of his neck.

"Are you okay?" said Laura.

He looked at her and every hurt faded. He told her about Jane and it was good to let everything go, and to let Jane go.

He said, "I tend to lose everyone I love," and smiled sadly.

He waited for her to say something, but she didn't. And he knew that what he'd said was true and not just a pathetic appeal for sympathy: he *did* lose them all. His shoulders slumped and any drop of hope he had in his heart trickled away.

"I can't stay," said Laura, seeing into him. "I have to be lost to the world, and you won't do that: you have Sophie."

He looked at her and nodded. They held each other's eyes for a good time. Laura, after a while, said, "I'm not an animal."

He said, "You're beautiful," and leaned in to kiss her, and they kissed, and pressed into each other, and made noises as heat came from their bodies.

They went at each other, and they made love deep into each other, and the deepness of it felt like it was love made for the first and last time.

CHAPTER 78.
PARTY TIME.

MICHAEL laughed as they moaned and puked and jerked about. "You're changing, guys," he said, "you're fucking changing."

They were down in the cellar. A single light bulb cast a weak light on the circle of men thrashing around on the flagstone floor.

Ross, his face pale and the skin around his eyes dark, said, "I'm dying, Michael, I'm dying," and then he jerked. His head snapped from side to side. Blond hair spouted from his cheeks and his arms. His back arched and bones cracked. He screamed, his face creased with agony.

Michael laughed. "Enjoy it, Ross, enjoy it."

Peter Straker had transformed. Michael looked at him. Peter had sprouted brown fur. His legs had bent backwards. He had claws poking out of his fingers. His face hadn't fully changed into a wolf's; it was still humanoid, but the nose and mouth areas were slightly pushed out. His teeth, bared in a groan, were sharp and long. Blood poured from his mouth where the teeth had ripped through his gums. He'd got taller, too: well over six-and-a-half feet. Muscled and powerful, he'd look terrifying out in the streets.

They'd all changed, or were in the process of changing. Their transformations weren't perfect: they weren't as wolf-like as Michael or Laura Greenacre; there was still a lot of human in them. But maybe that was down to the blood, thought Michael.

His had been poisoned from source: from a Greenacre. Her bite had been enough to reconstruct his genes. But Michael's blood, injected into his cousins, was still second-hand; it wasn't pure. And since their blood had been diluted by centuries of breeding with humans, Michael's wasn't strong enough to completely alter their DNA.

Sod the science, he thought; *I don't understand it, so it doesn't matter.*

What mattered was –

"What's the problem, Ralph?"

"Michael," said Ralph Cato, on all fours, straining, blood dripping from his nose and his eyes, "Michael, I can't change...nothing... nothing's happening."

"Come on, you twat," said Michael, "just get angry and let it out of you. It's easy after the first time. Come on."

"I'm trying – I'm – trying – just – can't – "

Ralph's face was red. The veins on his temples pulsed. He looked freakish, like he was giving birth. Michael laughed at the thought.

He said, "You're fucking pathetic."

The Templeton werewolves glowered at their unchanged cousin. They slobbered, the spit oozing from their jaws.

Michael smiled. He grabbed Ralph by the hair and dragged him to his feet. Ralph whined. His eyes were shut; tears of blood leaked down his cheeks. Sweat glossed his body. Holding him up by the hair, Michael looked around at the Templeton werewolves.

He said, "Ralph's not one of us. He must be a bastard. His mum must be a whore who shagged some waster. Not one of us, guys."

They growled and snapped their teeth.

Ralph said, "Please...please...Michael...I'm..."

"Take him," he said, shoving Ralph into them; and they fell on him and his screams pierced the mound of monsters pressing down on him and eating him.

* * *

Half an hour later, ten men smeared in sweat and blood were sprawled around the cellar. They picked meat from between their teeth. They licked blood and pieces of human from their hands.

Ralph's remains steamed. The smell of guts saturated the air. Blood smeared the white, plaster walls, and it ran down the rivulets between the flagstones.

Michael watched the ten men, and he felt mighty.

Everything was going well. He thought about fucking Ruth last night and the way she loved it. He thought about Ralph's death and how the guys killed as a pack. He thought about Elena McIntyre trussed up in a room upstairs and how she was bait to draw Laura towards her doom.

Ross said, "It tastes so good. I never thought I'd eat rare."

Jake Sears said, "This isn't rare – this is raw."

They laughed.

Michael saw how good this was. He said, "Can you see that we can do anything we want? Can you see how powerful we'll be?"

"What are we going to do next?" said Peter Straker.

Michael looked at them, their blood-soiled faces, their sweat-glistened bodies, and he said, "We're going to scare the living shit out of some tourists."

"Are we going to prowl around London?" said Peter.

"Yeah. Prowl around. Kill some people."

They froze and looked at Michael.

"Kill?" said Jake.

"Yeah. Like we killed Josh. Like we killed Ralph."

Ross said, "You killed Josh, Michael."

"Won't we get caught?" said Peter.

Michael pulled a face. "Who's going to want to catch us?"

"A zoo?" said Ross, and some of them chuckled.

"But I'm serious," said Peter, "we'll be seen and we'll be hunted."

"No we won't," said Michael. "They won't know it's us, will they. They'll see werewolves. They can't trace it back to you and me, Pete."

"That's right," said Ross. "We all just killed Ralph. You were happy enough to do that. You've still got bits of him in your teeth, you mucky sod."

Peter shook his head. "I don't know."

"So you didn't think," said Michael, "about this before you pounced on Ralph? What do you think we're going to tell his mum and Josh's parents? You think they won't ask?"

Peter shrugged. "I didn't think, did I?" He looked at Michael, concern wrinkling his face. "What *will* we tell them?"

"We can tell them they died in that terrible animal attack that's going to happen in London today. Or we can tell them we had them for lunch."

"Oh yeah," said Peter, "that'll go down well."

"So will Josh and Ralph's parents if they cause us any hassle."

The guys laughed, and Michael saw that he'd won them over.

"Are you with us, Pete?" he said.

Peter stared at him, and for a moment Michael thought he saw a challenge in his cousin's eyes. But Peter said, "You know I'm with you, Michael."

"Okay," said Michael, "let's go hunting."

CHAPTER 79.
BAIT.

MICHAEL, peering around the door, said, "Everything all right?"

"Why shouldn't it be?" said Craig, feet up on the table, reading a porn mag.

Michael looked at the woman on the mattress. She had a pillowcase over her head. Her right wrist was handcuffed to a radiator. A plate with some beans on it lay on the floor.

"She's not eaten," said Michael.

Craig shrugged. "She will if she's hungry."

"You slapped her around?"

Craig put the magazine down and sat up straight. "No, I fucking well haven't."

"Well," said Michael, coming into the room, "do it then. Push her about a bit. Make her scared."

"You want me to beat her up?"

"Just a little. Nothing bad. A few slaps, that's all. I want her to be scared of this."

"I think she's already scared, Michael."

"Yeah. Okay. I've come to tell you that we're going out. We can all change, now."

"You can?" said Craig, his gaze suspicious.

"Yes, and if you want to see some killing, you can come with us. Bring a gun, just in case."

"In case of what?"

"In case someone gets a bit to brave. In case Laura turns up."

"You think she'll come?"

"Of course she'll come. She's not going to leave the McIntyre woman lying here handcuffed to a radiator, is she? Would you?"

"Yes, I would."

"Well, so would I – but Laura won't. She'll be down here like a shot."

"How will she know we're in London?"

He looked at Elena's pillow-cased head and smiled. "I gave Mrs Garvey, the cook, a grand. She liked Thorn, but she was happy to stick the knife in for cash. Anyone can be bought."

"What did she tell him?"

"I told her to tell Thorn that we'd gone to London. He'd guess then that we'd got this one," said Michael, gesturing towards Elena.

"How did you know Thorn would go to Templeton Hall?"

"If you were a cop trying to find someone, and your suspect lived at a certain address, wouldn't you go to that certain address first?"

"So this cook's going to tell Thorn and that girl that we're here."

"Yes. They're probably on the way down – or if we're lucky, already here. I need her dead, Craig. If she turns up today, kill her."

"You sure about that?"

Michael thought about Ruth taking off her clothes and saying, "Kill her." He knew he wanted Ruth again, and for that to happen he'd have to get rid of Laura Greenacre. He'd intended to put her down at some stage, anyway; but he hoped for some fun with her, first. A pack of bitches headed by Ruth and Laura would've been great; but Ruth wouldn't have it and demanded Laura's head on a plate.

"I want her dead," said Michael.

"And the cop?"

Michael shrugged. "Dead too."

"And this one?" said Craig, indicating Elena.

"Do you actually need to ask?"

CHAPTER 80.
GOING UNDERGROUND.

"KEN Travis used to be a useful contact. He got me Richie Jarvis's details."

"Sorry," said Laura, "to have eaten your pal."

"I didn't mean that. He wasn't a friend. There's no one I can call, now, that's all. Ask them to find me Ross Andersson's address."

They walked from their hotel to Kensington's high street. It was a brisk ten-minute jaunt. Thorn thought about their night together.

A shaft of sun had woken him that morning. Laura was pressed against his back. He turned, and she tucked herself into him, nestling her face into his chest. He wished he could've held that moment and made it his life. It seemed right to him, and he didn't want things to change. She woke up. She raised her head and swept the hair from her face. She looked sleepy but smiled with her tired eyes. He cupped her face, drew it to his, and they kissed. He grew hard on her and she moved her thigh against it. He lay on his back and she straddled him, and they made love.

And they knew that this *would* be the last time.

He tried not to think of it as he walked along the busy Sunday morning pavement, but ridding his mind of Laura Greenacre was going to be impossible.

"Where are we going?" she said.

"I've no idea. I guess I'm looking for trouble."

"And what are you going to do when you find it?"

"Again, no idea."

"Good. You don't have a strategy in place, then?"

"No, do you?"

"I'm going to kill Michael, rescue Elena, and then – "

He looked at her, waiting for her to finish her words. When she didn't, he said, "I don't think much of your tactics, either."

She glanced at him and made a little smile.

He said, "What if Michael changes into a werewolf?"

"Doesn't matter. I'll be stronger than him. I've been doing this all my life. It takes time to fully control the transformation, and then to control yourself as a werewolf."

"I never thought I'd be having this discussion."

"You've come a long way since you gave me this black eye."

"It's healing up nicely, I'd say." He saw a Starbucks. "I need a coffee. Do you need a coffee?"

She said no, but she wanted water. Thorn went in, bought himself a black coffee, got a bottle of water for Laura.

They walked on, drinking. The coffee revived him. He felt sharp. He'd slept well the previous night. It was the first time in a while he'd been under for more than two or three hours.

They got on the underground at High Street Kensington station. The Tube was crammed with tourists. A babel of languages knitted together in the carriage. Laura wedged herself between a fat American who was going on about "The Queen of England" and a blonde girl reading a bible. Thorn stood, grabbing a rail as the train started to rattle into the tunnel.

He had no idea what they were going to do. He thought if he could find a police station he could wheedle himself in. He didn't have much hope for the "I'm a cop" line, but he'd give it a try; he had to. If they checked him out, they'd soon discover he was suspended – and even worse, they'd see he was wanted.

That's the nightmare scenario, he told himself.

But knowing cops, they wouldn't pay that much attention. If he could play the part properly, he stood a decent chance of getting in. Once he'd found himself a computer, he could access all the databases he'd need to find Andersson's address.

I must be mad, he thought. Running around London looking for a werewolf and an ex-stripper in the company of someone who was both a werewolf *and* an ex-stripper.

There was no way back, now; no job for him with Northumbria Police after this was done. He refused to think about the future. He'd deal with that when this was done.

He sighed, looked at Laura. She smiled up at him from her seat. She rolled her eyes at the loud American who was saying that "Mr Blair is such a fantastic guy". Thorn grinned. His gaze drifted towards the far end of the carriage. He could see into the next car along. That was packed, too.

Three guys stood at the rear end, nearest Thorn's carriage. Thorn had side profiles of the men. They were laughing. Thorn guessed they were being loud. They seemed to be swaggering, their gestures expressive.

Thorn shuddered.

Something cold crept up his spine.

He held his breath, his gaze fixed on the guy with the curly-blonde hair.

Thorn had seen him before. His mind started to filter through stored memories.

The blonde-haired guy, as if sensing that someone was watching him, turned and his eyes locked on Thorn. The man's smile dropped away. His face was cold.

Thorn's mind stopped rolling and found the man's identity.

It was Ross Andersson.

CHAPTER 81.
KURI AND HAMA.

KURI Endo turned her Tower of London baseball cap back-to-front so she could take a picture of the London Underground map.

The Tube train rumbled through the tunnels, so keeping the map in the viewfinder was difficult.

Hama said, "Wait 'til we stop. Take it then."

Kuri put the camera in her lap and turned the baseball cap the right way around. She said, "It's so old. Everything's like the ancient world here. I love it so, Hama. I'm coming here to university next year. I'm going to learn English and come here and be English. Very, very traditional."

Kuri and Hama laughed. The train jerked. Passengers glanced at the girls. Everyone seemed so dour, so quiet.

"They think we're loud," said Kuri.

"Do they?"

"Yes, they're frowning at us."

"Not all of them. They're smiling."

Kuri turned to look and saw three young men standing at the back of the carriage. They held on to the straps and their arm muscles corded. Kuri squirmed and felt herself blush. They were handsome Europeans. European boys made her feel funny. She liked them, but going out with one seemed wrong. She knew a lot of women who'd married Europeans, and it was fine; but her dad wanted her to have Japanese boyfriends.

Maybe I can have a holiday boyfriend from England, she thought.

Two of the guys were smiling and winking at Kuri and Hama. The other one – the one with golden curls – was looking into the carriage behind theirs.

Kuri was eighteen and a virgin. She'd had boyfriends, but nothing serious. She wasn't going to wait until she was married to have sex – no way – but she wanted to find the right boy.

Hama didn't care. She'd already slept with ten boys. She'd slept with two on this holiday – and they'd only been in England for a week. On Wednesday, they were going to France, and they'd spend a week travelling to Italy. They'd fly from Rome to New York, then across to L.A., and home for the millennium.

How many boys will Hama have let into her bed by the end of the trip? wondered Kuri. *How many will I let into mine?*

Perhaps one of these boys smiling and winking at them would be her first.

She felt a trill of excitement in her belly. She flushed again, and started to giggle. Hama nudged her, and they were both sniggering.

"Which one do you like?" said Hama.

"I don't know – I – I think I like the one with yellow hair."

"He's not looking at us."

"Maybe he's shy and sweet. Maybe he blushes like me."

"You should sleep with him, Kuri."

"Why would he want to sleep with me?"

Hama pulled a face. "All men want to sleep with girls. And English guys really like Japanese girls."

"Which one do you like?"

"All three," said Hama.

Kuri gasped, putting a hand to her mouth.

"But," said Hama, "if you like the blonde one, you have him – I'll take the other two."

"No, no, I don't" – she giggled – "it's not what I said."

Kuri looked over at the men.

The blonde one turned round.

Kuri winced. Goosepimples burst out all over her skin.

The man's face was red. His eyes were yellow like an animal's eyes. His mouth was open showing sharp teeth.

CHAPTER 82.
GATHERING FORCE.

THEY got off at Embankment underground station and walked to Trafalgar Square. It was packed with tourists. The sun beat down. Nelson towered above the bustle. Cameras snapped up at him. Voices knitted into each other. Traffic whizzed through, engines revving, horns blaring.

Michael sniffed the air and breathed in blood and sweat and oil.

"Okay," he said, scanning the square, "this is it."

He checked his watch. He wondered where Ross was. Ross and the Sears brothers, Jake and Sam, had stayed behind to clean up Ralph's remains.

Michael was with Anton Sears, and the Paleys: Will, Stephen, and Nick. Peter Straker had travelled here by cab with his brother Paul, and Kevin Muir. They should be milling about on the steps of the National Gallery. Michael stared across the square at the building's neo-classical facade. The tradition it represented made Michael's heart swell. *This is what I stand for,* he thought, *this is what I'm doing: reviving custom; respecting history; and* — he smiled — *making art.*

Yes — this Trafalgar Square, named for Nelson's victory, would be his canvas. It would be itself the scene of a battle; it would be decorated in the dead of this war.

Michael said, "One of our descendents was Marius Victor. He was a Tribunus laticlavius, a senior tribune. Marius helped crush the British druids on Anglesey in North Wales almost two thousand years ago. But he was there, at that battle, for another reason. Werewolves lived among the druids. Before crossing the water and entering the fray, Marius said, 'Today, and forever more, men will fight wolves, and men will triumph'. My dad told me that. I thought it was boring at the time, but it stayed with me and I can understand it, now."

Michael's eyes ranged Trafalgar Square. He didn't know if Anton and the Paleys were listening to him, but these words felt important.

He said, "I'm changing Marius's words. I'm saying, 'Today, wolves will fight men, and wolves will triumph'."

"Don't know what you're on about, mate," said Anton, "but it sounds good to me."

"Let's do it," said Michael, and he tightened his body, tensing every muscle, straining every nerve, and the animal that was inside him pressed itself outwards.

The Paleys and Anton did the same.

Their bodies snapped and swelled and sprouted fur, and their clothes ripped and flapped away. Tourists stopped to glare at them as they thrashed and roared. The audience pointed, mouths open in astonishment. Some took pictures, thinking it was a street-show. Then they saw it wasn't a street-show, and screams started to sweep through Trafalgar Square.

* * *

"Next carriage," said Thorn, tugging Laura from her seat.

The fat American said, "Hey, mister, you leave the lady alone," and he got up. The train banked. The standing passengers swayed. Metal screeched. The lights blinked.

The fat American grabbed at Thorn. Laura elbowed the man in the face. His nose spread out in red over his cheeks. He fell into his seat, and the seat shuddered. His wife screamed.

Laura and Thorn shoved their way through the commuters. The American wife wailed. Passengers were shouting. Screams filled the carriage. The lights blinked again. The train banked and rattled.

Thorn said, "Ross Andersson's in the carriage ahead. He's Michael's cousin. I saw him at Templeton Hall a few times."

Panic took hold. Passengers pushed and shouted. Thorn looked through to the next carriage. He saw Andersson and his two companions. There was something different about them. The commuters were watching the men with fear on their faces.

The lights blinked for a third time.

Screams pierced the darkness.

The lights came on and the screams were louder, and Thorn saw three werewolves rampage through the carriage. Commuters scattered. Passengers in Thorn's carriage had seen what was happening, and they were rushing towards the rear of the carriage. They were screaming and shouting, and Thorn and Laura had to shove through them, pushing them aside.

Thorn tried to yank the door open, but it was jammed.

"Jesus Christ," he said, watching the werewolves attack. The passengers were panicking. They scratched at the sliding doors, kicked at the windows, trampled other people. The werewolves pounced and snapped and tore. The victims screamed and their blood sprayed. Thorn said Jesus Christ again, then Laura grabbed the handle and tore the door away.

Wind sliced in from the tunnel. It whipped against Thorn's face.

Behind him, the commuters were screaming and trying to get out of the carriage. He turned and said, "It's all right, you're okay in here. Calm down, please," but the wind lashed his voice away.

The train howled. Laura stepped across the gap between carriages. Her hair flailed about. She shouldered the door and it bent. One of the werewolves turned around. It saw Laura ramming the door again. Blood seeped from its mouth. It held a body in its claws, the face of the body torn away.

"Stop her," said one of the passengers, "stop her from breaking that door, or they can get in here."

Thorn ignored the man. He moved towards Laura.

The train wailed. The darkness outside lifted. They pulled into South Kensington. The breaks screeched. The train rattled. Laura crashed through the door. The train stopped. She stumbled into the carriage, slipping on blood and flesh.

The train's doors slid open. The passengers waiting on the platform had already seen the carnage. They were running and screaming.

The passengers in Thorn's carriage spilled out on to the platform and raced for the exit. Some fell and were trampled; some fought, punching and kicking to be first away.

Thorn saw Laura crouching on the bloody floor. Dead and dying passengers were the only ones left in the carriage. Thorn could hear the moans.

The three werewolves turned on Laura and bent down, as if ready to pounce. They growled and showed their teeth.

A siren howled. Screams echoed through the station. London Underground staff tried to hold back the tide of fleeing passengers, but they were swept up, or under, by the flood of bodies.

The werewolves moved towards Laura.

Thorn shouted her name. He went to his pocket. He got out the Browning. He thought about the policeman who told him to keep an extra gun. This was a "you-never-know" moment if there ever was one. He shouted Laura's name again.

The werewolves closed on her and Thorn felt the fear of losing her and he shouted and aimed the Browning.

He fired.

Laura leaped to her feet.

CHAPTER 83.
FLORIAN AND RUDI.

"THREE came in today," said Florian Duka into the mobile phone. "Ludmilla, Marinka, and Katya. Very pretty. Lithuanians. Very good fucks." He laughed. "They'll be at the house tomorrow. Yes, yes, Mr Bitri, you can try them out, for sure. Okay, Mr Bitri. Yes. Yes. We need new I.D., Mr Bitri. Our I.D. run out last month. We don't want to get deported, no? Okay. Okay. *Shihemi.*"

Rudi said, "That old bastard think he's going to get first go at the bitches again?"

"Yeah, yeah. He thinks they're virgins from Vilnius. He don't know they've been fucked all the way here."

The brothers laughed.

"Hey," said Rudi, "is he going to get us new I.D.?"

"He said yes."

"What this time?"

"What do you mean?"

"What country?"

Florian shrugged, pushing past a group of tourists and picking a man's pocket. He slipped out a wallet. Florian checked it out. "Full of dollars," he said. He had a look at the credit cards. "Mr Peter Yarrow."

"Who's that?"

"I don't fucking know." He tucked the wallet into his back pocket. "So, who we going to be?"

Rudi was asking about the fake identities Mr Bitri would sort out.

Mr Bitri sorted that out when the brothers arrived in England five years ago from Albania. They didn't want to bother with visas and all that kind of shit. They were illegals and that's how they'd stay: in the shadows and on the black market.

"I don't fucking know, Rudi. Greek like last time. Who gives a shit, as long as we're here making cash. Better than starving in fucking Tirana – look at these fucking tourists."

Trafalgar Square was clogged. He bumped past a few more holidaymakers. They turned to look, but Florian scowled and that soon had them cowering. He just wanted to get home, start drinking.

He and Rudi had met the courier at a Soho sex shop that morning. The courier, a Lithuanian, said that the girls had arrived and he showed pictures of them to Florian and Rudi. The girls had been promised work in London. They were told they'd be nannies. Rich British families loved Lithuanian nannies, said the woman in Vilnius who pretended to be an agent.

Florian paid the courier, then got the address where the girls were being kept that night. Florian and Rudi would pick them up in the morning; take them to the house in Kennington where they'd stay until they got too old or too ugly to make money.

The brothers had walked from Soho. They smoked and drank takeaway coffee. They headed for Charing Cross, where they'd pick up a Northern Line to Kennington. Florian thought he might visit the brothel, fuck the Nigerian bitch, then go home and get pissed.

"Hey, what's going on?" said Rudi.

Florian's mind had wandered. He said, "What?" but then the screams made him stop walking. A wave of people swept towards him. He could see things leap above the heads of the crowd. The leaping things were dark and very large. Animals of some kind. Shit – wild animals loose in London.

"What is it?" said Rudi, moving forward.

"No," said Florian, backing away, "Rudi, let's go back."

"Why? Something's happening."

"Rudi." He stepped backwards. The crowd rushed towards him. Rudi craned his neck to look over the human wave. Panic flushed Florian's body. His legs went weak. He called his brother again.

A memory switched on:

Rudi twelve years ago: he's ten-years-old and standing in the middle of the road; a blaring truck hurtling towards him; Florian shouting his name; Rudi laughing, saying it would be okay; Florian screaming, covering his eyes; Rudi diving out of the way at the last moment.

Florian ran towards his kid brother. He grabbed Rudi's arm. The crowd swarmed past them. Florian tried to say Rudi's name but the screams drowned his voice. Florian tried again, ready to scream, pulling at Rudi, but Rudi staying put, wanting to see, playing chicken with –

Florian's scream locked in his throat. Ice water seemed to wash through his veins. His bladder felt heavy and cold.

Monsters his mind couldn't name bounded through the crowd. These terrifying things sank their teeth into fleeing prey. They snapped their massive wolf-like heads from side to side, breaking their victims. Blood sprayed from the rag-doll humans in the creatures' mouths. If the animals couldn't bite, they slashed with razor-sharp claws. Chunks of meat flew around, spattering the streets.

Florian found his voice.

"Run, Rudi."

Florian yanked at his brother. But he stumbled, lost his grip. Florian ran a few yards and looked over his shoulder.

It's not a fucking truck, Rudi, he thought, as two of the monstrous animals bore down on his little brother.

Florian stopped running.

The wolf-things sprang into the air, fell on a screaming Rudi, and tore him to pieces.

Florian watched his brother's remains twitch, and his killers spread out into the crowd. Shivering, he turned slowly. He was breathless. He wanted to vomit. He started running.

He'd only taken three steps when something like a truck hit him in the back. The blow snapped his spine. It broke three of his ribs, one of which punctured his lung.

Florian couldn't breath. His throat was full of blood. The pain was horrific.

The monster hunched on Florian's shoulders and crushed him into the concrete. It growled and pressed its claws into his broken back. Florian started to scream and he emptied his bladder. Claws tore his back to shreds and opened him up for eating.

CHAPTER 84.
ANGEL.

KURI panted. It was so hard to breathe. She felt cold, too. But the pain had drifted away, and numbness spread over her.

She coughed and blood spurted from her mouth. She cringed, a stab of pain in her leg. She looked down at herself and cried. Kuri knew she was dying. Her right side had been ripped away, and she could see her ribs and her insides. Her left leg was mangled and twisted, a bone jutting out from her thigh. Her left arm was torn away, and veins and skin draped from the stump. The arm itself lay nearby. Kuri saw the colourful bangles and the yellow watch her mum gave her on her fifth birthday still wrapped around the wrist.

Kuri wept at her own dying. She made the word mother with her mouth but couldn't make the sound. The blood was too thick in her throat. She cried harder, knowing she'd never go home, knowing she'd never see her family again.

She turned her head and gasped. The carriage was like a slaughterhouse. She tried to say *Hama*, but again couldn't make the sound of the name. She tried to see if Hama was here, but all around her was blood and meat.

The men who'd become monsters were still here. Fear rattled through her. She wept and hoped they wouldn't notice her; let her die as she was.

Then, a woman rose up as if from the ground. She was dark haired and beautiful, and her eyes were yellow.

A loud crack made Kuri jerk. One of the monsters yelped and stumbled, blood spurting from its chest. The woman who had risen looked behind her. Then she turned back to face the monsters.

Kuri stared at the woman. Kuri's vision started to blur. She gasped, praying that she could hold on to life. Her eyes focused again. The woman had gone. A great, wolf-like creature towered above Kuri.

I have gone mad, Kuri thought, *and I've plunged into hell.*

And the wolf-creature hurled itself towards the monsters.

★ ★ ★

Thorn came through into the carriage. He flinched at the bloodbath. Broken bodies lay everywhere. Blood sprayed the walls. The smell was awful: the coppery odour of blood, the sour stink of piss.

The werewolf Laura fought with two of the monsters responsible for the carnage. Thorn had floored the other one with the Browning. The downed werewolf had turned back into a man. He writhed at the far end of the carriage. The bullet had blasted a hole in his chest and his skin was turning blue.

The werewolves battled. Thorn gritted his teeth. He raised the weapon and stepped back. It was an unbelievable site: had anyone told him a week ago that he'd be watching werewolves fight on London Underground, he'd have arrested them.

But here I am, he thought.

He tried to follow the combat, but it was hostile and frantic. The creatures, a whirl of fur, heaved from side to side, crashing into the carriage, tilting it on its wheels. Windows cracked under the force of impact; the carriage's structure bent and buckled.

One of the werewolves, the blonde one, was flung from the fight. Thorn took a shot at it, catching it in the thigh. It yelped and spun round to face Thorn. He fired again, the bullet hitting the animal in the shoulder.

The werewolf staggered. It wailed and keeled over. Thorn watched as the injured werewolf turned back into Ross Andersson.

A screech snapped Thorn out of his stare. The third werewolf lay dead, its throat torn out. A cold hand gripped his heart...but then the carcass transformed into a man; early twenties; brown hair.

The werewolf Laura hunkered down, breathing hard. She drooled, blood mixed with saliva pouring from her jaws.

Andersson moaned. Thorn bent down and grabbed the injured man's hair, dragging him across the carriage. Andersson screamed. Thorn crouched next to him and pressed the Browning's barrel into the wound in Andersson's shoulder. The young man squealed and Thorn pulled the barrel out.

He said, "Got one or two questions for you, Ross. If you don't come up with the right answer, I'll do that again – and I'll keep doing it until I hear something that sounds like the truth."

* * *

Kuri heard the screams and came out of unconsciousness.

The wolf-thing filled her vision. It loomed above her, looked down at her. Kuri started to shudder, thinking she was going to be eaten by this thing.

Please let me die quietly, she thought; *please let me slip away.*

She felt no pain. Her body was cold. She was tired and wanted to close her eyes and sleep, but she kept waking up.

The monster bent forward, pink spit spilling from its mouth. Kuri started to weep, seeing her mother's face, hearing her father's voice, mourning the fact that she would die a virgin.

The monster's contours softened and the beautiful dark-haired woman knelt over Kuri. Kuri furrowed her brow. She didn't understand how this happened: how this woman changed into an animal and then changed back; how those men – the blonde one who she wanted to like – had changed the same way.

The beautiful woman smiled at Kuri. The woman's face and mouth were bloody but her smile was lovely. Kuri smiled back. The woman touched Kuri's face and Kuri felt the hand on her cheek; she hadn't expected to feel it because she couldn't feel anything else – but it was gentle and kind.

The woman said something but Kuri didn't hear and if she'd heard she would not have understood...*I'm going to learn English and come here and be English.*

She asked the woman if she was an angel, but the words didn't come out.

Somehow the woman understood, because she smiled and nodded.

And Kuri closed her eyes and slipped away.

CHAPTER 85.
WOLVES WILL FIGHT MEN.

EIGHT werewolves hunted in Trafalgar Square.

Five attacked from the south side; the other three came from the north. They circled the crowd, pushing them into a huddle. Many of the prey escaped: there were thousands in the square and only eight werewolves, so the odds of survival were high.

But the monsters caught dozens. They killed swiftly. This was a hunt for pleasure, not a hunt for food. They tore out throats with their teeth; they slashed out hearts with their claws.

It was rapid and brutal. They took whoever was nearest: men, women, children; it didn't matter. The crowd's screams swept across London. Helicopters growled overhead, watching the carnage. Tourists brandishing video cameras filmed the attack. Some got too close and recorded their own deaths. Others took photographs, amazed at what they were capturing.

A policeman screamed for back-up. He tried to stem the tide of panic, but was trampled to death. Another officer managed to get a call in. Sirens wailed in the distance. The policeman's colleague at the station said there'd been a report of an "animal attack" on the Underground at South Kensington.

"What the hell's going on?" said the policeman.

"I don't know. We've heard it's a bloodbath," said the operator.

"The crowd's going crazy. Jesus, what is that thing?"

"What do you see?"

"I – I don't know what it is? A huge animal. Like a – like a wolf but it's – Jesus, it's coming this way – Christ – like a giant wolf on – fuck, fuck – two legs."

"Oh, my God, are you running?"

"Yes – Christ – Oh, Jes – "

The operator had to throw her headset aside. The roar of the beast and the scream of its victim deafened her.

999 calls jammed the lines.

Story-hungry editors ordered TV crews to the scene.

The Underground was closed. Trains stopped where they were, and passengers stuck in tunnels had to be guided out by torchlight. There was panic, there was anger, there was confusion; fights broke out between anyone in a uniform and the pissed off public.

Tell us what's going on, they said.

We don't know, said officials.

Why do we have to walk through this fucking dark tunnel?

I'm sorry, but that's what we've been told.

Their fury echoed through the earth.

And in that earth, along the tunnels, in the shadows, a fabled animal hurtled towards its fate.

CHAPTER 86.
MARATHON MAN.

THORN ran from the station to the address he got out of Ross. The streets were clogged. The passengers who'd flooded out of the station milled around. Police tried to move them on. Thorn pretended to be a commuter, shoving through the police ranks. Cops barged past him into the station, down towards the platforms.

They'd find hell down there. Ten to a dozen dead commuters; at least two naked dead men – three, if Ross hadn't made it, and it didn't look good for him.

Thorn, leaving the chaos at the station behind him, thought about what he'd done to Ross. It terrified him that he could be so cruel: he tortured a wounded man. He tried to forget it. But his brutality stayed with him. It would always stay with him – a stain on his memory.

Could he live with it?

Yes, he thought, quickening his pace; *yes, I can live with it. If what I did saves a life, I can easily live with it.*

Ross said Michael and the others were headed for Trafalgar Square. He said they could all turn into werewolves, and Michael was going to kill as many people as he could – he wanted to be all-powerful.

Ross hadn't been very brave – but pain can bring the coward out in most people.

Thorn pushed on. His lungs burned. His legs filled with lactic acid. Adrenalin kept him going. He wove through pedestrians. They watched him, moving out of his way. He sensed panic in them. It was as if the crowd that spilled from the Underground had infected the rest of the population with fear.

Some passers-by were looking up. They were huddled together. Thorn threw a glance upwards. Helicopters filled the sky.

Thorn ran on. He panted, and sweat plastered his clothes to his body. The Browning was tucked into his belt.

Police cars whizzed by. Sirens blared across the city. Screams choked the air.

It sounds like a war, he thought – they must think Armageddon's coming; the end of the world; Y2K four months early. The prophets of doom would be saying, "We were right all along – this is the end time."

Thorn turned into a street of four-storey Georgian houses. The silence stopped him. The screams, the sirens, and the helicopters' roar dimmed.

He bent forward, putting his hands on his knees. He breathed hard and listened to his heartbeat. He closed his eyes and steadied his breathing. The pulse throbbing in his ears slowed down. Thorn took a deep breath and straightened. He looked around. Expensive cars lined the street. Iron bars fronted the houses. A row of trees ran down the centre of the road. The pavements stood empty.

He walked down the street, checking the doors...52...50...48...46 ...44...42 –

A helicopter rumbled overhead. Thorn instinctively ducked and looked up. The helicopter was quite low. It swept away, the growl of its rotors fading.

Thorn stopped outside No. 38. He touched the Browning.

He hoped Elena was here – if she wasn't, he had no Plan B.

Thorn stepped up to the door and knocked.

★ ★ ★

Ruth, getting out of bed, said, "Shouldn't you be with Michael?"

"He'll be fine," said Craig, rolling over to reach for a cigarette.

She pulled on a dressing gown. "Do you have to smoke?"

"It's traditional after sex."

Craig smiled. He lit the fag. He laid there, his broad chest bare and covered with silver hair. He slid a hand under the sheet and scratched his balls.

He said, "Tell whoever it is to sod off and then come back to bed."

"No," she said, going to the door. "You've got to go and see if Michael's all right. He told you to go with him."

"*Told* me? No one *tells* me."

"He's paying you, Ray, so he can tell. Get up, get dressed."

She stormed out of the bedroom and slammed the door behind her. She was regretting this already. How had she found herself in bed with Ray Craig? Twenty years ago, perhaps; but she was almost sixty.

I still look good, though, she thought, drifting past the mirror at the top of the stairs.

It was Michael who made her horny. She felt ashamed after sleeping with her nephew, her brother's son; but the sex was astonishing. Young men were often better – but Michael's strength, his passion, his energy, drove her wild.

Craig came on to her that morning after Michael and the boys had left.

The memory of Michael remained, and it made her dizzy, so she said, "All right, Ray – but hurry up," and led him upstairs to Ross's bedroom.

Craig was solid meat and muscle: wide across the shoulders and chest, heavy around the hips and thighs. He spread her 'til it hurt, but the hurt was good.

But that was it – once was enough with Ray Craig this time.

She trotted downstairs checking herself in the full-length mirrors Ross had placed at the top of each flight. She tightened the dressing gown's belt around her waist. *Who can that be?* she thought. *Maybe it's Ross, or Michael.*

A cold hand grabbed her insides and twisted. She gasped, put a hand to her belly.

What if something had happened to Ross, to her baby?

She'd kill anyone who would hurt her boy.

Her Ross: the handsome, blonde angel who made her so happy. The blonde came from his dad. Skipp was Swedish, a former Member of the European Parliament who worked for an oil company. His work kept him away from London. Ruth and he had drifted apart. They were separated but stayed together for show. She loved him, but found him tedious. She'd often been unfaithful during their thirty-year marriage. The affairs were always about sex, though; never love. She only felt love for her brother and her children. Catherine was in the States, an attorney; Ross was in limbo, a boy.

A pang of shame rushed through her: how could she have been bucking and moaning under Craig while her son was in peril?

She thought about Ross; about Michael. Had they changed, yet? Were they doing the stupid things Michael wanted them to do? Ruth had warned them against the plans. It would draw attention.

But Michael said, *Who'll know it's us?*

They may shoot you, she said; but he said they'd have to catch him first.

Michael knew he and his cousins would be faster and stronger and brighter than any animal – including humans.

He said that if things went badly they'd use their speed to run away, quickly change back into human form – and come home for tea. He'd laughed and reached for her, and she'd brushed his hand away despite wanting him again.

She got to the front door and swept a hand through her hair. She pulled the collars of the dressing gown together at her throat and opened the door. She stared at the gun pointing at her face.

CHAPTER 87.
TUNNEL VISION.

SHE sniffed her way through the tunnel. The scent of panic got stronger. Screams filtered into the Underground.

The werewolf knew she was getting closer.

She scanned the darkness ahead and it started to lift. She came to the mouth of a tunnel and pressed her body against the tunnel wall. She sniffed and peered around the corner. A train stood abandoned. The platform lay empty.

She ran from the tunnel and leaped on the platform.

Shouts and screams wafted down the stairs and the werewolf bounded up the stairs towards the noise.

A crowd clustered at the station entrance. They were trying to move up the stairs that led out into the street. Someone in the crowd turned and saw her. They screamed and pushed against those in front. A shriek rifled through the group. They ran, some pouring out of the station, others scrabbling right and left over barriers, down to the platforms – anywhere to get away from this monster.

She moved forward and then crept up the narrow stairs. People saw her, and they screamed. They ran from her, stumbling and tripping.

She came out into the street and watched the crowd spread.

Someone said, "They're everywhere. What are they?"

A bus lay overturned. Passengers squeezed out of the windows. Smoke streamed from under the vehicle. Cars tottered on their roofs. Two taxis had crashed head-on, their bonnets like concertinas.

She stalked into the square and the crowd made way for her. The fear she instilled was good; it kept people out of her way. She looked up at the towering column at the front of the square. Pigeons perched on the statue at the top of the column.

Snarls filled the air, mixing with the screams and shouts.

She moved forward, her gaze ranging the area.

She saw them, eight rampaging monsters hunting, stalking, and killing in Trafalgar Square. They were all different colours – the colours of their human hair. Two red ones; a blonde one; three light brown; one a darker shade of brown – and a black one, prowling around, watching the carnage. The black one was the only finished monster – a werewolf as perfect as she was. The others were ugly, imperfect – but still lethal.

A woman stood in one of the fountains trying to protect some children. Two of the monsters moved towards her, their backs arched, their faces close to the ground. They were ready to pounce. The children screamed.

CHAPTER 88.
GUNS AND GIRLS.

THORN, following her up the stairs, apologised for pointing the gun at her.

"It's not something I enjoy doing," he said.

"It seems to me, Mr Thorn, that it gives you great joy."

"I'm sorry, Mrs Andersson, but I can't trust you."

"Rightly so."

"Where is she?"

"Who?"

"Don't play with me, Ruth."

"Ruth now, is it?"

"I know she's here. Ross told me."

The woman stopped. Thorn, still moving, pressed the barrel into her spine. He drew it away. She glanced at him in the mirror at the top of the first flight of stairs. He saw the fear in her eyes.

She said, "Where did you see him?"

"Show me where Elena is, and I'll tell you."

She spun round, a hand on the banister. Her knuckles were white. She leaned forward. Glaring at Thorn, she said, "Tell me. I don't care about you, or Elena McIntyre, or me – tell me about Ross."

Thorn swallowed. "He was on the Underground. He was killing people, Ruth. He was" – he looked away, trying to find the right word – "a werewolf."

Ruth straightened. "Was he beautiful?"

"Beautiful? He was an animal. I don't understand any of this, but your son was an animal."

"But was he beautiful? Was he a beautiful wolf?"

"As wolves go, I guess he was all right – not my type, that's all."

"You spoke to him. Where is he, now?"

"I made him tell me – "

"Made him? What did you do to him?"

"Nothing. This" – and he jabbed the gun at her – "pointed the gun, that's all, and he said where Elena was. Now – "

"Where is he?"

"He...got away. Turned into a...and got away...down the tunnel."

Her eyes narrowed. "If you're lying, I'll kill you."

"Fine. Show me where Elena's at, Ruth. I'm getting fed up with you and your family. You're all making me a bit edgy."

She led him up another flight of stairs. A mirror was pinned to the wall here, as well. He saw himself in the mirror; he was pointing the gun at Ruth. He dropped his arm to his side.

At the top of the third flight of stairs, staring into yet another full-length mirror, Thorn said, "You like to look at yourself, Ruth."

"This is Ross's house. He likes to see who's sneaking up behind him."

They got to the fourth floor. Ruth pointed to a door and said, "She's in there."

"Lead the way."

She did, and they went in. He took the pillowcase off Elena's head and asked her if she was all right, and Elena nodded. He asked Ruth for the key to the handcuffs, but Ruth said she didn't have them. Thorn ripped the pipe that the cuffs were attached to from the wall. The water hissed out. He slid the cuff off the pipe.

Thorn held the gun on Ruth. "You stay there 'til we're gone," he said to her.

He backed out of the room, supporting Elena.

A shadow swept over the wall behind Ruth. Thorn ducked, turned, but he was too late. Someone grabbed his hair, yanked him out of the room, and tossed him against the banister.

CHAPTER 89.
BRIT HEG.

WHEN the demons came, Brit and Alrik Heg moved the children into the fountain and cowered with them under the arc of water.

They watched the horror and Alrik said, "We must pray. All pray," and they started to pray. Alrik said the Lord's Prayer; Brit started on Psalm 23; the children screamed for their mothers.

Brit came to the part about the valley of death and thought, *I am here; this is the valley the psalmist sings about.*

The hellish creatures looked like dogs and bears and humans all mixed together. *They are the Devil's breed,* thought Brit, *monsters made by Satan as he begins his war against God.*

The end days are here, she thought.

The millennium was months away, but this was the start of the great tribulation. And it would culminate in the return of the Lord Jesus Christ.

But we will have to suffer before we are saved, Alrik had always said.

And he was right – he was always right. Alrik knew God, and he knew man; Alrik knew everything.

The monsters raced around Trafalgar Square, hunting down the scattering crowd. They picked off stragglers, pulling them down and quickly killing them with teeth or claws. She tried to shield the children's eyes from the carnage, but she had ten youngsters in her charge; ten young souls to protect for God.

Their parents had said, *Will they be safe in that den of iniquity?*

Alrik promised that the children would be perfectly safe. Their church was conservative. Members regarded Stockholm, which was twenty miles away from their heartland, as a hell-hole; so to bring the children to London was a terrible risk.

But Alrik said, *We must go out into the world and show the children the great cities before they fall to the Devil.*

And the parents, tutting, chewing their nails, said, *All right, our children can go – but please keep them safe.*

Alrik nodded and said that God would keep them safe.

"Please, God, keep us safe," said Brit, drenched in the fountain.

"Oh, Lord in Heaven," said Alrik, his voice high pitched.

Brit saw what scared him. One of the monsters – an ugly, terrifying beast covered on coarse red hair – stalked towards them.

Alrik held his arms out, protecting Brit and the children behind him. Water rushed over them. Fear made Brit shake.

The monster stood on its back legs and seemed to grin at them. Its teeth were sharp and long. He lunged into the fountain. Water erupted around him. The children shrieked. Alrik yelled for God's help. Brit's scream locked in her throat.

The monster's jaws clamped around Alrik's thigh, and Alrik screamed.

Brit reached out, yelling her husband's name as he was dragged through the water. But she couldn't go after him; she couldn't leave the children, who were shaking and yelling and crying in the fountain. And Brit watched as the Devil's breed shook her husband by his leg.

His body flailed like a rag doll and he screeched.

The monster slammed Alrik's body against the ground and a terrible thud made Brit shudder. Alrik jerked and was still. Brit felt as if her heart had been torn out and she started to weep, staring at her dead husband. The screams filling the square dimmed as she focused on her own pain.

"Mrs Heg, Mrs Heg," said a voice, and she turned. Eleven-year-old Johan tugged her sleeve and pointed. She followed his finger and saw that the red-furred beast that killed Alrik had been joined by another monster; this one coated in brown hair, muscles bulging from its huge hindquarters.

The animals prowled towards Brit and the children.

She tried to press the children together; to compress them into a little ball of safety.

"God will protect us," she said, "God will keep us safe." But the children's screams showed they didn't believe her. And she wasn't sure if she believed it herself anymore.

The two monsters bore down on her and the youngsters. They would leap into the fountain and be on them in a second. Her legs trembled. She had no strength left; fear wracked her body.

God, she knew, had abandoned them.

And then, from the corner of her eye, she saw hope.

She turned to look. A lean, black wolf-like creature – more perfect; more beautiful than the ones rampaging through the square – sped towards them.

She looked at the two creatures approaching the fountain. They toyed with her. They seemed to be grinning, showing their teeth. They snapped and lashed out with their claws.

A flash of black barrelled into the pair.

Brit's eyes weren't quick enough to capture what happened. But her gaze chased after the furious, rolling mass of animals. The creatures crashed into a stone wall and separated. The red-fur and the brown-fur seemed dizzy. The black-fur sprang forward. It killed the red-fur with a bite to the throat. The brown-fur attacked, slashing with its claws. It struck the black animal across the shoulder. Blood splashed on the concrete.

The black struck out. The blow sent the brown sprawling, and before it could get to its feet, the black pounced on it. The black sunk its teeth into the back of the brown-fur's neck and shook it to death.

Brit watched, open-mouthed. The black-fur moved away, looking around. Blood poured from its shoulder. Brit looked back at the dead monsters. The monsters were gone, and two dead men lay in their place.

She almost fainted. She couldn't breath. She tried to avert the children's eyes, telling them to look away – not because the scene was any bloodier than she'd expect it to be, but because the men were naked.

This is truly hell, she thought.

Men have become monsters.

She scanned the square. People were running and screaming. She watched them being killed. Her eyes darted around and stopped at the Fourth Plinth that stood at the north-west corner.

A plinth stood at each corner of the square. She'd learned all about them before coming over here; it was something to tell the children.

Three of the plinths sported statues of Napier and Havelock, two British generals; and King George IV. A bronze of King William IV was supposed to have been placed on the Fourth Plinth, but the government ran out of money – so the platform had been empty for over a century.

Until today.

A monster had clambered on top of the pedestal. The creature reared up on its two hind legs. It craned its neck and looked up at the sky.

The monster howled.

The call whipped out over the noise of slaughter that filled the square and swept across the city.

★ ★ ★

Laura, in her werewolf shape, flinched as Michael bayed.

She turned to glare his way, and she snarled. His call was a call of triumph; of dominance – but she was ready to challenge that authority.

Pain shot through her back. She reared up and yelped. She leaped away, and twisted round to face her attacker. The second red-haired werewolf lunged towards her. His slashing claws dripped blood, her blood. The creature came for her, and she staggered away. Something struck her from behind. Her neck whiplashed. She was hurled across the square. She crashed against the base of the tall column, and bucked, throwing off her attacker.

She turned on him, growling.

His fur was dark brown. His face had fully developed into its wolf-shape, but the ears were still human.

A growl made her snap her head to the right. The red-coated werewolf who slashed her came bounding over.

Her back and shoulder throbbed. She knew she was bleeding, badly injured after fighting only two of them – now she faced these two, and another four who were still rampaging around the square.

The red-fur leaped. She ducked and it smashed into the concrete column. The thing yelped and sagged. The dark brown attacked, charging her on all fours. She met him face on. He sank his teeth into her arm. She pushed her arm into his mouth, and they rolled and rolled.

When they stopped, she grabbed the back of his neck and shoved her arm deeper into his mouth.

Teeth sank into her flesh. Blood oozed from her wounds.

His jaw stretched. His eyes showed white. He thrashed, but she was too strong. She jammed her limb deeper into his mouth. His jaw, wide open, cracked. He jerked and clawed at her, but she held him. And when his struggles stopped, she sniffed him and saw he was dead.

She skulked away and watched him turn human. The point of his jaw rested on his chest. His cheeks were split up to his ears.

She turned to the red-fur. He was on all fours, shaking his head. She went for him and clamped her jaws around his throat, whipped her head from side to side and let his limp body slip from her grasp. She sniffed him and then moved away.

★ ★ ★

"They're werewolves," said someone.

Another voice said, "They're men, look, they're changing back into men."

And Brit saw that the red and the dark brown that died over at the foot of Nelson's column had become human again.

They become human in death, she thought. Maybe it's God claiming them back from the Devil. The Devil makes them monsters; God makes them men.

But what about that one?

Brit's gaze followed the black-fur that saved her life and the lives of the children.

She's not from the Devil.

"Werewolves, they're werewolves," said another voice.

Brit looked around. Three of the Devil's breed were still marauding and killing, and the fourth stood on the plinth; but Brit gambled that it was safe for her to lead the children away from the fountain.

"We must go," she said.

"No, no, we're safe here," said Gala, a nine-year-old with a mind of her own.

"Gala, you lead the children. Take my hand."

"No, Mrs Heg, no – "

"Yes, Gala," said Johan, and he took Gala's hand and another child

345

took Gala's other hand. And they made a chain, following Brit out of the water.

"Run and don't look at the bodies," said Brit, "it is disrespectful to look at the dead."

And a daisy chain of kids, led by Brit, left a trail of water as they wove through the carcasses spread around the square.

Brit led them towards the crowd, and as the crowd parted to let them through she heard voices saying, "Armed police! Armed police! Get down!"

CHAPTER 90.
PUNCHBAG.

PAIN pulsed through Thorn's head. He saw stars and someone called his name. He got kicked in the ribs. He gasped and rolled on the floor. The breath had been knocked out of him.

Writhing on the carpet, he opened his eyes.

A large man wearing boxer shorts smiled down at him. The man stood wide and tall. Muscles swelled under his tattooed skin. His silver hair was in a crewcut. Scars crisscrossed his sunburned face.

Thorn looked across the landing. Ruth and Elena tussled. Ruth grabbed Elena's hair and twisted her into a headlock. Elena struggled, but Ruth punched her in the face.

Ruth said, "Kill him, Craig."

The large man said, "My pleasure," and he leaned down to reach for Thorn.

Thorn threw a fist. It caught Craig in the nose. Craig's eyes rolled back in his head and his nose went flat against his face. He stumbled back and his knees buckled.

Thorn struggled to his feet. The pain in his side made it hard for him to breathe.

Craig shook his head and blood splashed from his nose. "Bastard," he said, "bastard."

Thorn reached for the Browning. He patted his belt. He looked down and saw that the gun was gone. He darted looks around the landing. The gun lay between the banisters. It teetered on the edge.

Thorn lunged for the gun. Craig grabbed him, spun him around, and slammed him against the wall. Thorn grunted, the pain in his ribs almost making him pass out. Craig clutched him round the throat and lifted him off his feet.

Craig tried to headbutt him but Thorn turned away and took the blow on his cheek. It hurt, but it was better than being smacked in the nose.

Craig punched him in the stomach, and Thorn bent double, his chin resting on Craig's shoulder.

Thorn bit the man's ear. Craig screeched and pulled himself away, leaving part of his ear in Thorn's mouth. Thorn spat out the blood and the ear.

"What are you doing?" said Ruth. "Finish him off."

Craig squinted in pain. He put a hand over his ear. Blood leaked between his fingers. "He bit my fucking ear off."

He charged Thorn.

Elena pushed her head out of the crook of Ruth's arm. Ruth turned to face her. Elena swung an arm and caught Ruth on the temple. Ruth staggered away.

Craig hurtled.

Thorn kicked out.

He caught Craig in the balls. Craig folded in two, but his weight shoved Thorn back towards the top of the stairs, and Thorn almost rolled down. He grabbed the banister and pulled himself upright.

"The gun," he said to Elena, and Elena looked for the gun and went for it.

Craig, his face red, stood up straight. He grimaced. "I'm going to kill you a thousand times over, you fucking pig. You're going to beg me for death after I've finished with you." And Craig came for him.

Elena picked up the gun.

Thorn dragged himself upright and kicked out at Craig, but the large man body-slammed Thorn against the wall. He grabbed Thorn by the lapels, tossed him across the landing.

Craig turned on Elena. He held out his hand. "Give me the gun, bitch."

She pointed the Browning at him.

Thorn pulled himself to his feet. He ached all over. If he could only lie down, go to sleep, wake up when it was all done.

Craig said, "Give me the gun," and stepped forward.

Elena pulled the trigger. Craig yelped. His knee exploded in blood and bone. He bent down and grabbed his leg, saying, "You bitch."

Thorn rushed him, but Craig saw him coming and swiped out an arm. A fist struck Thorn under the chin. Stars whizzed in front of his eyes, and he spun away.

"You've crippled me," said Craig.

Thorn kicked out, caught Craig in the back of his bad knee. The man screamed and toppled over, crashing into the banister. The wood creaked.

Ruth had got up. She came flying for Elena. Elena swung the gun like a hammer. She smashed Ruth in the face, and Ruth crashed to the floor.

Craig stood on one leg, staring at Thorn. "The more you hurt me," said Craig, "the more I'm going to hurt you – and you've hurt me pretty bad."

Craig hopped towards him. Thorn ducked down and threw himself at the large man, rugby tackling him. Craig wheezed and stumbled backwards. He crashed into the banister and the banister snapped. Craig clutched at thin air and he shouted and fell.

Thorn, getting up, heard wood crack and then a thump as Craig hit the hallway floor.

CHAPTER 91.
PAUL FRENCH/
NICK NEVILLE.

INSPECTOR Paul French barged through the crowd.

His team of authorised firearms officers had spent ten minutes trying to get through the sea of people. It was chaos. The guys had spilled out of the armed response vehicle on Whitehall. They spread out and tried to force their way through the throng.

French held his Benelli M3 shotgun above his head. His body armour protected him from the elbows and fists carelessly thrown at him as he pressed on.

It was stifling. He hated the heat, he hated confined spaces and crowds – this was a nightmare.

Finally, he pushed through. He looked for his colleagues. He could hear voices saying, "Armed Police! Armed Police! Get down!" but that didn't get them through; they were stuck in that crowd.

French moved towards the square.

Unarmed colleagues rushed in from Northumberland Avenue to his right. *Here's crowd control*, he thought. They started to hem the crowd, creating an open space in the square. A few stragglers were running around, crashing through the fountains, racing around Nelson's column, trying to escape the –

Fuck me, he thought.

The animal stood on the Fourth Plinth at the north-west corner. It looked like a wolf or a bear; it was huge. It howled up at the helicopters hovering above the square.

And then –

"Fuck me," he said aloud.

Two monstrous things fought in the middle of the square. They rolled around, one black, the other brown. Blood sprayed as they slashed and bit each other. French heard them yelp and howl.

At the south-west corner, another bear-wolf thing was racing after people, and when it caught them they screeched before being killed.

What the hell is this?

"They're werewolves, officer," said a voice.

French turned.

A man in an Iron Maiden T-shirt was pointing at the square. "Can you see?" he said. "They're werewolves. I'm telling you. Werewolves in London – in Trafalgar Square."

French looked back at the square. Dead bodies lay scattered about. The pigeons had returned to see if they could scavenge some food.

Cartwright broke through the crowd about twenty yards away and said, "Let's get them, Frenchie."

They moved forward, shotguns at their shoulders.

Someone said, "Don't shoot the black one. It saved some people. It saved some kids. It's trying to help."

"Yeah," said a man, "leave it alone."

French turned and said to a policewoman, "Tell those people to keep quiet."

The policewoman nodded. But then her face showed terror. And the people behind her screamed. They pointed at French and French turned to see what had startled them.

A massive, sand-coloured creature dashed towards him.

★ ★ ★

Nick Neville said, "Get lower, for fuck's sake, get lower."

"Can't do that," said the helicopter pilot, "Civil Aviation Authority regulations."

"Fuck that. Get lower. We need shots."

"Come on, Nick," said Jed Long, "sort this guy out."

Nick peered round the pilot's seat. "Listen, mate, I'll give you extra. Just take us down. If we get the shots, we'll get paid – and then you'll have a couple of grand, cash in hand."

"I really shouldn't."

"'Shouldn't' is bollocks. 'Shouldn't' is for poofs."

"Shouldn't" didn't exist when Nick, Jed, and Dave "The Dog" Daniels – also in the 'copter – hired a car in Paris almost two years ago and chased a Merc into that tunnel. "Shouldn't" didn't get them those shots in the tunnel that no one will touch for a few years. "Shouldn't" never got Nick that pad in L.A. and a porn star girlfriend.

"Fuck 'shouldn't'," he said, "take us down."

They'd been tracking some bird said to be shagging a married England footballer. The Daily Mail put Nick on to it; Jed trailed her for The Sun; and The Dog was pay-rolled by The People. But if someone else offered them more cash, they'd go for the money. The editors wanted pictures, and they'd pay big bucks for them – they couldn't give a shit how they got them. They'd slag off the paparazzi in public then send them out a-hunting.

Nick, Jed, and The Dog had been hanging around outside a hotel in Victoria to pap this bird. Nick picked up a message on the police frequency. It reported "an incident in Trafalgar Square," "mass panic," "civilian deaths."

Nick, Jed, and The Dog hopped in a cab. *London Heliport in Battersea,* said Nick.

Rapid, said The Dog.

In the cab, Nick rang ahead to book a helicopter.

He was told they were busy, today – lots of hires; but they had one available.

The four mile journey to the heliport took twenty-two minutes. Fifteen minutes later they were swooping over Trafalgar Square and the three paps were going, "Fucking hell, look at that."

Thousands spilled down The Mall, Whitehall, up St Martin's Place, Pall Mall. The crowds abandoned Trafalgar Square.

Hovering two hundred feet above the chaos, Nick told the pilot again to take it lower.

"We want shots," said The Dog. "We'll pay buckets if you take us low. This guy" – he nudged Nick – "is richer than Al Fayed."

"All right," said the pilot. "I'll have to keep an eye on that police 'copter, though. If he tells me to fuck off, I'm fucking off."

"Yeah, yeah, whatever," said Nick. "Down we go."

And the helicopter dropped. Nick held on to his seat as the ground rushed towards him. The crowds grew clearer. The animals going berserk down there became detailed. The Dog and Jed started shooting. Nick aimed his camera.

They went lower and Nick could see the 'copter's shadow on the ground. Rubbish scattered. Pigeons flapped away. Armed cops waved their guns. The crowds ducked.

Nick rattled off some pictures: dead bodies, animals rampaging, crowds fleeing.

He ranged the camera around the square and rested it on the large, black animal perched on the Fourth Plinth. It was looking straight up at him.

"Look at that thing," he said, resting the camera in his lap.

The Dog said, "What the fuck is it?"

"Looks like a – I dunno – wolf or bear?" said Jed.

"Bit lower," said Nick, and the pilot dropped it. They were barely thirty feet off the ground. The rotors caused a whirlwind.

The Dog said, "Werewolves."

"Bollocks," said Jed.

Nick took a picture of the – What was it? A werewolf?

The creature, whatever it was, raised up. It stared up at the helicopter. It's fur rippled in the force of the helicopter's rotor blades.

"I can see its eyes," said Nick.

The werewolf squatted.

"What's it doing?" said The Dog. "Having a piss?"

"No – fuck, no," said Nick, "it's – "

And the werewolf leaped, stretching its arms above its head.

The pilot tried to swoop away. But he was too slow. The werewolf grabbed the landing gear. The 'copter slanted. Nick yelled and fell against the loading door. His face was pressed against the glass. He looked into the werewolf's eyes. Nick took its picture. The monster yanked at the landing gear. The helicopter tipped from side to side.

The pilot screamed, saying he was losing control.

And the 'copter started to plummet.

★ ★ ★

French raised his shotgun. Cartwright screamed for him to get out of the way. French heard gunfire but the sand-coloured animal still pelted towards him. He aimed; he pulled the trigger.

353

The gun jammed.

French's throat went dry and his bladder sagged.

More gunfire; his colleagues trying to kill the monster.

French heard screams.

He raised his arm over his face. The monster pounced. French saw its face – almost human; almost wolf.

I'm going to die, he thought.

A streak of black shot from his left, crashing into the monster and sweeping it away.

The werewolves tumbled, snarling and snapping at each other. A voice from the crowd said, "It saved *your* life, now, copper," and someone else said, "It's killing them all."

French watched the fight. He'd seen the black-fur fight and kill another monster in the centre of the square moments before. The woman in the crowd was right: this thing was attacking and killing the other creatures. *Maybe it's defending the people,* thought French.

"Jesus Christ, look at that," said Cartwright.

And French saw the helicopter.

It was spiralling towards the ground. He recognised it: a Eurocopter 120 Colibri. French got a helicopter lesson for his birthday a few years ago, and that was the type he had flown.

He and Cartwright ran towards the centre of the square. A huge black shape latched on to the 'copter's landing gear. The thing wrenched at the landing gear, making the pilot lose control.

"Shit, it's going to crash," said French.

The black thing dived away from the spinning 'copter. The machine hit the concrete. Screams as the people nearby tried to get away.

The 'copter exploded.

French cowered.

A fireball filled the square. One of the creatures, a brown-coated animal, was swallowed by the blast. The people he chased were cooked alive. A rotor blade spun out of the blaze and hacked into Nelson's statue. Tongues of fire lashed out of the inferno. The flames spouted over nearby buildings. The National Gallery started to burn. St-Martin's-in-the-Field-Church caught fire.

"Frenchie," said Cartwright, and French turned.

The black-fur that saved his life stood over the naked body of a young blonde man. Blood oozed from the black-fur's jaw. Wounds gashed its hide.

French raised his Benelli.

"No," said a chorus from the crowd, and a woman said, "It saved your life."

A man said, "It's human inside – look at the one it's just killed. It's human."

"Hold your fire," said French into the mike.

"What the fuck's going on?" said a voice in his ear.

French didn't answer; he didn't know. He watched the black-fur. It was sniffing the air. It looked towards the bonfire cracking and spitting between the fountains. Burning debris littered the area.

French scanned his surroundings. The crowd skirted the square like an audience watching a blood sport.

A howl broke through the tempest of noise, and French followed the call.

The black-fur that brought the helicopter down prowled Trafalgar Square. The bodies, the wreckage, the fires made the area look like a war zone.

The werewolf – he was calling it that, now; he didn't know any other word for it – that had saved his life bolted.

"They're going to fight," said Cartwright.

"We should kill them," said a voice in French's ear.

He said, "Hold your fire."

He didn't know why; he should be putting these animals down – they were a threat to the public. But the striking, sleek, powerful creature that saved French moments ago had looked him in the eye. And French saw human in there. The man in the crowd was right – it *was* human inside.

The two black-furs charged at each other. Teeth bared, they pounded the ground and clashed. The impact made French recoil. The animals rolled and snarled. They became one, a whipping cloud of black sweeping across the square.

They sliced through the water in the fountains, and the water separated. They crashed through burning metal, tumbled over fallen masonry. They slashed and hacked at each other, their yelps echoing across Trafalgar Square.

French said, "Move in," and his team started to approach the fight zone.

Uniformed officers tried to hold back the crowd. It's like a football match, thought French. The crowd cheered; they had their favourite.

"Can you tell the difference?" said Cartwright.

French said he couldn't: it was a mass of fur and dust and blood.

He couldn't let this go on. He'd get a lashing from his chiefs at Scotland Yard.

"Close in," he said into his mike, and he watched as his team pressed forward.

CHAPTER 92.
RUNNING ON EMPTY.

THE explosion rose over the buildings and the blast from it swept over the city.

"What the hell was that?" said the cab driver.

Thorn had been leaning on the driver's window, trying to persuade her to take him to Trafalgar Square. She wouldn't; said they'd never get through – the whole of London's gridlocked. Then the explosion hit.

And Thorn started to run towards it.

He'd left Elena in Kensington. She couldn't keep up with him, so he had said she should keep her head down; find a Starbucks, drink some coffee. He rang 999 anonymously and told them to get to the Andersson house.

Life still pulsed through Craig. He lay broken at the bottom of the stairs, and Thorn didn't want to leave him dying, so he'd called the cops. Ruth had been knocked out. She'd be all right. She wouldn't want police crawling all over the place, so their arrival would certainly piss her off. The thought cheered Thorn.

The roads were clogged with traffic and people. He'd raced through Knightsbridge, trying to hail cabs that were stuck in jams.

A fight broke out near the Harvey Nicholls store, and the two brawlers crashed through the shop's window. Passers-by spilled in and nicked a couple of dummies draped in expensive clothes.

Thorn ran on adrenalin. Each time he stopped, the pain in his body became apparent. His head throbbed and his ribs ached. Blood dried on his face and he limped.

"I'm a hospital case," he said to Elena before leaving her, "but I can't put myself back together until this is done."

He hobbled through Knightsbridge and made it to Hyde Park Corner. Londoners and tourists packed the place out. They listened to preachers of doom predicting the end of the world. Thorn believed for the first time that these prophets could be telling the truth.

Shoving through the crowd, Thorn remembered Elena's directions: "Up Constitution Hill, which is closed on Sunday, past Buckingham Palace – "

And Thorn wondered if The Queen would be watching her country's end from the balcony.

" – straight up The Mall, through Admiralty Arch, and you're there – Trafalgar Square."

"How long will it take me?"

She said it could take up to an hour, the state he was in.

He saw the taxi at the junction with Constitution Hill. He leaned on the window and panted over the driver. She tried to roll up her window, but Thorn said, "Please...please can you take me to Trafalgar Square."

The crowd streamed up Constitution Hill. Thorn swam against the tide. He saw the smoke blacken the sky.

"What was that explosion?" he said. But no one answered. They were too busy running. Thorn tried to shove through them, but his body protested. He stopped moving and the crowd swept him back. He saw a sign for Hyde Park Corner underground station and elbowed his way towards it. Thorn ducked under the plastic tape that said, POLICE: DO NOT ENTER and ran down into the silent, empty station.

CHAPTER 93.
HOWL.

LAURA, in her werewolf shape, snarled as the pain tore through her shoulder. Michael's dagger-like canines sank into her flesh. They rolled across the concrete kicking up dust and debris. The smell of blood and burning filled her nostrils.

She struck at him with her claws, lacerating his face. But he still held on. She got to her feet. Michael tore at her belly. She rammed him into one of the plinths. He yelped and let go of her shoulder.

Laura hunkered down and snarled at him. He showed his teeth.

She felt weak. Her fights with the other Templeton werewolves had taken their toll. She was injured and fatigued; Michael was strong and healthy.

Laura noticed the ring of armed police circling them.

Michael rushed her. She grappled with him, snapping her jaws near his throat. He twisted, tossing her across the concrete. She laid there, eyes closed. She heard Michael thunder towards her. She opened her eyes. Michael filled the sky above her. He fell on her, but she pushed out against him with her hind legs. He rolled away and yelped.

Laura got on all fours. She stalked after Michael. He got up and shook himself, dust spraying from his fur. Laura pounced. They tumbled again, crashing through debris and bodies. She tried to bite him; he tried to bite her. Laura dug her claws into his flanks and Michael thrashed about. His struggles got him free of her grasp, and he raced away before turning to face her once more.

"Which one's which?" said one of the policemen.

"Does it matter?" said one of the others.

"It does to me – one of them saved my life."

And another one said, "Saved some kids, too."

"Doesn't matter," the second voice said again, "safety first – we've got to kill 'em both. We don't know what they are, for fuck's sake."

Laura and Michael circled each other. They snapped and snarled. Laura attacked. Michael reared up on his hind legs as she lunged in. She struck him in the belly, and he stumbled backwards, Laura bounding after him.

He regained his balance and swiped at her as she dived in. Michael's claws gashed her cheek. She yelped and lurched away. Her vision turned red – blood in her eyes. It poured from her face and into her mouth. Dizziness washed over her.

I'm going to die, she sensed herself think; *he's going to kill me.*

She stumbled around to face his attack and it came. His teeth bared ready for the bite, Michael charged.

He pounced, pushing himself off the ground with those powerful hindquarters. His jaws opened, his head tilted so he could slide it under her chin and bite into her throat.

Laura ducked and thrust upwards. Her mouth clamped onto Michael's throat. He shrieked. He pulled her with him and crashed to the ground, crushing Laura under his powerful frame.

But she held on, her teeth sinking deeper into his flesh. His blood filled her mouth, warm and thick. She swallowed, salivating at its taste.

Michael struggled, yelping and scratching at her. She felt him weaken, and managed to roll him over. She was on top, her jaws at his throat. She snarled and their eyes met. Laura snapped her head from side to side, five rapid movements. She tore away Michael's throat. Blood spurted from the wound. He jerked and flailed.

Laura rolled away, his blood and flesh hanging from her jaws.

Michael panted. His body shrank. The fur sank into his skin. The nose and the ears shrivelled. The teeth pushed back into his gums. The claws contracted.

The human Michael, bleeding from his side and his throat, lay dying.

Laura moved to him and sniffed his body.

She ignored shouts of "Move away from him, move away," coming from behind her.

She looked at his pale face and he opened his eyes. He tried to speak, but blood bubbled in his mouth.

Laura lowered her head.

Michael, his voice a rasp, said, "You're...you're...you're my...my...sister – "

And her eyes softened, and she felt warmth in her breast for him.

He said, " – never, you...you bitch...never...you're my...sister..."

Laura narrowed her eyes and growled.

Michael spat in her face, spraying blood into her eyes.

She stepped backwards and shook her head, trying to clear her vision.

Michael screamed. He arched his back. Blood spouted from his mouth. He let out a howl. His body sagged and he died.

★ ★ ★

The werewolf turned to face them.

French tightened his grip on the shotgun. He had the weapon trained on the creature and he'd fire if he had to.

"We've got to kill it," said Cartwright.

"No," said French, "it's not an 'it', it's a – " He trailed off. Male or female? All the others were male. Men who took on the shapes of wolves. The black-fur that took down the helicopter had turned back into its human form.

The werewolf bolted through a gap in the circle of AFOs. It was five yards from French and he saw its powerful, sleek body; its strength, its beauty. He was frozen by it and he watched the animal pelt across the square.

"Come on," said Cartwright, and the guys followed him.

The werewolf sprang up on the Fourth Plinth.

What is it with that podium? thought French, running after his colleagues. That dead one, the one who'd brought down the 'copter liked that spot, too. *Was it high ground?* he thought. Did that elevation give them comfort?

The werewolf perched on the plinth.

The AFOs formed a ring around the pedestal. They trained their shotguns on the werewolf. French stepped through the cordon, weapon held down. He looked up at the creature and the creature looked at him.

And the creature faded away.

French held his breath. He almost dropped the gun.

The werewolf changed into a woman; a naked woman with long black hair and severe wounds all over her body.

She sat down and tucked her legs up, rolling herself into a ball. She started to weep.

"Oh, my God," said French, "look at that."

Cartwright said, "We've got to take her out, Frenchie. We don't know what she is."

She was beautiful, that's what she was; bloodied and dirty, perhaps, but still beautiful – and French couldn't take his eyes off her.

The woman craned her neck and started to shout.

"Johhhhhhn-eeeee! Johhhhhhn-eeeee! Johhhhhhn-eeeee!"

"What's that she's saying?" said Cartwright.

French shook his head.

"Frenchie, you're not taking action, pal – so I'm taking over."

French heard the shotgun primed behind him, and Cartwright said, "Take her out."

CHAPTER 94.
LOST SOULS.

THE shot echoed down the tunnel.

Thorn froze and stared into the darkness.

The tunnels were clear and he'd made good time. He'd guessed, heading down into the underground at Hyde Park Corner, that it would take him half-an-hour to run-walk-stagger to Charing Cross.

Using a map he'd picked up at the station, he followed the tracks through to Green Park and Piccadilly Circus where he veered left. Charing Cross was his next stop.

It was dark and damp down here. Rats scurried across his path. Voices leached from above ground into the tunnels. His footsteps echoed and chased him down.

The echo of the gunshot faded.

What the hell was that? he thought.

Goosepimples popped up all over his skin. A cold sweat broke on his back. He saw in his head that Laura had been shot. He started to run through the darkness. His lungs sagged in his chest. Nausea swam over him, but he gritted his teeth and pushed on.

A light flickered ahead. He stopped and heard scratching. *More rats*, he thought. He moved towards the lights. It was weak, pressed close to the tunnel wall. He got closer and saw the candle, and in the light the candle made he saw the tramp.

The tramp scratched at the wall of the tunnel. Thorn said, "Hello."

The tramp stopped scratching and turned to face Thorn. A grey beard covered his face. Silver hair tumbled over his shoulders. Thorn stepped closer and smelled the tramp. "What are you doing?" he said, putting a hand over his face before approaching the tramp.

He went back to his scratching, and by the light of the candle Thorn saw that the tramp was using a flint to scrape images on the tunnel wall.

He was making the image of a wolf fighting a wolf.

The tramp said, "In a thousand years time, when they find this place, they'll know how these days came to an end. They'll see my cave paintings and know that monsters fought on the streets of London. God told Ezekiel to warn the people of Israel that they should fear Him. 'And the cities that are inhabited shall be laid to waste, and the land shall be desolate.' That's what God said. And it's happening here, too. London's first. Then England and the world. The millennium marks the end for us."

Thorn watched him for a few seconds, then ran on into the darkness. A few hundred feet down the track, he stopped and glanced over his shoulder. He thought he'd see the flickering candle and the shape of the old cave painter. But the candle had gone out and the tunnel was dark.

★ ★ ★

Laura didn't flinch when the gun went off. She sat with her legs tucked up against her chest.

The policeman who'd fired into the air turned to look at his colleagues. He said, "You hold your fire until I give the order. Cartwright, stand down. I give the orders. I'm in charge."

Laura shivered. It was so cold and her wounds ached. Blood caked her body. It dried on her and it oozed out of her. Dust peppered her wounds and that made them hurt even more. Sweat and grime plastered her hair to her scalp. Fur and flesh filled her mouth.

"Miss," said the policeman who'd fired into the air, "I'll ask you again: please come down from the plinth."

Voices from the crowds that surrounded Trafalgar Square said, "Let her be," and "She saved us," and "Don't hurt her."

Laura's gaze roved the square. She had one hell of an audience. They'd all seen her change and seen her kill; they'd all seen her — she wrapped her arms around herself — naked.

I hurt so much, she thought; *I just want to curl up here and go to sleep.*
Where was he?

"Johhhhhhn-eeeee!" she said again, throwing his name over the city, "Johhhhhhn-eeeee!"

"Who's Johnny, Miss?" said the policeman.

"Get her down, Frenchie," said one of the other cops.

The one called Frenchie turned round and told his mate to shut up, then he looked up at Laura again.

He said, "Is there anything I can get you? Can I help you? Please, let me help you."

She looked around. All these people watching her. She wondered what they thought of it all.

Paramedics were taking care of the wounded, ferrying away the dead.

So many, she thought; and that explosion didn't help.

Dozens and dozens lay dead; so many more injured.

She saw men wearing white forensic suits put Michael into a body bag and zip him up. They rolled him on to a stretcher and scurried away. There he goes, off to some lab where they'll prod him and open him up and do all manner of things to his carcass. That's why she'd always tried to keep herself hidden. If anyone saw her as a werewolf, they'd be after her; they'd hunt her down.

Her gaze drifted over the crowd – the witnesses.

I can't kill them all, can I?

She called for John Thorn again, and his name came back to her in an echo.

Laura looked up at the helicopters. A camera pointed at her from one of the cockpits.

Laura squatted and marked her territory. Her urine poured over the plinth. The armed policemen stepped back like they'd never seen anyone take a piss before.

Voices from the crowd crisscrossed, saying, "She's pissing – that's disgusting – she's scared – leave her alone – marking her territory – "

Laura stood up and showed herself to them all.

A cheer burst from the crowd.

She leaped off the plinth and by the time she hit the pavement she was a werewolf again, and the crowd gasped.

The policemen lifted their shotguns and aimed at her.

Laura bolted, heading towards the Charing Cross exit.

The cop said, "Stop," and he trained his weapon on the flash of black whipping across Trafalgar Square.

The wind rushed through her fur and it cooled her aching body. The crowd parted and their shouts rang in her ears. She burst through the yellow tape strapped across the station's entrance. She bounded down the stairs into the Underground.

The armed officers chased her.

CHAPTER 95.
THE LAST EMBRACE.

I'M lost, he thought; *I've gone the wrong way.*

He looked at the Underground map, bringing it right up to his face. It was all coloured lines crisscrossing each other; they couldn't be followed like a map could be followed.

He stared ahead and saw only shapes in the darkness.

I'm going to be down here forever; I'm never going to see her again.

Grief gouged out a pit in his stomach. He wanted to fall to his knees, curl up, and fade out of this life. He was aching all over and was certain he'd done some permanent damage to parts of his body.

He took a deep breath and moved forward. He'd come to a platform in the end. The distance between these underground stations wasn't that far – it just felt far when you'd run halfway across London after fighting with a gorilla at Andersson's house.

His feet crunched on the gravel. The rats kept him company, one confident little creature running alongside him.

Thorn said, "Know the way out of here, ratty?"

Thorn laughed at himself and looked ahead. He stopped. Shafts of light hacked at the darkness. They were distant and dim, but they were coming.

He opened his mouth to call out, but a dark shape slipped across the tunnel and shut off the lights. Thorn gasped and took a step back. The shape shuffled towards him. Yellow eyes fixed on him. A snarl rumbled in the darkness.

He said, "Laura," and Laura stepped naked out of the dark and she cried his name and rushed towards him.

They embraced and they fell to their knees. They kissed and he tasted her mouth. He pulled her against him and stroked her wet hair, her bloodied and soiled back, and she trembled in his arms.

She looked up at him, dirty and tearful.

He said, "That's the third time you've run into me in the dark without your clothes on."

"It's my favourite thing."

He cupped her face. "You're hurt, you're hurt all over."

"So are you."

"I'm all right, but you – " He looked at her wounds.

"Where's Elena?"

"Safe. Everything's fine. Laura, we've got to get you – "

Shouts filtered down the tunnel. Dogs barked. The slashing lights grew stronger.

"They're coming for me, Johnny."

"Stay with me. I'll take care of things." He got up, pulled her to her feet and started to tug her away from the approaching lights.

"No," she said, pulling back, "They'll keep coming. I'm an animal, now. I'm hunted."

"No you're not. I've loved you and you're not an animal."

She lunged up at him and kissed him, pressing her lips against his lips. Her strength, her odour, and her taste brought longing to his breast. She slipped away and he felt her being ripped from his heart. She brushed past him and he glanced over his shoulder, and by the time he looked Laura was in her werewolf form again.

He turned to face her. She came to him and she nuzzled her face into his chest. Thorn held her head and closed his eyes. He stroked her velvet fur and buried his face in it and he sniffed it and her odour drenched his nostrils.

She drew away. He opened his eyes and saw her shape blend into the darkness as she ran down the tunnel.

She howled and the howl faded.

A voice behind him said, "Armed police. Down on your knees."

Thorn dropped to his knees.

"I'm Inspector Paul French," said the man behind him. "I'm an authorised firearms officer with the Metropolitan Police. We're all armed. Identify yourself, please."

Thorn smiled. He looked into the darkness where she went. He said, "I'm Johnny."

PART FIVE.

ENDINGS AND BEGINNINGS.

CHAPTER 96.
NOT QUITE THE END OF
THE WORLD.

Bwthyn y Blaidd, near Amlwch,
Anglesey — 11.59 p.m., December 31, 1999

JULIA said, "Do you want to count down with me?"

He gazed into his wine and scratched his beard. She looked at him and wished he would shave. The beard tickled her when they kissed; it itched when he moved down her body. His hair had grown, too, and it draped over his shoulders.

"You're a scruff, John," she'd sometimes say, and he would force a smile.

Big Ben tolled the year away on the radio. Julia looked over at the set as if pleading for the great bell to slow down, give her more time to bring this man round.

Looking back at Thorn, she said, "John."

And he looked up at her, and his eyes were like they'd seen her for the first time.

"John, I said do you want to – "

The time slipped away and the announcer said, "Happy new year."

Julia said, "Happy new year," and leaned over to kiss him. "And a happy new millennium."

"It's not really the new millennium," he said. He put an arm around her but it didn't heal her sadness. "The year Two-thousand," he said, "is not the end of the 20th century – it's Two-thousand-and-one. This is all meaningless."

She slipped away from him and went over to the window. She said, "So it was all meaningless, then – I should have realised."

She stared into the pitch black. There was nothing there. No stars; no moon; no lights from isolated homes.

The middle of nowhere meant just that: nowhere, nothing.

She turned to look at Thorn.

Nothing at all, she thought.

He rang two days after that London thing in August; all the chaos, all the deaths.

He said, "Do you remember me?"

She did. A man like John Thorn stays with you.

He asked if he could see her and her stomach flipped, and she said yes. He came to her and he was a broken man, so she took him in and did her best to heal him.

"They'll come for me," he said. "I slipped away at the time, but they'll come for me."

And they did. He was all over the news; him and that woman – the woman they said was the heroine and the villain of Trafalgar Square.

Sky, the BBC, and ITN; all the newspapers – they went after the story like it was the end of the world.

They had analysts asking, *Did she bring those terrible animals to the UK? Were they bred here? Was it some government experiment gone wrong?*

Footage from the massacre spread across the world. The internet buzzed with images of werewolves from Canada, Japan, Brazil, Ukraine, New Zealand, everywhere.

The myths grew and stuff that didn't happen *had* happened, and things that were not there *were* there. Witnesses cashed in. They sold their stories to newspapers and magazines. Even those who weren't there that day, they still claimed to have seen a werewolf and got their fifteen minutes on the back of it.

The truth got lost and changed into something else. And the two people who could find it again – John Thorn and Laura Greenacre – were missing.

John had wanted to see his daughter, but his wife stopped him. It broke him, and Julia could see this breaking down happening. Laura also obsessed him. Julia noticed a far away look in his eyes all the time, and she knew he was thinking about Laura.

Julia knew that he would never be hers; she knew that she would only be a companion, nothing more. She gave so much but got little in return. Only strength, that's all: strength that encouraged her to report Dr Lawrence Procter; strength to lead the other nurses who'd been assaulted by that pervert medic.

He was charged but fled before his trial.

Soon after Procter disappeared, she said to Thorn, "Let's go away for the new year."

He said all right, and found them this cottage. Julia's heart bloomed – he was making an effort, she thought; perhaps there *was* hope for them.

The cottage was on Anglesey in North Wales, lost in fields, far from towns. Julia thought Wales was all valleys, but the island was flat and bleak and beautiful.

When they were driving up here four days ago, she said, "What's the cottage called again? Booth-in-ee-Blade?"

"No," he said, "you say it, 'Bwth-in uh blithe', as in Blithe Spirit."

"What does it mean?"

He was about to say, then his brow creased and he turned away. She saw that he knew, but he said that he didn't.

And that's how things had been all week: him saying he didn't know.

Julia started to speak but he interrupted.

Staring into his wine again, he said, "This is where it all started. On this island, almost two thousand years ago."

Julia sighed and turned to look at the darkness again.

He said, "Their first battle on British soil."

She scowled and shook her head at the night.

"The Greenacres," said Thorn, "although they weren't Greenacres at the time, had crossed to Britain with traders from Gaul. The Templetons – who weren't Templetons back then – were Roman dignitaries, and they were always hunting their distant cousins. The first Templeton in Britain was Marius Victor. A senior tribune. Roman legions came to this island to wipe out the British druids. Marius came with them. He knew that a Greenacre was hiding out among the local tribes. She was a queen of the werewolf clan. He killed her, and blood was spilled. Laura killed Michael, and the circle was complete."

374

Julia tossed her glass at the wall and it shattered. The plaster stained pink.

"I don't care," she said, "can't you see that I don't care?"

He looked at her and frowned.

"Do you love me, John?"

His frown deepened, as if the question was a mathematical conundrum he had no idea how to solve.

After a few moments, Julia said, "There's my answer." She folded her arms. "You're a kind and gentle man; you're strong and I feel safe with you – but I deserve more. I deserve to be loved, and if you're not able to love me then I won't suffer like this. I adore you, John, but you don't adore me. And that's not fair."

His eyes held her for a long time. She gazed into them and they were new eyes to her. Not eyes that were distant; not eyes that held another woman's image.

"You're finally looking at me," she said.

"I am, and I'm sorry – you're right, Julia."

"I know I am."

"You deserve more. I only wish I could give it."

"And you can't?" Hope still lingered in the question.

He lowered his gaze.

Her heart punctured and everything that held her together slid away like ice off a roof. She sagged into a chair and cried.

"You gave me hope and strength," she said. "I loved you for making me new. But you've taken it all away, John. You've taken it back and trampled all over it."

"Julia..."

"Don't tell me not to cry or not to be sad. You're the *one*, you see. I do love you and that's it. I want to be with you, and I see us together, but" – she shook her head – "I know that can't happen. You can't make people love you."

"I'm sorry."

"I know things get better and I hope it'll change for me quickly because I don't want to feel like this – I can't take the anguish."

"No. And you shouldn't have to."

She furrowed her brow and said, "Then why? Why this lie? This false hope?"

"I never lied to you, I never said anything that was not true. But there wasn't any hope, was there."

"You being with me was hope."

"Then I'm sorry. I'm selfish and I should've stopped it. I'll go" – and he got up – "right now."

"And leave me here, in the middle of nowhere, all alone?"

He looked at her and smiled. And she saw his kindness and his heart and his love and wished they belonged to her and not to an animal.

CHAPTER 97.
ALPHA FEMALE.

"PUT it in me," she said.

"All right, all right."

He stuck the needle in her arm and pressed the plunger. The blood seeped into her vein. She grimaced and watched the syringe empty. After it was done she rolled down her sleeve and sat down at the Formica table next to the window. She looked down at the snow covering the city.

"It gets cold here."

"Freezing," said Lawrence Procter.

"Wouldn't you come back to England?"

"Of course I would. There's nothing I want more." He dropped the syringe into an old coffee jar. He filled the jar with water then poured disinfectant over it.

"Will you...use that again?" she said.

"Of course I will. The druggies don't mind."

"Was it clean when you — ?"

"Yes, yes — what do you think I am, Mrs Andersson?"

"I don't use that anymore. I'm Ruth Templeton again. My husband divorced me when I was in prison."

"I see," he said, pouring vodka into a shot glass. He swallowed it and made a face. He held the glass out to her and raised his eyebrows, but she shook her head. He said, "It's prison that worries me, you see. That's why I could never come back. I face charges I can't beat." He shook his head, anger in his eyes. "All I did was fondle them, put my hand up their skirts. It was a compliment – I only did the pretty ones. But they didn't see it like that, the stupid slags. Women are strange creatures."

"Yes we are," said Ruth.

"What's prison like?"

"Not as awful as one would imagine. Perhaps you'd be all right."

He shook his head. "Sex offender. They don't like sex offenders – all those morally upstanding murderers and armed robbers."

"Does he pay well, this hoodlum?"

"He's a businessman, and he pays shit."

He swept an arm over the miserable flat. Damp darkened the walls. Burned food caked the old stove. The pipes clanked.

"It's hell," he said, "but it's still cold."

He sat down opposite her and rubbed his face.

He looked at her and said, "How long did you do?"

"Seven years. Served four. Kidnapping and related offences. My name is sullied. My son is dead. My marriage collapsed. My daughter doesn't speak to me. But it's not all bad. I have a hobby."

"A hobby?"

"Yes: it's hunting John Thorn and Laura Greenacre. He killed my son, you see; she killed my nephew."

Procter hummed. "I wouldn't mind seeing that Thorn bastard suffer. Apparently he encouraged that nurse to report me."

"We have much in common."

"How did you know I had the blood?"

Ruth glanced out of the window. It started to snow again. She hoped her flight wouldn't be cancelled. She said, "That lunatic Ellis Cole. He's spent years trying to retrieve footage of Laura Greenacre from the vaults of Northumbria Police. Him and some former BBC reporter he's now married to."

"Karen Hughes."

"You know them," she said. "Ellis Cole made contact with me after I was released three years ago. He said a doctor had a vial of Laura's blood. Cole was after money to buy this blood. He wanted to test it for werewolf DNA. He'd use that as evidence in his fight to retrieve this film of his."

"I approached Cole after being charged. I hoped he would defend me, but he'd 'retired', he said, and was fighting the police over this footage. I told him I had the blood. But then I had to leave the country."

"Ellis wants to be on the bandwagon," said Ruth. "There's footage all over the place. He wants to be part of that with his own clips. Soon after the Trafalgar Square incident, the internet spilled over with film of werewolves. But that's boring, now, isn't it. The next stage is to find Laura Greenacre – find the werewolf, not the footage."

"Little bitch. Attacked me."

"Very clever of you to hold on to her blood, doctor."

"She seemed obsessed with destroying it. I slipped some into a vial, popped it into my pocket. Sent the rest up and, as we know, she got to it and destroyed it. I knew it would come in useful one day. Not like this, though."

Ruth rubbed her arm. She thought about the Greenacre blood leaching through her veins; werewolf DNA knitting with her own to spark life into those dormant genes.

"When will it take effect?" she said.

He shrugged. "I don't know. I don't understand this science. No one understands it. I warned you it could be dangerous."

Ruth felt hot. A flush ran through her and she patted her reddened cheeks. The veins bulged in her arms.

Procter said, "Are you all right? Do you need some water?"

"No," she said, feeling a monster rise inside her, "I'm fine."

She stood, and he got up, too. She took her coat from the back of the chair and slipped it on. She said, "Thank you, doctor."

"You've paid me; there's no need to thank me."

"I see." She went to the door, then stopped. She turned to face him. "What about travelling with me?"

"Travelling?"

"Yes. As my aide. I need an aide, particularly one with medical experience. I have money, plenty of money."

Procter scratched his head.

"I'll kill them for you," she said. "Thorn, the nurse; all the nurses, if you want."

"Kill them?"

"Yes. When I change. When I'm...like she is. I can do anything. What do you think?"

He hummed. "My boss – I don't know what – "

"Is he a bastard?

"Yes, he is. A brute. A bully."

"And you're his doctor?"

"He has a skin condition. He's terribly vain. Has me searching for a miracle cure."

"All right. I'll kill him too."

"Kill Vasili Kolodenko?"

"Yes. Kill Vasili Kolodenko."

"He's an influential man. Has links with the Kremlin."

Ruth shrugged. "Only a man, though. Flesh and blood and bone. Come on" – and she went to the door and opened it – "get your coat – and you can watch me eat him alive."

END.

ABOUT THE AUTHOR.

Thomas Emson is a writer who lives under another name. Born and raised in North Wales, he has been a singer-songwriter, an author, and a journalist. He has published fiction in the Welsh language, but Maneater is his first English-language novel. He lives in Kent with a wonderful woman, an elderly cat, and two house rabbits.